1971

A WAR STORY

Dr. Neelam Batra-Verma

1971 - A War Story
Copyright © 2018 by Dr. Neelam Batra-Verma

Cover designed by Qazi Raghib
creativeqazi@gmail.com

Tellwell Talent
www.tellwell.ca

ISBN
978-0-2288-0680-6 (Paperback)
978-0-2288-0681-3 (eBook)

Preface

Dedicated to the life and memory of my father who developed my writing skills and all those brave soldiers who sacrificed their lives for their countries.

Chapter 1

Final flight

December 15, 1971

One cold winter morning, December 15, 1971, to be precise, somewhere on the Line of Control between Indian and Pakistani Kashmir, a pilot of HF-24, an Indian fighter bomber, had to eject from his aircraft after it was shot down by the enemy. The aircraft went plunging into a deep valley below and burst into flames. Not far from the ground, the pilot thought, as he held tightly onto the ropes of his parachute – I hope I make it. The breeze was light, visibility low due to the winter fog, not enough to disrupt his vertical descent. He prayed that he would land inside his own country. Just a couple of feet more, he would be safe.

Safe from what? Maybe he would not have any broken bones as he was proficient in landing by parachute, but would he land in enemy territory, or his own? He didn't know how far he was from the border. He was trained to survive a few days in the jungles of no man's land, yet his big worry was being caught by the Pakistan Army, if he was in their territory. Suddenly, a gust of wind blew his parachute over the trees, far from the burning plane.

He found himself hanging on the trees, scraping and bruising his face, forehead, arms and hands. As he dangled there, just

a short distance away he could see people running towards the burning plane. Quite possibly, the villagers had seen him eject and would now come look for him. He struggled to free himself from the ropes as fast as he could.

He was just a couple of feet from the ground. Disentangling the parachute from the tree was next to impossible. He swiftly stretched his arm to his backpack, trying to feel his pocket knife. He knew it was somewhere in the outer pocket...yeah, there it is.

The shouts of villagers were getting louder and louder, closer and closer. He swiftly extricated himself from his parachute and jumped towards Mother Earth. Would he be able to save himself from the villagers in case they became violent once they realised he was the enemy? He crawled behind the bushes on all fours to hide himself. He changed his watch to Pakistan time, slowing it by 30 minutes and started tearing at his uniform so he could take the Indian Air Force Emblem, sown to his uniform, apart. He had to be careful in case he had landed across the border.

The voices were closer now and he guessed he would not be able to hide for long. Around him were only bushes and trees, with crows cawing above and the sun shining bright. He tugged and tugged at the IAF emblem with his knife till it came off. As he struggled, he felt a pair of eyes watching him. He looked up and found a little boy not more than 7 or 8 years old, watching him in awe. Whether the boy was scared or surprised, the crouching pilot could not tell. Slowly, the pilot buried the torn Indian emblem in his hand under the twigs and dried leaves he was sitting on.

The pilot smiled and put his index finger on his lips, gesturing the little boy not to make a noise. The boy, wearing a dirty blue salwar suit, kept staring at him open mouthed. The pilot couldn't decide whether he should stay still, wait for the villagers to spot him or try to hide in the jungle. Running was not be an option as he didn't know his whereabouts and looking for a way out would not be easy with the villagers on his heel.

"Saleeeeem......Saleeeem," the pilot heard a woman calling. "Where are you, dear?"

"Here," the little boy called out. "Come look," the little boy pointed towards the pilot.

The pilot now had no choice but to come out of hiding. He tried to stand but realized his knees were hurt and bleeding. He stumbled a little and the boy ran to hold him. "Did you get hurt?"

"Yes, looks like," the pilot said, smiling.

"Did you jump out of the plane?"

"Yes."

"Are you a pilot?"

"Salim! Come here," the mother called out. She looked scared.

"Are you a bad man?"

The pilot shook his head.

"Don't worry mother, he is not a bad guy." Then turning to the pilot, Salim asked, "Can you teach me to fly planes?"

Before the pilot could respond to that innocent request with a nod, swarms of people came running towards the little group. But the pilot managed to smile at the little boy, nodding his head. The little boy smiled back happily.

"Who are you?"

"Were you flying the plane that went down?"

"Where are you from?"

"Did you come from across the border?"

Everyone was speaking at the same time. There were about 40-50 people, some scared, others threatening, some curious, others anxious, some with nothing in their hands, others with bamboo sticks ready to pounce on the pilot. The pilot was confused. If he told them he was from India, they would lynch him right away. If he lied, he might get some time to plan his next move. Now was not the time to play Truth or Dare.

"Do you have something to say?" growled a big man in an off-white crisp *pathani* suit, bamboo stick in hand, his mouth

3

stained red with *paan*. Spitting to his side, he stared at the pilot, waiting for an answer.

He looks important, thought the pilot. He felt a streak of sweat flowing from the right corner of his head on to his cheek. As his mind raced for an answer, he saw that it was blood, not sweat. Suddenly, he had an answer.

He rolled up his eyes and started slurring. "Mmmmaqsooood… help help…my head…" Legs trembling, feet wobbling, hands shivering, he was about to fall when the big man reached out to support him.

"Come, you lazy men. Help Maqsood, take him to the *hakim*. Looks like his plane was shot by the Indians."

The pilot smiled to himself. Yes, he was in Pakistan and he had to remember that his name now was Maqsood.

As he was being carried on someone's shoulder, he thought of Anita, who would be waiting for him to come home. He had to find a way to get out. How, he didn't know. They looked like simple people who could be easily fooled, but not for long. A plane was burning, word would travel and Pakistani authorities would soon investigate. The longer the plane burned, the better for him as any signs of an Indian plane would be obliterated. He could not hide for long, he knew.

The villagers carried the pilot into an old man's house in the village. They called him Hakimji. Naturopath. There was a *charpoy* – a cot made of bamboo and strings – on the verandah of this little house where they laid him down. The little old man, maybe be 70-something, with a long white beard, came rushing out.

"*As-salamu alaykum, bhaijan. Kya hua?*" the old man asked with concern. Greetings, brother. What happened?

"Just come look at this pilot. His plane was shot by the Indians and we found him behind the bushes. I think he is badly injured. There is blood on his shirt and forehead. I think it is coming from his head," the authoritative man said with concern.

4

"Oh! He looks like he might be badly injured. He should be taken to the Military Hospital," said the *hakim*.

"That will take 5-6 hours. By then he might die. Just look at him," the big man bellowed.

Hmmm... the city is about 6 hours away – about 250-300 km. It might take some time for news to travel that someone has been shot. As long as these people remained under the impression that he was not an Indian, he could buy time.

The *hakim* bent down to check the pilot's head where it was bleeding. If I am badly injured, they will certainly take me to the hospital, the pilot thought. But if not, they might still keep me in the village and treat me. So if I have to feign illness, it should not be too serious, the pilot told himself. There were at least 50 people surrounding him at that time and he had to be careful. One bad move, and they would realize that he is not one of them.

"Where did he fall from?" the *hakim* asked casually.

"From the sky, Hakim Chacha," the little boy Salim blurted out before anyone else could respond, trying to sound important. "He was flying a plane and someone set his plane on fire. I think the Indians shot him."

"If he was flying in the Indian territory and the Indians shot him, he should have fallen in India. How did he land in Pakistan?" the *hakim* was inquisitive.

These people are alert, the pilot thought.

"Why do you care," the big man hollered. "We know he is our guy and his name is Maqsood. Just start his treatment."

"Allah-o-Akbar," the little boy's mother prayed with raised hands. "He is so young. I hope he doesn't die in our village."

"No, he won't die," said the *hakim*, examining the pilot's wound. "It is a superficial injury and he should be fine after I apply my medicine." Then calling to his wife, who was watching patiently from the doorway, "Mehra, can you start boiling the *kara* (potion)? You people, go do your work. No need to crowd around. I will take care of him."

5

While the women walked away, some men went into a huddle. "I never thought after 1965 we will have to fight another war with India," said one man.

"They are like us, Bhaijaan. It pains to see so many of our men dying just because the Bengalis want to form another country," said another elderly gentleman.

"Everyone wants independence these days. Azadi is the key word".

"If our fathers had not fought for Azadi, the British would still be ruling us."

"True, but we can't forget that it was Mahatma Gandhi who bought Azadi with his slogan of non-violence."

"Hey, don't forget that he is an INDIAN!! Or was."

"So were we before the British divided us."

"At the end of the day, we got Azadi with violent means, not because of non-violent methods of that old guy they call Mahatma," the man with a loud voice kept his tirade against Gandhi going. "Do you know how many people were killed, all because of him?"

"Hey, he did not ask for the country to be divided like this. He just wanted to get rid of the British in India. Don't forget the roles of Pandit Nehru and Jinnah. Since both of them wanted to be Prime Minister, they divided the country on religious grounds so they could fulfill their personal ambitions."

"Who knows what their intention was, but if the country hadn't been divided, we would never be at war and our people would not be dying at the borders. Gentlemen, let's hope history doesn't repeat itself," said the elderly man with a gentle voice, trying to calm the two parties down. "Instead we should concentrate on what is happening in our country now. Sad but true that India is trying to divide our country again."

So, these guys are not dunderheads, Flight Lt Ajay thought. He knew what they were discussing. Pakistan had held its first general election to elect members of the National Assembly a year

6

back. Like India, Pakistan too was a young country trying to get its house in order. But unfortunately for the people of Pakistan, the first general election scheduled for 1959 never took place. Instead, martial law was imposed and power was handed over to the Commander-in-Chief of the Army, General Muhammad Ayub Khan, who later promoted himself to the rank of Field Marshal after assuming the country's presidency.

The war Ajay was fighting was a result of internal political fighting, in which India got involved after West Pakistan's pre-emptive strikes on 11 Indian airbases. India sided with the Bangladeshi nationalist forces in an attempt to create a separate country for the Bengalis of East Pakistan. A year earlier, Pakistan's first official general elections had resulted in shocking results – it was Mujib-ur-Rehman's Awami League which won 162 seats out of 300. Yet he was not invited to form the government.

Yahya Khan, in collaboration with Zulfikar Ali Bhutto, who's PPP had won just 81 seats, somehow managed to form the government. Bengali nationalist groups started to protest against the military regime of Yahya Khan, which retaliated by slaughtering the East Pakistanis. India did not want to be involved in the internal affairs of its neighbours but the Bangladeshis called out to India to help. Pre-emptive air strikes were carried out by the Pakistan Air Force at the Indian borders, resulting in declaration of war by the then Prime Minister Indira Gandhi.

"*Hakimji*, do you have the transistor on?" someone asked.

Just then the old lady came out with some liquid in a porcelain cup. All this while Ajay, had been concentrating on listening to the people talking, without thinking about his throbbing head. He could feel his shoulders, elbows and knees were scraped from the fall and some blood on his elbows was now drying and sticking to his shirt. But the *hakim* was only concentrating on the blood that had now stopped flowing from his head.

The *hakim* lifted the pilot's head and tried to force the liquid down his throat. He pressed the cup so hard on Ajay's lips that the cup clanked as it touched his teeth. To escape from this misery, he voluntarily opened his mouth and drank the bitter potion, almost vomiting once. It tasted like rat poison, not that he had ever tasted rat poison before.

"There," the *hakim* said with some relief. "By tomorrow he should be fine. And then he can go back to wherever he came from."

"Do you think he will be able to walk around tomorrow?" the big man asked.

"Yes, Malik. He should at least be talking by tomorrow."

"Ok then, I will come and see him tomorrow," the man replied as he walked away. Then the bitter potion took effect and he went into a deep sleep while the little boy went back to the site where the pilot had landed to look for what the pilot was hiding.

When the pilot woke up, it was pitch dark. In the fading light from a kerosene lamp with a glass shade on a little stool, he could gauge that he was now in a small red brick room. The cement between the bricks was turning black. A door opened to another part of the house and there were clothes hanging on nails and any peg on which things could hang. It took a while for the pilot to recollect what had happened. Gradually, the events of the day started coming back to him.

Slowly and steadily, he tried to get out of the cot, the strings of which were so loose that his body was almost curved into a fetal position. The mattress too was wearing thin. It was too uncomfortable to be called a bed. As he tried to get up using his elbows as support, he almost screamed in pain as they were still sore from his jump. His head too was pounding inside the homemade bandage. But he did feel better.

Through the ray of moonlight coming from the tiny window above his bed, he could see there was a pitcher of water next to him with a twisted brass glass. He pulled himself up trying

to look at his watch in the fading light. He couldn't make out whether it was dusk or dawn. He angled his watch and could just guess that one of the needles was pointing upwards towards 12 but he couldn't be certain of the smaller needle. He lifted the lid of the earthen pitcher, making a slight jangling sound. He waited for someone to walk inside his room to check on him. When no one came, he slowly threw the cotton patched blanket aside. It was darn ugly and stinky yet it had kept him warm.

He dipped the glass slowly in the pitcher, as silently as possible. The December cold had almost frozen the water, yet he drank a glass full. The bed squeaked a bit as he moved. The coldness of the room made the ugly blanket inviting. But he had to get out of here. He had to find his way. Wobbling and feeling giddy, he tried to look for his shoes. He still had socks on, and his pants and shirt, and the military sweater underneath. He looked for a sweater or jacket amongst the clutter of clothing on the walls. It was still so dark that he couldn't make out whether there were shirts or pants or salwars hanging on the walls. He pulled at the blanket the *hakim* had thrown at him when he slept, that looked like woven wool and felt warm. He wrapped himself in it and slowly tiptoed outside the room, only to find himself in another room where he could see the silhouette of two, no, three people sleeping on the floor.

He saw another door, which he thought might lead him outside. He could see rays of blue light falling on the floor through the cracks of the door. He had to jump over these bodies wrapped in dark blankets and head to the door. The door led to the tiny kitchen packed with all kinds of brass and clay pots and pans, with the smell of burnt wood stronger here than anywhere in the house. The room he slept in had a strong smell too but it was bearable. He never had an aversion to the smell of burning wood. When they were in training in the jungles and trying to cook up a pot of stew as part of survival training, it was a comforting smell. But mixed with human sweat, it wasn't quite welcome.

He reached the outside door, which was unlocked. The two doors were held together with a metal rod on a ring which could be opened from outside too. The only way for it not to be opened from outside was a small little *chitkani* or locking mechanism. Soon, he was on the familiar porch. The old door squeaked as it opened and shut behind Ajay. Robbers could easily get in, but there was nothing to rob. That is why no one bothered to lock it, he guessed.

He was now outside and saw his shoes placed neatly under the string bed where they had first been taken off by the *hakim*. They looked shiny, though not up to military standards. It was 10 minutes past five by his watch. On his left, he could see silhouettes of a mountain while on the right, except for some twinkling lights from kerosene lamps and shadows of tiny village houses amongst dense trees and bushes, he couldn't see too far ahead. There was a big tall tree outside this little house, with a brick and cement parapet around it, a place where villagers would normally gather to share problems, hold court, pass judgments, punish the guilty and innocent, gossip, create or spread rumours, share news, etc.

As he started walking towards the mountains, it occurred to him that he would be easily recognized by his uniform. He had to look for something different to wear, something which the people here in the village wore. What is the name of the village, he thought as he looked around. "What am I thinking? As if people plaster the name of their village outside their houses!"

He changed direction and started walking towards the village. If people can leave their doors open at night, they might leave their clothes to dry outside their homes. He was right. He didn't have to walk too far before he found a shawl, then a man's shirt, dirty and crumpled. Surely, no one would miss it. He carried his uniform with him. That would unnecessary catch someone's attention if he left it behind.

The villagers owned cattle in plenty. There were cows, buffaloes and goats tied outside a few houses. As he walked past them, one cow stood up from its sitting position with a jerk and started mooing.

He was walking towards the mountains, the jungle was dense but the frost seemed to have made the little branches brittle, piercing Ajay as he walked past. There was a mud path that seemed to lead somewhere. Since the villagers used wood to cook and keep warm, the women must be following this path to collect wood, he thought. And others to do their business. The villagers didn't have bathrooms in their homes, or anywhere nearby. Men would be bathing near the wells while women would fill buckets of water at the well and walk to the privacy of their kitchens or homes to bathe.

The area wasn't known to be inhabited by a lot of dangerous animals. Maybe deer or snakes. Pilots are trained to deal with that eventuality.

He looked at his watch. It was 5:40 am. People would be waking up soon and heading to the jungles. If there was a school nearby, children would be up and about. Ajay hastened his gait. But it wasn't easy to walk as there were pebbles, roots of trees and branches sticking out and tearing at his clothes. Tucking his uniform under his arm, Ajay walked carefully as the baby birds were waking up somewhere, in their nests and chirping away. Daylight had started to spread though the sun was nowhere to be found. Grey clouds were ominous, hiding the sun behind them but edges glowing against still Prussian blue sky. It was a lovely sight, most beautiful – nature at its best glow – if only he had the time sit and stare. The scene reminded Ajay of a poem he was taught in school written by Robert Frost – *The woods are lovely dark and deep; but I have promises to keep; miles to go before I sleep; and miles to go before I sleep...*He couldn't recall the whole poem.

Making a path for himself through the bushes and trees, he didn't know where he was going. The mountains were so far away.

He was now thinking of the war that brought him here. Is it still on? The border should be close by since he knew he hadn't flown too far into the country when he had been shot down. Possibly from the ground. As he walked trying to weigh every step, he tried to gauge the direction he was going. Anita would be waiting to hear from him. So would Ma and Bauji, he thought. What kind of news would have been delivered to them, he wondered. Were they told that he died in the war or was Missing in Action? Or captured by the enemy and now a Prisoner of War (PoW)?

If they were told he died since his plane had been spotted going down, no one would come looking for him. Neither his family, who could barely do anything anyways, nor the Air Force or military personnel. Brushing away the negative thoughts that were haunting him now, he told himself that there was a policy in place to look for every soldier who went to war. And even if he died, it is the responsibility of the government to bring the body home and cremate it with dignity.

Next possibility is that my family is told I am alive but in a prison in Pakistan. They would be relieved to hear that but would have nightmares thinking that their son is being tortured. How would Anita feel? We just got married, hardly know one another but it was love at first sight for him. He didn't know whether Anita felt the same way about him. He never had the time to ask her. She never said anything anyway and when he had proposed, she agreed to marry him despite the fact that she had just started college and had a dream of becoming a teacher. Just like he had always dreamt of becoming a pilot and had fiercely followed it – maybe to the end.

He had wanted Anita to follow her dream too and once he had even told her to go back to college and finish her degree. Unfortunately, he had broached the subject when Ma and Bauji were there. Ma had shot down the idea with "She is the daughter-in-law of the house and your wife. Her responsibility lies with taking care of you and us. She doesn't have to worry about putting

food on the table or earning money. You don't need a degree to run a house."

Anita had just stood there and he had regretted opening his mouth too soon. He cursed himself for saying what he did. He could have waited till his parents had left Ambala, his new posting. Barely two months into his marriage, his parents paid an unexpected visit – just to check things out and see if their daughter-in-law, whom they had not selected, was taking good care of their son. Which didn't make sense as he was not allowed to take his family to certain field areas and lived mostly on his own. In fact, adjusting to living with another human being, no matter how much he loved her, was still a work in progress when he got called out to war.

A couple of hours had passed since he started walking. The sun had already come up but was still playing hide-and-seek from behind the clouds. He didn't know where he was headed – up and down the jungle, past a fast-moving creek, where he had stopped to drink as much water as he could, wishing he was a camel so he could retain something for future use. Sitting on the rocks surrounded by dense jungle on three sides and mountains, sometimes craggy but breathtaking valleys with air so pure, Ajay wasn't sure where he was going and what he should be doing.

Now he was hungry. He remembered he hadn't eaten for close to 48 hours. His last meal was a bowl of almond porridge before he started his sortie and then that awful potion the good *hakim* had forced down his throat. He could hear the birds chirping away fast and crisp now. That is what they do when it is time to get home to their babies – just like people, trying to go back to their children after a hard day's work.

Common sense told him that birds screech to warn each other about impending danger. Their morning call merely means that they are still alive, to wake their friends up and tell them it is time to get to work. Evening call, he thought, conveys it is time to hide as predators might be out. Since they can't see properly at night,

they warn each other "to be safe" and "go home." Sometimes if they see food, birds alert each other by making a noise so every hungry bird knows there is food nearby.

Darkness was descending on the mountains and he still he did not know where he was going. Crows were now circling on top of him. Did they think he was food? Or was there food nearby? He knew it was time to stop and look for a refuge for the night. Under the tree or a rock or a cave somewhere.

He felt the breeze pick up and blow through his clothes. He could smell the freshness of water – maybe a creek or river flowing by. He wrapped the shawl around his head and neck tightly. He threw away the parcel of clothes as there was no point carrying them. A familiar aromatic whiff filled his nostrils. But only for a couple of seconds and before he could place what exactly it was, it was gone. Even if the authorities had started to search for him, that he was a day ahead of them was a solace, he thought. Would they spare a helicopter to look for a lost Pakistani soldier, he thought when every piece of equipment was needed for the war? Unless they realized that he was Indian.

The fresh fragrant smell was closer now. It wasn't just a whiff any more. He stopped in his tracks when he recognized that it was wood burning. He had always loved the warm and fuzzy feeling of burning wood, whether it was used for cooking food or just keeping people warm. There were many occasions when he had found people sitting around the fire with hands outstretched, chatting away. He remembered the winds blowing the fragrance of wood on fire outside his home in Patiala. Security guards, roaming the streets at night, would always keep warm around a bonfire, chat and laugh loudly between rounds.

There could be a village close by or maybe Pakistani soldiers camping or training. He had to investigate to be safe.

As he got closer to the smell, he could now see smoke and light from a fire as well as hear voices. He could even smell the aroma of food being cooked. Rice or *dal*, he thought, and that made

him hungry. He crept closer slowly, trying his best to remain in the dark shadows and tread slowly so as not to crunch too many dry leaves and branches under his heavy boots. He stood behind a big bush and tried to catch the conversation going on. This was a vast flat land sprinkled with only a few trees and dense bushes. From where he was, he could see shadows of about 20-25 people, men and women. A couple of men were busy trying to set up tents, those sitting around the fire appeared to be elderly, their hands facing the fire. There was another smaller fire burning where some women appeared to be cooking food while others were chopping onions. A big pot was on the cooking fire and Ajay guessed that was where the fragrance of *dal* or rice was emanating from. There were 6-7 children and he could hear the cries of babies too.

They could be gypsies, passing through the jungles to reach somewhere else. But he had to confirm for himself and try to understand what they were talking about. Were they speaking Urdu? Though he could not understand the exact words, he guessed maybe it was Punjabi or Pushto, the language spoken in Jammu & Kashmir, mixed with Urdu. He didn't know.

After observing the group for a few minutes, he decided it was safe to approach. These people certainly would not be carrying guns or any other communication devices. They appeared to be simple villagers and would pose no danger to him, he concluded. In fact, they could be like him, running away from some place or running to another place. Or just hiding from authorities. He had to talk to them, he thought, otherwise there was no way he could ever get out of the jungle and cross the border. But he had to be careful. As he stood there in the dark contemplating his next move, a young girl emerged from behind the bushes where he stood and screamed, dropping a tumbler she had been carrying with her.

"EEEEEEEEEEEEEE".

Obviously, she had gone to relieve herself among the vegetation and was shocked to see him peering behind the tree at the group. The commotion alerted everyone and they came running. Some came with hammers, others with chisels and iron rods while others just picked up rocks or stones and shouted, "Oye oye!! *Kaun hai?*" Who is there?

Ajay was now alert and immediately put his hands up as a sign of surrender.

"No, no, please don't hit me. I am lost in the jungle. I am a mere wanderer looking for food. I could smell something cooking so I came to beg," Ajay blurted out without thinking and putting his hands up to show he had no weapons. There was no time to think or this mob would club him to death with their raw weapons.

Everyone stopped running and came to a standstill as if they have been hit by a boulder. They were now looking at each other, dropping their raised arms but not their weapons.

"I am not here to hurt anyone. I just want some food and then I will go my way. If only you can…please," pleaded Ajay, eyes filled with tears.

As the attitude of his attackers seemed to soften, Ajay thought, "What a good actor I can be. Maybe I am in the wrong profession". He soon realized the tears were genuine, so was the rumble in his stomach. His last meal was a distant memory and the words that flowed were *bona fide*. No wonder they believed him.

"*Kya bolte ho?*" an elderly gentleman asked. What language do you speak?

"Hiiii…UU.. Urdu," Ajay corrected himself. This part of the world did not speak Hindi, he reminded himself. This gentleman appears to be one of the people in authority and should be pleased. He was scared, what if they asked him to recite a verse from Koran to prove that he was one of them. For now, they seemed to believe his words.

"*Theek hai. Aa jao.* (Fine. Come here.) You really look famished. How long have you been wandering?" the gentleman who introduced himself as Chaudhury said. The group broke up and went back to what they were doing before the confusion. Then addressing an elderly lady, he commanded, "Feed him. He is our guest." The lady gave a blank look but smiled softly at him.

In chaste Urdu, Chaudhury started talking to Ajay as if they were close friends. This time Ajay gave his name as Iqbal Khan. What if they were looking for Maqsood and these guys got wind of it? Just the name would ring a bell. In half an hour, which felt like an eternity, women in the group started serving food. The girl he had scared, whose name turned out to be Rehana, served him food with a big smile on her face and longing eyes. She seemed to like him but Ajay was suddenly wary of her. He didn't want to send any signals and at the same time had to make up a story about himself before they started asking him about his family.

Soon everyone was seated in a big circle and the women started serving them *khichri* – a soupy concoction of lentil and rice cooked in spices – on big banana leaves. Of course, there were no spoons. He looked at the semi-liquid stuff wondering how to eat it. From the corner of his eye, he saw Chaudhury break the corner of the leaf to make it into a spoon and scoop up the *khichri*. Hah! He quickly followed the leader lest the crowd notice his confusion and decide he is an alien.

Soon the questions started pouring forth: Where are you from? Why are you wandering in the woods? Where is your family? What do you do for a living? What does your father do? How many brothers and sisters do you have?

He was expecting these questions but not in such a flurry. His first thoughts were that he had to play dumb and illiterate for them to trust him.

"Oh! I am from a little village near Sialkot called Tuntunwala. I have no family. My parents died when I was very little and my uncle and aunt took care of me," Ajay's mind raced to make up an

interesting story. "Now they hate me and want to get rid of me." Tuntun was his favourite actress growing up and now his saviour.

"Never heard of this village," a middle-aged lady said.

Neither had Ajay. He just invented the name and he knew that there are many places in Pakistan which ended in 'wala'. He was thinking of the actress Tuntun as one of the women in the crowd resembled her when he came up with this name.

"How can someone who brought you up, hate you like this," a voice asked, thankfully diverting everyone's attention from his hometown to the cause of the imaginary dispute.

"I think because now I am old enough to claim rights on the house we were living in and the little patch of land that belonged to my grandfather." That was easy. Every household has a property dispute. "I just asked them once for some money so I can start some business and they yelled at me. They just want me to slave in their farm without claiming any rights."

"That's not good. You have equal rights, lad," the Chaudhury bellowed. "Sometimes the elders in the family just don't know how to deal with young people. That is what property is for, so the next generation can have a better start in life and not go through the same struggle as their elders."

"They threw me out and I have nowhere to go. I don't know how many days I have been wandering," he said sadly, going back to his food now that his story seemed palatable enough to digest.

To divert attention from himself, he asked the Chaudhury, "Do you live in the jungles? Or are you travelling to somewhere? Or just collecting wood in the jungles?"

Suddenly everyone burst out laughing. "No, no, we are not wood pickers. Yes, we do pick wood to cook when we are in the jungle but that is not our profession. We are nomads, who move from one place to the other, from one city to a village and back to a city."

"Oh, that sounds interesting. But surely, you do have to do something for a living. There are so many of you. You would need

to buy food and clothes," Ajay queried, still digging into his food and suddenly realizing that he shouldn't sound too intelligent.

He realized everyone was now staring at him as if he had no business asking such personal questions. Or intelligent ones. He realized his mistake. "This *khichri* is so amazing. I can't understand how you can make such delicious *khichri* in the middle of a jungle. Can I ask who made it and what spices you used?" he blurted out, trying to change the topic. "Can I have some more, please?"

"Just one little spoon is all you can have. We have to leave some for the children who are sleeping," the elderly woman said with a frown, getting up to give him some more. "No one gets a second helping here but you are a guest."

"So what are your plans now?" the girl who served him food asked softly, trying to make eye contact. Ajay was thankful to her for breaking the awkward silence but he had to come up with an answer. A plausible one at that.

"Plans? What plans?" he asked. "I don't plan anything."

"But what were you thinking when you left home?" the girl persisted, getting up to wash her hands.

Ajay's mind was racing. He needed a logical answer. He had to play dumb, yet he had to reach the border. And go home to Anita.

"Don't worry, son. You can join us wherever we go. We seem to be alike here. We don't have any plans either," the Chaudhury said, laughing heartily.

Everyone seemed to nod their heads, smiling. He had no choice but to smile and appear to be happy. Something was telling him he was being sucked into a swamp. Should he or should he not agree to this proposal? At this point in time, he needed their support. He didn't know where he was heading, what side of the mountain he was, how far the border was and how long would it take for him to get there, if he ever did.

He said casually, "I remember my mother once telling me that she had a cousin brother living in Ambala in India. She

said that if I ever need help, he will always help. I was thinking maybe one day I will go to him."

The elderly woman looked at him and smiled. "You think you can just walk over to India like that? India and Pakistan are fighting. The Indian soldiers will kill you near the border."

"Amma, the war is over," the young girl countered. "I heard it on the radio when we were in that house where we…"

"Oh really!" the Chaudhury blurted before she could finish her sentence, staring at her angrily. "How come no one told me?"

"I thought you heard it too…" The mother was now staring at the girl, who was now scared and averted her gaze. She didn't say anything further and looked the other way. But it was enough for Ajay to understand that they were hiding something, that something was not right. Yet the girl had given him hope and the news that the war was over. There was no other way he would have found out.

Walking up to Ajay, the Chaudhury put his arm around Ajay and said politely. "Don't worry. You can be with us as long as you want, Iqbal. Crossing to India would be out of the question. The soldiers on both sides are on high alert these days and will not even blink before shooting anyone. For them, you would just be an intruder – bang – and your life has ended. You can work with us and stay in our community."

"Work? What kind of work do you do in the jungles?"

"Well, we do various jobs. We make terracotta toys and sell them in the villages or cities that come our way. We make baskets from twigs, from roots or barks of trees found in the jungles. Our people also sing and dance, entertaining people. You can also learn some folk songs and join the group. You look able-bodied and very fit, though hungry."

Ajay had no choice but to agree to this proposal. If he went anywhere near the border alone, he would definitely attract attention. But in a group of about 30-odd people, he could pass off as one of them. It was not long before Ajay learnt that the

group belonged to the nomadic Kanjar community who, in the garb of selling toys, were actually stealing from unsuspecting people's homes.

The group would set up tents close to the city and spread out during the day. Some walked the streets selling their wares, but actually spying. When women came out of their houses to buy something, one of them would try to peer through the window or the cracks of the door to see their standard of living, where they kept the money, from where the woman of the house was taking out the cash.

Amongst them were groups who sang and danced to entertain people. Some would take the residential areas, others fanned out in the market, keeping an eye on shops, especially jewelry shops. As the audience got busy watching the performance, one of them stayed at a distance from the dancing troupe. He or she would then sneak into the shop and steal whatever he could lay hands on. For them, anything would do – anything more than 10 paise was valuable. Even a hair clip, a piece of cloth, a dress, a shirt, a pot or pan, could be used or sold.

Young girls in the group like Rehana would play the most interesting part. During the dance sequence, the girls would deliberately fall on older men and try to attract their attention. After the performance, these men would pay them handsomely and sometimes even invite them to their homes and shops. This would give them inside information about the person and an opportunity to steal. Ajay was amazed at the amount of booty the group would bring at the end of the day and show Chaudhury, who then would decide who gets what after leaving enough for food, travel and other daily expenditure. There were bullocks too who needed to be taken care of and fed. There were little children who would fall sick as the weather changed.

Ajay had joined the group as he had no other option. Crossing the border just wasn't an option at the moment. Chaudhury spun a vague yarn about his community, saying that they once lived

somewhere in Rajasthan when it was in India and then had to hide in the woods as the Mughals were always trying to persecute them. They had to take to hunting to survive and often killed deer or boars for meat, buying other groceries, mainly rice and lentils whenever they happened to pass by a village shop. The Kanjars always married within the clan and protected each other.

Chapter 2

School

*I*t was dark. No light shone from anywhere. No shadows, no candle burning and not a soul in sight. But she was running, running as fast as her feet could carry her. As she ran, she wondered how she could run in the dark. "Do I have a sixth sense?" she thought to herself panting and out of breath. "How long am I running? Where am I going?" There was no guiding light yet her feet wouldn't stop.

She was scared. She was barefoot and the pebbles under her feet hurt. She could sense wetness under her feet and knew the dirt was now sticking. Oh no, she was bleeding. She knew she was scared but why, she wondered again and again. Was it a cat or a dog chasing her? A robber or a murderer? And then suddenly, she couldn't run any more as there was no earth beneath her. She was in thin air… flying, falling into a vacuum…feeling like she was being sucked into a labyrinth below.

Anita's eyes popped wide open. Soaked in her own sweat, Anita looked at her surroundings and was relieved to see familiarity. Her books were on her desk, her Biology guide book near her pillow, a faint moonlight shining through the open windows and her younger 13-year old sister slept on the jute woven cot with a thin cotton mattress, next to her. She sat up and held her head in her hands. Why these weird dreams? Do they have a meaning? Are they a sign of something that happened in her

life in the past that she does not remember? Or a premonition of impending doom?

She already had a discussion with her mother on the issue, who had always comforted her. Her mother had told her not to worry, dreams are mere dreams. Some are good, others nightmares. Maybe it's just a growing up phase, she thought. She would be turning seventeen years next week and her grandparents were already planning to get her married.

Anita had her own plans to go to college once she cleared her Grade 12 exams and do something positive with her life. She had thought of becoming a teacher and maybe one day land a job with her own Pandit Maharaj Girls Senior Secondary school in Rajpura near Patiala in Punjab. She wanted to go to the beautiful university spread over 600 acres on the outskirts of Patiala. It was so beautiful and her teachers at school who had graduated from there, just raved about it as one of the best in the country. The teachers also described the nice time they had there and also about the students who would come from all over the country. They would tell stories about how students from states like Tamil Nadu and Andhra Pradesh would come there and were ragged by the Punjabis.

Just the thought of going to college excited her. She looked at the little clock on her worn out desk. It was ten minutes past three in the morning. It was so quiet that she could hear the leaves move. There was slight chill left from the fading winter. She grabbed the dull grey sweater which she had worn since Grade 8. It was a size too small now but she loved it as it was knitted lovingly by her maternal grandmother, who passed away two years back. Since then, she had loved it all the more.

The year was 1970, the month of March when exams are held all over the country. Today was her Biology exam for Grade 12. She needed at least B overall to apply for the closest girls' college in the district.

She knew going to college was her wish but she still had to convince her parents. Her father, Chaman Lal, who was a soldier with the Punjab regiment of the Indian army, was away on field duty and was scheduled to be back around Diwali, which fell in October. Before he returned, she had to at least fill out the forms and gain admission. She loved Biology with its colourful diagrams and thought maybe she could teach the subject one day. Out of a class of 50 students, her teacher Mrs Lal did not have many favorites. Luckily, Anita was an exception.

As she opened the door leading to the courtyard to use the bathroom, a cool breeze not only blew her long open black hair but also her fears away. The family cow Champa looked lovingly at her, perhaps waiting for a pat on the nose, as usual. Anita just smiled and ran to the washroom to freshen up. "Not now, Champa", she whispered. "Have to revise for my exam."

The night was quiet, she could hear the leaves rustle. Far away she could hear the hoot of a railway engine. Patiala railway station was not too far away and in the quiet of the night, it felt really close. Though she had completed her syllabus in detail a few times already, she was never satisfied. She wanted to do it once again and ensure she didn't miss anything. In her last mathematics exams, she had missed a formula during her preparation. But just before keeping her books outside of the class, as directed by the teacher, she opened it randomly and saw that formula. Wonder how, but it stuck in her head, maybe out of fear that she had missed it. Lo and behold! That was the fifth question on the exam. She thanked God for it – for she believed a supernatural power directed her fingers to that page.

Her school was on the outskirts of the village, and catered to a number of surrounding villages. Some children from her village would take the local bus to school. Anita would instead walk as she not only enjoyed the walk through meandering green fields, but could breathe the early morning fresh air. It also saved some money. Anita knew her father barely scraped through with

his meager salary of a soldier and had eight mouths to feed. She was the oldest, there was her 13-year old sister Tina, 15-year-old brother Shyam or Shamu as he was lovingly called. The youngest brother was merely seven years and just starting school. She was more like a mother to him and would pamper him a lot. She enjoyed playing with him, holding his hands to teach him to write, just like her father and mother had done for her.

Being the first child, she knew her father had pampered her a lot. As she grew older, she realized that he would cut into his own expenses to fulfill her wishes. There were also her grandparents to take care of, with hefty medical bills. The local dispensary could never provide all the medicines free. "We have to treat hundreds of other patients and don't know when the next stock will arrive," the compounder would tell her when she went for refills.

On normal school days, she would wake up at 5 am, catch up on her studies for an hour, and help her mother clean the house, prepare breakfast for everyone, milk the cow and prepare the younger children for school. But now that she had her exams, her little sister Tina promised to help along with her grandmother. While Tina would help little brother Sunny get dressed, her grandmother would prepare breakfast for everyone. That was not an easy task. Due to her severe arthritis, she could neither stand nor squat for too long. Anita's mother would come into the kitchen to keep check on her while she milked the cow, cleaned the shed and gathered hay.

Anita's mother Shobha was a very hardworking woman. With her husband away for long periods of time, Shobha was bringing up the kids mostly on her own. Apart from the children, she had the additional responsibility of taking care of his aging parents and their little field where they grew some potatoes and basmati rice. The field being just 2 acres, yet her mother was able to harvest at least 150 kilograms of rice a year. She would sell half to the local middleman who would in turn sell to an exporter, the

rest she would put in sacks for the family to enjoy all year round. "The older the rice is, the better it is," she always told Anita.

The bumper harvest of 'basmati rice' in their field was a result of the green revolution taking place in India in the sixties. In an attempt to make India self-sufficient, increased use of fertilizers and irrigation was encouraged by the government, to make famines a thing of the past. Growing up, Anita had heard stories about how grain and wheat was sent from other countries. When it landed in India, it was inedible either because the developed countries were sending substandard food or it had rotted in transit.

Her mother often told stories about how, before the Green Revolution, it was common for crops to fail and get destroyed by pests. "Lal Bahadur Shastri brought in these changes in agriculture and dams were built so farmers would not have to depend on monsoon only for their crops. The government encouraged double cropping," her mother would tell her.

At school, the principal would talk about how their country was progressing every day. He was well aware that children don't read newspapers and most families did not even get one at home. Anita's grandfather would always go around looking for used newspapers when he went for an evening or morning walk. Sometimes, he was able to lay his hands on one from the local tea or *paan* stall owner, who would gladly call out for him if one had been left by a customer. Anita would always wonder how he read the ones that were crumpled and greasy.

Due to lack of space and the fear of pests, they could not keep too much rice at home. Sometimes, before the new harvest, the previous year's stock would still be there. Shobha would ask the children to distribute it in their schools to children whose parents were labourers and were not able to afford quality rice. The children loved the fragrance and for days the school would smell of basmati rice. Shobha was happy about that as this would not only keep the pests away but also make her feel good about

doing some community service. The children's mothers would drop by to thank her and the ladies would stand at their door chatting for hours.

At 8 am, Anita said goodbye to everyone in the house and started for her neighbor's house to call her friend. On the way, the two friends asked each other questions on the syllabus so they could revise together. Despite being in the same class and good friends, when the two got back home, they did not study together. On Sundays, sometimes Anita would hop over to Shikha's house to watch the Sunday movie as Shikha's was one of the few houses in the village which owned a television set. Shikha's father worked at the post office.

Ironically, due to hours of power cuts each day, it was not very often that villagers were able to watch the film. Prime Minister Indira Gandhi had announced that every village would have at least one television set so all villagers could get together and watch in a community hall. The villagers had asked the *pradhan* (headman) to send an application to the state government. But since Shikha's family had allowed everyone who wanted to watch the Sunday movie, no one really cared much. Shikha's father Babu Ram would take out the television on the verandah of the house and open the main door. People would bring their own mats to sit on, while children would just sit on the bare ground. There would be pindrop silence in the village when the film was on. Only the occasional moo of a hungry cow or the bark of stray dogs could be heard till 10 pm when the film ended.

Doordarshan, the public broadcaster, was the only channel that was beamed in the seventies. In the middle of the week, the channel would telecast another popular programme called Chitrahaar which was the compilation of a few good songs from movies. But no one dared go watch as they did not want to intrude, though little children would try to peek in through the cracks of the door.

The exam went very well for both Anita and Shikha. All the way, they compared notes and when they got to Anita's house, they opened their books to reassure themselves they got the answers right. "I think I should get a first division in today's exam," said Anita. "Yeah me too. I answered all questions and labeled the diagrams. Hope I got the spellings right, though."

"This is Biology. I don't think they should deduct marks for spellings," consoled Anita.

"I hope you are right. But in the board exam, we don't know which examiner is going to mark our exams," Shikha was worried.

"I just hope he doesn't check my paper after he had a bad day or fought with his wife."

"You never know," laughed Shikha. "Now let's go out and jump rope before the sun sets and then I have to cook dinner."

"Good idea. I have to get back to helping Mummy more now that my exams are over. The last one month, I hardly helped her. Poor Dadi. With her arthritis, it's not easy to stand or sit when she is cooking. She is always shouting at Sunny to bring her stuff."

"What? She wants Sunny to help her! Does he really?"

"Of course not. He is just a baby. How do you expect him to do anything?" Anita defended her kid brother.

"He is seven years old, Anita," reminded Shikha. "When you were seven, you were washing pots, cleaning and even started cooking."

"Well yeah, because I was the eldest and had to help anyway."

The two chatted as they took turns skipping rope just outside Anita's house. This was a game they enjoyed immensely and were allowed to play by their parents as it was a girlie game. Once when Anita and Shikha were younger, they went to the field where boys played cricket and asked to join in. The boys had teased them, saying girls are not supposed to play cricket.

They came back home in a fury. While Shikha picked up Ramu's cricket bat and ball, Anita called out other girls in the village and soon formed a team of 10 girls. But the girls couldn't

play for long as their parents wouldn't allow them to. Even Shikha and Anita's parents did not allow them to play a boy's game. "Cricket is a man's game. The ball is heavy and you will get hurt. It's not nice for girls to run around the village chasing a ball," chastised Shobha. "Your Papa would not like it if he comes to know."

That was it.

Chapter 3

Dreams

The holidays dragged for Anita and Shikha. They had to wait until June for their results and then think about applying to the nearest Government College for Women. As eager as both Anita and Shikha were to go to college, they were both scared of broaching the subject with their parents, aware that they would discourage the idea. Her dad would talk to anyone who cared to listen at the post office where he worked that he had a young daughter of marriageable age. "She just finished her intermediate exams. For girls, this should be enough. She is almost 18 years old and very proficient in household chores," he would proudly tell anyone who cared to listen.

But that had Shikha worried. One day she told her friend, "I am scared that Papa is in a hurry to marry me off. I don't like it when he keeps talking to people as if I am a burden on him."

"I know what you mean. That is how parents in our village think about their daughters. Marry them off and it's all good. My grandmother is also talking to my mother about my marriage." Anita was talking to Shikha on the terrace as she was hanging laundry to dry in the sun.

"Your father is not here until Diwali. So you have a few more months of freedom and can at least apply to college. Once you

get in, you can try to convince him. I don't think I have that much time."

"So, talk to Uncle now and try to convince him to let you go to college," advised Anita.

"But our results haven't been declared yet. What if I don't get admission?"

"So, if you don't get admission, you want to be married?"

"It's not a question of what I want. It never has been and it never will be."

"You are right," rued Anita. "Our wants are never a priority for anyone. It's always what others want us to do."

"Yet, you can't forget that these others are our parents who love us no end. Remember, we love them too," reminded Shikha.

"Yes, I know. But I wish we had a say in our lives. I know the day Papa gets back, this is going to be the topic of discussion at home too. Dadi has already told the village priest about me, given my *kundli* (horoscope) and all," lamented Anita.

"Remember, Sudha, she was married when she was in grade 9. Her parents didn't even let her finish Grade 9. She cried so much in class, Mrs Lal had even gone to her house to try to convince her parents to let her study. All in vain. She turned seventeen this year and already has two children. We are lucky to have at least completed Intermediate," Shikha reminded her friend, trying to bring some cheer.

As summer wore on, it was just impossible to leave the house before sunset. The village bustled with activity in the early morning hours as men would finish their farm work before noon so they could sit and chat under the shade of the big banyan tree in the afternoon before returning to work after sunset. Going out in the sun would be a torture. Women too would be stuck indoors and sit beside open windows and doors where they could feel some cool breeze. Only the younger children could be seen still running on the streets, playing cricket or just chasing each other.

One day in the month of June, one of Anita and Shikha's classmate, Prema, came visiting. Prema lived on the other side of the village and was close to their former school and therefore, they met only when they were in class and not otherwise.

"Did you know what happened to Mrs Lal?" asked Prema

"Mrs Lal? Did something happen to her?" asked Anita, worried.

"Oh! So you don't know. Mrs Lal's husband passed away in an accident."

"Oh no! What happened?" asked Shikha, shocked.

"His scooter collided with a bus coming from the opposite side. He died before he was taken to the hospital."

The three friends sat there in shock. Though Mrs Lal was very strict and never hesitated to punish the children when they made mistakes, yet the girls liked her. She helped her students become better, conscientious citizens and made them feel proud of their country. She also rewarded her best students. Her students had a love/hate relationship with her.

"She didn't deserve this," muttered Anita

"Yes," agreed Shikha. "It must be hard on her and her little children."

"We should visit her. Do you think all ceremonies would be over?" asked Anita.

"No, I don't think so. The accident happened just last week. Cremation should have taken place by now. I think we can still go and pay our condolences at the ceremony they have on the 13th day," said Prema.

Anita's mother just walked in. "Your teacher will be sur-rounded by so many relatives that she will not have time to even look at you," she suggested. "Why doesn't Prema first find out what time they are holding the ceremony and then you can go all together," suggested Shobha.

"Okay then. I will ask the neighbours and will let you know. I have to go now. My mother must be waiting," Prema got up,

checked her *chunni* and started to leave, patting her two tiny braids. She was always hoping that one day she will have long hair like Anita's and Shikha's.

"Why don't you girls walk her down half-way? Get some fresh air," suggested Shobha to the other girls as Prema appeared morose.

The evening sun had dropped below the horizon, scattering its last rays of orange and red hue. The air was cooler at this time of the day. Some peasants were still at work. As the friends made their way through the fields, they could see a farmer spraying his fields with fertilizer while another was trying hard to make his animal move faster. Just before their row of houses, there was a big banyan tree and a small parapet was built around it with brick and concrete. The tree overlooked the vast emptiness of fields, giving a clear view of where the sun was going down.

Thanks to regular power cuts for the past few nights, their neighbourhood was bustling with night-time activity. Almost every other night, fans would stop working around 2 am and for the next 2-3 hours, everyone would have to come out in the open. Men would then sit together or take out their cots and lie down while women and girls would either go to the terrace for some air or just stay in their courtyards fanning little children with their portable jute fans. At that time of the night, they did not want little ones crying and disturbing the neighbourhood nor did they want to see them running around and asking for food. Fanning them as they slept was the easiest way out.

It was two days before they heard from Prema again. Anita and Shikha were outside Anita's house one evening, sitting on a jute cot trying to catch a glimpse of Anita's little brother Sunny who was running around with the other children sucking sweet sugarcane. "Hello there," Prema shouted with drops of sweat dripping from her forehead and sides of her face. "I hate it. It is so hot and muggy and I don't want to leave my house at all during the day. Now it is almost 6 o'clock and my mother

wants me home before 7. Shucks! Have no time to sit and chat," complained Prema.

"Yes, it is. But don't worry. They are predicting the monsoon soon," consoled Anita.

"They aren't always right, you know," said Prema.

"I wish we had telephones so I did not have to come all the way," Prema continued whining.

"Well, we don't. So, when can we go to Mrs Lal's house?" Shikha came to the point.

"Tomorrow at 4 pm. They are having the *uthala* ceremony and anyone can go."

"Do you know if any other of our classmates are going?" Shikha asked.

"The girls from 11 and 10 should be going. It would be nice as she will be teaching them again next year. I don't think our class now cares," Anita offered her friend a glass of cold water from the pitcher.

"Well, we are from 12th and we care," said Shikha.

"They will come if they care and if they know about Mr Lal," said Anita sitting down.

"It was in the papers today. Mrs Lal's family gave a small advertisement in the newspapers. But then, not everyone buys newspapers," mumbled Prema, drinking the water in one gulp.

The three friends chatted for another few minutes before calling out to their mothers to inform them that they would be back in a few minutes after dropping Prema to the bus stand.

"It will be dark soon. Walk fast, lazy girls," shouted Anita's grandmother from inside. "You could have gone a few minutes earlier. But no, you wanted to sit and gossip first."

"Yes, Dadi," shouted back Anita. The three friends grinned at each other. They were all too familiar with Dadi's condescending attitude towards girls' freedom.

The next day, both Shikha and Anita left their homes when the sun was burning hot at around 3 in the afternoon. The prayers

at Mrs Lal's house were to start at 4 and the girls had never been to her house before. They had the address and a vague idea that it was close to the school.

Anita's grandfather was concerned at the girls going alone. "Do you want me to come with you girls? Though it is day time, people prefer to stay indoors during the afternoons."

"No, no. We will be fine. I have an idea where her house is," assured Anita. "We will head back as soon as the prayers are done. Besides, we might have to walk a lot in this sun. And you are not too well."

"Okay then, take care. Here, take some money in case you have to hire a rickshaw," advised Dadaji after handling them Rs 10 note.

By the time the girls reached Mrs Lal's house, it was past 4:15 pm. There was a big crowd of people, most wearing white clothes. The women wore white sarees and men white shirts. There were children running around. Both Anita and Shikha had taken care to dress in lighter clothes though none of them owned anything white – except the white school dupatta which they had worn with their blue uniforms for years, and now hated.

As the two entered the house, they saw Mrs Lal sitting in the centre of a room surrounded by women. Her three children, who looked anywhere between 9 to 15 years old, were sitting quietly beside her. Her youngest daughter had her head on her mother's lap while the two older boys sat cross-legged facing a garlanded picture of their father. A priest was citing some *shlokas* – holy verses – and the crowd was listening intently. Mrs Lal looked up and smiled as the girls made their way to the back of the crowd. They folded their hands in Namaste at Mrs Lal who nodded her head at them.

Anita and Shikha had never been to this kind of ceremony before. From the back, they could barely see Mrs Lal as she was a short woman. She sat with her back straight and a stern look – as always. She didn't look like she had been crying at all.

With her small eyes, nose and mouth, to Anita she looked the same 'strict ole small woman', as the children always called her. She was barely 35 years old and the fact that she was already a widow gave Anita goosebumps.

Mr Lal too had been a teacher who taught Physics at the local boys' school. Everyone thought they were a perfect couple. They had similar jobs, similar work schedule. The couple, with their children, were known to take a number of holidays every year. Since their older son entered the eighth standard, that had declined. But at least once or twice a year, the family paid regular visits to their village in Bihar where their family still lived. No, theirs was not a love marriage at all though their families knew each other before they were born. Boys and girls of the 1950s and '60s were not allowed to fall in love and get married back then, Anita knew. Well, she thought, nothing has changed – even today they will not be permitted to choose their own life partners.

Anita could not help overhearing the whispers around her. Friends and relatives were talking softly. Some had genuine tears in their eyes while others merely nodded their heads. Among the women, Anita recognized some teachers from her school. In fact, former teachers now. And former school, thought Anita wryly.

From the talk around, Anita gathered that the Lals owned their small house with five bedrooms. They were not financially too sound yet could not be called poor in any sense of the term. They had a comfortable life.

"But that was when both husband and wife were earning. Now it will only be Lalita," commented one of the women who appeared to be a neighbour. Lalita Lal – so that was her teacher's full name. She never knew until now.

"You are right. Now they will have to get by with just one salary," pitched in another wide-eyed middle-aged woman.

"Vinod worked in the government school. I am sure he will have some pension and insurance," said a younger woman who was the only one not wearing white. She looked like she had

recently been married and perhaps was forbidden to wear white. She wore lots of jewelry and henna on her hands.

Vinod must be Mr Lal's first name, thought Anita. As the women talked, Anita and Shikha learnt a lot about their favorite teacher. Then, all of a sudden, one of the older women who had silently been sobbing and listening to the preacher blurted out, "I wish Lalita would just cry. She needs to cry and let her feelings out. She cannot remain silent and hide her feelings. Once everyone is gone, there will be no one to console her."

"Oh! You mean Lalitaji hasn't cried," the younger woman almost screamed in apparent shock. Other women sitting in the front and the back all turned their heads and stared at this woman with colourful clothes in anger.

"Sorry," she hissed.

"Yeah, she hasn't cried since the day Vinod died. She is trying to be strong for the children, I think. She has been talking to them as if nothing has happened," continued the older woman, now in tears. "It is so not good for her."

As the women talked, both Shikha and Anita, later joined by Prema, who was obviously late, could not help crying. Tears started welling up in their eyes as they looked on, trying to concentrate more on the service than the women blabbering away.

When the remembrance service came to an end, everyone started getting up to pay their respects to the departed soul. Mrs Lal and her children along with some other close relatives stood near the gates with folded hands. People were saying their goodbyes and assuring the family of all help. As Anita and Shikha went up to Mrs Lal with folded hands, she gave a faint smile as if appreciating their gesture of coming all the way. The girls did not know what to say and left the place quietly.

On the way back, they decided to take the bus as it would be dark soon. They did not talk much but felt a heavy burden on their hearts. Their sadness was apparent in their eyes and face. When they almost reached their house, Anita casually said,

"I have never felt this way before. I don't know how to describe it but it's like I want to cry and cannot."

Agreed Shikha, "To lose a close relative I am sure is not easy on the family. They will have to think a lot now as to what to do, how to do, where should the children go to school and if they will ever go to college."

"This was the first *uthala* I went to in my life. Have you been to one before?" Asked Anita.

"Never. My first as well. But I don't want to go to another one. I swear, I cannot bear it," said Shikha vehemently.

"We should be getting our results next week," reminded Shikha, trying to change the topic.

"Feels like forever. I think I even forgot how it feels to be in school. We should go to pick up our college forms soon."

As the two neared their homes, Anita's grandmother was standing outside the house waiting for her. "There you are. It's almost dark. Did your mother not tell you to come back before sunset," she scolded Anita, who ignored her and waved Shikha goodbye.

Stepping in, the friendly aroma of fenugreek greeted her. She loved it as a side dish with lentil and *chapati*. She went straight to the hand pump to wash her hands and feet, calling out to her mother that she was back.

"You were gone the whole day," complained her grandfather, who was sitting in the verandah with a table fan blowing air directly at him.

"No Dadaji. We left at about 3 in the afternoon and it takes an hour to get there."

Chapter 4

Nightmares

*I*t was dark and lonely. Someone was whispering...trying to say something but could not...she was being pushed. But there was no one around. Not a soul. Not a sound. No moon shone. Yes, there were clouds forming. The clouds started taking shape of a man, an old man. Are those clouds? Or fumes of a fire burning somewhere? No, there is no fire. The figure is still running. It is scared. Cannot see anything. Wondering if the direction was right. Does the path to the right lead to....lead to...lead to where? And the path to the left?

The wind. The goddamn wind. Every gust sends another chill through her body. As if the surreal night wasn't scary enough. Why am I alone? Where is everyone? How about the road? Yes, the road. I should make sure that I take the road. All roads lead somewhere. Will this one? Then...which one. There is no road. Are my feet touching the ground? No, there is no ground. What? No ground what is it? It's thin air.

And suddenly the clouds burst. There is lightning. And the face of an old man appears...big flowing white beard, long flowing salt and pepper hair, a cute nose, beautiful youthful eyes but in pain, pleading for help. And then a scream.

Anita woke up with a jolt, sweating profusely. That dream again. Her white salwar suit was soaked with sweat. She looked at the fan above, thinking the lights went out again. No, it is

running and her sister is sleeping peacefully beside her on the same bed. But she is panting, out of breath as if she had been running. O Lord! Why do I get these dreams? Not dreams, nightmares, she corrected herself.

She looked at the clock beside her desk – 3:59 am. It was still two hours before daylight and I don't have anything to do at this hour, she told herself. She wanted to go out to the washroom to wash her sweaty face. But then thought of pampered Champa, who might moo to get her attention and wake up everybody in the house. No, I will try to go back to sleep or at least lie still. She wiped her face and neck with her chunni. But dared not close her eyes for fear that the nightmare would return.

These nightmares had become part of her life. But do these have a meaning? It is said that early morning dreams are pre-monitions of things to come. No, she convinced herself. Her mother had told her dreams are merely dreams. "Make sure to wash your face and brush your teeth before you go to bed. You won't get any dreams then," her mother had tried to pacify her then. "I always do all that," Anita told herself.

The day came when results were to be declared. Both Anita and Shikha got up early, finished their chores, bathed and prayed for a little longer time than usual. Then they crossed the road to the other side and went to the temple. Though the girls visited the temple a couple of days a month, it was never regular. Both prayed, said Namaste to the priest, ate the sweets as devotional offering, that the priest lovingly gave them with his blessings and set out for school.

As they neared the school gates, they could see a stream of girls walking from all directions towards the school -- as if the school was in session and they were late for class. Others were already leaving the premises.

"Are we late or something?" asked Anita

"What is there to be late about? They display the results on the notice board and all you do is write them down in your

notebook," said Shikha casually. Both of them had remembered to bring their notebooks and pens. Official results always came in the post.

"Hey there," called out a hoarse voice they had heard a hundred times before.

Both of them turned and saw Prema walking towards them. "Did you get to see your results? How was it? Did you see mine? Did I pass or fail? I am so scared. If I don't pass, I don't get another chance. My father is planning to marry me off to this stupid boy who is a son of a friend of his."

"No, no! We are just going in. We haven't seen anything yet," replied Shikha.

"Oh, don't worry. You both will pass, I know. It's me you should be worried about," said Prema sadly.

"Nothing can be done now," replied Shikha, angry that someone who called herself a friend was just thinking about herself.

"O God! Please have mercy. I promise to work harder next time," Prema pleaded with folded hands and closed eyes. "Okay God! I am lying. I know there is no next time. So please, pass me this last time. Last time please!"

Both Shikha and Anita glanced at each other and rolled their eyes. Prema had always been like that – lazy and careless. Mrs Lal knew about Prema's laziness and therefore always picked upon her to distribute homework notebooks in class, handing out tests or cleaning the lab. At times, Prema would be the last one to leave class as Mrs Lal would deliberately give her things to do. Other teachers simply ignored her and called out other children ready to volunteer.

As they neared the notice board, there was a big crowd of girls, different shapes and sizes, and very colourful. Unlike during school time, when the girls had to be dressed in their skyblue shirts and white salwars with a *chunni* tied to the shirt, the girls that day wore bright coloured shirts and ribbons. In fact, it did

not look like a school at all. There was so much shouting and screaming, like in a stock market.

Anita and Shikha had to push their way inside the crowd but they allowed Prema to go first so she could make way for them. Prema was good at pushing and shoving while screaming at the top of her voice to be allowed in. "Watch me use my weight," she would joke at her own plump body. As she reached the front, she started looking for her roll number with a finger on the board. But there were so many fingers on the board that it was difficult to keep steady.

And then a scream so loud that other girls standing and talking with their fingers on the board, jumped up. It was Prema. "I passed. Hey!! I passed. Unbelievable! Shikha, Anita....did you hear, I passed. Barely but I did," she screamed at the top of her voice as she made her way out of the crowd. As she came out, both Anita and Shikha were able to make their way to the notice board.

Ten minutes later, both of them emerged smiling. Finally, the butterflies in their stomach had stopped fluttering.

"So," queried Prema who was watching them standing at the back of the crowd.

"I got 66%," said Anita.

"Mine is 64%. Very close. But then you always scored more than me," Shikha consoled herself.

"And you don't want to know how much I got?" asked Prema anxiously.

"Yeah how much?" asked Shikha.

"53%. I know not as good as yours but I wasn't expecting this much either," said Prema with a broad grin. "At least I can tell Ma and Bauji that I have passed. They will be happy to have at least one educated person in the family. They don't care about percentage anyways." Prema's two younger sisters and a brother were still in school. Her youngest sister was just four

years old. Since both her parents had never gone to school, they were adamant that all their children learn to read and write.

The three started walking towards the school exit. The crowd of girls now had started dispersing. Some fathers were coming on their bicycles to pick up their daughters while some had mothers in tow. "Now what? We have been waiting for this day for so long," said Anita thoughtfully.

"Let us go to Government College for Women tomorrow to pick up the forms for admission," suggested Shikha.

"What? You are planning to go to college," Prema was alarmed.

"You know that was the plan," Shikha said curtly. Shikha did not have too much patience with Prema's foolish talk, unlike Anita.

"I heard you talking about it. But are your parents okay with that?"

"I will talk to them tonight," said Shikha.

"Bauji is not back until October. I am not sure if I should be talking to Dadaji. He might not agree," said Anita thoughtfully.

"By then it will be too late."

"I know. Admissions would be over by then," said Anita.

"I don't have to worry about college. This is it for me. My aunt has arranged for a few boys who will be coming over to look at me and then I will be married in a few months," said Prema excitedly.

"Bauji was talking about my marriage a few days ago. One of his friends' son and all that." said Shikha.

"Being a girl is so difficult. You cannot take your own decision. Everything has to be decided by someone else," said Anita solemnly.

"Those someone else are your parents," reminded Shikha.

"True but I am scared of marriage. All that extra baggage of so much work, children, fields, cows, in-laws and what not. It makes my mind boggle just to think how I will ever manage that," said Anita.

"Boggle? What is that?" asked Prema.

"I don't know. Maybe like dizzy, I guess." replied Anita.

"Will you come to my house when the boys come to see me?" asked Prema excitedly. "You are my only friends who I can rely on."

"What will we do there?" asked Anita.

"Well, just what friends do – dress me up really nice, do some makeup, change my hairstyle and make me look pretty for the boys. I don't want any of them saying no to me," said Prema.

"Yeah, let's go, Anita, and dress her up. It will be fun," winked Shikha, who was now excited as well.

"I hate all this trend of showing off girls," said Anita. "Um! Will have to take permission, I guess."

"If we go together, there will not be a problem."

The three had reached the bus stop. "Okay then, my bus is here," said Prema. "I will let you know when they are coming and make sure you come." Some passengers got off the bus, Prema climbed in and waved her friends goodbye as the two started walking in the other direction.

By the time the two reached their house, they had decided to meet in the morning at about 9 o'clock to see if they could go to pick up the forms. Anita's grandparents were sitting near the shade of the wall in the verandah when she stepped in. Both looked up at her expectedly as if waiting for her to say something. With her results out of the way, there were again butterflies in her stomach since she was now nervous about seeking permission for going to college. How to broach the subject that she had been avoiding so far? But she had to or her dreams would shatter.

"Did you pass, *beta*?" now her grandmother was impatient and shouted at her as she headed to the hand pump.

"Yes, I did," replied Anita, wiping her face with a kitchen towel and walking to the charpoy where her grandparents were seated. The best way to get something out of them would be to be sweet and cute. "Do you want me to make some tea for you Dadi and Dadaji?" she asked sweetly.

"No, no. Just sit under the shade and dry off your sweat. It's too hot to drink tea. Let your mother come and then we can have it together," said Dadaji.

Dadi folded her legs under her and shuffled so she could rest her back against the wall, gathering her billowy salwar kameez under her. About 70-75 years old, she always wore a pastel coloured shirt with matching salwar and chunni. Sometimes it was a flowery pattern and sometimes just plain light colours, which she changed twice daily. She never got more than one or two new sets per year and with regular washing, the colours were mostly faded. Every Diwali, she would make sure everyone in the household had a new pair of clothes and that was the only time she bought herself a new set. Mostly, she would go out around Diwali and buy one big roll of cloth for all the females in the family. Then she would have a set stitched for herself, her daughter-in-law and her two granddaughters. While Dadi and Anita's mother would get the loose-fitting salwar, Anita and her sister always opted for the tights, just like their favourite heroine Mumtaz wore in the film *Do Raaste*.

Her grandfather, who was 10 years senior to his wife, took care of the male members of the family and would go out to buy shirt and pant material for everyone before giving it to the neighbourhood male tailor. He would take an old shirt and pant from Anita's mother for his son and keep a set ready for him when he came on vacation.

In some of Dadi's clothes, Anita could not distinguish whether it once had a flowery pattern or was just plain from day one. Anita noticed how her grandmother put on so much weight in the last few years and had cut her morning and evening walks to less than an hour. Anita's mother would always pester her to go for regular evening walks but whenever she went out, she would always meet a neighbor or an old acquaintance and would start chatting for hours. Sometimes she would just walk over to their house, sit, chat, have chai and come home saying,

"Oh! It's too late to go for a walk now. I will go tomorrow. I will start dinner." Shobha would always tell her mother-in-law that she was plain lazy. "No, I am not." Dadi would retort. "It's just that I met this friend of mine after a year and she was talking about how bad her new daughter-in-law is. She is from the city and more educated than her son and tries to tell her mother-in-law what to do. She is so arrogant that..."

"And then you told her how bad your daughter-in-law is. She does not give you food or clothes and makes you work all day and by the time you get to bed at night your legs are so tired with arthritis that you cannot sleep," teased Shyam, who would always interrupt this discussion.

"Of course not," Dadi would shout back. "I am not like that".

And so it went on almost every other day. Shobha never indulged in neighborhood gossip and did not care what the neighbors were up to. She had no time. The only time she could relax was when her husband was home and then he would tend to the fields and take care of other such stuff.

Chapter 5

The lost soldier

Sometimes in July 1977

Ajay had now spent more than six years travelling with the group of Kanjars. He had tried to escape to India whenever they were close to the border – so he thought – but it never worked. Crossing the border from any point was close to impossible. He was caught three times by the border security guards and given a good thrashing. Many times, he was even thrown behind the bars. Every time he was caught, the Chaudhury had come to his rescue. He had pleaded with the guards that he was his son and dumb-witted. "*Saabji, murkh hai. Maaf kar do. Hindustan jaane ki pata nahi kya sanak pad gai hai.* Please he won't do it again. Please let him go." (Sir, he is dumbwitted. Wants to go to India.) Ajay too had played stupid when he was caught, trying to prove that Chaudhury was right.

This was at the Wagah border near Lahore. Ajay knew if only he could sneak from any point into India, he will be able to convince the guards on the Indian side there that he was one of them. The Pakistani guards were a major hurdle and he definitely knew if he was caught again, it won't take them too long to find out he was not a Pakistani. He hardly knew the Koran. Only

once, Chaudhury had asked him how he prayed. He had casually said, "I don't. No one taught me."

"Your relatives certainly have neglected you. They should have at least sent you to a *madrasa* to learn the Koran," Chaudhury said.

"Maybe they tried and I didn't want to go," Ajay said casually, to change the topic.

"No child wants to go to a *madrasa*. They could have taught you some Ayaths at home. Did they not pray at home?" Chaudhury's wife was now concerned.

Ajay had merely shrugged and looked away sadly. How could he hold a discussion on such a topic? He prayed when he was alone, at night, mumbling to himself the *Hanuman Chalisa*, the *Om Jai Jagdish Hare* and whatever little he had learnt at home. His dad always came out of his bath singing the *Hanuman Chalisa*. The words which he had never paid any attention to as a child, which had no meaning in his childhood days, now were engraved in his mind. Maybe, that was the reason his father sang it loud, so he and his sister could memorize it. He missed his dad, his mother who was not very pleased with his marriage to Anita, yet feigned happiness for him. He missed them all and cried himself to sleep every night. The nights were dark and lonely, no silver lining in the cloud. He didn't know how to get out of this deceitful situation. Every word he spoke, every step he took had to be with caution so as not to be caught.

"Don't worry, dear. I shall teach you some of the Koran's Ayaths. These are very easy. Little children learn them too. For example, *Ola-ika A Aala hudan minrabbihim waola-ika humu almuflihoon*. This means the Lord guides you and gives you all bounties in life –which could be food, houses, gardens or even spiritual gifts."

"*Wala talbisoo alhaqqa bilbatiliwataktumoo alhaqqa waantum taA Alamoon.* This means never conceal the truth or mix it with falsehood. Some people will barely hide the truth with whatever means they can, be it by dress or their own shadows." The truth!!

There is no truth in my life anymore, Ajay thought. My whole existence is fake, based on falsehood. Allah was watching. I am a liar, a thief, how will I ever face Allah or God, whoever I meet on the other side of the world. But I was just doing my duty to my motherland. "I was merely fighting for my country and following orders. I did not start this war. I did not choose to kill so many people. It was not my decision to land this side of the border. But I know, O God or Allah, you chose for me to be alive. You did not kill me. It was your decision that I do what I am doing now – living this deceitful life." His own thoughts and justifications made him feel better. Chaudhury went on and on, not realizing that Ajay was hardly paying attention.

Ajay looked at him and couldn't believe that this nice-looking kind gentleman who had taken him under his umbrella led a pack of thieves from one place to the other. What a farce! Ajay couldn't decide whether he liked this man or hated him. Who cares, he thought. All I want is to get back to my family.

Once he tried escaping from the Pakistan-Afghanistan border along the north-western Balochistan area near Quetta, not realizing it was heavily guarded. The group preferred to stay closer to the cities and villages and not near the mountains during the winter because of the snow and lack of living spaces. They would hire a *haveli* for everyone to live in together and as summer approached, went on their nomadic ways. During the winter, the group lay low and their only source of earning would then be the terracotta toys the women made and the entertainment the girls provided on the streets. Their stealing was kept to a minimum as the group was aware that it would not be possible to run in case one of them was suspected. The men would just wander in the villages collecting wood for burning. They also took care of the oxen or bullocks they kept to pull carriages.

In Quetta, Ajay had ventured into the popular old market which crumbled during the famous earthquake of 1935. He had heard his grandmother talk about the ill-fated quake which

had taken many lives, close to 50,000. "I remember the city like the back of my hand," his grandmother always told him fondly. "There were nice buildings, beautiful market, so neat and clean that people had started calling it Little Paris. I was so proud to be living in that city. When this happened, your grandfather was helping a customer in his shop. The tremors were so strong and sudden that not many people could come out in time. Many of us had never experienced this kind of thing before. We all ran out of the houses just to see what was going on. But your grandfather, who was always very faithful to his customers, couldn't. The customer and the little boy helping him survived. They heard him screaming for help. For three days, he was alive and stuck there but no one could reach him."

That was more than forty years ago. Ajay was glad he was able to visit the spot where his grandfather breathed his last. He stood outside the shop, now a pretty shoe store with glass doors and shelves, and prayed. Paying homage to his grandfather was never on the agenda. For him prayers were just the *aartis* he had learnt while growing up and having the image of Gods from the temples his mother had taken him to, in his mind. In all the six years in Pakistan, he had not seen any temple, merely ruins where a temple may have stood. There was just one picture of his grandfather in his house, which was probably 50 years old. His mother would be happy to learn that he had visited the site no one had ever dreamt of visiting. He felt some solace at his kindly act and for a short while, the guilt and frustration of leaving his family in the lurch, lessened.

All these years, Ajay had tried to keep himself abreast of the political situation in Pakistan and somewhat in India. Again, that wasn't easy. Most newspapers were in Urdu, a language he could not read. English newspapers were scarce and he did not want to be seen reading one. He did not have much money anyway. After every theft, Chaudhury would give everyone an *anna* or a couple of *annas* to buy whatever they wanted. He always thought

of saving up enough to buy a small transistor so he could hear the news once in a while. But he never had enough. Chaudhury would give more *annas* to people who actually did the deed. Since he was not considered to be reliable and professional, they had given him the task of taking care of the animals, setting up tents or carrying groceries if they happened to pass by a village and other mundane tasks.

Chaudhury always made sure he did not go alone since the three times they had allowed him to go alone, he had fled to the border and caused trouble for the group. Since then, he wasn't able to even buy an English newspaper, but when he did, he would read it either in the jungle or in a public toilet. He was aware that Bangladesh had been created after the war; that Indira Gandhi, his favorite leader, was still the Prime Minister of India; that the Pakistan People's Party led by Zulifiqar Ali Bhutto had come to power since.

He read about the prisoner exchange after Pakistan signed the Shimla Agreement. India had released about 90,000 prisoners. He felt proud to learn that all the fighting had finally paid off and he was instrumental in giving birth to a new country called Bangladesh, yet he couldn't help feeling sorry for himself. Politics had ruined not only his life but the lives of so many other soldiers and their families. There was a prisoner exchange but there were accusations that not all prisoners were released. Unfortunately, he could not be a part of the process. Pakistan too released some PoWs but not all. India believed Pakistan had hidden some of their armed forces personnel but Pakistan kept denying the charge. It kept saying that all the Indian prisoners in Pakistan were Indian spies and would be dealt with by the court of law. The thought that he could have been part of the prisoner exchange kept him awake at night. Maybe walking away from the burning plane was not a smart decision after all. But then, the probability of him being caught by the villagers and being lynched, had been higher.

Chapter 6

Hope

July 1971

Sitting on the charpoy with her grandparents, Anita was wondering how to broach the subject of college. She had to convince her grandparents first before trying to convince her own parents. She really was confused now. She cursed herself for not working out a good strategy to talk about the issue sooner. Before she could say anything, Dadi beamed, 'Good that you passed. Now you can be married with no problem. Chaman should be home in 2-3 months and we will have some boys lined up for you by then."

Shocked, Anita almost screamed, "No Dadi! I don't want to get married right now. I want to study to become a teacher."

Her Dadi, who was half asleep, opened her eyes with a jolt, almost jumping up. "What did she just say?" she asked her husband.

"What was that, *beta*"? Dadaji asked calmly.

"I DON'T want to get married right now," she said softly but sternly.

"But why? All girls your age have to get married." Dadaji was apparently shocked.

"If not marriage, what will you do? Girls from decent families don't roam the streets of the city. It is your age to start your own family. You are already seventeen and not married yet. I was married at thirteen years of age," said Dadi.

"Our times were different then," said Dadaji, looking at Anita as if trying to convince her that he was on her side. "Look at you. You went to school only so you can read and write your name and count some paise. Once you learnt that, your parents asked you to stop and tied you to me." Dadaji was trying to make light of the situation. Anita was his favorite grandchild. She was sincere and hardworking like her mother and very responsible, unlike her siblings, who were brats.

"I know times have changed. That is why she spent twelve years in school and Chaman did not say anything. Neither did I as all girls these days are going to school. Indira Gandhi wants all girls to go to school, so did Anita. But then, there is a limit," said Dadi, ignoring her husband's joke.

"Very true. We did not have to spend a lot of money on you," said Dadaji to Anita. "Except for some stationery, the government was kind enough to give everything else. But college is not free, dear. You have to pay a lot of money to get a college education."

"I know. But then if I go to college, I can become a teacher and earn some money myself," argued Anita.

"How long will that take?" asked Dadaji.

"Three years at college and one year for Bachelor of Education," said Anita excitedly, thinking that she was getting somewhere.

"What?" screamed Dadi. "That means by the time you finish you will be 21 years of age. We will not be able to find a groom for you as you will be too old by then."

"Twentyone is not old. Plus I will bring in some money and help Shyam go to college," Anita tried to sound convincing, realizing that this discussion was not going her way. Maybe my choice of words is wrong, she thought to herself.

"Don't worry about Shyam. He can go to college if he wants," Dadi was stern.

"But that is not right. He can go without a problem but I can't just because I am born a girl," argued Anita, her voice quivering in anger. "You are partial."

"No, *beta*. This is not being partial. We love all children equally and so do Shobha and Chaman. But it is our culture that girls have to leave their parents' homes and make their home with their husbands' families," Dadi tried to explain.

Dadaji touched her head lovingly and said, "Dear, every girl one day leaves her parents' home and goes to her husband's home. That is how your mother came to our house and so did Dadi. We will miss you a lot but can't do anything. That does not mean we don't love you."

"I am not saying that I will not get married at all. Just not right now. I really really want to go to college and become a teacher," pleaded Anita, sobbing now.

"Ok, let's leave this for Chaman to decide, *beta*. Don't cry your heart out. If he says you can study further, you can. But he has been saving up for your marriage and that will mean he will have to spend that money on your education. It will be difficult for him. You have to understand. Once you are married, he will have to save for Shamu to send him to study further or for some training. Then again save for Tina's marriage. It takes years of planning," said Dadaji, trying to convince Anita.

Anita knew that grandparents were right. Her parents have been saving up for her marriage and her mother bought a couple of sarees and new utensils whenever she found a good bargain. They had to prepare a big dowry which included clothes for her and the prospective groom. Gifts had to be given to his family. And then there will be so much money given to the groom's family, not to count the money spent on ceremonies. Tons of food will have to be prepared for the whole village on the day of the marriage and guests from outside the village who would

come and stay in their house for weeks would be treated with respect and showered with gifts. Indian marriages are such an expensive affair because every relative or friend has to be pleased. Or they might curse your relationship with your spouse. No one wanted to jinx their marriages.

"I hate marriages," Anita thought. "Why can't life go on just the way it is?"

Chapter 7

New Beginnings

It was late July and mid-morning, with the sun blazing hot. Anita was trying to make the cows drink water while she herself was sweating profusely, when Prema barged in.

Anita was startled as Prema's short but big frame banged the main wooden door open and cried out, "Anita, listen to this."

"Gosh Prema," screeched Anita's grandmother who was sitting on the charpoy under the wall shade peeling vegetables for the afternoon meal, shocked. "Can't you ever knock the door or at least not scare us by barging in like a criminal? You scared me to death!"

"Sorry Dadi!" apologized Prema softly. "I did not want to scare you. But the news is so exciting that I had to tell Anita."

"What news?" asked Anita, walking towards her while dusting hay from her clothes. "Come sit here," pointing towards another cot opposite her grandmother's.

"No, let's go over to Shikha's house. I want to tell both of you together," insisted Prema.

"Sure, if that is what you want. Dadi, I will be right back," called out Anita as they went out. She was in no mood to argue with Prema, knowing fully well that she wouldn't get too far anyway.

The three were seated in Shikha's living room with glasses of lemonade which Shikha's mother had made with cold water from the earthen pitcher. "Okay Prema, now out with it," said Anita. Shikha had asked her brother to get some ice from the corner store but he refused, saying it was too hot.

"You won't believe this but a boy is coming to see me tomorrow. I want you both to be there," said Prema excitedly.

"Really?" Shikha was wide-eyed. "Who is he? What does he do and where does he live? Tell us more about him."

"Yeah really! That is why you are so excited. A would-be groom coming to see you!!" Anita could not believe her ears and sounded more sarcastic than excited.

Prema ignored the sarcasm and turned to Shikha "He is from Patiala. They have a business of making cricket bats or sports goods. Whatever. They are rich, have loads of money. They are five brothers and three sisters. My Bua is somehow related to him or his mother or something to that effect. Not sure about the details."

"That is exciting. So, you are not going to college," stated Shikha.

"No way. I never wanted to go to college," said Prema, frowning in disgust. "What about you? Are you going to college?"

"Not sure. My dad wants me to get married too. He said I could take admission if I wanted to and if midway I have to leave, I should be prepared for it. What about you, Anita?" asked Shikha.

Anita heaved a big sigh. She looked stressed and sad. "I don't know myself. I tried to convince Dada-Dadi but could not. I have to wait till Papa gets back. But by then admissions will be over."

"Why don't you ladies at least get the forms and fill them up before it is too late if that is what you want to do? Let your parents decide later but if you miss the deadline, there is no looking back," suggested Prema, hugging Anita. "Don't look so sad."

"I don't know. These adults don't really see our point of view," rued Anita.

"I know what you two can do. You are coming to my place tomorrow. Just come an hour early, go to the college, pick up the forms and then come to my place. Your parents won't stop you from coming to my house, I know that," said Prema excitedly.

Shikha and Anita looked at each other with a smile. Till now, Anita had not had the courage to talk to her mother about even going to pick up the forms. "Yes, that is a good idea," Shikha was excited too.

"Right. Thank you Prema. You are turning out to be smarter than we thought," Anita was delighted."

"No worries. I was always smart but you never appreciated me," said Prema cheekily.

In the event, both the mothers smiled and gave permission to their daughters to visit their friend the next day.

That evening, Anita decided to talk to her mother about going to college. She had never lied to her and did not intend to start now. If I don't tell her, I know I will feel bad later, she thought. It just does not feel right to not tell her.

At dinner time, when everyone was sitting together on the mat and had been served, Anita talked to her mother

"Since I am going to the city tomorrow, can I will also go to Maharishi Girls College, as it is near Prema's house, and pick up the college forms, Ma?" asked Anita casually. Her mother had never heard Anita talk about going to college but knew that she was always good at studies, and had guessed that one day she might want to go to college too.

"Do you want to go to college?" Shobha stopped eating and looked at her. She did not appear shocked, as Anita had thought.

"We have already talked about this. I told you Chaman will not be able to send you to college. We don't want you to study so much that we cannot find a groom who is more educated than you are," said Dadi angrily, before Anita could respond.

"I know you did. But I want to go to college," pleaded Anita.

Shyam had stopped eating too and was staring at his sister. He knew about his sister's intentions but never thought she would ever have the courage to talk to any of the adults at home. He said, "Why can't she go to college if she wants to, Dadi? The fee is not a lot of money for poor students like us in government colleges."

Anita looked at her younger brother, her eyes thanking him; he returned her look as if to say: No matter how much we fight with each other, when it comes to our rights, we are in it together.

"I thought we had ended this discussion till Chaman got back," Dadi retorted.

"But by then it will be too late. The last dates would be over and I cannot get in then," said Anita slowly, almost in tears.

"Since you are going tomorrow, might as well get the forms and fill them out," agreed Shobha, who could not bear to see any of her children in distress.

"Yes, do that. I will give you the money to gain admission. If your classes start before Chaman comes, go to them but you have to agree to quit when he tells you so," said Dadaji, trying to pacify her.

Wiping her tears, Anita smiled. "Thank you, Dadaji. I will do what he tells me after he gets back, I promise." Dadi stared at both her husband and Shobha but could not say anything as the two ignored her angry look. There was silence and rest of the dinner was eaten peacefully except when Sunny spilled water on the mat.

The next day, the two friends left the house around noon as they wanted to be at Prema's house by 3 pm. They went to the college in Patiala and went straight to the office. There were other students at the window, some asking for the forms, others depositing them. Anita applied for Sciences with Biology, her favorite subject. Shikha applied for Political Science as her main subject. At about 3 pm, they left the college grounds, excited at taking a step towards their future.

It was past four when the two friends reached Prema's house. She was getting dressed, wearing the same chiffon saree that she had worn at their farewell ceremony at school -- red and bold pink with black embroidery at the *pallu* and the corner with matching jewelry. Except for a light lipstick, she had no other makeup on.

"You are looking pretty," smiled Anita at her friend.

"Yes, the saree does not make you look fat at all. I am sure the boy will immediately say yes," cooed Shikha.

"So, indirectly you are saying that I am fat," said Prema, with fake annoyance.

"Hmmm! Not really. A little bit of your mother's makeup will beautify you," joked Shikha.

"So now you are saying I am ugly. She doesn't want me wearing any makeup. I am not allowed to use anything of hers, just the lipstick she was kind enough to loan," Prema rolled her eyes.

Prema's house was bigger than Anita's. Prema had her own bedroom with a decent bed and matching dresser with a long mirror, in front of which Prema stood adjusting her saree. There were four more rooms around a verandah and a big living room with a television set. They even had a dining table in the verandah and a set of two rooms on the terrace which were rented out. The rental income gave them the additional income to buy some luxuries which Anita's family could not afford. Also, since Prema's father was the only son, the fields that her grandfather owned all came to him and he had a good harvest coming from there. He never did anything himself but gave out his land on contract to whoever was ready to pay him some money and a portion of the produce. He instead ran his own business of selling cloth material in the city. He would buy directly from the manufacturers and sell the same at a higher price to small-time retailers. By caste, they were Agarwals, who were supposed to lead a frugal life and keep lots of money in the bank. But this family was different.

"Instead of making fun of me, why don't you help me put this saree together? I can't get the creases right," Prema had to shout at her friends before the two got up to help her.

"You have a nice room, all to yourself," commented Anita, getting up. "I have to share mine with my sister and brother."

"Yes, I too share with my brother. I don't even have a mirror in my room," it was now Shikha's turn to show envy.

"Don't you worry. Both of you will marry rich charming princes and will afford tens of those silly mirrors, which just make me look fat. You know, it's this mirror, which shows all the bulges. I hate it. I know I am not fat," said Prema while the others laughed.

"Those are not bulges, dear. Just a couple of samosas dangling here and there," chuckled Shikha as Prema picked up her hairbrush to hit her. Shikha made a sharp turn to avoid the brush and bumped into someone just entering the room.

"Sorry," said Shikha sheepishly and looked up to see a handsome young man with crew cut hair and big built looking down at her. He was tall, fair, with round eyes, chiseled chin and a nose just the right size for his clean-shaven face. They both stood there, staring at each other till Prema said, "Oh! Don't worry. This is my cousin Amar. He just came today from Manipal. Amar *bhaiya*, meet my friends Shikha and Anita. We were together in school."

As Amar walked past Shikha towards Prema, he was still ogling Shikha. "You never told me you had such pretty friends."

"*Bhaiya*!!" begged Prema. "Don't you start teasing my friends?"

"Why not? You don't bump into pretty earthlings every day," Amar teased. Shikha couldn't get herself to look up to him and was blushing now. She felt her face go red and her palms were sweating. Amar was still looking at her as if checking her out from head to toe while she stood there embarrassed, very pretty in her light yellow and white outfit.

"Okay *bhaiya*, what brings you here," Prema almost yelled, irritated that her brother was teasing her friends.

"Oh yeah, sis. I almost forgot. What magic have your friends spun that my brain stops functioning?" He was still staring at a blushing Shikha. "The guests are here. So, when we signal you to enter, you make an appearance with your friends in tow, Your Highness," teased Amar. "All eyes are going to be on you."

"But should she not be in the kitchen and bring the tray of snacks with tea?" asked Anita as Shikha had just gone numb.

"Right. That is what Masi said – for you all to go to the kitchen and wait for the signal to go red. Sorry green," still in his teasing mode.

"*Bhaiya*! Can you please stop staring at Shikha? You are embarrassing her," Prema was now clearly irritated as she watched Shikha standing like a statue.

"Okay okay. I am leaving. You got the message." He finally walked out of the room but turned around to give Shikha a quick glance.

"Yes we did. We are going to the kitchen now. Prema, are you ready or you still need to do something?" asked Anita.

"No, I am ready. Shikha, don't take him seriously. He is always in a jovial mood. I get irritated at times too but otherwise he is really nice and cute and I don't get to see him often."

The three friends walking towards the kitchen could hear a clamour of voices coming from the living room. The elders certainly were having a good time, Anita thought, while the girls in the kitchen were nervous.

"Why don't you get to see him often?" asked Anita.

"Well, because he has joined the Air Force and doesn't come home months together. But we sort of grew up together and I really like him. He always wanted to fly planes. He always played with toy planes as a child. But he can really be annoying at times. He just doesn't stop."

They had reached the kitchen. Shikha had been silent all this while. Prema's mother was there waiting for the girls. She had

already set a tray of biscuits, samosas and sweets and there was a pot of cinnamon tea boiling on the stove.

"You look so pretty, Prema, in that saree," said her mother.

"I would have looked prettier if only you would let me use some of your make-up, Ma," sulked Prema.

"You know your Papa does not like to see you all made up. Besides, the boy has to like you as you are and not some made-up doll," her mother said patiently.

"Yes, so when you take that make-up off, he shouldn't die of a heart attack when he sees you," Amar had popped his head in the kitchen and was listening to the conversation.

"*Bhaiya*!!" screamed Prema. "Ma, tell him to stop please. He's been teasing us all day." Before Prema's mother could say anything, Amar left the kitchen and joined the others in the living room.

"The tea is almost ready. You can carry the tea in this pink tray while Anita and Shikha can carry the snacks. I am going out now and you girls come out once the tea is ready. Don't forget to pour the tea in the kettle and cover it. The sugar and spoons are here," pointed Prema's mother before walking out of the kitchen leaving the girls to themselves.

Prema stood watching her mother leave in silence as the tea boiled over. Anita quickly pushed Prema aside and put off the stove almost screaming, "Watch out, Prema. The tea is almost done. What's wrong with you?"

"I have butterflies in my stomach."

"I thought you weren't excited,"exclaimed Anita.

"I wasn't until now. What if they reject me, Anita? What if he does not like me?" Prema was now clearly worried.

"There is nothing you can do about that. What if you don't like him? Should he feel bad?" queried Anita. "In this kind of situation I guess it is best to expect anything and don't fret or think about it. Now let's start moving."

"Shouldn't I be carrying the samosas?" Prema was looking at them with longing eyes.

"Sure, so by the time the samosas reach the living room, there is nothing left for the guests," frowned Anita.

Prema and Anita set up the trays, one with tea kettle, cups and saucers and the other with sumptuous smelling snacks. Prema carried the tea while Anita carried the rest as Shikha remained grounded. "Are you going to come with us or not?" called out Anita as they were leaving the kitchen. "What has got into this girl?" Anita was now visibly irritated by her friend.

Everything went off smoothly. Prema was all smiles after seeing the would-be groom, who was just 21 years old. He was short, somewhat on the heavier side with a small moustache, hair parted neatly on the left. He worked with his father, who manufactured sports goods and was now trying to get into exports. The father had started with a small shop decades ago and now had factories that manufactured cricket bats, wickets, hockey sticks, nets, balls, etc. They still owned the small shop of sports goods in the local bazaar, their first venture which they considered to be a good luck charm. It still made good money and the would-be-groom would spend a lot of time there. He had two other sons who were married and had children but had not come with them.

The boy, who Anita later found out was named Mahesh, was just staring at Prema, who was acting coy. Anita could see that she was trying too hard to fight the urge to directly look at him but instead was looking at his shoes, which looked new, as if bought especially for this occasion. "How many girls have seen those shoes?" thought Anita as she knew this family had been looking for a bride for some time. It was the dowry, maybe, that would be the deciding factor. "He shouldn't demand a heavy sum as he is not at all good-looking," whispered Anita to Shikha, who was standing beside her just behind where Prema sat on the sofa.

"Shut up, Anita," Shikha whispered. "This is not a good time for jokes."

"So you are alive. I thought you have been stung by a snake or something since you haven't uttered a word after we came out of that room."

Amar, who was sitting on Prema's side, walked over to the opposite side and squeezed himself between the wall and the chair where Mahesh sat. Now he had a clear view of Shikha and Anita. Once again, Shikha's face turned red when she saw him staring at her and she averted her gaze, looking down. All she could see was the top of Prema's head now. She started adjusting Prema's *pallu*. Prema looked up, irritated, while Anita stared at her.

"Stop playing with her saree, Shikha," whispered Anita.

Without saying anything, Shikha moved her hands to her side. Amar was now smiling. Anita then realized why Shikha was behaving so weirdly. Anita nudged at Shikha to go inside if she was uncomfortable. But like before, Shikha was carved in stone.

Half an hour later, the girls were asked to go in while the elders talked with each other. Prema's mother cleared the table and took everything to the kitchen. A few minutes later, she walked into Prema's bedroom with a plate of samosas where the girls were sitting.

"Thank you, Aunty, for bringing the samosas. I have been dying to eat those," said Anita as she jumped from the bed to take the plate.

"I know you must be hungry. Now eat them all and try to leave before it gets dark so your parents are not worried. The buses will be full at this time too," said Prema's mother walking out the door.

"Sure, Aunty," said Anita with a mouthful of samosa. "Shikha certainly is not interested in samosas today. Something has bitten her."

"What? Was it a snake or a spider?" asked Prema, shocked. "We don't have those in our house, you know. Sudha, our part-time maid, cleans the house every day."

"No, no, it is not an animal or an insect," continued Anita, more interested in grabbing another samosa. "Looks like the Amar bug."

"What? What did *bhaiya* do to you, Shikha?" yelled Prema. That jolted Shikha out of her trance and she looked at Prema. "What what?"

"I asked what did *bhaiya* do to you that you are not eating. Have you gone deaf and dumb as well, Shikha? You have been acting so weird. You don't look yourself."

Prema picked up the last samosa before asking her friends if they liked the boy and his family.

"Well, he is not bad. He is not Rajesh Khanna or Dharmendra of course but decent enough to be your husband," teased Anita, as Prema lunged at her. Anita dodged her and spilled potato filling on the bed.

"See what you did, Prema. Now clean up. See you later." Anita and Shikha got up and hugged their friend before saying Namaste to the rest of Prema's family. The guests had by now departed, leaving the family to discuss the boy and his family. Before leaving, Anita had whispered in Prema's ears to let them know if she is marrying this boy. Prema smiled and blushed.

All the way back, there was not much conversation. Anita was more excited about filling out the college forms than Prema's new found love. "I just hope Papa allows me to go to college and doesn't decide to marry me off," she told her friend.

Shikha finally spoke up as they were nearing their house and said, "There is no harm in marrying someone you like. College may not be important but we have to get married one day."

Anita stopped walking and stared at Shikha, who had turned around to face her. Anita's mouth was open with astonishment. "Seriously Anita, I don't think it is bad either."

"So, now that you have filled out the forms, you are not interested in going to college. May I know why," asked Anita, as she slowly started walking again.

"I don't know. The thought just occurred to me. Anyway, forget what I said and if Papa allows me, I will go to college with you."

"No, you are not going to college for me or with me. You have to go for yourself or you will not be successful, Shikha."

"I know. I am just confused. All of a sudden college does not seem important," whispered Shikha, walking towards her house. Anita stood there watching her friend, wondering if she really knew her.

Chapter 8

Friends

Two weeks later, Anita and Shikha got mail from their college. While Anita was given admission in her first preference, which was Biology (Honours), Shikha got her second preference, Bachelor of Arts with Political Science instead of Political Science (Honours). Dadaji opened the letter and called out to Anita, who was on the terrace helping her mother dry washed wheat kernels before dispatching them to the grinding machine. She came running and took the letter from her grandfather's hands.

"College starts in August," she said excitedly to Dadaji.

"Good, have you paid the fees?" asked Dadaji, going back to other letters delivered by the postman.

"No, not yet," Anita's excitement had now waned. "Dadaji, do you think Papa will let me go to college?"

"Um...how can I say? We can't talk to him till he comes home." Opening another letter, he said, "This is from him. He is coming around Diwali."

"But that is too late. Classes start next month and we have to pay the fees. What should I do?"

Dadi came out of the kitchen as her mother came down the stairs from the terrace. "What are you confused about, dear?"

Anita just looked up and said nothing. Just the thought of asking her dad about college gave her goosebumps. How should I approach the subject, she thought? Should I send a letter? I should have done that a long time ago, she thought. But never had the nerve to pen one down. Too late for that.

Anita looked at Shobha pleadingly. Her mother always understood her inner turmoil without having to be told and always seemed to have solutions. "So, you got a letter from your college. Oh yes you did. I can read your face," Shobha said, trying to lighten the mood.

Shobha took the letter Anita was holding and looked at it impressed. "You know, Anita, I have never seen a letter of admission from a college before. They really must like you and want you to study there. Isn't it, Bauji?" she looked at her father-in-law.

"You are so right, Bahu. Come to think of it, even I have never seen a letter from any college, leave alone an admission offer. This is my first time as well," he said, taking the letter from Shobha's hands. "If you go, Anita, I would be so happy to brag about you to my friends and relatives."

"Girls in our community don't go to college. In fact, girls are taught only basic stuff so you can read and write enough to make budgets for household expenses. You have done more than that and your life will be fine. We should start looking for a groom for you," said the elderly lady sitting next to her husband.

Shobha lovingly stroked her daughter's head and sat down near her. "I really want you to go to college, Anita. But the question is not what I want or what we all want. It is true all girls your age have to get married. You friend Prema is getting married too. And so will Shikha eventually. Her family is looking for a boy for her, you know."

"I know, Ma. But till I get married, can I go? I'm not saying I will not get married. And the tuition is not so much and I promise not to spend too much money on books. You know in

college, you don't need to buy books. You can get them issued from the library, make your notes and give them back."

"You are being adamant now," said Dadiji sternly.

"Till her father comes and says something, I think she can start going to college and we will see later. Maybe we will find a better groom for her as we can say our girl is in college," said Dadaji cheerily.

"Why do you want to waste money? No, I don't agree that she will get a better groom. Boys don't want to marry a girl who is more educated than them," said Dadiji lying down on the charpoy and closing her eyes. "Do what you wish."

She ran to the terrace excitedly and called out Shikha. "How about you, Shikha? Will you be coming to college too?"

"I guess so. Papa keeps saying he has to get me married as soon as possible. But there is no boy in sight," said Shikha, sitting on the terrace parapet on her side of the roof as Anita stayed on her own side. Both friends would be there for hours chatting about everything under the sun. So would their mothers at times when they were working on the terrace, taking a few minutes to exchange domestic notes.

On the Sunday, just a day before the girls started their classes, Prema came to Anita's house with her mother. It was her first ever visit to their house and Anita was surprised.

So was Shobha but she welcomed her with a hug. The two women had never met before but knew about each other through their daughters.

"Namaste," said Shobha bowing her head. "Welcome to our house. It is nice meeting you."

"Namaste," said Prema's mother as the two friends hugged each other and Anita shot an inquisitive glance at Prema, who merely fluttered her eyes.

"What brings you here today?" asked Shobha, seating the guests in her modest verandah which served as a sitting area for guests. It had an old bamboo three-seat sofa and two lone chairs

with cushions. Shobha always tried to keep the covers clean but frequent washing had taken off the pretty flowery print. There were two matching glass-topped coffee tables.

Shobha started the ceiling fan. Prema's mother opened her purse and took out a wedding card.

"I came to invite you all personally to Prema's wedding next month," she said handing over a wedding card to Shobha. "You should all come."

"So Prema is marrying the boy we saw," said Anita excitedly as Prema blushed.

"Yes, they are very nice people and want the marriage as soon as possible. It is a rush for us, of course, as we have a lot to do in a very short time. Our functions start from 15th August starting with Roka and you should come to all the events," said Prema's mother.

"Yes, of course," assured Shobha, taking the card.

"Behenji, if you don't mind, can I ask you a question?" asked Prema's mother hesitantly.

"Sure."

"Prema tells me Shikha and her family are your neighbors".

"Yes, they live right next door. Very nice people. But why do you ask?"

"How long have you known them?"

"I have been married for almost 20 years and they have lived next door since I came to this house. Shikha's father works at the post office and they have a piece of land too on which they do farming."

"Actually, my sister's son Amar really liked Shikha and wanted me to talk to her parents. He had to go to back to his station but should be here for the wedding. Do you think I should talk about the issue with them today? Do you know if they have already met someone for Shikha?"

"That is so exciting," said Anita looking at Prema. "Is he the cousin of yours who we met when we were at your place? He couldn't take his eyes off Shikha."

"Yes, that is the one. He was so drawn to Shikha, always talking about her till he left. I wanted to come and tell you but mother did not let me come," complained Prema, looking at her mother sadly.

"This was the reason I did not want you to come so you don't create a scandal for both the families. Behenji (Sister), do you know if they are seriously looking for a boy for Shikha?"

"Oh yes. I know they are and they haven't found anyone decent yet. They got two proposals which Shika's father rejected," replied Shobha.

Anita looked at her mother. "Seriously, Ma. Shikha had two proposals? She never told me."

"Maybe she doesn't know either but her mother told me the other day that her father is looking for a boy actively. Behenji, if your nephew is serious about Shikha, you should talk to them right now. She is a nice girl just like our Prema and Anita and we all know each other's families. I don't think there should be a problem."

"Thank you, Behenji. I am so relieved now. I have Amar's horoscope and his picture and I will go right away. I will invite them and talk to them too. I should make a move now."

"No, no. Have tea at least. You have come for the first time. Anita, can you make some tea for Aunty?"

Anita rushed to the kitchen followed by Prema. The two friends chatted excitedly in the kitchen for a while before Prema and her mother left for Shikha's house. Before leaving, Prema's mother warned the two friends not to talk about the proposal with anyone else.

Anita couldn't sleep that night. Every cell in her body was filled with anxiety. She was excited about not only starting college but also about Shikha. She wanted to know how her friend's

family had reacted and if they were going ahead with the proposal. She could tell that Shikha had somehow fallen for Amar too and had seen the change in her behaviour after their meeting at Prema's house.

Her nightmares continued.

By 7 the next morning, Anita was all ready to go. Their classes started at 9 am and it would take about 45 minutes to reach college.

Dadi merely stared at her silently when she said goodbye. The old lady was still angry at not only Anita but at Shobha and her husband for allowing Anita to go to college. To appease her, Anita gave her a hug. "Dadi, please smile. I need your blessings." She merely said, "Beware of strangers, girl. Don't talk to boys. They can be dangerous."

Shikha's father was sitting on a charpoy reading the newspaper and her mother was in the kitchen as Anita walked in. Anita greeted them with "Namaste, Uncle. Namaste, Aunty."

"Namaste, *beta*," replied Shikha's father. "I don't think Shikha will be accompanying you to college for long. She might get married in a few months."

"So, you too liked Amar, Uncle?"

"Yes, he appears to be a nice boy. Good job, good family."

"Shikha likes him too."

"Oh, she does?" Shikha's father was shocked as Shikha glared at Anita. Apparently, Shikha's father was not aware of his daughter's feelings.

"We are getting late, Uncle. Come, Shikha," said Anita hurriedly, tugging at Shikha's arm.

"Phew! That was close," sighed Anita as the two were some distance away from Shikha's house.

"It sure was. Papa does not know that I have actually met Amar. He thinks Amar just saw me at Prema's engagement and liked me and sent his proposal. You embarrassed me, Anita."

"I'm sorry. It was just a spontaneous reaction. But you like him, don't you?" teased Anita. On the way to college, Shikha blushed every time Amar's name came up.

The two friends reached college just before 9 am and barely had enough time to locate their classrooms. They ran in different directions as their departments were on opposite side of the campus.

On the way back in the afternoon, the two chatted about their teachers and new friends. Though it was a girls' college, the two could not ignore the glare of boys on bikes, a common sight outside girls' schools and colleges. Growing up, the girls had learnt to either avoid them or only react if they got too mischievous. Most of them were harmless, out to have some fun.

Chapter 9

Friends with similar destinies

*S*he was on the floor...six pairs of eyes stared down on her... *she lay there helpless wanting to scream but could not. It was dark, dingy, and the concrete floor was cold. A pair of hands was tugging at her shirt, his hands were big and rough, her skin soft and silky, he had no face, only white teeth – too white. Her hands were tied with her chunni, her screams muffled, a piece of cloth stuffed in her mouth. Surprisingly with so much commotion, it was eerily quiet. They were hurting her but still there was no sound, except the scuffling of her body moving under the weight of those big men. Suddenly, all of them left but one and she felt something entering her. A monster, a depraved monster, sullying an innocent victim... No no...Anita woke up horrified. She was sweating profusely. Her clothes were all crumpled. Her breath was rapid, her heart beating fast. She looked around her. Where was she?*

Anita was safe, in her own little apartment in Gulmohar Park, New Delhi. There was a calendar on the wall, above the tiny desk in the corner of her bedroom. There was a pile of books and diaries on the corner of her desk. Every year that had gone by since she left college, she had kept a diary. Prior to that, she thought writing a diary was for the weak, for those who had no social skills and those who wanted to hide behind white expressionless blank pages who never talk back, never argue,

76

never pass judgments but just believe you – trust you enough that you can go on pricking at them and they never scream. Paper made of bark from a tree which is a living thing. So, paper is a living thing with feelings and could understand what was being written…yet…

She looked at the calendar. The year was 1999. Twenty-eight years has gone by since that day in 1971 when her husband, Flight Lieutenant Ajay Singh, had left home, promising he would be back soon. But he did not keep his promise. It was so unlike him. He always kept his word and never went back on it. The six months they had spent together were the best in her life. Memories of those days, 186 to be exact, felt like a dream – a dream is short and one wakes up fast, dreams are normally about people, the faces of those one sees in real life. That is why psychiatrists describe dreams as being very meaningful, helping to interpret behavior, motives, thoughts and feelings. However, the superstitious describe dreams as a premonition of things to come – good or bad – and consider dreams as a warning. For some, dreams help in resolving complex issues. Like her mother always said, "If you can't find a solution to your problem, close your books and go to sleep. By morning, you will have all the answers."

Every morning, Anita waited for news from Ajay. Long ago, she used to wait for good news, for a messenger to knock on her door and tell her that Ajay is safe, he will be back soon. But none came. Today, she just wants closure. She wants to know where he has been, what happened to him.

Anita looked at the stack of diaries on the side of her small desk. There were now some on the floor. She first started writing diaries in December 1975, four years after Ajay disappeared and almost five years after she got married to him. All these years, she had tried to keep that memory alive – the scene like a black and white movie playing in her mind all the time – sometimes she felt that she forced herself to think about the day again and

again and that was scared that it might fade one day if she did not. He had his backpack, dressed smartly in his Air Force uniform, cap and all. Just before he stepped out to the official jeep waiting for him, he turned around, kissed her on the cheek and said lovingly, "Wait for me here. I will be back soon. Wars don't last long these days. Take care." He waved to her. She waved back with tears in her eyes, apprehensive and fearful. Is this the last goodbye? No, no, she scolded herself. "How dare this thought come to your mind, Anita," she shrugged. She had been shrugging for the last 28 years.

It felt like yesterday when she first met him. Her dad had finally given in and allowed her to attend college when he came for Diwali that year. As was expected, Dadi made a big fuss about it. Finally, Dadaji reined her in. "The fee for the year is already paid, she has a bus pass to go to college, she is not spending money on books, so let her do what she wants till you find a suitable boy for her. Do you have anyone in mind?" Dadaji asked, looking at his son.

"Not right now," he replied.

"Okay then, look for a decent boy and we will continue this conversation when you find someone," Dadaji said, sternly looking at his son and daughter-in-law and winking at Anita slyly.

The next few months floated by. In August, Prema got married and in the next few days, Shikha and Amar's wedding was fixed. Amar's family insisted on an early ceremony. Amar and Shikha were engaged at Prema's wedding and married by December that year.

Ajay, being Amar's best friend and cousin, had come to attend the wedding. Amar and Ajay had schooled together at Rajpura, both wanted to serve the country and fly planes, went for training together at the Air Force Academy to train as pilots. Their professional and personal life was so intermixed that the fine line just wasn't visible. Their families were related and their grandparents had moved from Pakistan during Independence

and had remained together forever. The families had been each other's support much before Ajay and Amar were born. Both of them were Flight Lieutenants in the Air Force now.

Therefore, it was but natural that both the families were present during Amar's wedding and one thing led to another. And Ajay rightly was Amar's *sarbala*, his best man. In some cases, the *sarbala* wears similar clothes as the groom and comes to the rescue of the groom in case he is teased by the bride's sisters and friends during rituals.

Anita, being Shikha's best friend, was with her throughout the wedding. She helped Shikha tie her green and yellow saree with bright yellow blouse during the engagement. Instead of the usual two braids, Anita suggested a bun on top of the head. "You look like Mumtaz in *Khilona*," pulling Shikha in front of the mirror. The two had sneaked out from college to watch the film when one of their classes had been cancelled, unknown to their families.

"Shh...someone might hear us," whispered Shikha. "There are so many people in the house."

"Don't worry. In a few days no one will care anymore. How do you like yourself? Amar will drop to the ground once he sees you," teased Anita.

"Do you have a lipstick? That might help," Shikha whispered.

"No, I don't. Do you want me to ask your mother?"

"No, no. She said no makeup, like all mothers," Shikha frowned. "All mothers seem to have the same issue with make-up. They think too highly of their daughters, as if they are little princesses, and the whole world will view them so. Boys like pretty girls, made-up or not."

"Ok, ok now, don't start crying or you will smudge whatever little *kajal* you have in your eyes. And Amar will freak out," teased Anita.

"I am here, I am here," the girls heard. As they turned around a big pink ball came flying towards them, crushing Shikha's bun

as Anita fell on top of her and Prema on top of them all just before Anita called out, "Watch it."

"Watch what?" asked Prema, still on top of both the girls.

"Get up, you fatso," Shikha managed to screech. "Anita, move"

"Prema, get up now. Look what you have done to Shikha's saree and make-up. It took me two hours and now we have to start all over again."

"Oh no! I'm sorry. I'm so excited to see you. And look what I got for you girls. My make-up kit! Now that I am married, I have my own and I can share with you," said Prema excitedly trying to pull herself together. Finally, when Anita was back on her feet, she pulled Shikha up with her saree under her feet now showing her delicate waist, bun on the floor and loose hair hanging on her shoulders.

"You are a total mess. We have to start all over again," Anita said, slapping her forehead and sitting on the bed.

"I'm so sorry," Prema said, pulling her ears. "But don't worry, it will take less time now since there are two of us to help Shikha. You do the beautiful bun and I will help her with the saree."

Shikha stared angrily at Prema. "You know two people cannot work together. To tie the saree I have to stand and for the bun, I have to sit."

"Are you girls ready? It is almost time," Shikha's mother called as she walked in the room. "I want to see how my princess looks."

Shikha's mother was shell-shocked when she saw her daughter – eyes wide and mouth open. Before she could say anything, Anita tried to calm her down, "Don't worry, Aunty. We will fix her. It was an accident."

"Yes, yes, an accident." chipped in Prema. "We will beautify your princess in a few minutes ..."

"Oh my God! Can't trust you girls at all. The boy's family will be here any minute."

"The boy's family is already here and we know how she looks anyway," laughed Prema. "I am from Amar Bhaiya's family, remember."

"Okay okay! Do your magic fast, I will help," said the mother.

"No, no Aunty. You take care of other things. It won't take more than 10 minutes," Anita tried to convince her, pushing Shikha on the stool in front of the mirror. She picked up the yellow comb with one hand and gathered Shikha's long black hair in the other.

An hour later, Shikha was seated on the bamboo sofa in the living room opposite Amar, who was squashed between his parents. His best friend Ajay was next to him and Prema was sitting on the sofa armrest to the left of Amar's mother. An uninvited guest, Amar's best friend Ajay too had shown up. "The two have always been there for each other. They went to school together, trained together but unfortunately have been posted to different parts of the country. When Ajay came to know that Amar was planning to get married, he came down from Hindon."

Ajay was tall, fair, charismatic and deliriously handsome with deep dark grey eyes under thick eyebrows on a heart-shaped face. His hair was heavy, jet-black wavy and parted on the right. His thick wavy sideburns and the small moustache reminded Anita of Randhir Kapoor in the recently released *Kal Aaj Aur Kal*. No, she hadn't seen the film, only the posters.

Anita was standing next to Shikha laughing at the funny stories Amar and Ajay were telling about each other. Amar was telling a story when they were almost 5 years old and one of their uncles had taken Amar to watch a cricket match at the University campus. Since Amar did not want to go, he dragged Ajay along.

"None of us understood the game. For us it was just like playing bat and ball," laughed Ajay. "I did not want to go but Ammaji said I should go with Amar as she could see his sad face."

"Uncle wanted to take me to the match so I could start loving the game and play cricket with him. He was explaining the rules

all the way there, right in my ear as I was the one standing in front of the scooter and Ajay was on the back seat. I remember getting so bored at people running about the field for a stupid little ball. Since both of us played football more, we found it a waste of time running after that small heavy ball."

"Once one of the players caught the ball, I was happy and shouted 'Let's go home," laughed Ajay with a twinkle in his eye, looking at Anita. Everyone was laughing. Anita tried not to look into Ajay's eyes.

But Ajay couldn't take his eyes off her. All through the ceremony, he was staring at Anita, unaware that Amar was watching him. Anita saw Amar whispering in Prema's ears, whose already big smile was now ear to ear. She jumped up with joy and ran to the verandah where all the elders were while Anita wondered what the excitement was all about.

After the ceremony, Shikha and Anita were sitting on the bed chatting in Shikha's room. "I don't get it. Where is Prema? I haven't seen her in a while," wondered Anita.

"Must be eating in the kitchen corner," said Shikha. "Why doesn't she eat here as usual? God, I am so hungry. It's been 7 hours since I ate anything and no one has offered me any food. Aren't you hungry, Anita?"

"Wait, I will go and look for some food," Anita said, getting up from the bed and adjusting her *chunni*. Just then Prema came running into the room and bumped into Anita. Anita grabbed the door to prevent herself from falling. "Prema, can't you ever walk straight -- or see straight?" squealed Anita, trying to keep her voice down.

"Oh my dear Anita Anita Anita." Prema grabbed Anita's shoulders and hugged her. "I am so happy today. Happy happy happy."

"Why are you so happy? You are already married and my marriage is nothing out of the ordinary. Forget about that, why didn't you get me some food," said Shikha.

Prema pushed Anita aside and ran towards Shikha. "Oh Shikha Bhabhi! Stop thinking about food. I am so excited today." Prema hugged Shikha so tight that she almost screamed.

"Stop thinking about food! Look who's talking," exclaimed Anita.

"You will stop thinking about food when you hear the good news. Anita is getting married too," said Prema with a big smile on her face. "Amar Bhaiya's friend Ajay liked Anita so much that he convinced his parents to speak to Anita's parents. All elders have agreed and are now working out the details."

"I don't believe you!" exclaimed Shikha as Anita stood frozen near the door, her head spinning. She could see her dreams crashing, her wings being cut. She felt like that injured pigeon she had once seen fall from the sky, its flight cut midway by naughty children who had used it for target practice. She had saved that pigeon, nursed it to health and one day it was able to fly again. She had named it Dumbo, since it had not dodged the pebble coming towards it. She now felt like that helpless bird. Would she fly again? Ever?

The sun went down, the full moon shone through the clouds as bright as the electric bulb Grahm created. "Everyone is a moon, and has a dark side which he never shows to anybody," Mark Twain once said. The sky was darkening as lights of all the houses started twinkling. The stars were lighting up in the sky above.

Anita's mind was spinning. "I will be a bride – 'a woman with a fine prospect of happiness behind her', as someone had said." She heard the bells ringing in the temple far away…mingling with the sound of muezzin reciting evening calls to Muslim prayers.

Chapter 10

Missing Anita in Pakistan

One day in 1977, when the pilot woke up, he heard a lot of commotion outside the *haveli*. People were running around shouting, "*Bhutto gaya, Bhutto gaya.*" (Bhutto is gone). Others were screaming, "*Zia ne kabza kia! Zia ne kabza kiya*"! (Zia has taken over the country!) There was a lot of commotion around tea stalls, *paanwallas*, mosques, under trees and any other location used by villagers to gather and chat. There was panic in the air. A hundred radios were blaring at the same time and groups of men were standing around the radios listening intently. Strangely, even women had come out of their houses and were standing in groups chatting away. "*Fauj ne kabza kar liya!! Ab kya hoga hamara. Zia to bahut zalim hai suna.*" (The military has taken over the country. What will happen to us? We have heard Zia is very cruel.)

Outside, people were going about their business as if it was an ordinary day but were very scared inside. News on the radio was being filtered and there were rumors galore. People were uncertain of the future. Government officials were being fired, captured and thrown in prison for no reason. Days after the coup Zia-ul-Haq, the military commander of Pakistan's Army, declared Martial Law. This resulted in killing the opposition by throwing the members of rival political parties in jail and

public flogging of popular student leaders, journalists, trade union leaders and government officials working for the previous Bhutto government.

Though Ajay was not able to follow Pakistani politics in detail due to his limited access to newspapers and other material, the group he was part of was least concerned about what happened in other parts of the country. They were planning their next heist. It was only during their evening meals that they discussed the news, if at all they had heard something

"Zia-ul-Haq got rid of Bhutto. Now he is the President of Pakistan."

"People don't like him. He is supposed to be very harsh."

"All of Bhutto's men are in jails right now. No one to confront him."

"Even the policemen have been jailed. Only his men can be police officers. No one is allowed to say anything against him."

"But that is not good," Ajay tried to encourage a debate to get more information. "They said Bhutto was a good man and he got so many prisoners from India." He stopped himself from saying 'our men'. That would have been the right word to use but his patriotism got to him. "Bharat Mata *ki jai* (Hail India!)", he muttered under his breath.

"We don't know who is a good man or a bad man. But remember, we should all mind our own business. Don't talk to anyone about what goes on in the country. For the government, we don't exist. *Iqbal Mian, hoshiyar rehna,*" Chaudhury reprimanded Ajay. "We don't want any trouble."

End of discussion. During his stay with the group, he had made friends with men his age. But most elderly people in the group were wary of him and would clam up when he was around, especially when they were discussing their next plan. Chaudhury initially had trusted him with lots of responsibility because he thought he was physically capable, a strong man who could carry a lot of stuff during burglaries. But after the time when he created

trouble for the group, they just used him to lift loads, set up tents, take care of the cattle and at times baby-sit a group of kids when the women went out.

He regarded the job of lifting loads as a good way of keeping fit. He was happy that they did not take him out during their larceny as his conscience never approved of that. He was a favorite of the women, as he would always volunteer to lift heavy hot pots from the *chulha*. As a goodwill gesture, they would serve him more food than the others, which kept him going. While minding the children, he would play games with them of lifting bricks and made them compete with each other. And then he would show them how much he could lift and keep challenging himself every day. At other times, he would ask the children to hang on to his arms and swing them around. He would do that with all the 17-18 children from 2 years of age to older.

After all, he had to gain strength so he could run.

As the turmoil in Pakistan was at its peak, curfews became the norm and so did public flogging. There were unwarranted arrests of civilians and public servants. Sheer barbarism was unleashed on hapless people, left at the mercy of the military might. Elections, which were supposed to take place in October 1977, were postponed. Soon after, the mighty leader declared political parties defunct and barred political leaders from political activities. Just to set an example of his ruthlessness, Zia publicly flogged well-known leaders, union members, journalists and anyone raising voices against his regime.

In fact, Zia imposed medieval Islamic punishments – like amputation of the fingers – for theft and banditry, calling for death penalty or public hanging, taking the country back to the time before British rule. Student agitations and political activity resulted in imprisonment of up to 5 years and/or whipping; crimes against women got 5 years in prison. Death was certain for resisting police or armed forces. The military dictator tried

to reassure the public that severe punishments would only be imposed by the civil courts or the highest military.

Newspapers became scarcer and government fed news on radios. However, looking at the brighter side, Ajay would get more news about India than he ever did. In an attempt to play down the atrocities committed by the Pakistani General on his own people, he dictated the media highlight news from India and the changes in government taking place there.

So, India had already exploded her first nuclear device a couple of years ago, he learnt. Peace talks had been initiated between India and Pakistan to avoid any armed conflict between the countries like in 1971 and 1975. 1971 he knew about but 1975? Did India and Pakistan fight another war? How come there was no news ever and no hint in the countryside that the countries were warring? Ajay couldn't sleep that night wondering about what happened in 1975. Were more of our men killed? Or went missing like me? Were they rotting in Pakistan jails? By now, he had started doubting the news Pakistan media was feeding its population.

Just the thought of a Pakistan jail sent shivers down his spine. The conditions were inhuman, not to mention the brutality of the torture prisoners underwent every day. He was hung upside down, beaten on the soles of his feet, denied food and sleep, water and salt thrown on his open wounds. All this when he was considered one of them. He couldn't imagine what they would do to him if they ever learnt he was an Indian. Thanks to the sweet-talking Chaudhury, he was rescued every time. He would call Ajay his wayward son who spent time in the company of bad people and always got into trouble. It had taken months for the women in the group to nurse him back to health using their grass and herb-based concoctions. None of them was allowed to see a doctor or visit modern chemist shops to buy medicines. He had thanked them a couple of times but now some of them were getting sick of taking care of him. Especially Chaudhury's wife,

who was ready to abandon him in the jungle. Though vocal about her views, she did not have the courage to talk to her husband about her intentions.

He prayed silently for the wellbeing of his family. He thought of Anita all the time: was she waiting for him? It had been six years since he had seen her and didn't know her whereabouts. Pakistan radio, which he would overhear when passing by a shop, was talking about all the agitations against the government that had taken place in different parts of the country, resulting in Indira Gandhi imposing an internal Emergency. He wondered if Anita had gone back to her parents' house or was waiting for him in Ambala. Would the Air Force still allow her to live there – give her the house and the amenities that came with being an officer's wife? He had his doubts about that. And his parents had never approved of Anita – so going there would be next to impossible.

How would she cope? Ajay always had the fear that Anita's parents would get her remarried. After all, there would be no news of him. Soldiers Missing in Action (MIA) are mostly considered dead and the families given pensions. Since his name could not be on any lists dead or alive, he would just be declared MIA and his file would be closed. He was as good as dead for both the countries and after six long years, there would be no one looking for him.

He hoped Anita got the letter he had written years ago. While his mind wanted Anita to go on with her life, marry again and find love somewhere else, his heart would not agree. He was positive that one day he would find his way back and once that happened, he wanted Anita to be waiting for him so they could live happily ever after. He decided to write another letter but couldn't find a post office. This time he thought he would write a long letter telling Anita about what he had been going through since his plane was shot down. "I will have to buy pen, paper,

envelope and a stamp," he thought. That would cost a lot of money and raise suspicion. So he bided his time.

The troupe of Kanjars now retreated in the forests of Sindh in the Punjab province. One day over dinner, a couple of weeks after Martial Law was imposed in Pakistan, Chaudhury said in a hushed tone, "With the new government, it will be difficult to do business. The military people have no brains and will not think twice before beheading you."

"You mean have no heart," an elderly woman with two teenage daughters said, correcting Chaudhury.

"Business?" Ajay thought. What business is he talking about? Stealing, looting people, selling their wares?

"And you think anyone with a uniform has it," countered a young man named Rahim, who preferred to be called Amir, Ajay never understood why, looking at the woman, then giving a fleeting glance at her daughter sitting next to her. She looked about 20 years old, about the same age as the young man.

Ajay had always wondered about the marriages that took place within this community. In the last couple of years since he had been with the group, he had observed a few of the children he saw grow up, get married to each other. When exactly the ceremony took place was a mystery to him. He observed that before the wedding, the couple and a few elders along with the parents of the bride and groom would be gone for a couple of days. When they got back, the young people were a couple. The bride and groom would be wearing new clothes, the girl some shining new jewelry and they would be carrying shopping bags. Ajay once asked a younger woman whose two little children he took care of, "Where do these people go for their marriage, Appa (Elder Sister)? Why not have the marriage here when the whole family is together?"

"Because no one is a priest here. So they have to go to a temple and look for someone who can get them married," the woman replied casually.

"You mean the mosque," Ajay looked at her questioningly. Ajay had gotten used to calling all women in the group Appa and men Bhaijaan (Big Brother).

"Ah! Yes, yes. That is what I meant," the young woman with an oval face, the fairest of all the women in the group said, avoiding Ajay's gaze. She was knitting a bamboo basket and tried to speed up the process.

"Who decides who should marry who? No one can marry anyone from outside the group?" Ajay further questioned her, picking up some bamboo sticks to make a basket himself. After watching for years, he could make one faster than anyone in the group and was always ready to help.

"It depends. The girl and boy have the liberty to choose and so do their parents. Sometimes, Chaudhury will decide. They have always preferred that marriages take place in the same *biradari* (community). Our *biradari* is scattered and therefore, we can't find anyone from outside. Then we don't live in one place for long. Which means, that if anyone decides to marry anyone from outside, they will never see their family ever again. It is very rare that we go to the same place twice. Why do you ask? Do you want to marry one of the girls?" she mocked. "You know Jamila likes you so much. She is a nice girl and will make you a good wife."

"No, no. I am not the marrying kind. You know about me. I want to go to India and look for my family. I have no one here." His sorrow was reflected in his eyes. Phuki, the young woman, looked at the lonesome distraught man with a forced smile and went back to knitting her basket. "Don't worry. We are all your family. If ever you think I can help, I sure will. I will elope with you too. I may be your Appa but when it comes to some fun and adventure, I am ready," she laughed heartily.

"I meant the government is becoming strict with bandits and thieves like us," Chaudhury was saying. The sun had set on that August evening and it was getting dark. Only the orange yellow light of the fire that burnt in the middle of the group with

a big pot of hot water boiling on it reflected on the old man's face. As Ajay looked at him, he was reminded of the first horror film he had seen. It was about this man who was murdered; his family disappeared into thin air. The man with sunken eyes and cheeks, white teeth reflecting the dance of the fire and flowing white-orange beard, long fingers of a skinny hand moving up and down from his leafy plate to his mouth holding a *roti* and that moving aquiline jaw, could scare any child. The film was shot in a jungle where the family had lived in a huge bungalow. Was it *Bhooth Bangla* or *Bhootiya*, he couldn't remember. But the setting seemed to be as eerie as his present circumstances. Dark silhouettes of human bodies with shades of fiery orange yellow reflective of their clothes, super white teeth shining in the darkness of nothingness.

"We will be moving tomorrow morning. Iqbal, wake up early to pack," the master ordered Ajay. Everyone looked at Ajay for a moment and went back to their chomping.

"Don't worry," the young man called Raju assured Ajay. "I will help Iqbal."

"So will I."

"Me too."

And then there was a chorus from many in the group. Even children as young as 6 years were ready to help Iqbal. He had made many friends along the way and they all liked him because of his modesty, charm, friendliness and good looks.

"Where are we going this time?" Iqbal managed to ask. It was very rarely that he asked Chaudhury any questions but he knew everyone else wanted to know too.

"I don't know but let's stay away from major cities and towns so as to keep the army at a distance. We should follow the Indus River running a few kilometers from here. It might take us close to somewhere near Bahawalnagar."

"Why Bahawalnagar?" a young man asked. "It is so close to the border with India. What if they start fighting again and then

we are caught? Indians will say we are Pakistanis and Pakistanis will say we are Indians. In the end we lose our lives." The young man was shaking his head while others couldn't stop laughing.

"And with the lunatic General in charge, anything can happen," a middle-aged man they called Ali said.

"Of course, this will also give another chance to Iqbal to try to cross the border again," Chaudhury's wife said angrily. "And all of us will be in trouble."

"Okay okay...we will proceed towards Narowal and then to Shakar Garh. But it is important to stay away from main cities because so many people are protesting and cities can be under curfew. Moving in large groups will attract attention. We will try to stay away from the border but I can tell you, it will be a long journey and might take months. But most importantly, we have to stay together and stay safe," Chaudhury looked around at everyone. "I will tell you when we can do business but every day for a few hours when we rest, we shall continue to make our toys and baskets as selling these will be our main source of income for some time. So, everyone needs to help."

Chaudhury's word was final.

How Ajay wished he had a map or a compass so he could gauge exactly where they were and how far was the border. His memory of the map of India was fading. Anyway, memorizing every little detail of any map was out of the question. Every time he thought he had gained enough knowledge about an area, they would move. With no books, maps or library, it was not easy. His sources of information were only the people he talked to. And he had to be very careful while talking to them so as not to arouse suspicion.

It was not until December that year that Ajay was able to send another postcard to Anita asking her to wait for him and that he would be home soon. Since the group had not pulled off a heist for months, money was scarce. The money they made selling wares was barely enough to feed so many mouths. They

traveled to Godhuwala from Bahawalnagar. He wasn't sure if the route was pre-planned or they were moving on the whims of the leader. Was there a destination they were heading to? Or were they merely escaping the military ruler and trying to lie low till the political situation was under control?

He noticed that they seemed to be following the Indus River. Maybe it was just so as not to get lost. He had a vague idea that this river was one of the largest and flowed between the two countries in the Northern part of the country. He had studied about the rivers and its history maybe when he was in class 5 or before. How long ago was that, he tried to remember – fifteen years, twenty years? It seemed like a century ago when he was a child at school and everything around him was just so perfect. His parents made sure of it.

How he missed his parents today! The ring of security was broken the day he left home for the Air Force, his dream job. His father had inculcated a sense of patriotism in him to the extent that he had never thought of any other career. His grandfather had fought for Independence of India alongside Mahatma Gandhi and had been jailed a few times but every time he left jail, he said his resolve to get rid of the British became stronger. His father had regretted the fact that to gain independence, the country was divided on religious lines. He himself had vague memories of his grandfather, who had died when he was about 5 or 7 years old. Children his age were told to be doctors and engineers while he was told to serve his country whichever way he could.

"A healthy mind can only be in a healthy body," his father always told him. "Any job requires that you have to be alert at all times. Feed your mind but don't forget your body. You have to be fit in body to be fit in mind."

Chapter 11

My Bro Amar

As a result of these repeated talks, both he and Amar had decided early in their childhoods to serve their country. Amar and Ajay were distant cousins and also the best of friends. They went to school and college together, started their Air Force training together and unfortunately, went to war together. And both are missing, Ajay thought.

"Did you get back home safely, Amarua," Ajay asked. Recently, he had taken to talking to himself more than to real people. "This is because other people here don't understand me. They don't know who I am and what is my purpose of being with this group of nomads I have no relation to," he muttered to himself.

"But I like them now. They are nice, decent and kind but all their activities are illegal."

"Why do I care? I am neither the police nor the government and they haven't stolen anything from me. Well, they have helped me survive difficult situations. If it hadn't been for them, who knows, I could have been rotting in a Pakistani jail, inside filthy grey walls. Or I would have been killed by the wolves and my body eaten up by vultures or jungle dogs would have killed me anyway. Would it have been better if I surrendered to the Pakistan Army? Maybe the Indian government could have helped me. Maybe they would have let me rot in Pakistan or have me killed in jail so

I don't divulge secret information." The ifs, ors and buts wrestled in his mind for a long time.

"Or I could have crossed the border and reached Patiala and might be sitting with Ma and Bauji drinking tea in the verandah and reading *The Times of India*." Anita would be hovering in the kitchen and who knows, I might have been a Papa by now. How old would my child be at this time? Maybe ready to go to school and I would have been helping him with homework. Him? No, no, I will tell Anita that we need a daughter. Yes, I like girls – so pretty, delicate, and docile. She would look exactly like Anita – beautiful with long black hair, mesmerizing eyes, fair complexion, running after him on little feet. Just the thought brought a big smile on his face.

Ajay had called Amar Amarua since his school days. Amar had teased Ajay too, calling him Ajua. At school, no student dared mess with them, as their strength was double. Their chant of 'Amar Ajay Bhai Bhai' scared other children.

Amar went missing before he did. He had promised Amar's family that he would try to find Amar but at the time was certain that the Pakistani Army had captured Amar. They had trained together and knew how to jump out of a burning plane and land safely. They had learnt and mastered the techniques of Parachute Landing fall. They had practiced the HALO or the High Altitude Low Opening as well as HAHO – High Altitude High Opening techniques of getting off a burning plane.

Their trainers had praised them no end and encouraged them to pick up more techniques. "There might be an opportunity to train in Russia or America when we buy new planes. I will definitely forward your names for further training." Like little kids, both of them had almost jumped with joy and when in their quarters, hugged and congratulated each other for their own performances.

"I know for sure that you are alive, Bhai. Or you are lost or have you been found? Never mind what the authorities say -- that

you were killed in an air attack. But it's only me who knew that you wouldn't go down with the plane. That is why they never found your remains. Because you are somewhere. But where?" How he wished he could get answers to his questions. If only he could get hold of a phone. But how? The Kanjars mostly moved on the outskirts of the city, crossing villages, jungles, creeks, mountains and deserts. Most places did not even have basic amenities like water and electricity. Every house or hut was lit by lanterns, which were carried wherever they went, including doing their business in the fields.

It has been years. Just once, only once if he could get in touch with an Indian border guard, he would be able to convince them he was one of them. Not that he hadn't tried but Pakistani police and border guards were very vigilant and rough. The minute they saw anyone lurking near the border, they just pounced like a lion on a prey.

Pakistani border guards were also known for their brutality. Every time he was caught, they thrashed him with batons, belts, sticks or whatever they could lay their hands on before handing him over the local police. The last time, they broke a tooth. They had hung him upside down in a cell for hours before Chaudhury came to his rescue. He was sure that the soldiers would kill him that day. No food or water for three days had left him too weak to even speak – fighting was out of the question. All three days, he prayed that the soldiers don't find out that he is an Indian – for that would be the end of his life for sure. He had promised Chaudhury that he would not try to escape again for the leader too was sick and tired of his games. That was more than four years back and he had kept his promise.

Last year, he realized that they were passing the city of Sindh, which was very close to the Indian states of Gujarat or Rajasthan or both, he couldn't remember. Long years of wilderness had started taking a toll on his memory. Though he had tried to keep his strength and stay in shape by taking over all the hard

labour of the group, scarcity of healthy food had started taking a toll. Age too was catching up and he wondered if that was his fate – to die uncared for, unwanted and forgotten. There would be no tomb of an unknown soldier.

He was alone in his suffering – he had seen Chaudhury and his wife grow weak. They looked 10 years older than they were. Other older men and women, like Chaudhury's brother, his wife and wife's sister and her husband too were growing weak. Thankfully, the elders had enough knowledge of therapeutic roots and herbs easily found in the mountains and didn't have to see a doctor. Ajay guessed that their knowledge would have been passed down to them by their parents, just as they were now passing it to their children.

"Don't worry, we will get it fixed once we are in a safer place, dear." Chaudhury had assured him when Ajay was rescued from the jail, his last attempt till then. Ajay was massaging his cheek and moving his tongue to where his canine should have been on the left. He was asked to carry cloves all the time. But it was 4 years now and he knew his tooth was infected due to the food lodgments. Root or leaf-based concoctions were able to control his pain. Turmeric was one spice that the group relied on for all illnesses, from cold, cough to diarrhea, aches, pains and bruises. If someone were bleeding, they would heat turmeric powder with jaggery, stick it on a roti and tie it around the wound. If you had a body ache or fever, they would boil it in milk or water, depending on availability and make you drink it. Cinnamon, ginger, onion and garlic were other wonder healing agents, which the group replenished at every stop and threw in every meal, whether to add as a flavor or for their healing properties, he didn't know. All he knew was, the group did not suffer from major illnesses.

The *modus operandi* of the group had not changed – girls danced and marked the houses to be looted by the men at night, some sold their wares while others created ruckus on the street

so that when the shopkeepers came out to see what was going on, the trained children would sneak in and grab whatever their little hands could carry. Most could identify a cash safe immediately as most shopkeepers kept it close to where they sat. In his fifteen or twenty years of wandering with this group, there had been just six deaths, three children were lost or ran away while 6-7 couples decided to part ways with the group. That was not easy for the group. The elders were really upset as they had wanted to stick together and hand over the reins of their clan to the new generation. It was apparent that the youngsters had decided to part ways as they did not want to continue wandering the jungles.

"We want to live like normal people, Tauji (Uncle). We want to have a house and children going to school to read and write. We don't want to run for the rest of our lives," argued Wasim, who had recently married 14-year old Rubina.

"Because that is what our ancestors did. That is what we were taught to do and is a way of life. It is our tradition to help the community by entertaining them and earn our living. We are not trained to work in a *daakkhana* (post office) or be *masterjis* (teachers)," Chaudhury had responded.

"But we don't entertain, Tauji. We steal from them and then hide for days and months wandering in the jungles and it never ends. I suggest that everyone who wants to leave, should be allowed to leave," the young man was adamant.

"But when will I get to see you again," his mother wailed. "When dear, when? Oh, why do you want to leave us? I can't live without you." Crying, she sat down on the hard mud floor strewn with dry twigs and leaves, with a thud.

"Then you have to come with me too, Amma. Abba too should come with us so we can all live like a family of normal people."

"But this is our family. I have never lived without this family. Where will we go, what will we do?" The old man sat down on the rocky ground, hit his forehead with the palm of his hand.

"What has come over you, my dear son? Looks like you are not feeling well."

"I think he is possessed. The devil has overtaken his body," Chaudhury's wife's sister suggested. She went by the name Badi Amma (Big Mother).

"I think we should take him to the *bhooth-wala baba* (exorcist). I know where he lives. Just the other side of this jungle, I think, because I heard someone screaming last night." Putting her hand on the weeping mother, she asked, "Do you want me to go look for him? He might suggest we take your son to him."

"I am not going anywhere," Wasim had screamed at the top of his voice. "And I am not possessed. I am warning all of you. I AM NOT possessed. I wanted to leave this group all my life, since when I was a child. But now I am older and I can take care of my wife. And Amma and Abba too."

"How will you take care of them? What work will you do? You don't have any education. Who will give you work? If you steal, you will have to run anyway or they will put you in jail. Once you go to jail, we will never see you again," Chaudhury said calmly. He was still trying to control the situation and bring some peace with this shouting and wailing match going on.

"I am NOT going to steal. I can find some work. I can work in a factory or work as a construction laborer. And it is not difficult to find work like that where no skill is required. I can load bricks on my head and climb stairs. I can carry people's luggage and things. Abba can also work in a shop or start his own puncture shop. For so many years, he has been fixing wheels of all the bullock carts. Anything to get out of this miserable life in the jungles," Wasim had then walked away in a huff. "AND I WANT TO MAKE AN HONEST LIVING"...he had shouted back.

It was apparent that no one could change his mind. When they reached the city of Shakar Garh, the family of eight had parted ways, never to be seen again. Wasim took with him not only his family but also Rubina's parents along with their little

boys. The elders had touched Chaudhury's feet and apologized for their defection. The women and men had hugged each other and cried but still parted ways.

Wasim and Rubina were the only two people who appeared happy to be leaving to start a new life. Ajay felt relieved. Why should two young people have to spend their entire life in the jungles like fugitives? They have a right to try their luck elsewhere. Which reminded him of how his own life would have been, living a quiet life in Patiala with Ma, Bauji and Anita. So many years, of course I would have fathered a couple of children and would be taking them to school just like Bauji walked me to and from school every day.

His life was taken away by fate or politicians fighting wars from the comforts of their cushy offices, a life which he had a right to live but couldn't, a life he did not choose to live. He remembered a quote from Mother Teresa, "A life not lived for others is a life not lived." Such quotes from learned people had always been his inspiration and his will to sacrifice for his country was generated after understanding the deep meaning they conveyed. "I gave my everything to my country, which would have forgotten me by now." Was it worth it? Are other soldiers' sacrifices worth it? These thoughts had plagued him all these years.

"If I ever have kids, I will always tell them to take up politics as a career and never, never to join the armed forces. I will guide them to pay respect to the learned people but never to follow their preaching. Those words look good on paper, but when it comes to practice, they ruin your life. After so many years of delving into his soul, he understood the real meaning of "Shaheed". So true, it's better to die for your country than live a life like this.

Chapter 12

Missing my baby

July, 1999

It is 7 am. Anita has to get ready and head to class. Her first class starts at 9 but she has to be in the staff room by 8 am. She does not want to go today. Not this week, not this year, never. Going to school, spending time with those innocent children is not a choice. It is not a profession, not a career, not a way to earn some money. She considers the school her hospital, where she goes every day to heal herself. The children are her pills – pills to sanity. Spending time with innocent young children, with twinkling naughty eyes, untainted hearts, pure souls, asking honest questions, is the best time of her day.

As the years go by, the pills don't work their magic. In fact, her wounds are still raw, still oozing pain, scalding and aching.

She looks at the phone, that green instrument with rotating dials, her mode of communication with her family. Her father calls her once in a few days, her sister now married to a UP government employee with three grown children, lives in Aligarh and calls once a month. Her brother Shyam, who joined the army, is now a Major posted in Jammu. His wife and two children live in Patiala so his children could continue their schooling without their having to move station to station, which he has to do every

two to three years. He calls her at least once a week, whenever he feels lonely, maybe sitting in the mess nursing a drink. Every festival, he would be the first to call and talk for hours, trying to console her, convince her that life is not as cruel as she thinks, not to lose hope and that he is still doing his best to bring Ajay back from the jails of Pakistan, where he is believed to be living, still alive, waiting to be released.

Today, the phone call she awaits is from Ajita, her daughter, whose only dream is to meet her father. Ajay was not aware that he had fathered a child when he went to war, as Anita did not know she was expecting their first child. She was excited when she learnt of it and waited to give the news to Ajay when he got back from the war. He never did.

Ajay's picture in Air Force uniform hung on the wall opposite Anita's bed, so his would be the first face she saw every morning. Black and white, yes, it was black and white when she had first nailed the frame on the wall, but now it was yellow. On the wall next to the window is a picture of Anita and Ajay on their wedding day. Both of them look into the camera with garlands of big red and white roses around their necks. The black and white photo too is now yellow...the roses were never red in the picture. Anita still remembered the smell of roses – their sweet smell lingered in her senses. She still had the bright red wedding dress, she had worn that day. Also Ajay's shiny embroidered maroon *sherwani* with the closed neck collar looked so elegant. That was the only day he had worn it.

Her friend Prema had teased her all through the wedding. "My God, Anita! Why didn't I meet Ajay before? I sure would have married him, not this big lollipop of a husband." Prema's husband Mahesh was a little on the plump side and was eavesdropping on the friends' conversation. His blood boiled, his face red as lava and his fists clenched in anger – all unbeknown to Prema.

"Shut up, Prema," whispered Anita. "All this started with you. Just because you wanted to get married, your brother met Shikha. And Ajay came to meet his friend."

"'Thus Anita now has to stop college and is now sitting here on this stage decked as a bride," whispered Shikha, standing behind Prema. "Let's ask the photographer to take at least one picture of the three of us so we can each take one with us." That was the day the three friends had decided that no matter where they were in life, they would make it a point to visit their parents' homes every July and share their lives.

A promise they did their best to keep, but not for too long.

Excitedly, a picture was taken; Anita dressed as a bride and the two friends on each side – their first and last picture together. The smiles on those young faces were short-lived. Life was waiting to hug them with thorny arms, ready to prick and bleed.

That picture now hung on the wall opposite Anita's wedding picture, turning the pages of time. Age had set in. John F. Kennedy once said, 'Change is the law of life. Those who look into the past or present, are certain to miss the future.' Anita wanted to believe that, to look into the future but there was nothing there. Everything she remembered was in the past. The future held nothing for her. Those pictures, those pieces of paper, could never be reproduced yet held memories that were once true and a life that smiled, that laughed and was always alive. Unlike today, when life is on a waitlist. Again!

By the time of the friends' first reunion, a lot had changed. Ajay had gone to the war on December 1, 1971 and hadn't come back. Nor had Amar. On December 16, 1971, the allied forces of the Indian Army and the Mukti Bahini had defeated the West Pakistani forces deployed in the East. As a result, a large number of prisoners of war were taken on both sides. The newspapers and radio had called the rapid conclusion a result of the objectives set by Mukti Bahini in East Pakistan and executed with excellent co-ordination with the Air Force and the Indian Army.

The Indian Army took about ninety three thousand Pakistani soldiers as prisoners, which was considered the largest number of PoWs taken since World War II. But after the Shimla Agreement, India had released them, without getting all of her own soldiers back. Pakistan had vehemently denied that it was holding Indian PoWs in jails. Families of fifty-four soldiers missing in the war had time and again brought to the government's attention eyewitness accounts that Indian prisoners had been seen in Pakistani jails, yet no action was ever taken. A newspaper in Pakistan too had published Amar's picture and his name was on the list of people Pakistan was holding initially. But it was officially recorded that Amar was killed when his plane went down despite eyewitnesses suggesting that he was captured alive. Ajay was still fighting when he heard about Amar. He had sent Anita a postcard dated December 7, 1971, which she received twenty-two days later.

"*My dear Anita,*

> *I hope you are doing well and keeping strong. We are told the fighting will not last long but till then, I have to follow orders. I will be back soon. I have some bad news for you. Amar's plane was shot down two days back. They were announcing that he probably died when his plane went down. But I know him very well. He knows the tricks and would have gotten out timely. I will try to find out more information and tell Shikha, I will do my best to bring him back. You take care of yourself and wait for me. Wish I could fly my plane over Ambala just once and see you. I miss you.*

> *Truly yours Ajay.*"

In that little postcard, Ajay had said a lot. Anita knew. Had Ajay been given more paper, he would have gone on and on told

her everything that was going on in his life at that point. But maybe, as of that moment, only a postcard was available to him. He was always a big talker. Right from the day when she first set eyes on him to their last day together, he talked – about school, college, his training days, friends, parents, and hobbies. When he ran out of topics, he talked about Indira Gandhi, Pakistan and the refugees that were crossing the border into India from Pakistan. Pakistani Army led by Yahya Khan was committing atrocities on the people, especially on the Hindus, resulting in people fleeing Pakistan and entering India from the East. "Did you know that as many as one hundred and two thousand refugees are coming into India daily? Which means seventy-one refugees per minute, can you imagine, Anita? And this figure will only go up. How long can Indira Gandhi ignore what is going on in her neighborhood?"

"You mean India cannot ignore," Anita tried to correct Ajay.

"One and the same," Ajay quipped. He idolized Indira Gandhi to the extent that he considered her as the country. "She is smart. She will strike when the time is right. Pakistan cannot continue killing its people like that." Ajay would at times talk about how difficult it was for his grandparents when they were pushed out of their homes in Islamabad, walking for miles, hiding from people bent upon just killing anyone they saw, taking the first train to India and getting off at Patiala, living in refugee camps. It took years to restart their lives after India split. "They worked so hard but when they died, they had not reached the status they had in 1947." Ajay was both angry and sad at the same time. Anita would look at him awestruck but couldn't decide his mood – bitter, dismal, heartbroken or pensive.

Anita had waited six months at the Ambala Air Force station, trying to live the life Ajay had left behind. She had kept everything the same, following the same routine – wake up in the morning, shower, do her prayers, clean the house and cook as if Ajay would walk in and ask for his evening cup of tea and then

eat dinner together. But now she had an extra job: the 20 minute walk to Wing Commander's office, waiting outside his office for a couple of hours before being called in and told that there was no news. Every day, the Wing Commander would tell her to come the next day as he might have some news from his sources.

"I am sorry, Mrs Singh. There is no more news than already given. Flt Lt Singh's plane was shot down by Pakistani Air Force when he crossed the Line of Control. There is no possibility that he is alive."

"But, is there any evidence that he died?" Anita had asked, voice quivering. "Is his plane found? He told me once that he is very good at jumping from the plane with his parachute. Isn't it possible that he jumped from the plane and landed in enemy territory?" She was told that Ajay was flying the HF-24 aircraft, also known as Marut, when he was shot down.

"I understand, Mrs Singh. It is difficult to believe without evidence. But wars don't always leave evidence and there is not always a reason to it. I am sorry but we have now come to a conclusion that Flt Lt Ajay is dead. His death certificate will be issued next week," he said matter-of-factly.

Maybe these guys are trained to act tough, Anita thought. How callous, indifferent can this person be. As if nothing had happened. As if Ajay had merely crossed the border because he wanted to get himself killed. As if Ajay was so naive that he didn't know the danger around him. No, Anita couldn't believe what this middle-aged man sitting across this big table on a big chair with a big back and large glasses and moustache on his face was saying. Utter nonsense, she thought. He just wants to get rid of me.

Maybe he is being held somewhere in a Pakistani jail, she had suggested in a hoarse voice, trying to be strong.

"We have got a list of all detainees being held in Pakistani jails. His name is not on any of the lists, Mrs Singh," the man said now, rather softly. Anita could gauge that he was going to

say something serious. "You will have to vacate the apartment on the station and move out. We have to give this place to another family who has just got transferred to Ambala. But don't worry, you will have access to all facilities at the station."

"But I don't have anywhere to go! And I want to keep everything the same when Ajay comes back," Anita almost screamed, with tears rolling down her cheeks.

"Why don't you go spend some time with your parents? Or in-laws?" the big man suggested, getting up from his big chair and offering Anita a glass of water and caressing her head lovingly. "By the time you come back, I will look for a room for you here and then you can live here and keep everything the same for your Ajay."

She looked up at him; his eyes didn't radiate sincerity. He was smiling – no, more of a smirk. All these days she had been coming to him for help, not once thinking that this man was probably… She couldn't believe it. This man, who is her father's age, is having dirty thoughts. This had been going on for six months and her tummy was now showing. The baby had started kicking and she had gone to the doctor just once to confirm her pregnancy though the doctor had told her to come back for a checkup at least once a month. But she never went back. She always remembered Dadi's words: "A baby is God's gift and he takes care of it. The doctors just want to make money and give unnecessary medicine. Just eat for two people instead of one and you will be fine." This is what she told women who came to her for advice.

This big man was still caressing her and now touching her shoulders. "Don't worry, Anita." Anita! So now he is calling me by my first name. What happened to Mrs Singh? Is she too dead in his eyes? "In a few months, you will have the baby. Rest with your parents and then come back to me. I will take care of you and the baby just like Ajay would. I will look for accommodation for you either inside the station or just outside. You are still young and have a long way to go, my dear."

"My dear, so he is calling me with yet another name," Anita thought. No, this is not right. She jumped up to walk away. "Not so fast, dear," the big man said holding her arm. "You are pregnant, remember. Be careful what you are doing. Come with me, I will drive you home in my car."

Car! Anita had never sat in a car. This should be fun then, Anita thought. She remembered how she and her two friends always fancied sitting in a nice lavish car. But none had ever done so. Ajay had a scooter and she had always enjoyed riding pillion, holding him tight, her scarf flying in the wind, Ajay looking at her lovingly in his rearview mirror and Anita always scared that he might run into someone. "Watch it, Ajayji. I think the first rule of driving a scooter is look in front of you." Ajay had always laughed her fears away.

"Come, let's go," someone was putting his arm around her shoulders and walking with her. Anita jerked his arm away. "No thank you. I can go on my own," she said rudely, walking out the door. She had looked up to this man as a fatherly figure who was trying to help her when she needed help. When Ajay was here, he had always respected this man, called him "Sir" whenever he met him. And now this man was leering at her, his eyes boring through her clothes.

"Good morning, sir," an officer passing by in the corridor said politely to this big man and stopped to talk to him.

"Good morning," he said and had no choice but to let Anita go.

That night, Anita's nightmares included a giant with big feet and big ears. Ears like Mr Spock from Star Trek and Jack the Giant-Killer. Big ears flapping, inviting her to come to him, just ears with an invisible face followed by a big body and big feet. She stood under the tree in this barren dark jungle all alone, with arms folded across her chest in fear, shivering and frightened. She wanted to run but couldn't, she wanted to scream but couldn't. She stood there frozen. And then those Big Feet started moving towards her. She stepped back. Another step back and there was no ground. Anita was falling. She

was suspended in air, her arms now flapping in the air, her chunni flying away and…

Anita woke up with a jolt. She was sweating so profusely that her pale pink shirt was soaked, almost transparent. Her hair disheveled. Her forehead sweaty and salty tears flowing into her mouth. That big man, why does he disturb me so? He is not related; he is just a stranger, my husband's boss who should be responsible for his staff. Instead of trying to find Ajay, he was giving excuses not to do anything.

Anita looked at the clock on the wall. 6 am. She is not in a hurry today. It has been six months since Ajay disappeared. And she is 7 months pregnant now. The baby has started kicking. In two months, the baby will be here. And I don't have anyone with me, she thinks. "Maybe I should go home to Ma and Bauji. Dadi will help. But should I not be going to Ajay's house to see his parents?" she thinks. "If I don't, they might feel bad. But they haven't called once since Ajay disappeared. Not even a letter, a postcard, no communication at all. Would they really like to see me? This baby is their grandchild. Maybe, they will want to see the baby."

Anita had not felt welcome when she had gone to Patiala after the wedding. There were no special ceremonies, no reception, nothing at all. In fact, the very day after her arrival, she was expected to go to the kitchen and make breakfast for everyone. Her mother-in-law taunted her by saying, "Once a daughter-in-law comes to the family, mothers-in-law take a back seat. From now, Anita will take over the kitchen and everything else in the house." Ajay's sister-in-law too took advantage of the situation and left everything for Anita to do.

Trying to pacify Anita, Ajay had said, "Don't worry, Anita. It is just a matter of a few days and then we will go back to Ambala. You don't have to do this for too long. I am just waiting for information about family accommodation then we will go. Then, it will be just you and me"

Chapter 13

Back home

In her confused state of mind, Anita decided to give a call to Dadi. She had to first call the post office where Shikha's dad worked. She had to let him know that she will call again in the evening, so he could send a message home to let them know that she would call again. The post office was the only source of communication in her village. She walked to the nearest telephone, which was in the local grocery store. The shopkeeper would charge 1 rupee per call but when a call was received and he had to send his young boy to call people, he would charge 2 rupees.

On the way back, she thought of visiting the doctor at the Station Hospital. It has been five months since she was told to come every month. In the waiting room, she met Sheila, Warrant Officer Akhtar's wife. The couple had had a love marriage, against their parents' wishes and therefore, had no family contact or support. Sheila had come to see the gynecologist as she was expecting her third child. Her first son now was in kindergarten; the second was on her lap.

"How are you doing Anita?" asked Sheila. "You should be expecting soon. Is your mother or mother-in-law coming to be with you?" The two had gotten along together whenever their husbands had an opportunity to socialize.

"I don't know yet," replied Anita with a big sigh. "I know nothing about my life." Anita could not control her emotions and tears flowed down her cheeks freely. As if her tears were locked up and Sheila had inserted the key. Anita slowly sat down on an empty chair next to Sheila. It was about lunchtime and most patients had already left. The waiting area was almost empty, thankfully giving her privacy.

All this while, she had kept her distance from everyone: neighbours, Ajay's friends and colleagues, in fact her own family. She did not have the courage to answer their questions, to look them in their eyes and see the sympathy. She knew they all wanted to make her believe that she was now a widow – a widow at nineteen.

"Oh Anita," Sheila tried to console her. "I'm so sorry. How I wish I could help you." Sheila took Anita in her big fat arms as if she was a mother trying to control a sobbing child. Sheila was fat, broad and tall. Till a few years ago, she was a pretty, delicate, thin and tall girl with big kind eyes. Sheila's pretty face still oozed innocence, but with the birth of two children and the third one on the way, she had become curvaceous. Her upper arms now hung like flaps, her love handles clearly visible as her shirts became tighter with every day the baby was growing. Her bosom was so big that Anita looked like a baby bear tugging it for security.

Anita sobbed and sobbed and sobbed, till she couldn't anymore. Sheila couldn't stop her own tears from flowing and falling on Anita's head. Her little one on her right lap was now falling asleep. Sheila hugged both of them tightly and kept saying "Shh, shh…don't cry, dear. Everything will be fine. Oh! Please don't cry."

"Anita," called the nurse. Anita lifted her head, wiping her tears with her *chunni* and breathing heavily. Sheila let her go, saying, "Go dear. See the doctor. I will wait for you here. Then we will go home and drink *chai*. Go." Turning to the nurse she said, "Nurse, can you give Anita some water."

A few minutes later, Anita walked out of the doctor's office with the nurse following her. Talking to Sheila, she said, "Madam, you need to take good care of her. The baby is growing but she is becoming very weak. She needs to eat a lot of fruits and drink milk." Sheila nodded and thanked the nurse.

When the doctor mentioned it, Anita realised she had not eaten a single piece of fruit after she heard about Ajay. Whatever she ate was merely for survival: 2 chapatis with lentil for lunch and the same for dinner. She would make 4 chapatis for herself and Ajay every morning. Every night, she had waited for him and when he didn't come, she would just eat his leftover food for dinner. She felt the hunger pangs but ignored the signals. Her own life and dreams had come to a standstill but not the baby growing inside. He was growing and kicking inside her, seeking her attention.

Sheila got up and shifted Anas, her little one, to her right arm, putting her left arm around Anita. "Come, let's go home," she said. "You must be hungry. It's time to eat."

"You go home, Didi. I already cooked. You should take care of Anas. He needs milk," said Anita, walking out with her friend.

"No dear. You are coming with me. Someone needs to take care of you. You have been hiding way too long. Now come out of it. We need to talk too," said Sheila stubbornly. "When was the last time you had milk, Anita?"

"Milk?" Anita looked blankly at Sheila.

"You know a pregnant woman should drink at least 3 glasses of milk every day. Didn't the doctor tell you that?"

Anita nodded. "I haven't seen milk since Ajay left. I never felt the need," Anita said thoughtfully, her low voice barely audible. But Sheila easily guessed what Anita said without asking her to repeat herself. Anita's sad eyes gave away the glimpse of her soul – depressed, lacking energy, confidence and the will to live. Sheila vowed to herself to nurse Anita back to health till someone from her family came to take her home, for staying at the station

appeared futile. As the two pregnant women walked together towards Sheila's second floor apartment, she tried to pep Anita up by talking about Anas and his funny antics.

As the two women climbed the stairs, Sheila was panting as she had to carry the sleepy child. Anita asked if she could carry Anas. "Yes please. He is heavy. But will you be okay?"

Anita nodded and took Anas from Sheila. She held him close to her chest and immediately felt a heavy stone being lifted from her heart. She couldn't describe the feeling she had, the baby's heart beating against hers, the soft cheeks touching her neck and his little hands around her neck. She felt wanted, loved, connected. It had been months since she had held anyone's hand, cuddled anyone or was cuddled. She felt her pain taking flight. Suddenly, she felt light.

Sheila unlocked the door to her apartment and walked in. "Come, lay him down on this bed." Anita looked around the sparsely furnished but neat apartment. There was a foyer, two bedrooms and a small living room.

Anita held the toddler tight to her chest and sat down on the bed, holding on to the baby. "I will make some *chai*," said Sheila walking to the kitchen.

"I don't drink *chai*," said Anita softly.

"Oh yeah, I forgot," Sheila said, slapping her forehead. "I'll bring some milk for you first and we will have lunch later."

Sheila took care of Anita for a week, nursing her to health. Spending time with Sheila's two little ones alleviated her pain. She played with the children and laughed after months of living in a cocoon. Her zest for life was slowly coming back. But when she smiled, she missed Ajay, when she laughed she missed Ajay, when she ate, she wondered if Ajay had eaten. She felt guilty all over again and would go back to her cocoon, which Sheila found hard to penetrate. Her six months of loneliness were like a vast black hole, surrounded by a world of lustreless tones of grey. Anita

had no social life – no family, no friends. Ajay had left before she had a chance to make any friends in her new environment.

Her worry for Ajay had not ended or abated. Sheila tried to counsel her, "Worry will not empty tomorrow of its sorrow. It empties today of its strength. Stop thinking too much and take life as it comes. We will continue to look for Ajay but don't let this affect your child."

Sheila had nursed Anita back to health. Some color and cheer had come back on Anita's innocent face. Sheila was able to convince Anita to go back to her parents' house with an assurance that she and Akhtar would take care of things at the station. She promised that she would send letters in case there was any news from Ajay, yet tried to convince her to prepare herself for any eventuality. Anita's heart and soul wouldn't accept that.

Chapter 14

Meeting and losing friends

As the three friends had promised, Anita and Shikha were on Anita's terrace waiting for Prema to arrive. The two friends were happy to see each other and were smiling and laughing after a long time, months after both their husbands had disappeared in the war.

"I still can't believe it. How can both of us have the same destiny?" Shikha wondered. "We went to school together, we were married almost together and now here we are like we never got married. Same terrace, same house, same village, same hot summer of July and waiting for Prema."

Anita merely looked at her friend and nodded.

"Except that baby of yours trying to burst your little belly," Shikha smiled, pointing at Anita's now full-blown pregnancy. "When that little guy comes, your life will change, Anita. Have you thought about it?'

"No. I don't know what life has in store for us. How can one ever be prepared for such an eventuality, Shikha? "Anita whispered. Shikha put her arm around her friend and held her closer.

"You know what they call us around here?" asked Anita.

"By here you mean…"

"In Rajpura. They call us the unlucky duo."

"My mother-in-law says it was all my fault. I was a bad omen for Amar. But what did I do? I am suffering too." Now it was Shikha's turn to choke as tears welled in her eyes and Anita's turn to put her arms around her friend. After Amar's disappearance, Shikha had gone to her in-laws' house in Patiala. Within a month of the Air Force declaring Amar dead, her father-in-law made her sign some papers and then called her dad to come pick her up. Since then, Shikha has been living in her parents' house.

"That our in-laws don't want us back is yet another common factor between us," Anita sniffed.

"That I am your friend is yet another common factor between you too," a little voice chirped. The friends turned around and saw Prema walking towards them, not running to hug them, as was her wont. She was walking slowly, with tears flowing on her cheeks, as if she couldn't decide if she should smile or cry. Wearing a pale blue sari, Prema walked over and put her arms around her friends; the three friends just stood there crying their hearts out, as if their emotions had been blocked for a long time – until the orange glow from the setting sun signaled that it was time for Prema to go home.

Prema's silhouette was almost dark grey as the sun went down behind her. Prema and Anita were sitting on a string charpoy while Shikha was on a stool facing the two. The three shared their experiences after marriage. Their first marriage anniversary was nothing to celebrate. As Anita and Shikha shared their story with Prema, she just sobbed.

"Prema, you have been so quiet. How is your family? How is your baby boy?" asked Anita.

"How old is your little boy now? In all our grief, we didn't even congratulate you. Congratulations, Prema," said Shikha a little excitedly, trying to bring some cheer in their emotional conversation and hugged Prema tightly.

Once again Prema's eyes swelled and she started wailing. Anita once again hugged Prema, "Shush, Prema. See, we are

not crying any more. Both of us are not sad any more. Look at us, we are happy to see you. Now come come, don't cry." All this while, Anita and Shikha thought Prema was crying for her friends. Prema was, that day, not only sharing her friends' pain but also crying at her own misfortune.

"They named my baby Atma Ram and I don't like it at all," bawled Prema.

"So change it to what you like," said Shikha.

"Can't!! No one in the house listens to me. I am just a maid for them. You call them my family! They are like insects, always crawling over me," whimpered Prema.

"Prema, are you not happy in your new home?" questioned Anita.

"Happy is a feeling I have not felt after your wedding day, Anita. That was the last day I was happy,"

"What? What do you mean?" questioned Anita, looking guilty. "Did I do anything to hurt you?"

"It wasn't what you did. My destiny, what else."

"But what happened, Prema? The last time we met you, you were so excited and all praise for Mahesh and his family," persisted Shikha.

Prema looked down at her hands which looked like a laborer's hands, with minute cuts and bruises. There was no trace of nail polish any more on her small fingernails. Anita remembered that Prema was excited about getting married so she could use make-up whenever she wanted. For months after her marriage, applying make-up was her favorite pastime. Her mother-in-law had told her she need not worry about household chores and treated her like her daughter. Prema was very impressed by her and held her in high esteem. "Thankfully, she is not a typical mother-in-law who just wants to use me as a maid," Prema had told her friends when they last met at Anita's wedding.

"Looking back, that never happened. You know Anita," Prema looked at her and took Anita's hands in hers, "Remember Anita,

when we were taking pictures on the stage, we were joking about how Ajay was looking so handsome in his *sherwani* when you were getting married."

"Yeah, maybe," Anita was trying to think hard. "So, how is an innocent girlie conversation related to your present life?"

"Because, like a fool, I was joking that if I had met Ajay earlier, I would have married him and not Mahesh."

"Prema, we all joke around during weddings. What's the issue?" questioned Shikha.

She started sobbing again. The shock of watching a giggly, bubbly Prema turn into a whimpering, watery, hysterical mess was overwhelming. They could hear footsteps coming up the terrace.

"Shhhhh," Shikha said trying to console Prema but couldn't control her own tears from gushing. "I think they can hear you downstairs. Someone is coming."

Just then Shobha walked up with three glasses of lemonade and some biscuits on a tray. "What's going on? Who is having a bad day today?" she asked with genuine concern. Both Shobha and Shikha's mom had cried non-stop for days when the war happened. Their hearts bled for their daughters. Marriage was going to transform their daughters' lives, both of them had thought. Shobha had indirectly blamed her mother-in-law for Anita's marriage. "What was the hurry? She could have easily stayed in college for another two years. She wasn't getting too old." She always thought in her own superstitious way that if that moment had passed, it would have changed her daughter's destiny.

"Prema, what has gotten into you? And you certainly have lost some weight," Shobha tried to cheer her up.

Wiping her wet face, Prema gave her a smile and hugged her. "Aunty, I want to go back to our days when we were in school. So happy and carefree. Why did we have to get married? All three of us are now in a soup."

"I know about these two, but why are you so sad? Don't they treat you well?"

Before Prema could break into another of her frightening howls, Anita offered her lemonade. "Drink this first. Calm down and tell us everything."

It was a few minutes before Prema gathered herself and started talking. When she did, all listened in pin-drop silence. No one expected this. "Aunty, everything was fine till Anita's wedding. Mahesh was very nice and sweet and his family was nice to me too. Mahesh heard my comments when I was joking with Anita that if I had met Ajay before, I would have married him. He looked so handsome that day. Remember Anita, I called Mahesh something like a roly-poly ball. He overheard me and has been angry with me ever since. He calls me names, is rude to me and his mother now just treats me like a free maid."

"*Beta*, you could have apologized," suggested Shobha. "Things happen during weddings."

"I did, a hundred times, Aunty. But he doesn't listen to me now. Some days he is nice but most days, he just can't forgive me. He says that I insulted him in front of my friends. Even today, he did not agree to let me come and visit you. I had been pleading for a week. He kept taking the excuse that who will take care of Golu, who will cook lunch, etc., etc. He screamed at me yesterday calling all three of us a bunch of whores and that I should stay away from you as you are bad news. I cried and cried all night and this morning his mother finally asked him to let me go, saying maybe I will 'behave better' after I meet you. That bitch. I swear I will kill her one day."

"No one should treat you like that," Shobha said loudly. "That is so unfair. Have you talked to your parents?"

"I did when I went home before Golu was born. I told Mummy and Papa but they said everything will be fine when I have a son. Now I have a son but still things haven't changed, Aunty. Sometimes I feel things are better but other days, he also hits me when he is angry," sobbed Prema.

"Mahesh hits you!" exclaimed Anita.

"I am getting used to his slaps now," whimpered Prema.

The three stared at Prema in astonishment, wondering what to say. Shock was not enough of a word to describe how they were feeling. They felt like lightning had struck and they were all smoldering in anger.

"I will come and talk to Mahesh," said Shobha wiping away her own tears with her yellow *chunni*. Shobha, who had always looked graceful, evergreen and elegant, was showing signs of aging, her rosy cheeks now ashen pale. The last few months since Ajay went missing, Shobha had been weeping silently till late nights, when she was cooking, when she was doing the dishes or working in the fields. Every moment that she was alone, she was worried about Anita.

While she worried about Anita, now she had to worry about that unborn baby Anita was carrying and whose birth was just a couple of weeks away. "How will my baby take care of a baby? Why, God why did I not put my foot down and let her go to college like she wanted? God, why did you not give me sense then? Only if I had the courage to speak up for my baby, she wouldn't be suffering. Just nineteen and already a widow! God forgive me, please!" Shobha did not have control on her feelings and living with guilt was not bearable.

And now Prema, this innocent child who had played in her arms too, is suffering. This little girl, who was the most excited about getting married so she could live a free life, wear what she liked, could apply make-up at will – all those rosy dreams of little girls had crashed. Married life, which should have been full of happiness, was now a burden for the trio and their families.

"Oh no, Aunty. Please don't talk to Mahesh. In fact, please don't talk to anyone about what I have told you. Because if they find out that I have been talking about them, they will make my life more miserable. They will be angry and might kill me," Prema was now trembling. "I now understand Mahesh very well. I hurt his big fat ego. For days, he didn't talk to me and then one day, my

mother-in-law told me that I should call my father and go back to them. I was shocked. I pleaded to let me stay and that I will do whatever they want. No one ever told me until a month ago."

Prema was trembling as she sobbed. Her pale blue sari with printed flowers and a mustard blouse appeared worn out, the fabric so thin that her bra was exposed. Anita knew Prema well – she would never wear such clothes, given a choice. Looking good had always been Prema's passion and clothes her priority. Clearly, that pleasure had been taken away from her.

"If Mahesh comes to know I have told anyone what happens in the four walls of the house, they won't like it."

"But *beta*, we have to find a solution to this problem. You can't allow yourself to be tortured like this."

"I know, Aunty, but maybe this is my destiny. There is a bus leaving Rajpura soon. I think I should start off so I can reach home to cook dinner." Prema stood up to go.

"As you wish, dear. Don't hesitate to contact any of us whenever you need anything." Shobha hugged Prema tightly. "How can your mother allow such barbarism?" Shobha mumbled, wiping away her tears and walking towards the stairs. "I will have Shyam take Prema to the bus stop. Anita, you don't need to walk that far. Shamuuuuuuuuuuu!"

"I can walk with Prema. I will tell mother as we walk out," volunteered Shikha.

Anita and Prema hugged each other tight. Prema's body felt stiff and tight, none of the spongy flesh the friends were used to. They never got to talk about Prema's son Golu.

None knew then that that would be their last hug.

Chapter 15

First Prema

July 1973

Prema did not come the following year to meet her friends as they had promised each other once a year. Anita and Shikha had waited that day and sent Shyam to her in-laws' place. Instead of coming, she had sent a letter with Shyam:

> *My dearest Anita and Shikha*
>
> *I am so sorry that I cannot make it to our annual meeting...doesn't this sound so official and important. Except, I am not that important and I am glad to have had friends like you who still care for me. Mahesh is planning on getting a phone in the house and if he does soon, I will call you at the post office and maybe chat for hours.*
>
> *Because I am expecting my second child, and am so round like a golguppa, I can barely walk. I don't feel good too. I am always tired, cannot eat food, not that they give me samosas to eat. But whatever I get to eat, I can barely keep it down. I am due anytime and I hope I have a girl and then I can sew pretty gold and pink clothes for her, buy her red ribbons and tie them*

on her braids and red socks and red shoes. And some yellow clothes too. You know yellow and red are my favorite colors. I am sad to think that Mahesh and his family do not want a girl. They are still planning for a boy and I am sure, they will not be happy with a girl. But I so want a girl. Sometimes I think if I get a girl, I hope I die so they don't get to torture me. They might then torture my little girl as they don't have girls in their family. I don't know where the mother goose came from – did they buy her at the farmer's market?

Can you come visit me 'cause I can't? Anita, bring your little girl with you. I haven't seen her. I so want to meet up with both of you and want to know what is happening in your lives. I know Amar Bhaiya is still not traceable and about Ajay. They sometimes talk about them. Why did God write the same destiny for the three of us? None of us is happy in our lives and yet God won't take us away. Sometimes I want to run from here and come to you and then all three of us can elope to a world where there are only red and yellow flowers, which smile at you lovingly. Flowers are so pretty, so non-judgmental, so non-demanding, so non-critical. All they want is water and the bright yellow sun. I wish I could sit in a place and just stare at them for the rest of my life. Will this ever happen? Then I think, who will take care of my little Golu.

Like they say: If wishes were horses, beggars would ride. I think it should be if wishes were dreams, out would they fly. Whatever, I feel nice for having written this letter. It makes me feel as if I have been chatting with both of you. I so miss you and want to meet up with you. Please do come. Don't worry about these people. They don't like anyone from my family visiting me. But I don't care. Do you know when I last saw Ma…4 months ago when she came to see me on my birthday! She wanted to take me with her but these people did not let me go. I wanted to write letters

to you but who would post them? Thanks for sending Shyam. I should stop now because if I go on, Shyam will have to sleep here.

I will wait for you with lots of hugs. Take care

Your true friend Prema

Anita had read the letter out loud on the terrace, Shikha sitting next to her with Ajita on her lap.

"Since she can't come, I think we should go visit her," suggested Shikha, stroking the baby's hair. Since Ajita had been born, Shikha was with the baby all the time. She would go home only to sleep and be back first thing in the morning to take care of the baby. That would give Anita more time to help her mother and take care of her grandmother, who was ailing. Her arthritis was getting worse and moving around the house was a chore.

"Yes, I want to meet her too. I am just worried about how her family would react. They don't seem like nice people. Wish we could help."

Shikha nodded. They had been sitting on the terrace for two hours now, trying to get some fresh air for the baby, as Anita's mom had always suggested. The baby was now 9 months old and still there was no sign of the dad. Through newspapers and the radio, Anita realized that there were hundreds of PoWs being held on both sides of the border. Shikha and she strongly believed that their husbands were one of them. None had heard anything from the Indian Air Force except for a letter that came for Anita asking for her bank account number so she could be paid Ajay's family pension.

Till that time, Anita did not have a bank account. Only a widow collects her husband's pension, she found out. They would give her a couple of hundred rupees every month in place of her husband! They send your next of kin to fight for the country and then forget all about him.

Two days later, the two friends set out to meet Prema. They knew the family lived near Moti Chowk bazaar. They did not

have the exact address, as Prema did not write the address in her letter and they had never been to her house before. But Shyam gave them some vague directions. "I am sure someone at the shop can guide us to their home," said Anita.

The bus meandered through Patiala and stopped near the University. Some people got off, others got in. Anita, who was sitting close to the window, was looking longingly at the beautiful buildings, pretty gardens, and the library so far yet so close. She saw her dream pass her by. The wind blew them across the fields, over the University and under the ground. Buried deep, so deep, never to be excavated.

"Bazaar! Bazaar! Bazaar", the conductor shouted. Shikha and Anita got off the bus and started walking towards the narrow streets of the market, crowded with people walking, shopping, strolling with children, and jostling their way among cyclists, rickshaws and scooters. Cars, buses or trucks were not allowed inside the market. Walking towards Mahesh's shop, they had to jostle through hundreds of people. Many young boys would deliberately try to bump into the women. Some passed lewd comments, others just stood outside *paan* shops or tea stalls whistling or singing. At times, just a bold stare did the trick, at other times, faking daintiness or cursing loudly did the trick. Most of these boys were harmless and would back off the moment the girls retaliated. If the boys got close, there were many elders or shopkeepers around who would scold them. Many would just whistle, sing a stanza of a popular song and move on.

They were soon outside Mahesh's shop but they couldn't see Mahesh anywhere. Though it was a small shop, it was full of customers — mothers with little children trying to buy cricket bats, balls, hockey sticks as the employees were busy trying to sell their ware. Mahesh's older brother was sitting at the cash counter, taking payments, giving change from his big desk drawer and putting their stuff in plastic bags.

Both the girls slowly walked into the shop and waited for Mahesh's brother to take a break before they asked about Prema. The girls didn't even know his name, nor had they ever been introduced to him. But the resemblance to Mahesh was obvious. It took about 10 minutes for him to look up and notice the girls standing there.

"Girls, are you looking for something in particular?" he asked politely.

"Yes, Prema," Shikha managed.

"What do you mean," he asked.

"Bhaiya, we are Prema's school friends. We just wanted to meet her since we were in town. Can you tell us where you live?" Anita elaborated.

Mahesh's brother was suddenly alert, measuring his words.

"You are Prema's friends? She is not at home right now."

"Not at home? Has she gone to her mother's house? We know where that is. Thank you, Bhaiya," Anita said as the girls stepped back to leave the shop.

"No, no, not her mother's house. Actually, she is in hospital. She just had a baby girl," he said and then smiled. "She is very pretty."

"Really!!" Both the girls exclaimed in excitement.

"But I thought she wasn't due until another 3 weeks or so," Anita suddenly became sober.

"Yes, but suddenly two nights ago she was not feeling well and Mahesh took her to the hospital. They had to perform an operation to take the baby out."

"Oh no! How is she now?" Shikha was concerned.

"She is in the civil hospital. When I last heard, she was still in the maternity ward," he informed them, getting back to counting the money a teenaged boy had given him for a cricket bat. The girls got the hint.

"Thank you," said Anita slowly walking out of the shop with Shikha. They hired a cycle rickshaw, as it was easier to get out

of the market on a rickshaw and escape all the Romeos idling on the streets.

"I hope Prema is doing better," murmured Anita on the way.

"Our Ajita has a friend. I hope the two children become best friends like us," said Shikha excitedly.

It took the girls just a couple of minutes to reach the hospital but more than half an hour to get to the information desk to inquire about Prema. The hospital was a busy place with men, women and children everywhere. There was a long line, patients lining up to get their names registered to see a doctor. Patients had to first fill up a form, get their number and then wait. There were not too many chairs to sit on. Therefore, some people were sitting on the floor, crowding the alleyways. Doctors and nurses were finding it a challenge to tread their way in and out of the examining rooms and the Emergency but they were doing so without complaints and very efficiently.

Finally, they found their friend. Prema was lying with an intravenous drip on her left arm. There were just 2 patients in this room, which presumably meant that Prema was too serious to be placed in the general ward. This was not a private hospital where you had the option of choosing your room.

There was a flimsy curtain between the two beds. Prema's mother was sitting next to her, holding her daughter's hand. There was a baby cot next to her and the girls could see a baby happily moving her little arms and legs. The little child was giggling and squeaking loudly, bringing some cheer to the gloomy room.

Prema's mother looked up as the two girls walked in and the friends greeted her with folded hands. She smiled and said, getting up, "What took you girls so long to come see your friend? Prema has been waiting. Come now."

Prema appeared to be sleeping. She opened her eyes slowly at the sound of footsteps and tried to smile at her friends. "Prema,

congratulations. Your wish is fulfilled. You have a baby doll you can dress up in yellow," Anita said excitedly.

"How are you, Prema?" asked Shikha.

"Did you get my letter?" Prema asked slowly, barely audible.

"Of course, Prema," Anita moved forward and held her hand. "Remember our pledge to meet at least once a year. We waited for you but when you didn't come, we came to visit you."

"We missed you on our annual meeting," said Shikha cheerily. "Though for both us, it's kind of a daily meeting now. It wasn't supposed to be that way. We were supposed to be happily married and living somewhere else in the world and coming in the summer to visit each other. Someone said it right, destiny is not in our hands."

"Man proposes, God disposes," Anita said slowly, sitting on the foot of the bed where she could see the baby. "Shikha, aren't we happy to be having our round bed conference today? And look at this little baby. Prema, she looks exactly like you. So beautiful and pink."

"What have you named her? I want to call her Pinky, she is so pink," said Shikha bending down to pick up the baby. "By the way, what has your family decided to name her?"

"Which family?" asked Prema slowly.

"Mahesh and his parents, who else, Prema," said Shikha, playing with the baby's little fingers.

"I have no family now. This doll has changed my destiny," said Prema, weakly.

Shikha and Anita turned to look at their friend shocked. They could see that Prema was very weak. Her face looked drained, dark circles around her eyes. Tears trickled down her face, but she did not have the energy to wipe them off. Her mother, who was standing at the foot of the bed, walked up and wiped those tears with her handkerchief tucked into her waist.

"Don't say that, dear. They will come back to you and take you home. Please don't cry."

"Aunty, why is she talking like that? Prema, this is a time to celebrate. Why are you crying?" Anita was now concerned. Shikha too stopped playing with the baby and looked at Prema.

"Anita, Shikha, don't you remember? I told you, Mahesh and his mother wanted a boy."

"Yeah, but you already have Golu. So, now you have a baby girl. Isn't your family complete now? You have one of each," Shikha tried to convince Prema.

"I always wanted to have a girl but not Mahesh and his mother. They are too rigid." said Prema.

"This is not your fault, Prema," argued Anita. "Remember what Mrs Lal taught us. Giving birth to a boy or girl depends on the male chromosomes."

"I know. But how do I convince them? I tried, Anita. For months I tried. They wouldn't listen to me. I also told them if they did not trust me, we could go and talk to a doctor about it. Mahesh's brother too tried to explain to him that these things are not in my hands."

"We went to your shop before we came here. Your brother-in-law appeared excited about Pinky," said Shikha, astonished.

"Yes, Bhaiya is really happy. He comes to the hospital morning and evening to play with Pinky. Oh! I have already started calling her Pinky," smiled Prema for the first time. A very faint smile.

"So, it is Mahesh who has a problem with our lovely Pinky," said Anita.

"Yes, and his mother. Mahesh left the hospital after Pinky was born and hasn't come back," added Prema's mother. "It's been more than 24 hours and none of them have come to see the baby or Prema. They haven't even brought Golu. We haven't seen him too. He must be missing his mother, the dear child."

Aghast, Anita and Shikha did not have words to console Prema. She was sad, weak, unhappy, and inconsolable and in pain for being rejected by Mahesh, her husband who she wasn't even sure she ever loved. She never got a chance to know him

really. Their short-lived marriage was not a happy one. In those few years, Prema had lived a lifetime of abuse, unhappiness and sorrow. She was deprived of the only two things that brought happiness to her life – food and make-up.

In the end, even her grief was short-lived. She died, leaving behind the life she had wanted to live in colours of yellow, pink and red and the two tiny lives who were going to miss her the most.

After Prema's death, the friends were told that while Mahesh took Golu's responsibility, he wanted to send Pinky for adoption. Instead, his brother, who had always loved Pinky, decided to raise her against Mahesh's wishes. Later the friends learnt that, disgusted with his own mother and Mahesh's attitude towards Pinky, he left the joint family home with his wife and moved to Delhi. He told Mahesh never to ask for Pinky as he was adopting her legally. He had two little boys of his own and his wife welcomed Pinky. She promised to raise her like her own daughter.

"For once, God listened to us," sobbed Anita, still mourning for her friend. "Prema wanted to die if she gave birth to a baby girl to escape future torture. I can't imagine the torture she would have gone through to make a wish like that."

Chapter 16

And now Shikha

September 1977

Prema's departure left a vacuum in Shikha and Anita's hearts. When they were little girls, Prema had clung to them in school and in the playground just because other children never talked to her, teasing her for being fat. In the beginning, they did not want to be friends with her either, but would stop other girls in school from teasing and bullying her. Eventually, she had become one of the gang.

Around Ajita's fifth birthday, Shikha was remarried. Her family had portrayed Shikha as a widow and not as the wife of a missing soldier. Amar's family had already disowned Shikha, there was no question of their being in picture. Anita was hopeful but scared too that after her baby was born, Ajay's parents might come to claim their grandchild. Fortunately, she gave birth to a girl, and they did not want to see her face anymore. Not many in India are happy when a girl is born and Ajay's family was no different.

This time, Shikha's family was careful. They found an English Professor working at the nearby college, where both Anita and Shikha had earned their teaching certificates.

The only catch was that for the Professor, Shikha was a second wife. His first wife had died under mysterious circumstances. Police had started an investigation but later declared her death a suicide. There were rumors that she was tortured for dowry but there was no evidence. She had died leaving two children – a five-year-old boy and a two-year-old girl. The family needed someone to take care of the children.

"They basically need an *ayah* to take care of the children," Shikha had told Anita. "But I am happy that I can live so close by and visit you whenever I want."

"Are you happy? Do you like the Prof?" asked Anita.

"Obviously he is not a Rajesh Khanna. Nor is he like Amar. I have to move on, Anita. No one has heard anything from Amar or Ajay, for that matter. You also have to move on, Anita."

"Remember, that postcard from Ajay that came in the mail? It gives me hope. It is easy for a father of two to get married again but not a woman with a child. Even if I want to, I cannot get remarried. And I don't want to. I still believe Ajay will come back. He is just lost somewhere. He will find his way home."

"You are not even sure that it was Ajay's letter. All it said was 'I am trying to come home. Wait for me.' He didn't even sign as Ajay."

"But if you reverse what was signed, it spells Ajay." The postcard Anita had received was signed, as Yaja and Anita strongly believed that Ajay was using a code so no one could identify him. "He did tell me once that they are supposed to use code language when in danger. Maybe he is in Pakistan, in enemy country, and managed to sneak off a postcard."

Shikha had not argued. She too had started believing it was really Ajay's note. It came to Anita's parental address and not to the station commander or the Air Force headquarters. The house number on the postcard was 62 instead of 26 but because Shikha's father sorted the mail, he made sure it went to Anita. Despite Anita being a common name, there were not many

around. Working for the department for 30 years, he knew that in that area, there was no House No. 62. The postmark said Sialkot and the date was July 17, 1972, four months before Anita received it.

Chapter 17

Vacuum

1977 and after

After Shikha left for her husband's house, Anita felt another vacuum in her life. Shikha's marriage ceremony was very low key. This time there was no Prema to bring cheer to their lives or bring her make-up to dress up the bride. Years later, when Shikha would compare the pictures of her two weddings, the contrast was stark. Her second ceremony was dull, her face lacked the glow, her eyes were sad as if looking for her first love. Shikha had come to terms with her widowhood, accepted it and was trying to move on – that is what she told everyone. Unbeknownst to anyone, Amar still lived in her heart, her eyes always looked for him in the crowd, yet her mind said, "Forget him."

Two years later, Anita had received a letter from one Colonel Mattu from New Delhi, who had formed some kind of association to trace missing defence personnel of the 1971 war.

> "Respected Mrs Ajay Singh
>
> I have been collecting addresses of families of our missing personnel. Many families like yourself have been waiting for their family members to come home. As you

are aware, many of our army people have been imprisoned in Pakistan and the government is doing nothing to get them released. We have received bits and pieces of evidence percolating down to us proving that they are alive. Our family members in Pakistan jails are suffering and need our help. The government wants us to believe that they are dead but we know they are not.

Since 1971 when the war ended, families of fifty-four officers are waiting for them to come back. Indian government refuses to take responsibility, saying that they are sure that these people are dead and pension is being paid to families. We strongly believe that the officers are alive and the families should be paid their full salaries, not pension. We are all uniting to talk to the government to get the officers home.

I am sure if all speak in one voice, we can be heard. Our aim is to stay in touch. If you ever hear from your husband or get a clue, please do share with us so we can present the evidence to the government to take action. If ever you come to Delhi, please do visit us on the address on this letterhead.

Meanwhile, I will try to keep you informed with as much information I get on the news of our missing men. I am trying to come up with a newsletter, which I plan to send to the families of our missing men whenever there is a new development and you should be receiving these as well. Hopefully, we will have enough funds to continue our fight for justice. International Red Cross has also been trying to help us find our missing men and recently Pakistan has agreed to allow a team to visit their jails and see for ourselves if any of our men are there. If we find anything, we will keep you posted.

Please take care of yourself and if there is any help you need, we will do our best to ease your pain.

Signed Col. Mattu

The letterhead had a Mayur Vihar address in Delhi and a phone number. For the first time, Anita felt she was not alone in her struggle to get her husband back. And she was not alone in her belief that Ajay was alive and lost somewhere. Just trying to get back home. Anita wanted to go and meet this colonel who appeared to be a nice man.

But it wasn't easy for her to go at this stage of her life. She was now teaching Biology at the new private school that had opened up near Rajpura. Her grandfather had passed away the year before, her grandmother's arthritis had worsened and now even her mother always seemed sick and weak. She had persuaded her to go to the army hospital a few times but they would just say that she was tired with all the fieldwork and will be fine if she rested a bit. As planned, Shyam had joined the army and after training was on his first field posting in Manipur while Tina was to be married in a few months. There just was so much to do at home and at times Anita was relieved that she was at least there to help her family when they needed her.

Ajita too needed to be looked after. Now that both her mother and grandmother were ill, Anita got Ajita admitted to the nursery section of the school she was teaching in.

Shobha was growing weak and was always fatigued. Some days she couldn't hold down food, other days she appeared fine and went about her day as if nothing had happened. Anita had persuaded Shobha to hire some people to work in the fields at least till Tina's marriage. With the fieldwork taken care of, Shobha was now able to rest more till late in the morning. Before going to school, Anita would cook breakfast and lunch, help her grandmother take a bath and take medicines. After coming back from school, she would take care of other household chores.

She had mothered her little brother too but now he too was ready to face the world. After clearing his NDA exams, he was now preparing to follow the family tradition of going to the army. Anita had tried to talk to her little Sunny out of it. "Sunny, there

are so many professions out there. Army is not just the only option. Just because Papa and Shyam went to the army, doesn't mean you too have to go."

"Dada too was in the army, Didi," Sunny had argued. "Isn't it obvious that I too should join the army? Or our family will get a bad name."

"My baby, I don't want what happened to Ajay to happen to you too. And to Amar. You can go to college, become a teacher or become an IAS officer or even a police officer. Anything but the army, dear."

No argument worked. So, off he went, leaving another vacuum in her life. Slowly, everyone around her were leaving her – Ajay was gone, then Dadaji, Prema. Shikha's marriage brought a lot of responsibilities and her day was filled trying to be a good wife, mother, daughter-in-law, tutor and everything else that comes with marriage. The children may not be her own but she had to nurture them as her own, love them and take care of them. She had no time to think about Anita. Or listen to her own thoughts and feel her emotions. She was like a robot, doing everything for everyone else, yet they always complained.

The Professor was a good husband at first. He showed concern for Shikha and whenever he saw the children making a fuss, he would come to Shikha's rescue. Once in a couple of months when the children were at school, he would come back from the University early, and take Shikha out for a movie and lunch. They always watched the afternoon show, ate lunch at a nearby restaurant and come home by the time the children were back from school.

The Professor was well aware of the fact that their marriage was a compromise and love between them was yet to grow. Though Shikha never mentioned Amar, he knew that Amar still lived in Shikha's heart and a few times had taunted her about him. The first few times, Shikha ignored him but after their son was born, she had retorted, "If Amar lives in my heart,

so does Sunita in yours. Amar was my first love, just like Sunita was yours. Stop hurting me so I don't hurt you too."

That was the end of discussion on that subject but the Professor now found other ways to hurt her. Every day he would find one fault or the other with Shikha or her work or the children. "The children's grades are going down." he would say, his eyes shaming her. "*Dal* is excellent today, just missing the green chilies. Did you forget to buy from the market?" "This *aloo gobi* is not the same as the one you made last time. Did you forget the recipe?" "Baby's skirt is looking crushed today. Don't forget to tell the *dhobi* to do a better job next time."

The criticism was so regular that Shikha learnt to ignore his grumbling. Whatever he pointed out, Shikha made efforts not to repeat the same mistake. She would make an extra effort to please him, to find different recipes she thought he would like but nothing she did was ever good enough. Most of the time, he compared her cooking with his mother's. "The *dosa* is good but not the same as my mom's. When she is here next time, learn from her if you want to cook."

"If I want to cook?" Why would I want to cook? It was like he was on a daily fault-finding mission. As years went by, Shikha reached a stage where nothing mattered and whenever he made a negative comment about her cooking or the children, she would smile and walk away thinking, "This guy is innovative. This is a new one."

Apart from his judgmental views, Shikha had started liking him. He earned well and spent well. Never stingy with her or the kids, he continued with their tradition of movie and lunch once a month after their third child was old enough to go to school with his older siblings. Now he had added another Sunday outing where he would take the whole family to a children's movie, then lunch, to the zoo or some park, then have early dinner somewhere to be home by 7 pm to prepare the children for school the next day. Every couple of months, during Diwali, or their marriage

anniversary or her birthday, he would make it a point to buy her gold jewelry. "This jewelry that I buy is our investment. Especially yours. If ever something happens to me, you can use it. Or if tomorrow we fight or split, take this jewelry with you. This is something I have no right over. But I will always have a right over you and hope nothing of the sort ever happens." The love in his eyes for her was unmistakable. "This is also a thank you for taking such good care of me, my children and everyone else." These words would melt Shikha and she would fall in his arms in a tight hug. All the bitterness would just flow away for a few days. Slowly, the Professor was creeping into her heart, which was mostly occupied by Amar.

Chapter 18

Shobha

1984 and later

Ajita was now almost 12 years old and was growing up to be a chubby little inquisitive angel. She was always asking questions about her invisible Papa, Anita's father, about her uncles in the army and anything related to the army or the war.

Anita now focused more on taking care of her mother and Dadi. Yet she wanted to go to Delhi to get more information about the missing defence personnel. But she didn't have the heart to bring up the subject with her family. It was years since Col. Mattu contacted her, telling her nothing had come out of their discussions with the government. Once in a while, there would be a small item in the newspapers about how the missing defence personnel's families were talking to the government to bring them home and how the government was denying their existence. Newspapers were now a scant property in her house. After her Dadaji passed away, no one was interested in them. Once in a while she would go to the school library to read up any news about the war, the borders, India-Pakistan relations, the army or any news that would give her hope.

Shobha was becoming weaker by the day. The doctor at the army hospital had told Anita that there were many people from

her village and surrounding areas coming to him with similar symptoms. "This looks like an epidemic," Dr Khan at the Army hospital had told her. "The symptoms are all too similar in many patients – diarrhea, nausea, itchiness, loss of appetite, redness of the eyes. This is very strange, as these cases have started coming only in the last few years. I am talking to other hospitals to see if they too are receiving similar cases."

Then he would prescribe a heavier dose of antibiotics and vitamins, which made Shobha sleep more. She would feel better for a couple of days, eat more, walk more and then would relapse to her weak, nervous self.

In August 1984, when she visited the Delhi Army Hospital again, the doctor suggested that Shobha be admitted for a couple of tests. "I suspect cancer, Anita. I am sorry to say that, dear, but I have been talking to other hospitals round the country. Mainly people who have been working in the fields for years are visiting the hospitals with these symptoms. We suspect it is the fertilizers used in the fields to grow rice and wheat. These fertilizers contain potassium, which under certain conditions is harmful to human beings. Researchers in America have discovered potassium chloride interferes with nerve impulses. In some cases, this could also affect the heart."

"How long will she have to stay in hospital?" asked Anita.

"It could be weeks, maybe months. I can't give you a definite date. But these treatments take long. It will not be possible for you to come every day and travelling so much will not be easy for Shobha. After each session of chemotherapy, she will feel weak. I suggest that you live close to the hospital so it is easy on Shobha and will also save you time."

Anita was not only worried about Shobha but also Aju. Every time she visited Delhi, she left Aju behind with Shikha's mother, who was always happy to take care of her. But she wouldn't be happy if Ajita was left for so many days. Every time she came to Delhi, she had to take leave from school and her Principal

had to arrange a substitute teacher, which wasn't easy. "Anita, I understand your mother is really sick. As much as I want to accommodate you, I am still answerable to the trustees who have now started questioning the extra expenditure on the substitute teachers."

Anita had called her father that night looking for advice. Unfortunately, she had to tell him what the doctor had told her about suspecting cancer. Her Bauji had stopped talking for a few minutes. She knew he was shocked. "Bauji, Bauji, are you there? Please Bauji, say something. Are you alright?"

It was a few minutes before he could say anything. He had been crying silently, she knew but couldn't do anything. "Bauji, don't worry, she will be fine. That is why I am in Delhi. The doctor is suggesting that she should be in Delhi for further treatment. My Principal too refuses to give me so much leave. Looks like I will have to shift to Delhi to take care of Mummy."

Shobha was admitted to hospital for two weeks. Anita resigned from her job and asked for Ajita's transfer certificate from school, so she could be admitted to a school in New Delhi. Shyam had come down for three days to help Anita pack and shift. His silent tears couldn't stop flowing. All three days, not once did he smile or played any games with Ajita, his favorite niece.

Shikha's mother was very sad to see her friend Shobha leave for Delhi. "Anita, I still insist you can leave Ajita dear with me. I promise I will take good care of her. How can I live with an empty house next to me? The house which was filled with so many people and happy times, will now stand empty," Shikha's mother sobbed as she hugged Anita. "I will miss you all." Shikha's mother had promised she would take care of Dadi till Shyam got back from Delhi to take her with him.

Shyam had a friend whose parents lived in Gulmohar Park. They agreed to rent out a room on the terrace to Anita. "Don't

worry about the rent, Anu. I will take care of that. You just take care of Mummy," Shyam said.

Once in Delhi, Shyam realized there was much work that needed to be done to settle Anita and his mother and niece and he did not want to leave his favorite sister alone to handle so much stress. Ajita had to be admitted to a school, he had to help Anita set up her basic kitchen, buy some furniture and other things. He extended his leave for another 10 days and his Major was kind, as he knew about Shyam and his family. The Major had used his sources whenever he could, to try to get some news about Ajay.

They had not brought any furniture from Rajpura as that would have changed the feel of the house they grew up in. Neither Anita nor Shyam had the courage to do that. Both wanted the house to look the same, to feel the same whenever they returned. "Anu, I have now lived in so many nicer houses, but this is the only place I call home."

The doctors recommended chemotherapy. There were times when Shobha felt good and would cook lunch and dinner at home before Anita and Aju got home from school. At other times, she would just lie in bed all day, growing weak. And, when her little Aju had topped Class 9, Shobha had left for her heavenly abode, following her mother-in-law.

Chapter 19

Destiny

July 1999

Anita had learnt to curse her destiny and wait. Her wait for Ajay wasn't over yet, now she had to wait for Ajita. The girl had followed her father's footsteps and joined the armed forces after passing the Combined Defence Services exam. Aju appeared passionate about joining the Air Force, "serving the country just like Pa did," she would say. Yes, she called Ajay Pa – her father, an individual she had never met or seen and had just a couple of yellowed pictures of him in Anita's only album. Ajita was a big fan of his; always asking for stories about her Pa. Anita had no real stories about him but made some up to tell the child. She had known Ajay for merely six months but was married to him for twenty-eight years.

As Ajita grew older, she realized how hollow those stories were. She spent hours in the school and college library reading articles about the Indo-Pak war and the exchange of prisoners that followed. Her father's name appeared only in the first few articles as Missing in Action, nothing else.

When Ajita was sixteen, she had decided to buy a new album and had very carefully and meticulously moved the pictures to the new album. While transferring those pictures, the youngster had

realized that most pictures of her father were from his marriage only and a couple from his graduation. And then on the last page was a postcard from somewhere in Pakistan.

The day she had seen that postcard, she had made a pledge to herself, "I will bring Pa home. Yes, I will. For you, Ma."

That was more than a decade ago. This album too was now falling apart – six months of memories and twenty-eight years of wait with less than twenty pictures to hold on to. Shobha had died a painful death just a year after Anita had moved bag and baggage to Delhi and just as Ajita was trying to settle in her new school. Shyam and Bauji had suggested that she continue to live in Delhi as relocating Ajita once again would not be a good idea. Bauji had dipped in his pension funds and savings and bought her a small two-bedroom apartment. "What good are my pension funds as I can't share these with my wife now," he had said. "The fields and my little pension will be enough to keep me alive".

"But Bauji, who will take care of you? I want to come back to the house and be with you," Anita had tried to argue.

"No dear, I can take care of myself. Have always done it and now it is my turn to take care of the house and the fields. You take care of Aju, dear. She is growing up and moving her at this stage might disturb her again. I would again suggest you forget about Ajay and move on with your life. You have to find someone to spend the rest of your life with."

"I have Aju, Bauji and I have you," Anita argued. "Alright, I will stay in Delhi but promise me you will visit me often."

"Yes dear, I will. All my life I had looked forward to retirement so I could spend some time with Shobha and go on a pilgrimage with her. And now, I have nothing to look forward to," he sobbed, cupping his face in his hands. "I have now lost her forever." Looking up at the ceiling, he cried more, "Shobha, please forgive me. Please, please forgive me. I did not take care of you but you took care of my responsibilities."

Someone said it right: Don't leave anything for later. There is no later. Life is only about now.

It was the first time in her life that Anita saw her father so weak. In her mind, he was always big burly strong man in uniform. She and Shyam had slyly joked about his ears when they were little but never in front of anyone. And now the same man was sitting in front of her – a weak, broken man, his face wet with tears, feeling guilty about the life he did not live, crying over a wife he did not know, a woman whom he considered just a mother of his children and a caretaker of his parents, the fields, the house and even his wishes. "Maybe if I had paid more attention, I would have hired more people to work in the fields so she did not develop this deadly disease," he moaned.

"But the doctors don't know how she developed cancer. There is no evidence that working on the fields caused it. The doctor is merely speculating because there are other people in the village showing similar symptoms, Bauji. Don't be so hard on yourself."

Time never stands still and never comes back, they say. They also say, time is a big healer but for Anita, nothing had healed. And she knew, it will not heal for her father either.

One day, Anita gathered enough courage to make contact with Col. Mattu. "Mrs Singh, how happy I am to hear from you. How have you been?"

"I'm okay. I am in Delhi now and I thought maybe, I could come and see you…that is if you have time," Anita was hesitant in talking to him. "But I am not sure how to come and see you. I will look for a bus if you give me your address."

"Mrs Singh, don't worry about that. I will come and see you myself. There are lots of updates that you may not be aware of. We have been working hard trying to bring back our soldiers still left on that side of the border."

Col. Mattu came the next week with bundles of paper, all neatly arranged, which included articles of newspapers which Anita had never read, letters written to the Government of India

which had gone unheard, accounts of various soldiers who had been in Pakistan jails, evidence that some of the prisoners of the 1971 war were seen or heard.

Anita was shocked at all the papers given to her and the availability of so much information. How could I miss so much in life? Anita had just sat there with tears welling, not sure where to start reading.

Ajita had walked in the living room and took them from Anita's hands. She merely flipped the papers and asked, "Uncle, where is my father's name in all these articles? No one cared about him all these years. No one tried to find out about him."

Anita looked at her daughter. How could she tell without even looking at the papers handed over by this kind gentleman that her father's name was never mentioned?

"Yes, *beta*, I am aware that your father's name does not appear in these articles. But his name was there in the first few lists being circulated after the war. Pakistan never acknowledged his presence in any of the prisons. There have been a number of goodwill gestures between India and Pakistan since the war when we were allowed to go to Pakistan and look for our men but couldn't find anyone. In 1981, Pakistan allowed International Red Cross team to help trace the missing defence personnel but they couldn't find any evidence. Then again in 1989, at the constant hammering by our group, a fresh search was launched to trace our people. We do believe the solders are still there but Pakistan is hiding them in other jails which are not accessible."

Col. Mattu continued, "For some of the soldiers, we even got evidence over the years about them being alive. For example, Major Ashok Suri's father had evidence that he has been shifted from Karachi to NWEP and then to somewhere in Malakand. Mukhtiar Singh, who was repatriated from Pakistan sometime in 1988, also said that Major Ashok Puri was in Kot Lakhpat jail at that time. Another of our brave soldiers, Flight Lieutenant Lamba's name appeared as one of the five Indian pilots captured

alive but we couldn't find any trace of him either. He was last seen in 1988 at the Lahore Interrogation Centre. Unfortunately, we have never received any information about your husband."

"You don't know this, Uncle, but my father also sent a letter to Mummy after the war, so we know he is alive too," said Aju as she walked towards the chest of drawers where Anita had kept the only album she had and the letter Ajay had sent years ago pasted on the last page. Anita had told Aju about the letter years ago and never discussed it since. Aju was smart and intelligent but now Anita was thinking that there were parts of her daughter's personality she was unaware of.

Aju opened the last page of the album and handed it to Col. Mattu. He put on his glasses and tried to read the faded words, "I am trying to come home. Wait for me."

"I know people think anyone could have written this letter," Anita said slowly. "But I ..." Anita couldn't finish the sentence.

"You are sure that this letter was sent by Flt Lt Ajay," he completed the sentence Anita couldn't. "I am sure too. Who else do you think would write such a letter? Who would want you to wait?"

"Mummy HAS waited for seventeen years, Uncle," Aju was now angry. "It is not fair on her."

"*Beta*, I want you to understand that you are not alone. There are 54 families, maybe more, who too are waiting for their family members and friends to come home," he said. "When you get a chance, Anitaji, please make a few copies of this postcard. I would like to keep a copy as this is another evidence of one of our men still living in Pakistan."

"Uncle, do you think my Pa is still alive? In Pakistan?" Aju was not the little Aju anymore but a teenager who had grown tall like her father. She was big and strong and had started taking care of all the heavy chores around the house. When they went shopping, Aju would carry the bags. She would carry the heavy wet laundry to the terrace to dry every Sunday. In fact, she had

started behaving like the man of the house without asking too many questions about her father, like she once did.

In school, she took part in athletics and played cricket with the boys but never wanted to join the school teams as she called that a waste of time. She had joined NCC instead. "For me, sports is just a way of keeping fit, Mummy. I don't have time to play games. I don't want to waste time running after big and small balls." Aju had ignored her mother when she had asked why she didn't have time and why she didn't want to play competitively.

That night, before going to bed, Aju had come to her and said, "Mummy, don't worry, Pa will come back. Like Uncle said, he is alive and I will bring him back."

"You, my dear? You are just a child. Look at me; I haven't been able to do much. Even your Shyam Mama has tried to find information about him but couldn't. It is not easy, dear. Two countries which are always fighting with each other are involved."

"Yes, and the two governments have made our defence men and women pawns in their game of power. Wasn't Pakistan supposed to follow the Geneva Convention and release all Prisoners of War just like India did?" questioned Aju.

Anita looked at her baby. Her little girl, with a baby face and two little braids with red school uniform ribbons but inquisitive eyes was waiting for an answer.

"Mummy, I read about the Geneva Convention in the school library. Everything was in the newspapers. India had released thousands of Pakistani prisoners but Pakistan kept a few. Maybe, Pa is not even in any of Pakistan prisons. Maybe he is somewhere else. I know when they bombed his plane; they did not find anyone there. Not even a dead body. Is it possible that he walked away from the burning plane?"

"But they told me he was captured by the Pakistani army," Anita said slowly.

"They lied to you, Mummy. Where they found Pa's plane, there was no army around. There was just a wreckage of the plane but no body or anyone."

"Are you saying the Wing Commander who told me about Ajay's fallen plane lied to me?"

"I think so, Mummy. Maybe he just made up information to give to you because you were going to his office every day and he didn't want to appear like a buffoon sitting on that chair of authority. There have been no newspaper reports saying he was ever captured. Like Amar Chacha. I am sure he would have used his parachute to get out of the burning plane and because it was winter and foggy, no one would have seen him eject."

"But then, where is he now? Why hasn't he gotten in touch with us?" Anita questioned.

Looking at some of the bundles of pages Col. Mattu had brought, Aju said, "Look here, Mom. This paper talks about Kishorilal, who spied for India and was released three years after the war. He says that he met two of the missing people in this Kot Lakhpat Jail."

"Does it give any names?"

"Yes, Flight Lieutenant Lamba and Major Ghoshal. Newspapers had reported about Lamba immediately after his picture had appeared in one of the newspapers in Rawalpindi. That was the time when Pakistan was bragging about how many Indian soldiers it had captured like trophies and was letting the photographers take pictures of these captives. But now, it is hiding. If today Pakistan accepts that it has captured soldiers from 1971, it will be considered an inhuman act in violation of Geneva Convention. There is no way that after seventeen years of war, Pakistan will accept the presence of Indian soldiers they had captured and still rotting in their jails, no matter how many times Red Cross sends its team to Pakistan jails."

All these years, Anita had relied on information from the government, newspapers and radio but never had sat down to analyze the situation herself. Like her baby had.

"Mummy, I am sure Pa is alive and trying to come back. We will find him." Anita was amazed at her daughter's stubbornness. And a little scared of her resolve.

Chapter 20

The missing message

1989

Almost a year later, sometime in the autumn of 1989, Bauji called, as he did every other day now that he had a phone at home.

Aju picked up Bauji's phone and after exchanging pleasantries, handed over the phone to her mother. She was now talking more like her mother, showing concern for her grandfather's health and asked him to take care of himself, unlike the time when she would scream with excitement whenever her grandfather called and begged him to come visit them.

"What's wrong with Aju, dear? She sounded different." Bauji asked.

"She is growing up. She is too mature for her age. I feel like in two years, she has aged 20 years. She is more like a mother to me than I am to her."

"You know about Shikha's father. He just retired a few days ago. Before leaving, he decided to clean out his office and you know how at the post office letters with wrong or incomplete addresses tend to get lost and stay in a hole till someone really gets to them."

"Yes, Bauji," Anita was slightly impatient, not knowing where the conversation was going.

"He came last night and handed me a letter with just your name and House No. 62 on it. He said since this letter does not have the right address, and there is no House 62 in our village, it was not delivered. But he said that there was a similar letter, which had come for you a few years ago, and it turned out to be Ajay's. So he brought it to me."

Anita was shaking with curiosity and happiness. "Bauji, what does the letter say?"

"Sorry dear, I read your letter. I was curious too. But it doesn't say much just '*Main ghar ka rasta doondh raha hoon. Phas gaya hoon. Inshallah jald aaonga. Tumhara Yaja.*' (I am trying to find my way home. I am stuck. By God's grace will come home soon. Yours Yaja.)

"Inshallah!" Anita was confused. "Ajay never used that word."

"I don't understand either. But there is a similarity between the names of the two letters," Bauji said. "The letter is stamped December 1977."

"1977! That was twelve years ago."

"Yes."

"How could a letter remain undelivered for this long?'

"It looks like this letter came around the time when Babu was busy with Shikha's second marriage. He had taken a couple of months off. Whoever replaced him did not know us."

There was silence for a couple of minutes. Neither said anything, as if trying to digest the unexpected news.

Anita broke the silence.

"But still he hasn't found his way home. It has been twelve years."

Bauji had no words to console her. He felt that Anita had wasted away her life waiting for a man who would never return. He knew about the complicated relations between India and Pakistan. The two countries had fought wars and skirmishes had

never ended at the borders. Army men from both countries were being sacrificed at the altar of politics. The continuing hatred between the two countries showed no signs of ending.

Aju walked in and stared at her mother, who was now sitting on the chair next to the telephone, sobbing silently.

"Is Nanu ok? What happened?"

Anita looked up at her grown baby. Till today Anita had always told her stories, trying to keep her pain to herself. Yet Aju was aware of her agony and her anguish and understood it well without Anita having to put her feelings into words. This little girl was now more a mother to her than she was to her.

"Nanu, is everything ok?" she asked, snatching the receiver from her mother's hands who just sat there staring into space.

"Yes, dear. In fact, there is good news that your Pa is alive and trying to come home. I am sure he is just stuck somewhere." Bauji told her about the letter.

Both Anita and her father knew that these days no one could hide any news whether relevant or irrelevant from Aju. Everyone knew and strongly believed that Aju had more news about her father and current affairs than they did. She had admitted that during her free periods or during recess, she would go to the school library and read newspapers, current or old and even the files of some news items the school library kept for references.

The news got a smile on her face. "Mummy, Pa is alive. He sent another letter. I always believed he was and he is just waiting for me to find him. And I will." Aju couldn't control her excitement. She jumped up and down with joy while Anita just sat there stone-faced. Anita had never seen Aju so happy and excited in years. But Anita didn't know what to make of this news.

"What's wrong with you, Mummy? Are you not happy to hear the news?"

"*Beta*, don't make too much of this news. This letter was sent twelve years ago, not yesterday. So much more would have

happened by now. Situations change, governments change, neighbours and friends move on."

"I know, Mummy," Aju had now sobered down. "But see, this just adds to our belief that he is alive and just waiting to be found."

"I think we should let Col. Mattu know about this letter," suggested Anita.

"Oh! Mother, don't even bother. They can't do anything. All that group does is sit in their homes and write letters. They have to physically go there and look for OUR MEN in the jails or streets of Pakistan." Anita was shocked at how Aju had stressed on those words 'our men' as if it was her responsibility to bring them home.

"But he did say that Government of India had sent a few teams to Pakistan jails but they didn't find Ajay or any other missing army men."

"That was a useless exercise. When they knew the date and time Indians are coming to look for their people, it's not difficult to hide them for a few days. It's like the police going to a thief's house after making an appointment. Such operations should be done discreetly," argued Aju.

"We are talking about two countries who are always fighting with each other. It is not possible to enter those jails or that country without the governments talking to each other, Aju."

Chapter 21

July 1999

The full moon was playing hide-and-seek with the clouds. Were those clouds or was there a fire nearby. Maybe someone was burning leaves. This looked like a park somewhere…was it Lodhi Gardens? Or was it Ma burning leftover straw from rice fields. Ma did that after every crop just like every other farmer in Punjab did. She could easily recognize the smell of burning hay but she couldn't see the fire. Just then, a young girl in white came running out of the clouds. She was running hard and there were pairs of feet in hard shoes running behind her. They were too many feet and the girl had just two feet. How far could she run? Her white chunni was flying on her face and she could barely see in front.

The girl tripped on the protruding root of an old tree. EEEEEEEEE….

Anita woke up with a start. As usual, she was sweating profusely. Her breathing was heavy and it felt like her heart had skipped a couple of beats. Unlike other times, today she was scared. She switched on the tube light over her bed. Aju had installed a switch close to her bed. "Mom, you shouldn't have to hunt for the lights when you go to the bathroom at night. You might trip and fall. Who will take care of you if you hurt yourself?" Aju had smiled asking Anita.

"Why, you won't take care of me if I get sick? You always take care of me anyways like you are my mom," Anita had joked.

"Of course I will but only if I am here with you."

"What if I get a job somewhere else and have to go? What if I get selected for the Air Force and have to fly somewhere and you are living alone here."

"You know Aju, I don't want you to follow your Pa's profession. See, he has not come back. He left me alone. He doesn't even know you exist, that he has a daughter. I missed him terribly all these years. Now I don't want to miss you, dear."

"Oh Mother. Don't panic. If I have to go, I will always come back. Won't leave you like Pa," her baby had assured her. "I will come back." Aju had expressed her desire to join the force numerous times but Anita was relaxed at the thought that the Indian Air Force did not allow women pilots.

"Wait for me. I will be back soon," Ajay's last words had haunted her all her life. That is what Ajay had said before leaving and he never did, Anita thought, hiding a tear. Only a broken heart can shed tears. She wanted to believe that her heart, broken by Ajay's long absence, had now healed. These are mostly for Aju, she thought. I don't want her to follow her father's footsteps, yet every day Aju was growing up to be like the father she had never seen. She thought like him, spoke like him, was passionate about the country just like him.

Sitting on her bed now, Anita remembered the day just before Diwali when Aju was in her last year of college, there was a letter amongst many others in her mailbox addressed to Ajita. It looked like an official letter, just like those she had received from the Indian Air Force when Ajay had gone missing. Anita had the urge to read the letter before Aju got home but she knew Aju never liked her mother reading her letters. She had always said, "Mom, I am grown up now. I will get mail but please let me open my mail. If there is anything you need to know, I will definitely tell you."

Anita had decided to leave the letter on the dining table near the entrance for Aju to open. Aju had screamed with joy when she had opened the letter – excited like she hardly ever was. She had come rushing to the kitchen and hugged Anita tight.

"Ma, I will be joining the Indian Air Force. I have been selected and have to go for pilot training soon. Oh Ma! I am so excited."

Anita had stared at her beautiful daughter open mouthed – she didn't have words to express her shock. Aju had learnt to never express her emotions. She had learnt not to shed tears when her mother was around so as not to sadden her. She had never expressed her desires to her mother nor shared her happiness. Unlike other girls her age, Aju never wanted new clothes, never wanted to go shopping, never wanted to watch movies or any other activity which other girls would argue with their moms about. She hardly had any friends and if she did, they were restricted to school or college. None of her friends had ever come home. Aju was a quiet, hardworking, intelligent girl who always minded her own business, her teachers had written in her report card. She never got into trouble but had always helped in resolving disputes in class. She was well liked by everyone wherever she went. Most people were in awe of her and even the boys had steered clear of her, maybe because she was well built. Just once, she had thrashed a boy in college who had merely winked at her. But that was the last day anyone dared to mess with her.

Aju had cleared the NDA exams in her first attempt and had gone to Khadakwasla for training, leaving Anita alone. India was changing and girls were being given opportunities everywhere. Aju was among a group of just 25 women who were allowed in. Of course, Anita couldn't stop her.

Aju called her every day and always sounded excited and happy. She would describe what she had learnt and would always try to cheer Anita up. She had talked about parachute training, different kind of controls she learnt about in a cockpit of a helicopter, some kind of training on air warfare, navigation, learning the maps, the compass… Aju would be sad when she would tell her mother that women were not allowed to be fighters.

"Isn't this gender-based discrimination, Ma?"

"Well, dear, you are lucky that at least they have given you a chance. We did not even get a chance to apply." Aju would listen quietly and at times Anita got the impression that she was only talking to the telephone.

Not a single day had passed when Anita did not go to bed in fear of losing the only precious thing she had. She thanked God for giving her this beautiful gift of life but now she prayed for Aju's safety.

The Kargil War had ended a month ago but Aju hadn't come home. The Air Force had played a very significant role there. While Anita considered it a full-fledged war, the newspapers had at times called it a conflict. How can they call it a mere conflict or a skirmish when MiGs were used for deploying missiles? She read up everything on Kargil, the whys and hows, the whens and also the whos. Ajay was always right about wars – a war can be defined as a slaughter of innocent men and women for the benefit of the elite few, who live in forts, to distract the people from the politicians' misdeeds.

Anita was aware that the Indian Air Force played a major role in Indian victory as well as demoralizing the Pakistan army. While the skirmish was a result of infiltration of Kashmiri militants from Pakistan, India suspected that they were Pakistani soldiers in the garb of militants. The Indian Air Force had played a major role in the capture of Indian positions at Himalayan heights of 18,000 ft, a feat unprecedented in the force's history.

One month after the Kargil skirmish ended, when the afternoon sun was still hot and days in Delhi were long, Anita picked up her mail and sat on the dining table with a letter from the Air Force in her hand. The letter was addressed to Ajita, not Anita. Which meant, this letter was not about Ajay. She opened the envelope and stared blankly at the subject line: Court Martial of Ft Lt Ajita Singh on November 12, 1999.

Her heart sank. Her hands were shaking. Her head felt dizzy, her face turned red and hot. The letter fell from her hands. Court

martial?? Why? What did my baby do? She had gone to war as ordered. She obeyed as commanded. How long Anita sat there, she didn't know. Her thoughts were playing *kabaddi* in her mind. Her hands and legs were shaking. She was shivering with fear and couldn't utter a word. Not that there was anyone there she could talk to. Before the tears flowed and made her weak, she told herself to be strong - strong for herself and for her baby.

It took her an hour to gather her thoughts and emotions. Finally, she decided to call the number on the letter. One Air Marshal Khuranna had signed the letter. She dialed the number. It connected to Sena Bhawan. After a couple of rings, a Mr Nair picked up the phone. "Why do you want to speak with him? What is the issue?" Mr Nair queried.

"I am a mother of one of your members and I received this letter from him. I want to talk to him about this," Anita said slowly.

"What does the letter say?" Nair quizzed.

"It says that my daughter should appear before a board to be court mar….." She couldn't bring herself to say the words. She had never said those words in her life. They appeared so heavy and were weighing her down.

"Madam, I am sorry. I don't have all day." Mr Nair was now getting impatient. "What is the name of your daughter?"

"Flight Lieutenant Ajita Singh," Anita responded without hesitation this time. She realized that if she did not get over her shyness, she could never get any answers to her questions. Yes, they were busy people.

"Oh! That one. So, she is your daughter, Behenji," Mr Nair sounded amused, almost insultingly so. Anita thought she heard a chuckle.

"Yes, she is." Anita wasn't amused, of course, but something was building inside her. She realized after years and years, the emotion she was feeling was anger. Anger at someone who was not only insulting her, but her daughter who had fought for the

country. Now, when the country should come forward to protect her, these officials of power were ridiculing her.

"Thanks for calling, Behenji. But it is Flight Lieutenant Singh we should be talking to. Can I talk to her please?" Mr Nair asked a little more politely.

Anita was shocked to hear those words, coming from an official of the Sena Bhawan! Doesn't he know that her daughter had not come back from the war they had her sent to fight? How callous of him not to know.

"What are you saying, Bhaisahab?" Anita was now furious. She had raised her voice, maybe for the first time in so many years, yet wanted to sound polite. "You think my daughter is sitting at home and waiting to talk to you".

"She has not reported for duty after May 27. The Air Force would like to know her whereabouts. Surely, you are the mother, you would know her whereabouts."

"Her whereabouts!!! Shouldn't YOU know her whereabouts? You sit in your air-conditioned offices after sending our children to fight for the country. You got so many of our young children – who have not seen anything in this world but were passionate about their country – killed and now you tell me you don't know where my daughter is!!! I want to know from you, right now, where is my daughter? You asked her to be alert and fly the helicopter when Pakistani army was shooting anything Indian in sight. She told me that you had asked her to fly over Kargil and evacuate injured soldiers. She did as ordered but I haven't heard anything from her since. She went to do her duty to save lives as you ordered."

Anita vividly remembered the day when Aju had called her just before taking off. It was seven in the morning and she was getting ready to go to school on May 26, 1999. The phone rang and Anita dashed to pick it up, hitting her knee against the corner of the coffee table. The phone was her only hope and only connection to Aju and the rest of the family.

"Maaaaaa," Aju had screamed as soon as Anita got the earpiece to her ears. "Group Captain Gupta wants me to fly and bring the injured soldiers back. Ma, I am so excited. It will be my first real flight in a real fight – my flight. This is what I always wanted to do, Ma. Finally."

Her daughter was in a war zone. So was her husband. So were her brother Shyam and Sunny. Her whole family was dedicated to the country.

"Isn't this dangerous, Aju? Aren't there other pilots who can do the job?" Anita couldn't help but remember what Ajay had told her before he left. "I will be back soon." And he never did.

"No, Ma. Every pilot we have here right now is fighting. Don't worry, everything will be fine. I have a fully loaded revolver and this INSAS assault rifle."

"What is that?"

"Oh! It is a like a small weapon Indian Air Force has started using. It is very efficient but I am to use it only when required, in emergency situations."

"When will you be back?"

There was a pause.

"I don't know, Ma. No one knows how many of our jawans are injured and how many will need to be hospitalized. Just think like this, Ma – your daughter is going to save lives. Those people who might die if I don't reach in time. You take care of yourself and I will be back soon. Who knows, when I come back, I will bring your life back too."

"Of course, I guess I can't talk you out of it now. But be careful and always remember, in your heart beats my life and in my heart, beats your life. Don't take my life away from me."

Anita couldn't control her tears when she said goodbye to her baby.

What Anita didn't know that after Aju hung up, her daughter had made another call.

Another call to the country her own country was fighting.

"Mrs Singh, you are right that she was sent to save lives. But she didn't. In fact, she diverted from her assigned route and flew the helicopter near Poonch close to LoC. She wasn't asked to fly there. Our soldiers were waiting for her."

"How can it be? She was passionate about saving lives and that is what she wanted to do. She deliberately wouldn't have diverted her helicopter." Anita was in disbelief.

No, that was not her baby. She could not deliberately have left soldiers to die. Surely something had happened to her.

"Behenji, we wouldn't be court martialing her if she had obeyed orders. The Air Force does not have so much time. But discipline has to be maintained and everyone here has to obey orders. And she did not."

"But where is she? Was her helicopter shot down? Did no one go to rescue her? And you are telling me now! A month later! I called so many times and no one said anything. I have been trying to speak to the Air Force for a month but no one; NO ONE ever returned my calls. And now …"

"Behenji, please calm down." Nair interrupted. "The only reason this letter was sent because the Air Force presumed that she went home and decided not come back to service. We thought she got scared of the war. But if she had told us, we would have given her ground duty."

"Bhaisahab! My daughter is not a coward. She joined the Air Force because she wanted to give to the country and not leave it in the lurch during the time of war. She called me and told me she was so excited and happy to be given an opportunity to fly during a real fight. I can tell you and I say this very strongly, SHE IS NOT A COWARD!! What did you do to her? Tell me…I need to know where my baby is? If she crashed, no one went to rescue her?" Anita was now crying.

"Behenji, please don't cry. Did she not get in touch with you after the war?"

"NO, I haven't heard from her."

"Sending a letter like this is government protocol. We have to follow rules and we cannot divulge confidential information. Even for your daughter, I know you have a right to know, but I cannot tell you more on the phone. She is still our employee and we have to protect her information. Especially during the times when misinformation can spread like a rumour."

"But I need to know more. Where is she? What happened to her?"

"If this makes you a little happy, we never found her body near the helicopter wreckage."

"Wh…What does that mean?"

"That means she is alive somewhere."

"You mean she is taken prisoner by Pakistan?" Anita could only whisper now.

"We don't know. Her name is not on the list of prisoners Pakistan sent us."

So wasn't Ajay's…so what? That doesn't mean anything.

"Then where is she? You have not tried to locate her?"

"We are doing our best. Another officer who was with her was injured badly and is in induced coma right now. If you hear from your daughter, please remember that it is your responsibility to let us know. Namaste!" Mr Nair had hung up, leaving her holding the receiver in frozen hands.

First Ajay and now Aju. How can history repeat itself so soon, in one lifetime and to one person? Oh God! Is it because of me? Is it my bad deeds that have come back to haunt me? God please tell me, what did I do wrong that you keep punishing me like this? You took Ajay away from me but gave me Aju. I accepted her as a gift from you – like you gave me hope to live – hope that one day, if I could stay alive, Ajay will come back to me. Instead of sending him, you took my baby away from me. Now where do I find her? I know no one will help me.

Anita sat there for hours, cursing her fate, sobbing like a child, pulling her hair, slapping herself, an emotional wreck. No, she could not take this anymore. Not again…

The last rays of the setting sun were peeking through the mesh curtains of her balcony door, indicating that another day in her life had passed. She should talk to Shyam and Sunny. Or just Shyam. He was more mature, in a better position to help her. He was now a Colonel posted in Jammu and headed a battalion during the Kargil war. She hadn't talked to Shyam since before the war started. On most days, Shyam would call her at least once a week and the brother and sister would talk for hours about everything under the sun – their village, their school, their families, their mother – most of the time now they talked about Bauji. They were both worried about his health and Shyam made trips to see him as often as he could. Sometimes he would send his son, who was now almost 19 years old, and bring him to stay with them. But Bauji would get bored after a month or so and would then ask Shyam to book his train tickets. "In the village, at least I had something to do. There are people I can talk to, and I like to work in the fields too. Once upon a time I wanted to run away from these fields and therefore joined the army so that I had a good excuse not to work in the fields. Now, the same fields call me to them. I can't stay away from them. I feel like they are scolding me, like they are complaining that why did I leave them. Shyam *beta*, I will come back again but let me go now." And Shyam would become emotional and do as told.

Yes, she should talk to Shyam, Anita decided. Only he will be able to understand her situation. She got up and went to her bedroom in search of the tiny telephone diary she kept near her bed. The pages of that old diary were folded in a number of places. Aju had promised her she would make a new diary for her one day. Most of the time Anita never had to consult her diary, as Aju knew all the numbers by heart. She had a photographic memory. Any new number she dialed the first time, it would get

etched in her mind somewhere and Anita never had to consult any telephone book or her diary, which she had not updated in a long time. Before Aju had left for her training, she did write down some important numbers like the Bharat Gas agency, MTNL etc. She didn't keep her promise – will she, won't she? Will she come back to complete her unfulfilled tasks…

Her heart began to sink when she thought of Aju again. She could see her own life pass before her eyes…the day God gave her this little princess who became her motivation to live. How can he be so cruel as to take her away now? No, she was not yet ready to believe that life had come a full circle. No, this could not be happening to her, not again.

She had sat near the phone for hours, she didn't know how long. She didn't remember when her weak legs carried her to Aju's room. The room was as she had left it – Aju's books neatly stacked on the bookshelf, her bed well made, and a little lamp on her bed stand, her slippers and a pair of her favourite sandals near the closet, ready to be worn when she got home. Not a single piece of clothing hung on the nails or behind neither doors or on the bed or outside the closet. Aju had always been well organized – Anita never had to clean her room since she turned 7 or 8 years old. Especially when her mother was sick and was sharing Aju's room, Anita had once talked to Aju about hygiene. "Your Nani is very weak, her immunity is very low and she can catch infection easily. Both of us have to try to keep the house, the bathroom, the kitchen and everything around her very very clean. Will you help me take care of Nani?"

Aju had understood right away, "Ma, you have too much to do. Take care of Nani and I will take care of cleanliness. Of course I will help you. I love Nani. I want her to be with us forever. God please help us." Little Aju had clung to her and cried.

Chapter 22

Operation Pa

May 27, 1999

This was the first time Aju was flying a fighter jet after training. She was excited when Commander Gupta had called her into his office and said, "Ms Ajita, we are running out of pilots and personnel. We need as many trained officers as soon as possible."

"Don't worry sir, I am ready to fight," Aju had said excitedly.

"No Ms Ajita. You don't have to fight. We don't expect our women pilots to fight wars. But yes, we do need your help." Yeah, all that men and women talk – not again, you gender discriminator, prejudiced sexist son-of-a-…Anger was building up inside Ajita but she had to control herself.

"It is time now for you to prove that you are a trained pilot," the Commander was saying authoritatively. "Our men on the field are tired and injured. Some of them have lost their helicopters and jets and are injured, lying somewhere in the mountains, others are fighting and need supplies in the Dras and Batalik sectors. I would request you and Fight Lieutenant Rajni Patel to drop supplies and bring back the injured soldiers. Be careful. The enemy is still out there and we are in the middle of a war. You not only have to evacuate our soldiers but also report enemy

positions. You will carry with you a fully loaded revolver and INSAS assault rifle to be used in emergencies only. You will start at 6 am tomorrow morning and we expect you to be back in the camp after your successful mission by 6 in the evening. All the best, Flight Lieutenant Ajita. I will also talk to Flight Lieutenant Rajni now and you will meet her on the tarmac."

Ajita had clicked her heels, saluted the boss crisply and marched out with a fake smile glued to her pretty face. Her brain was racing faster than her feet were carrying her.

The day after, Ajita was on the tarmac much before the scheduled time. She was on a mission. She had to inspect the cockpit, the engines, load supplies to be carried to the injured soldiers but most of all check if parachutes were in working order. It was important that she get there before Rajni. She and Rajni were a little more than acquaintances; actually she could call her the only friend in the regiment. For Rajni too, Aju was the only friend she had confided in.

Now was the time to accomplish her only goal in her life – to make her mother happy. And her mother's happiness was her Pa.

"Had it not been for these terrorists invading Kashmir, we wouldn't be flying this beauty, right, Ajita?" Rajni was saying. They were both in their camouflage flight suits with their parachutes strapped to them. Both Aju and Rajni had trained together at Pune, Hyderabad, Bidar, Deolali and were now posted in Srinagar together. Unlike Rajni, Aju had to ask to be posted in Srinagar as she was looking for some action. After a stint in Assam, Aju got a posting in Udhampur. At a time when no one wanted to go to Kashmir, Aju had not only volunteered but also asked to be posted there. She had been watching the Kashmiri conflict for a while, and had been looking forward to her mission. Being close to the border, especially Kashmir, from where her Pa had started, would only further her goal. Her mission had finally taken wings.

They were flying over the Srinagar-Jammu highway, a stretch, which had been easy, targets for militants like Lashkar-e-Toiba or Hizbul Mujahideen. Looking down, Rajni was saying, "So many of our soldiers have died on this stretch of highway, Aju. On this stretch from Qazigunj to Srinagar, the militants attack our convoys. It is a strategic road for supplies but so life-threatening. Look down, what a beautiful sight. Still some snow on the mountains."

"Right," Ajita nodded. Though she liked to chat with Rajni, today was not the day. The chopper was soaring higher and higher. Both of them wore masks to supply oxygen to prevent hypoxia symptoms and were talking through a microphone. Their conversation could be recorded to be heard later, if required.

"You know, Aju, this has been my childhood dream – to fly a fighter jet in a war – and be above all. I used to watch all those Hollywood films where fighter pilots would zoom across the sky, throwing missiles and bombs. Anyway, I still consider myself lucky that I got an opportunity to fly this Cheetah helicopter. Had it not been for the helicopters, it would be difficult to fight any war in this terrain. Don't you think, Aju?"

"Yes, but remember, we are not fighting," Aju said nodding. "It has been my childhood dream too, Rajni, not to bomb or anything, but to fly HF-24, Indian's first fighter aircraft."

"Really? You never said that before."

"I know. Because I wasn't sure if I will ever be able to fulfill my dream. Did you know that my father was flying the Marut when he disappeared in the last war?"

"Oh no! Seriously! He would be so proud of you," Rajni was astonished.

"Only if I get to meet him. He doesn't even know that I exist. I have never seen him but just have an old photograph of him on my thigh."

"Thigh? How can you have a picture on your thigh?" Rajni was now laughing through the mask and her helmeted head was bobbing side to side.

"I have a tattoo of his picture on my thigh," Aju said casually. She was concentrating on the controls of the helicopter.

"Did your mother give you permission for that?" Rajni asked.

"Of course not. She doesn't know because I never asked her. I got it done after I finished school and no longer had to wear skirts."

"Wow! Aju, aren't you a smart aleck!"

"Don't know about that but all my life, I have dreamt about seeing my Pa. I know he is lost somewhere and needs to be brought home. He needs help," Aju was serious now.

"It has been 28 years, Aju! You think he would be still alive? That too in a dangerous place like Pakistan where they hate Indians? Forget Indians – an Indian soldier!"

"Of course he is alive. He was younger than me when he went missing. Our government has not done a serious job of looking for our men lost in Pakistan. Only when families insisted, the government sent these missions as eyewash. No politician has done anything to seriously look for our men."

"Shh Aju, let's not talk about the government right now. Remember, we work for the government. Let me look at the map and see where we are going," Rajni now wanted to change the topic as she knew that their conversation could be overheard. She did not want any problems for herself and Aju later. She was aware that when it came to talking about her Pa, Aju would get emotional. "Concentrate where we are going, Aju. We should be flying north but as per this compass, we are going East," Rajni now was worried.

"You know Rajni, even my mother, the only person I have loved and lived for all my life, doesn't know that my goal has always been to cross the border and look for Pa. That opportunity

is NOW," Aju said slowly and deliberately, almost whispering. "If I don't come back, can you do me a favour?"

"Come back? We will be back in the evening. That's what Gupta Sir said, remember."

"YOU will be back in the evening Rajni. Not me."

"What? Why?"

"Because I am going to Pakistan to look for Pa."

"You can't be serious, Aju. Not now. Do what you have to after this mission. Don't get distracted from our mission – we have to report back in the evening, drop supplies to our soldiers who have been fighting for so long, help the injured."

"Of course. You can do all that. After I drop, you take the copter where it is needed the most and help our people."

"Drop? Aju, I don't know what you are talking about," Rajni was flabbergasted and nervous. "Please let's follow the assigned route. Turn around. We are in the danger zone. Aju please turn around."

Just then a Pakistani missile barely missed the chopper and crashed in the mountains below, violently shaking the helicopter. Both the girls were now trembling with fear, as this was their first near-death experience. Too close.

"Oh Aju! We can be easy targets here. You know that. And we don't have the capability to fight. Please turn around." Rajni was now hysterical and was regretting the decision of letting her friend take control.

"Just five more minutes, once we cross Poonch, I will drop down and you can go back," Aju said, trying to calm her friend.

"Operation Safed Sagar! Operation Safed Sagar! Flight Lieutenant Ajita and Rajni, please return to your assigned route. You are on the wrong route", the radio was blaring as Rajni looked scared. She had always loved adventure and was looking forward to her first action, but not this. What did Aju have in mind?

"Oh my God! Both of us will be Court martialed for this. Aju, where are you going?"

"Only I will be Court martialed – that is, if I come back alive. Listen to me, Rajni, I will fly the helicopter close to the border and drop down so I land in Pakistan. As soon as I do that, you fly the chopper towards Southwest direction first and then return to North when you feel safe. This will confuse the enemy and give you time to escape."

"And you think you won't get killed when you drop down? They can shoot you when you are in the air, Aju. Please, let's go back, this is not a good plan. Try something else later. I promise, I will help you," Rajni pleaded, trying to convince Aju.

"Thanks, Rajni. You are helping me even now, though I am forcing you to. As per Geneva Convention, no one is supposed to shoot a parachute, Rajni. They won't shoot me but you have to get away as soon as I jump. Promise me, you will go and help our people. I am sorry for dragging you into this but the Commander wouldn't let me fly alone. I had asked him if I could take the chopper alone, but he wouldn't agree. Keep in mind we are entering Pakistani territory and quite possible they won't hit you thinking this is their helicopter. As soon as I eject, you have to turn around and enter India before Air Headquarters of both countries gauge what is going on and take action. But anyway, in my absence, you will be able to bring another injured soldier to safety," Aju tried to smile as Rajni looked on shocked. She had no words to convince her friend anymore.

"Why now? Why here?" Rajni merely whispered in desperation.

"Because I want to follow the trail my Pa might have taken."

"How can you be so certain?"

"His plane was seen last in this area. When you go back, can you tell Ma that I love her and will miss her? Tell her what I am doing now is for her happiness. I just want to see a little smile on her face and I am going to look for that smile. Wish me luck, Rajni. Thanks a lot for your help." Without waiting for Rajni's response, Aju used her right hand to put Rajni's left hand on

the controls, and used her left hand to unbuckle herself. "Please pray for me Rajni."

"Aju, this is too dangerous. We are at least at least 2,000 or 3,000 ft high. Can you not do this when it is much safer?" Rajni pleaded.

No use. The helicopter had slowed to 20-30 knots speed and shook violently as Aju ejected, lifting the glass topped cabin door. The Cheetah helicopters are capable of nib of the earth (NOE) flying – they can fly really low and gain height immediately. It didn't take long for Rajni to take control of the chopper immediately after Aju ejected, though her heart was crying for her friend and her visibility was reduced due to tears flooding her eyes. Her body was shivering for fear of the unknown but they were trained not to let emotions take over their duties and responsibilities towards their country. Aju was right. Maybe the Pakistanis were confused about this chopper's origin and the enemy refrained from firing for those couple of seconds. Rajni was safely able to fly the chopper back inside Indian terrain and return to her mission. She knew that for the rest of her life, she could have to live with the guilt of not being able to help her friend but she could not live with the guilt of not being able to help the injured soldiers. Wiping away tears, she brought her thoughts back to the mountainous region and the GPS in front of her to guide her to the assigned task.

Though she safely entered India, Rajni could not complete her mission.

Chapter 23

Mission Pa

Yes, that is what she had named her search for her dear Pa. Operation Pa was more important to her than Operation Safed Sagar. She did feel guilty about not performing the onerous responsibility she was assigned in times of war. She was patriotic enough to understand the importance of her role. But she had been waiting for this opportunity since she was a child. What other option did she have but to go to Pakistan and look for her father, who was lost somewhere? Going through the legal channel would never have been possible.

As she tumbled down from the helicopter, she kept her fingers on the ripcord, which would pull a closing pin, releasing a spring-loaded pilot chute and open the container. This results in the pilot chute being propelled into the air stream by its spring. It then uses the force generated by passing air to extract a deployment bag releasing a parachute canopy. She was now smoothly flying towards the earth. She had to be careful that the wind didn't push her back to India.

Far far away in between the mountains, valleys and canopy of trees, she could hear firing, see smoke, tankers, which meant that someone somewhere would be watching her fly down. She wouldn't be able to hide for long. Looking down, she knew she would be landing among trees and bushes, somewhere in the

jungles across from Poonch and had to get to Muzaffarabad. She had prepared for this day for as long as she could remember. Years of research, hard work, staying focused, role plays, the NCC training, reading maps and etching them into her memory, the tough Air Force training – all this was now going to come handy.

She was almost certain, remembering the map of Poonch and surrounding areas that she was landing in Pakistan Occupied Kashmir (PoK), a region flush with terrorist camps. The Pakistan Army had a base in Uri close to the border and she was sure someone would have spotted her coming down. Looking down, all she could see was tops of trees, bushes, a silhouette of a village close by, little huts and houses made of stones growing bigger as gravity pulled her inexorably down. The sun was shining; visibility was at its peak, yet she could not spot a lot of movement nearby. In times of war, the governments mostly get the villages close to the border vacated to minimize casualties. That is why, she thought, she couldn't spot humanity but only stray dogs.

She closed her eyes as she dropped on top of a big tree and the branches scraped and bruised her body. She was now dangling in the air with the strings of her parachute entangled among the branches. She had to cut herself out. That didn't take too long as Aju had prepared for this contingency. She felt relieved as her feet touched the earth, with dried leaves and branches welcoming her with their crackle.

Aju immediately took off her Air Force uniform to reveal a black salwar kameez that she had been wearing all along. Under her uniform was tucked a small shoulder bag containing another set of men's salwar kameez, a pocket knife with a small torch at the back, an antiseptic ointment, some dry fruits, a bottle of water, a pair of black canvas shoes and a monkey cap to hide her hair. She had considered carrying a burqa too but then thought a lone woman walking in a war zone would attract attention. She also carried a light pashmina shawl to hide her breasts and face if need be.

Before heading towards the village down the mountain, she examined herself. Her arms and knees were bleeding and she had a nasty cut near her lips, which she could not see but feel the warmth of blood oozing and taste its saltiness. Thankfully, her ankles and feet were fine, which for now were the most important limbs of her body that needed to be intact. She decided to give herself first aid and relieved herself before making her way.

She was not far from her destination city – Muzaffarabad, about 100 km. She should have carried a map, she knew, but was afraid that if she got caught with the map or compass paraphernalia, she couldn't give any excuses to stave off suspicion. Anyway, the map was etched in her mind. She had to walk northeast to come close to the city. While she had learnt navigation using the location of the sun, she had bought herself a wristwatch with a magnetic compass. She had to get down the mountain, through the jungles and reach the closest village she could see from the air. Though she didn't see any sign of life, yet she had to be careful. She had to get to Muzaffarabad as soon as she could and find a telephone booth to call her friend Sultana Rehman, who was a lawyer and human rights activist. She was now married to a police officer, who she thought might be able to help her in her search. Anita was unaware of her daughter's long-distance friendship, which had grown beyond a school project.

Aju had already received a letter from Sultana who, with the help of her husband, had tried to locate Ajay in the various jails of Pakistan where Indian PoWs were housed – Kot Lakhpat Jail, Multan Jail and Bahwalpur jail, where Indian PoWs had been spotted by a number of people who were in jail with them and released by Pakistan. In one of her last letters to Aju she had written,

"My dear friend Ajita,

I have done my best to locate your father here in Pakistan. Salim, my husband, has talked to various jailors who were on duty during the time of the 1971 war and after. No one has confirmed any Ajay Singh in his or her jails ever. He even made inquiries at the Lahore Interrogation Centre.

My dear, I don't want to dishearten you but it doesn't look like your father was ever taken a PoW. Also keep in mind; it has been 28 long years since your father disappeared. That is a long time to bear the kind of torture meted out to prisoners, especially Indians, in Pakistani jails. During my research, I have come across prisoners who have converted to Islam to escape torture and now are living here with names changed and started a new life as they were very disgruntled with their governments be it Indian, Bangladeshi or Nepalese as they feel that their home country doesn't need them anymore. These people are so bitter that they changed loyalties. Many prisoners live in such subhuman conditions that they have now become lunatics and don't remember even their names.

Please don't let this letter discourage you from looking for your father. I know it means a lot to you and is the only mission of your life. If you still want to come here, whatever method you choose, I am here to help you. My address and phone number is below and please call me when you are here.

Your true friend
Sultana

Aju had cried that night when she received this letter when she was posted in Assam.

Sultana was a human rights activist lawyer now, practicing in the District Courts of Muzaffarabad. Being a woman in a male-dominated profession was not easy, she had once told Aju in one of their phone conversations. Growing up, they had exchanged letters and were pen friends only. They sent letters to each other just a couple of times a year when an English teacher had asked Aju's Grade 5 class if they wanted to have pen friends. The teacher had a list of names and addresses from Russia, Pakistan, Afghanistan, Nepal, etc. Aju was the only one who chose Pakistan. Writing letters to pen friends was an English project that the teacher had encouraged and at the end of the year, they were graded on the quality of letters they had received. Though the project was just for one year, the two remained friends even after and would write letters to each other till one day, Sultana sent her a phone number of her new home. "I am married now. My husband is a police officer and works in Muzaffarabad. I am sending you my phone number so you can call me any time." Aju had just been posted to Assam then and had called her friend at least once a week, from a PCO, talking to her about her plan of action.

Aju wasn't disheartened easily. Like her mother had once told her Nanaji, "No rock can break my Aju's spirit. You need a mountain to do that." How mothers truly understand their children, is an amazing fact of life. She loved her mother so much that she had decided to sacrifice her own life just to bring that elusive smile on her face. She had never heard her mother's laughter, she would smile occasionally, that too when Aju was around. Other than that, even the best joke in the world had never raised a laugh, not even a muffled one.

For almost two hours, Aju walked down the mountain to the village. The sun was up and it was getting hotter. Soon she will run out of water, though she had been very frugal with it. Whenever she felt thirsty, she would just rinse her mouth with the one bottle she was carrying. It should not be difficult to find

a hand pump somewhere. Every village in India had a hand pump or a well somewhere from where the women could bring water for their families. They should have one here too.

Now she was passing through the village and there wasn't a soul in sight though the sound of war was audible far way. Oh, what a traitor she is, she thought. Everyone in her family would be embarrassed of her, she thought. She belonged to a family who has sacrificed their lives for their country but she had sacrificed her country for her own mission. While her conscious mind told her what she did was not right, her heart told her to follow it as far as she could. After all, her brain and heart were never connected. Like India and Pakistan, there was a line, which controlled each side – not to be crossed at any time. Just like India and Pakistan could never be on the same side, so were her body parts.

There was a row of thatched huts on one side, followed by small houses built with stones and roofs made of tin. Rocks and bricks were placed on the tin to prevent the wind blowing them away. Locks hung on flimsy doors of most houses though, if she wanted, she could easily break those with the locks still in place. But she had no reason to. A little further were a couple of concrete houses, which looked like they belonged to the rich of the village. Beyond, she could see small fields of maize or wheat or barley in the low-lying areas.

She looked at her watch compass. She had to walk northeast towards Banjosa Hajira road and should be around Ali Sojal in PoK. While she had to stay away from the war zone, she also had to be careful of the terrorist camps proliferating in the area. She had to walk parallel to the road, though not near it, so as not to draw any attention. For years, ISI had made Muzaffarabad their haven for activities against India and the Kargil conflict was a direct result of this. In a way, Aju was thankful for this as now she had the opportunity to complete her mission. All she wanted was to be able to find her Pa and the insurgency in

Kashmir had given her this opportunity. She knew no other way to complete her mission.

As she passed the haphazard row of houses, she saw wooden children's toys strewn outside houses, cattle feed, worn-out shoes and slippers, some clothes left drying on strings still flapping in the cool Himalayan wind, some pots and pans left to dry outside houses and other everyday items used by normal people. Vividly, everyone in the village had left in a hurry.

Suddenly she saw a stray dog coming towards her. As it came closer, it started barking, scaring Aju. If there were people nearby, more so anti-social elements, they would be alerted.

Running away from a barking angry dog is never an option, Nani had told her. "Remember, never look the dog in the eye and never run away. It will always run after anything that moves at a speed. Threaten it by picking a stick or stone from the ground or just your shoes." Slowly, Aju picked up a thick branch of a broken tree. The dog whined and moved back. Aju looked up and prayed, "Thank you, Nani." Most parents believe that their children don't listen to their lectures. Not true, Aju thought. Children may not seem to be listening but their subconscious mind is absorbing the information. That is why it is said that children are like sponges: they learn from their surroundings.

As she walked away from the dog, it followed her. Maybe it is lonely, Aju thought. It might be beneficial to befriend the animal. One friend is better than a hundred enemies. She stopped, looked back at the following animal, which also stopped and looked at her with questioning eyes. Aju bent down, kept the stick on the ground and called the dog, "Come doggie, come. Will you be my friend? See, I have no friend and neither do you. Together we can be a team and be safe. Come."

She fondled the dog when it came closer, rubbing its ears and the top of its head.

"Okay, now that we are friends, let's go together. Why don't you show me where the river is so we can drink some water?"

At least the dog had stopped barking and was quietly following her. There has to be a river somewhere close by, according to the map in her head. Could be the Poonch or the Neelum. Sure enough, they found one.

By sunset, Aju had walked for 8-10 hours straight and her feet were no longer ready to carry her. They had reached outskirts of a village and needed to spend the night somewhere. The nights in the Himalayas were cold. She had crossed various big and small hills, valleys, coarse wooden bridges over creeks and on her way also collected some walnuts, apples and apricots from abandoned farms. Unfortunately, she had heard helicopters too, flying closely above her, an indication that the authorities had been alerted about a parachutist coming down. She knew she had to be very very careful.

It was time to rest and spend the night in a safe place. The farther she went from the border, the less activity she could hear. Sounds of war were vivid enough not to be ignored. She had heard a passing truck or a vehicle, though she still had to see another human being. She had to stay away from the National Highway, which was somewhere nearby but definitely not close. Meandering through the narrow paths, mountains and lakes, she had almost lost her sense of direction. What she remembered from her years of studying the maps of Kashmir, she could be near Chamyati or somewhere near Dherkot road. Maybe in the morning, she could get a local bus going into Muzaffarabad. But she didn't have any Pakistani currency. That was a problem she had to deal with till she could call her friend.

Thankfully, there was no electricity in this part of the world and no fear of being seen in the dark. Looking down from the little hill she was at, she was able to see a flickering of light, maybe a candle or an oil lantern in a hut or small house. No, not one, there were a couple of flickering lights, which meant some people in that village had decided to stay put. So going too close to the village might attract attention. Aju looked at her accomplice

and said, "My friend, you have to stay very quiet. No barking, no acting funny or we will be caught." She patted the dog as it lovingly wagged its tail as if it totally understood what was going on. "Good boy. Now let's go."

Moving forward, Aju could see the silhouette of a dilapidated house across a field. Slowly Aju moved towards the shack, hoping it was just a godown used to store cattle fodder or crops. Since no flickering light could be seen there, Aju hoped the place was vacant and safe to spend the night. She had to carefully meander through narrow elevated pathways created in fields to hold water. Dried twigs and thistles crackled under her feet as she walked. The crops, maybe wheat or maize, did provide her some cover till they reached the vacant building made of stone. There was a flimsy door hanging crudely from heavy iron nails with a round iron ring which would be holding a piece of wood stuck to the doorframe from the inside. She had seen that kind of contraption at Nani's house in Rajpura and knew how to operate this antique locking mechanism.

Slowly she rotated the ring, controlling it with her strong hands so it wouldn't flap on the other side with a bang. It did click as it came down. Gently, she pushed the door, holding it by its edges so it would not make a sound but the door creaked. The old wooden door seemed to have lost shape due to weather conditions. It was dark inside and Aju could not hear any movement or sign of life.

With the faint moonlight coming into the structure through cracks in the door and windows, Aju could see the place was used to store wood, hay and old broken furniture along with farming tools. Quite possibly, people would come early morning to pick up their tools. Most people worked in the fields early morning before the sun beat down and then late evenings for a couple of hours. But in this part of the world, it did not get too hot even during the day.

"Shhh," she whispered to her companion as he too walked in behind her. Aju closed the door slowly, once again lifting it from the edges.

Once inside, Aju looked around at the available items that she could turn into a bed. There was a charpoy or jute cot hanging on the wall. She couldn't make out if it was broken or usable. She put her bag down; heavy with the fruit she had collected on the way, and pulled the charpoy down. One of its legs was hanging limply but she could easily tie it with the jute ropes. Once done, she spread a pile of hay on the cot to make a somewhat comfortable bed. She could have easily spread the hay on the floor to sleep on, but she wasn't sure if there were rodents who might bite or jump on her. Near the door, she laid another pile of hay for her four-legged friend to stay warm. As soon as she was done, he jumped excitedly on it and looked at Aju, lovingly wagging its tail as if thanking her. She smiled and patted its head saying, "Thank you for being my friend. But before we sleep, let's eat some apples and walnuts." She sat down with her friend and offered him two small apples while biting into one herself.

As she lay down on her make-shift rickety cot using her shawl as blanket, she had to remember not to move too much as the temporary leg might give way to jerky movements. Looking up into the broken asbestos ceiling through which blue moonlight was filtering, she felt Nani was looking down at her. She was missing her mother and knew her mother must be worried, waiting for her call in the evening. "I'm sorry, Ma, for not calling. I'm sorry for leaving you alone and hiding my mission from you all these years. But I know, if I had told you, you wouldn't let me go and be so stressed. I am sorry but please pray for me." A tear trickled down her eyes onto the hay and husk she was using as her pillow. "I hope Rajni has called you. Please take care of yourself. I will be back."

Chapter 24

Rajni

Aju's thoughts now went to her friend Rajni. She had seen difficult times growing up and getting into the Air Force had been an escape from the abuse she had been through since a child. Both of them had difficult childhoods. While Aju had missed a father figure in her life, Rajni on the other hand had a father who did not care about her and despite knowing what his daughter was going through, preferred to ignore it so as not to annoy his older brother who would shower expensive gifts on his little brother and had promised that he will pay for his two daughters' marriages.

"I will do Rajni and Manji's *kanyadaan*. Don't stress too much, Somu," Rajni's uncle, who she called Kaka, was older to her dad, had assured his younger brother when the girls were very little. Somnath Patel, Rajni's father had taken his brother on his word and since then, had almost danced to his tune.

Rajni's parents lived in their grandparents' house in Bhuj where she had grown up. It was a big *haveli* on which Somnath and her uncle Ramnath had inherited. Rajni's family had taken care of her grandparents till they passed away years ago, and, as per the law, the property was to be equally divided between the two brothers. While Rajni's father was still in school, the older brother had ventured out to Ahmedabad to start a textile

business. He had started off by selling children's clothes on a handcart, graduating to owning a shop selling children's clothes and now had a few factories churning out clothes of all shapes and sizes for export. By the time Rajni was 7 or 8 years old, her uncle was minting big money in business.

Every year when he came home for the holidays with his wife and two boys, the older one, Gopala, being just a year older to Rajni, would bring big gifts for everyone. He had bought almost every gadget Rajni's family owned. One year, he gifted her father a scooter on Diwali, something her father could never have afforded in his government job as a junior clerk in the municipality. He would get the house painted and repaired sometimes, telling his younger brother, "This is my house too. I too should spend money maintaining it." The next year, he had bought a kitchen grinder, then a fridge, TV and so on. Rajni's father had always lived with the fear of his brother claiming his share of the property. In that eventuality, they would have to sell the house and buy a small one far from his office. Though Ramnath had a few such houses in Ahmedabad, there would be no reason for him to sell this ancestral property unless the two had a breakdown in relations. Somnath made every attempt to please Ramnath and keep him in a good spirits during his visits.

But no one at the time understood the uncle's intentions or the motives of pleasing his brother's family. The uncle always sounded very cheerful and happy when he came to Bhuj, as if he had been waiting for this family reunion for a long time. As a child, even Rajni waited for her uncle and his family to visit them during summer vacations and Diwali holidays as he would come with lots of frocks, dolls, toys, pens and pencils for her, her little sister and brother. He would pick her up and shower Rajni with kisses as he tickled her and she giggled happily. He would make her feel so special to the extent that even his sons would start feeling jealous of her. He would not leave her alone and sit her on his lap when he had tea, ate his lunch or talked to adults

in the family while he held her on her waist in one hand and gently caressed her soft little legs, arms and other parts of her body, with the other. Excited at her favorite uncle's visit, Rajni would sit with him for a short while and then would want to go and play with the toys he had got. She had to scream at the top of her voice so he would let her go. At times, his wife admonished him, "Leave the child alone. Don't make her sit with the adults. Let her play with her brothers."

"After dinner, he would quietly invite her for ice cream, just a little wink from him would be a sign for me to sneak out and meet him so he would buy me ice cream," Rajni told Aju. He was careful not to invite the other children and that made Rajni feel special. He would tell her, "This is our little secret. Don't tell anyone we had ice cream." Little Rajni kept her promise and never told anyone for a long time. Her father could never afford to buy the kids the yummy chocolate cone at Kwality cart. Whenever he did, it was always the cheap orange ice, which she did not like any more. Uncle would play with her, run after her calling her "*meri bitiya*" (my daughter) and had everyone's trust.

At night, he would ask her to come and sleep with him as he was going to tell her a story. Other children too would want to hear his story and then he would ask Rajni's mother to lay out a couple of mattresses in the day room where he would sleep with all the children. But he made sure that Rajni was next to him despite his younger son crying to be close to the dad. "It's okay, dear. Rajni can sleep with me when we are here. I can sleep with you when we go home." "But you never do. And you never tell stories. You only love Rajni and not me," the little boy would cry. Once again, it made Rajni feel so special.

Listening to his stories, Rajni and the other children would fall asleep but every time Rajni awoke in the middle of the night, she would find her legs tightly clenched between her uncle's and something hard and warm making her uncomfortable. She would pull herself away and turn the other side but a couple of hours

later; she would find herself in the same sleeping position. By next day, the innocent child in her would forget the night before and in the excitement of listening to another story, would again compete to sleep next to him with the other children, especially Gopala, uncle's older son. He would get mad at his father and stomp out of the room.

This went on for a couple of years, without Rajni or her family realizing that anything was amiss. Once when she was about 12-13 years old, he had come as usual with gifts and after hugging and greeting everyone, came to her. He always hugged her last to get more time with her. Rajni was now more than 4 feet tall and he couldn't lift her anymore from the underarms like he always did. He held her close to his chest, pressing her small breasts against his thin cotton shirt till she pushed him away. "You are hurting me, Uncle," Rajni had to scream then, already confused at the changes taking place in her body.

"Oh! I am sorry *bitiya* but look at you! You look so pretty. What did Somu feed you?" he looked at his brother, who looked almost embarrassed. The uncle would find any excuse to touch and caress her lovingly, even in front of the adults. As Rajni grew older, she started feeling uncomfortable in his presence and his touch did not feel right. There was something wrong but she did not tell anyone. At night, Rajni started making excuses not to sleep with this uncle; before the mattresses were laid out in the living room, Rajni would go to her own room and pretend to be asleep. Her dad would come to her room and wake her up.

"Why are you sleeping here? You know your Kaka is waiting for you."

"I am tired. I want to sleep, Papa. I am fine here," she would pretend to be half asleep. She could sense some changes in her – she did not like Kaka's presence in the house, she did not feel special when he took her out for ice cream, she did not look forward to the gifts he brought but would look forward to Gopala's visit. As they grew older, Rajni and Gopala had

started sharing a special bond. Any time they found each other alone, they would talk for hours about anything under the sun – school, teachers, parents, friends, and books. Gopala was the studious kind and would buy lots of books, which Rajni could not afford. So, every time he came over, he would bring books for her. And since he was a year ahead, all his old course books would become hers. Books of fiction, literature, foreign writers, math guides, chemistry workbooks and even his notes would help Rajni throughout the year and she did not have to ask her father for any books.

The best part was, he was now no longer jealous of Rajni being his dad's favourite and buying her ice creams. He cared less and never wanted to be close to him anymore. In fact, Gopala just wanted to stay away from his father.

"No, no. Your Kaka is waiting for you. Go and sleep with him." And her own father would then physically pull her arm and push her towards the uncle. Like most times, the uncle would pull her pillow closer to him and every time Rajni awoke in the middle of the night, one of her legs would be tightly clenched between his legs, touching something hard and warm. Now she would even find his hand on her breasts. Slowly, she would disengage herself and go and sleep in her parents' room, still unaware of the uncle's intentions but aware of her own feelings of discomfort being close to him. Words like sexual abuse, groping, molestation, incest, rape had not been introduced in her vocabulary. No one talked about it in school or at home and such issues were taboo then. There were no books available in the school library, nor did the children have access to any other source to gain knowledge or talk to anyone. Her father's main concern was keeping this uncle in good spirits so he would keep bringing gifts and never asks for a share in the only property he half-owned.

The summer when Rajni had given her Grade 12 exams, the uncle had brought forms for a college in Ahmedabad. "Somu,

I found a good college for our *bitiya* in Ahmedabd. She can do her graduation there."

"Motabhai, I don't have the money to send her to college. I have two other children who still have to finish school. Then I have to think about her marriage."

"Marriage? She is just 17 years old. Don't worry about the money. I will pay for her education and she can live with us," Kaka announced. His words were always final in this house and no one dared argue. For the first time, Rajni's mother intervened.

"Motabhai, you don't have to take all responsibility. There are nice colleges in Bhuj and you can pay for her here too," she ventured as her husband glared at her warningly. The big brother had to be kept happy at all times.

"What responsibility, Sadhna? She is like my *bitiya* too. Let me enjoy her before she goes to her husband's house." Addressing Rajni, he said, "Here, take the forms, *beta*, and fill them out. I will submit them in college. Prepare to go to Ahmedabad, my dear." He patted her head lovingly.

Let me enjoy her before she goes to her husband's house... these words resonated in Rajni's mind for a long time, yet she could not understand their hidden meaning.

Rajni wasn't sure if she should be happy or sad. Yes, she wanted to go to college but living in Ahmedabad away from her parents was a thought that had never crossed her mind. But now, this uncle was taking over.

"I don't want to go to Ahmedabad to study. I can study here, Papa," she had tried to argue. As usual, her father intervened and half admonishingly said, "Don't worry, *beta*. Your mother and me will come and see you every month. Motabhai will take good care of you."

"Gopala too goes to the same college, *bitiya*. You and he can go together," her uncle tried to entice her. Well, that worked. She enjoyed spending time with Gopala. Whether it was a math problem or physics numerical, he could explain it to her with such

ease so she would remember it forever. She knew Gopala would help her, come what may. And her aunt, whom she called Kaki, was a noble soul who dedicated her life to either cooking for the family or going to the temple attending *kirtans*.

A week before college, Gopala came to take her away. He was really happy that she was coming to Ahmedabad. She cried a lot as she bade goodbye to her parents, brother and sister. "Don't worry, Kaka. I will take good care of your Rajni," Gopala assured Rajni's father.

"I know you are a good brother, my dear," Somnath had said. "*Beta*, I will come and see you soon. You work hard and get good marks."

Rajni's first couples of weeks at Ahmedabad were busy as she settled down. She was given a small room close to the younger son Varun's room. Her room had got a fresh coat of paint, new furniture with a small bed, a matching dressing and writing table and a Godrej cupboard with keys and locker. For the first time in her life, she had a dressing table. She decorated it with her cosmetics – a comb, a bottle of coconut oil, talcum powder and nail polish, which she would use sparingly, only when she had to attend weddings or go to someone's house.

Her uncle stayed away for a few days and she saw him just a couple of times at dinner table. He would eat with the family only 2 or 3 days a week. He travelled often and would mostly be busy in his books whenever he was home. Rajni noticed that Gopala mostly ate in his room whenever his father was home. They would walk to and from college together. He never let her walk alone and talked to her freely about his aims and ambitions. "I want to finish my accountancy, pick up a job and go to Bombay and live there. I don't like Ahmedabad."

"I think Ahmedabad is a nice place. I like the market, the college and you know I have made a few friends," Rajni had chirped.

And then it started. The days when the man was home, he would come to her room at night asking how she was doing, how she was settling in, how was college?

"I know you girls like to eat snacks in the canteen. College snacks are always so tasty. Here is some money."

And he would leave a couple of hundred rupees on her bedside. He would then lie down with her, caress her just like he did when she was a child, as she lay there in the dark, unable to say anything. "And don't forget to pay your tuition fees. You take money from me every month and pay it on time, my dear. If you don't, they will not let you finish your studies."

He would talk softly and touch her all over – under her shirt, her arms, legs and plant kisses on her cheeks, forehead, lips and take her in his embrace. Rajni would squirm, close her eyes, try to push him but nothing worked. She remained silent for she did not want other family members to know what he was doing to her.

This would go on for an hour or so after which he would leave, leaving Rajni feeling dirty and depressed. In the middle of the night, she would go to the bathroom, which she shared with her brothers and sit under the tap, crying for a long time. She could not understand the emotions she was going through. Why did she feel dirty, what was wrong, why did he do what he did and so on. One thing she knew about her situation – no one should know about it, as people would talk about her character. Rajni wasn't aware that every time she went to the bathroom after the man left, Gopala would be awake. He could hear the sound of the tap running for a long time.

That had gone on for a few months, when one day, on their way back from college, Gopala showed her a form to enter the National Defence Academy. "Prepare for this exam Rajni and get out of here."

Rajni had looked at the forms for a few minutes. "NDA? How? Why? I can't".

"Why can't you? You are smart; Rajni, but you are wasting away your talent here. Go out into the world and leave the Patel family. It's not worth it."

"How can I leave the family? That is all I have."

"Because you know no other. You have not seen the world. You have a world to explore. All you have seen is Bhuj and Ahmedabad. Get out of here," Gopala had sounded madly desperate.

"What makes you so angry with me, Gopala? What did I do?"

He stopped walking. Then pointing towards a tea stall, he said, "Come let's have some *chai*."

After they had ordered two teas, Gopala said slowly, almost whispering, "Rajni, I know what Papa had been doing to you all these years. As a child, I used to feel jealous that he loved you more than he loved us. But what he does to you is not love. It is called lust. And it is not right."

Rajni had never heard that word "lust" nor read it anywhere. It came as a shock to her that Gopala knew everything that went on in her room. She was embarrassed and could not control her tears. She could not face him anymore. She wanted to run and hide somewhere. She was looking down at her glass and her tears were plopping in it. Gopala put an arm around her to console her.

"Don't feel bad, *nanu*. It's not your fault. You were just a child. It's his entire fault and I hate him for what he does to you every night. I feel like vomiting every time I see him. You don't know this, but I cry every night when you are in the shower for hours. I know exactly why you spend so much time in there and there is nothing I can do to correct the situation you are in. But I want to help you and get you out of here so he cannot follow you. If tomorrow you finish your graduation and go back to Bhuj, he can continue with what he has been doing to you all these years. There is no stopping him. Even if you get married and go to your husband's house, he can still follow you there. And because every human being is greedy and selfish, he will come carrying with him big gifts and presents, which people love. Just like Chacha

turned a blind eye when Papa did what he did under his very nose, other people might do the same. The only solution for you is to get out of here and filling up this form is the only escape. Fill this and fly away. Once you get in, you will develop wings and the confidence to fly away from your miseries. You surely don't want to spend the rest of your life in self-pity."

Rajni had cried with her cousin's loving arms around her. What she had been hiding for years now was out in the open. Should she feel embarrassed or relieved, she did not know. Her feelings were mixed. At least now she could talk to Gopala about everything – literally speaking. Until then, she did talk to Gopala about everything else but this.

She knew he was right. She was in a miserable situation. Yes, I shall try to escape.

"But what about Mummy-Papa. They would never let me go."

"Don't worry, I will take care of that. I will convince them that what you did was right and you did not have a choice but to escape the way you did. But, till then, don't tell anyone about our plans."

"Our plans." Rajni liked that. Wiping away tears and standing up, she said, "I promise I will clear these exams and fly. Yes, I want to fly. I don't what to spend the rest of my life in self-pity. But you have to convince my parents and the rest of the family after I am gone."

Gopala got up excitedly and shook Rajni's extended hand. "That is a promise. You clear the exams and I will take care of the rest."

Three months later, she bade farewell to her Ahmedabad family on a day when her uncle was away and took a taxi with Gopala to the station. Her Kaki had stood there at the door, shocked beyond belief.

Days later, Gopala had called her to tell her he too was leaving home. "I wanted to leave home too but not just yet. Papa kicked me out. When he came back from his tour, he blamed Ma for

letting you go and was about to slap her when I intervened and told him I had helped you leave. He told me I should have left with you and that my time in their house was up. He even refused to give me any money but I have been saving for this day. I will survive till I find a job in Mumbai."

"I am so sorry, *bhai*. What happened to you is because of me," Rajni had cried.

"And you think I did not invite trouble or I wasn't aware of the repercussions."

"But not now. You still have one year before you finish your graduation."

"It's fine. Don't worry about me, Rajo. I have a friend in Mumbai and am living with him till I find a job. His father has promised to help me after I told him about you. He is a police officer and was really mad at you for keeping silent."

"Oh no, Gopala. Don't talk about him to anyone. Kaka would be so embarrassed."

"And you are still thinking about him?"

"I don't know, *bhai*. I just thought he wouldn't like it. I have some money saved in the bank. Give me your address and I will send you a cheque."

"I can take care of myself. You keep your money in case."

"It's not my money, *bhai*. It's yours. It is all the money Kaka gave me every night he …" she trailed off. "Of course, if I had spent that money, you know how I would have felt. I never used that money and never will. But it is your father's money and you have a right to it. Besides, you need it right now. And I never thanked you enough for helping me. This was the best decision of my life and you were always there to help me. Thank you, *bhai*."

After sending the money to Gopala, Rajni had closed that bank account. She wanted to close the chapter of her life that reminded her of her past. Her own family had cut her off too. Before going to Mumbai, Gopala had gone to Bhuj to explain her decision but her father refused to believe what Gopala told them.

Rajni's mother had cried a lot and when Gopala was leaving, had given him some money, kissed his forehead and said, "Thank you, *beta*, for taking care of your little sister. You have kept the honour of the *rakhi*, that sacred thread which Rajni tied on your wrist. May God be with you. Now take care of yourself."

Filling up the NDA forms, Rajni had given Air Force as her first option – a reason she herself did not know – but turned out to be best choice. There were no regrets here. Rajni and Gopala were still close and they continued to exchange letters and phone calls.

Chapter 25

In enemy territory

Daylight was streaming in from a number of holes in the asbestos roof in the shanty where Aju had spent the night as she opened her eyes in the morning. Did she sleep or did she just lie there thinking about her only friend Rajni? Both of them had shared something special with each other – for both were each other's first real friends. Aju had never made friends as she did not want any distraction in her life and Rajni had to hide her secret that friends might extract from her. But now they had found each other and did not hesitate to share anything under the sun. Except for her latest plan – Aju felt guilty about not sharing her intentions of escaping to Pakistan in the midst of a war.

Aju was wondering if she really got some sleep. Her mind certainly was at work as various thoughts came and went but she couldn't remember them. Her mind was occupied, she concluded, but her body felt well rested. After a whole day of walking, her body should have hurt but surprisingly, she felt relaxed. The rickety cot squeaked under her weight as she moved to get out of it. The broken leg, which she had tied, gave way and she fell on the floor. "Ouch," she said aloud, trying to muffle her scream. Her four-legged friend came running, wagging its tail and started licking her. "Go away, you licker. I am fine."

Picking up her shawl and dusting it, she hung the cot from where she had picked it up and the hay bed that she had made for her friend. She did not want to leave any clues behind. "Come, let's eat some breakfast before we head out. It is late anyway." She shared her fruits and nuts with her friend and looked at her watch. It was 7:20 in the morning. She should leave before anyone came barging in looking for their tools.

She closed the antique door behind her and started walking away from the direction she had come the night before.

There were some people walking on the road, some cycling and some people, including women, could be seen working in the fields. The sun was hiding behind the clouds. The cold and crisp morning smelled fresh of wet soil and grass. The air felt pure and earthy. She looked at her compass to check the direction she was going. By evening she might reach a village around Kohala and cross the Jhelum River and then she would be on Muzaffarabad Road. She had learnt the map of the area by heart after looking at it for years and drawing it on paper a couple of hundred times at least. She walked closer to the river, her heavy boots carrying her through the rough hilly terrain, protruding roots of old trees, shred leaves and twigs. She and her friend had stopped a couple of times to rest and fill the water bottle. On and off, she would go up to the road, which she thought should be a highway connecting PoK to Muzaffarabad. Sultana had told her finding a phone would not be easy but some shops in the villages do keep a phone and she will have to request them to let her make a call.

Passing through Neelum valley, Aju couldn't help but notice the beauty of the place. There were vast stretches of greenery and at this time of year, she could still see the snow-capped mountains. During her research of the area, she had come across a beautiful waterfall called Kutton and learned that there also was a Hindu pilgrimage site called Sharada Peeth. Wish I could bring Mummy to this place for a holiday, she thought. Not once during her entire growing up years, had she and her mother taken a holiday

to Shimla or Mussoorie as her school friends often did. Every summer vacation, they had gone to Rajpura to spend time with Nana. Shyam and Sunny Mama too would come down for a few days with their families. Nanu would be so happy to see everyone together, to have meals together and he would tell the kids stories of his time in the army and about Nani, whom everyone missed. Every evening, when he came back from the fields, he would bring little treats for the children neatly wrapped in newspaper. Sometimes it was peppermint, sometimes dates, jaggery-coated peanuts or just fresh baked biscuits from the local bakery. All the children would cluster around him, excitedly waiting for their turn.

She now was walking on the road and had seen trucks, including army trucks and tempos, pass by. She also saw a couple of buses but where they were going, she didn't know. Everything was written in Urdu, which she could not read. Walking on the side of the road, she noticed a tea stall or a small makeshift hut at a distance, where there were a number of people crowded around. Some people were sitting on benches, others just standing sipping tea. A bus was parked nearby. It appeared like a long distance passenger bus, which had stopped to take a break so the passengers can relieve themselves and drink some tea. While she didn't know where the bus was going, she thought about getting on it. Wherever it was going, she might find a phone somewhere.

She walked closer to the bus but stayed behind the trees so she wasn't easily visible. It was getting dark and the sun, which had played hide-and-seek throughout the day, was ready to call it a day too. There were no streetlights but a couple of lanterns in the tea stall were spreading their flickering yellow light on people's faces. Aju observed there were only men of various ages at the stall. She could see a couple of silhouettes of women in black burqas inside the bus. A few children too were inside while some played outside.

Whispering to her friend she said slowly, "Buddy, looks like we have to part ways here. I have to try to take this bus as it starts to move. I will climb at the back of it so no one can see me. You, my dear, go wherever you find comfort. Thank you for your company. I will miss you and remember you as my best friend. And when I find Pa, I will tell him about you." Aju rubbed the dog's ears lovingly and said, "Don't make a noise when I go or the people on the bus will be aware that someone is on the roof. You take care, good dog, okay." The dog stood there looking at Aju with sad eyes and tail wagging, as if it understood, then started licking her shoes.

"Muzaffarabad Muzaffarabad Muzaffarabad," the conductor called out in five minutes. *"Teen minute mein bus chalegi! Sab chadh jao."* (The bus leaves in three minutes. Everyone on the bus now.)

Aju was now excited as never before. Till that moment, she had the fear of being caught, of being seen and then never being able to accomplish her mission. All her fatigue vanished as if a wave of electricity had passed through her body, energizing every tired limb and rejuvenating it. Pa, here I come!

As soon as the vehicle started moving slowly, Aju moved to the right of the bus so the people at the stall could not see her and climbed the iron ladder at the rear. At the top, people's belongings of all shapes and sizes occupied the carriage. There were big and small trunks, sacks of rice, vegetables and bundles of clothes. This meant that she had to get off the roof before the bus came to a full stop as someone would climb up to unload passengers' belongings. She had to stay alert at all times. She looked back and saw her friend running alongside the bus. This was a sight she had never seen before. She had seen street dogs bark at moving vehicles or strangers and running after them. But not running silently.

She made a little space for herself between two trunks. Even in the month of May, the air in this part of the world felt like ice on her face. She pulled a warm blanket from one of the bundles,

changed her shoes, wrapped herself in it tightly, throwing out her military boots one at a time, and squeezed herself further between the trunks.

Almost three hours later, the bus entered a populated area. Aju woke up to sounds of chatter and honks. The bus had reduced speed and was honking away at tempos, bicycles, pedestrians, rickshaws, bullock carts and everything else on the narrow road, with small shops selling everything under the sun lining the sides. Hawkers were selling their wares cheap now that it was time to go home. Time for me to get off, she decided. Small bulbs shone light on the streets at the objects and every earthling there. Slowly, she started climbing down the ladder and jumped from the moving bus, running with it for a distance to stabilize herself. She bumped into a cyclist riding behind her and her shawl almost fell off. Thankfully her monkey cap had stayed put.

"*Oye, ankhein nahi hain kya,*" the cyclist shouted. Hey you! Can't you see?

"*Moaaf kijyega, bhaijaan,*" Please forgive me, brother, Aju said, trying to sound hoarse like a man and moved to the side of the road to avoid eye contact. Aju had practiced some key words of Urdu so she could at least survive a few days. Saying "*moaaf*" instead of "*maaf*", took her a while. She taught herself to roll her tongue by watching videos during her posting in Udhampur and learnt some more common Urdu words.

There were too many people on the road. It was almost 9 in the evening and the shops would close soon. She had to find a phone. She started walking purposefully, looking at both sides of the roads, between people and bullock carts. She felt like she was in Chandni Chowk, Old Delhi. People did not follow any traffic rules, there were no traffic lights, human beings jostled between big, hideous vehicles and cycles. Anyone could cross the road from anywhere. All they had to do was find a way out of the maze. She felt that she was playing a game she had played during childhood where one hit a small ball, and then let it roll

to the end, zig-zagging its way through a few obstructions before reaching its destination.

Worst of all, she had noticed some policemen on the streets watching people go by as if looking for prey. They were conspicuous by their presence with their black and khaki uniforms and Pakistani flag on their uniforms. She had to be careful and not create suspicion or attract attention. She didn't know where she was – was this Muzaffarabad? Everything written on the shops was in Urdu. Aju walked purposefully along the road lined with stores selling shawls, sweaters, cloth material, children's toys, pots and pans, artificial jewelry, a small restaurant, a tea stall and everything else. Every store she passed by, she slowed down to see if it had a phone. She did not ask anyone so as not to attract undue attention.

She must have walked about half an hour after she got off the bus; it was getting darker now as shops were downing shutters. Finally, she saw a man standing outside a grocery store with a phone receiver in hand. The shopkeeper was taking down hanging packets of chips as if preparing to close shop. Cautiously, Aju crossed the road and very casually stood behind the man on the phone. The shopkeeper looked at this man in a monkey cap and shawl and asked, "What do you want?"

In her best hoarse voice, Aju said, "Nothing. Just want to call my friend."

"Come tomorrow. I am closing now."

"It won't take too long. Just one minute, I promise," Aju pleaded.

"I said come tomorrow. I will close when this *bhaijaan* leaves," the shopkeeper was adamant.

"Please, *bhaijaan*. Just one call. I am lost and want to call my friend who can come and pick me up."

"Where are you from?" the shopkeeper now looked at Aju suspiciously.

"From Chamyati," Aju continued in her hoarse voice, without hesitation. She knew this place was somewhere in PoK and she had crossed it on her way. "*Yahan dost se milne aya tha but rasta bhatak gaya*". I had come here to meet a friend but got lost.

"Ok, I will wait for you. But it will be two rupees."

"I lost my wallet on the way. That is why I don't have any money to buy a bus ticket."

The shopkeeper looked at Aju angrily. "Want to make a call but don't have money! What do you think, I run a charity here?" Then looking at her bag he asked, "What do you have in there?"

Aju was now very careful. "Oh nothing. Just some almonds and walnuts and water."

"You have to give me something if you want to use this phone. Or shoo." The customer making the phone call had now left and the rude shopkeeper now went in to pull the phone inside so he could drop the shutter.

"Okay okay, I will give you all that I have." Aju promised. She immediately dived into her bag and took out a handful of almonds and walnuts. The shopkeeper stopped what he was doing and looked at the fair hands going in and out of the bag.

Picking up the dried fruit Aju had laid on the counter, the shopkeeper said, "Ok, be fast. I have to go home." Then he stepped outside. Without watching where he was going, Aju hurriedly picked up the receiver and started dialing Sultana's number. It took a couple of rings before Sultana answered.

"Hello Sultana," Aju said slowly.

"Who is it?" Sultana asked on the other end.

"Me, Ajita. Remember?"

"Oh my god! Oh my god! Are you here? Where are you? It is so late. Are you safe?" Sultana bombarded her with questions.

"Yes, I am safe but I don't know where I am. I am in a busy market, which is now closing, and it was so difficult to convince the storeowner to let me make this call. You know I have no Pakistani money."

"Shhhhh…be careful what you say, Aju. There might be people around you. Just describe me the market where you are and I will make a guess."

Aju looked around and started describing the shops, the crossing ahead, and the vehicles there and also the number of policemen there.

"Looks like you are in Madina Market, Aju. What are you wearing?"

Aju described the black salwar suit, the monkey cap and olive green shawl she had around her.

"Ok, Aju. Stay there. Salim will come pick you up. I told you Salim is in charge of the local police station. Let me check if he is at the station today or somewhere else."

"You know I will not be able to call again. This shop is closing now."

"I know. Just be around and look out for a police jeep. See you soon, my friend. I have been dying to meet you."

Aju put the phone down on the cradle and peeked under the half-down shutters to thank the storeowner. He wasn't there. She looked around and saw him walking towards her. Two policemen behind him were looking in her direction now. She looked away and started fiddling in her bag.

"*Shukriya, bhaijaan,*" she said as he came closer and started walking in the opposite direction from the policemen.

Without replying, the storeowner went inside, pulled the phone inside and closed the shutter. Aju had a feeling he had informed the policemen about her. She wondered what had raised his suspicion. Most shops were now closed and street was almost empty now. She marveled at the speed with which hundreds of people just disappeared in less than the hour she had been here.

She was in dangerous territory and Aju knew this part of 'Azad Kashmir', as Pakistanis called it, was where everything had started – the war that the two countries were fighting right now and the infiltration of ISI-sponsored terrorists to Kashmir.

If only this place was still a part of India, her Pa wouldn't have been missing for almost three decades and she herself wouldn't be walking in enemy territory. Both the countries in an attempt to show their might, had conducted nuclear tests the year before, creating tension not only in the region but the entire world. The international community felt a threat of impending nuclear war and the tests invited wide spread condemnation.

As the conflict intensified, other countries threatened economic sanctions against both the countries, forcing the two nuclear powers to initiate a peace process to ease up tension resulting in signing the Lahore Treaty by the Prime Minister of India Atal Bihari Vajpayee and Pakistan Prime Minister Nawaz Sharif. Vajpayee travelled to Pakistan on the inaugural bus service from New Delhi to Lahore, thus creating the first ever road transport link between the two countries. The two governments committed to creating peace and stability in the region and to follow the Shimla Agreement in letter and spirit, thus creating an atmosphere of hope and peace among the populations of both countries.

However, peace was short-lived as Pakistan, under the aegis of its intelligence agency ISI, started sending terrorists to India. There was also talk about Pakistan Army Chief Pervez Musharraf himself sneaking into Kargil and spending a night at the Pakistani camp before India reacted.

Whatever the reason, Aju was now in a situation of her own making and had no choice but to complete her plan of action. She chose to deceive her own country at a time it needed her the most just as the country deceived her when she and her mother needed the country the most. If Nani had not pushed her mother to go back to college, they would be living miserable lives on the pennies the government flipped at them in the name of pension. Her mother did not touch the pension the government had been giving them, as she always believed that Pa was alive. "When he comes back, he should have some money to fall back upon. Who

knows whether the Air Force will take him back," her mother told her once.

It was now pitch dark as the shops had closed and there were no streetlights. There were just a sprinkle of people on the road but she could still feel eyes watching her. There were fewer vehicles on the road and she had to be on the lookout for a police jeep, as Sultana told her. I should have asked her how Salim looked like at least or what kind of uniform he would be wearing. Does he have a beard or a moustache? Was he fair, soft-spoken or gruff?

She concluded it might take at least an hour for Salim to come for her, presuming he was close by. Till that time, it was not safe for her to look as if she had no place to go. She tried to stay as invisible as possible by staying in the dark areas of the street. She wished she had eyes on the back of her head so she could see if she still was being followed. Turning her head around to see would confirm their suspicion, if they had any.

The *paanwala* was just closing up when she passed by. She stopped and greeted the man.

"*Assalaamu alaykum, bhaijaan*," she greeted the man who turned around to look at her.

"*Walekum salam, bhaijaan*," the vendor said politely. "Sorry, I can't give you any *paan*. I am closing. Please come tomorrow."

Before answering him, Aju quickly chanced a glance to the left to see if the policemen were still following her. She could see them now but they were at a distance. She thought she could see three of them, not just two. This could be dangerous.

Aju bowed her head with her fingers touching her forehead. "Sure. *Adab*", she greeted without making eye contact and started walking away briskly. She had to be on her guard. She felt suspicion had already been raised and now she had to be extra alert. She was walking a tightrope and hiding in the shadows seemed to be the only option.

Chirping crickets and croaking frogs could be heard as she stepped into a narrow lane with dirty *nullahs* running on the side. Stinking wet black garbage was heaped on the side of the small lane as if someone had cleared the drains but did not pick up the muck.

She stepped into a narrow back lane, the darkest she could find. There were no streetlights and the moon, just like the sun, was playing hide-and-seek. The lane was stinky but empty. Perfect for a short waiting period, she decided and stood close to the edge of the lane so she could watch for the police jeep Sultana had talked about. She knew this was the most dangerous part of her mission – getting to Sultana. If she could get there safely, half her battle was won. Battle! She thought, that is what I fled from and now I want to win the battle. How can you win a battle if you haven't fought one, Aju? Once again the guilt of deserting her country at a crucial time surfaced. Could I have done it later? "Later!" Aju thought. "How late is later? No one can ever define how late is later. I hate the word later as that is just an excuse for dilly-dallying. Nana had left the time to spend with his wife for later. He never found that time. For me, 28 years is very late," she justified to herself. "This is final, it is now or never."

She didn't have to wait too long. She heard a vehicle pass by and people talking. Most vehicles in this part of the world were government owned while the citizens mostly cycled around or used local buses, just like the one she had jumped from. Some people also owned small tempos or trucks. She should go out and check, she decided, or no one could find her. But what if it wasn't them? That is a chance she had to take. Moving closer to the street, she saw a vehicle was now coming from the direction she had come from. In the glare of the headlights of the vehicle, Aju couldn't ascertain what kind of vehicle it was. It was moving slowly, but there were two constables looking at the shops, behind tempos parked on the side of the streets and inside lanes. These

people were surely looking for something or someone. Maybe it was her they were looking for.

She moved back inside the lane to let the vehicle pass by so she could confirm it was a police jeep. The men looking for something or someone were policemen, she concluded. She came out of hiding just behind the vehicle. The man sitting at the back of the jeep saw her and tapped the driver in front. The vehicle stopped and a policeman who was on the driver's seat jumped out of the vehicle brandishing a gun. Two other policemen, who were behind the vehicle came running, pointing their weapons at her. Why are they pointing their guns at me, Aju wondered, when it was me who came forward voluntarily?

"Salim *bhaijaan kaun hai?*" Aju stammered, looking at each one of them. Who is Salim? They did not appear friendly but very threatening.

"Salim? Who Salim?" the driver asked.

"SHO Salim," Aju said hesitantly. "Haven't Salim sent you to get me?"

The policemen looked at each other and smirked.

"Oh yes. Salim *bhaijaan!* He said to bring you to the station. Get inside the jeep," said one pointing his gun at the back of the jeep.

Their smiles and gestures didn't add up. Were these really the people sent by Salim? Or was this a trap? She had no time to think now as the policemen had surrounded her threateningly. Reluctantly, she climbed into the back of the jeep with the three policemen blocking her exit. Now she felt trapped and immediately guessed that her judgment was wrong. So, I have landed myself in trouble, she said to herself.

"Take off that cap," one policeman ordered.

Panic had set in and her mind was not working any more. Aju felt her life was in the hands of the enemy and her years of planning had failed. She had trusted herself to be smart enough to avoid such a situation. Ok, now what? Her clever mind, which

was always on its move, always thinking of the next strategy, was now frozen shut. As if someone had sown it shut, as if the brain shop had closed down.

One of the policemen suddenly pulled at her cap and off it came, revealing her shoulder length hair and fair face.

"Hey, brothers! Look what I found…a woman trying to pass off as a man," he roared loudly, as the others joined the laughter. "So, the shopkeeper was right. He had just looked at her hands and suspected them to be a woman's."

"Not just the hands, we have a full body of a woman," laughed another short policeman with a pork belly sitting right in front of her, so close that she could smell the garlic he may have eaten for dinner.

"Please, can you take me to Salim? He must be looking for me," Aju said slowly. "He is the SHO of the police station."

"Of course, of course," the driver laughed. "We will take you to Salim."

"Why not," said the policeman sitting next to her on the right and trying to brush her thighs with his. "But only after we have known each other."

"Please, *bhaijan*! Let me go. I am lost and have to meet my friend. Please let me go and my friend will come and get me," Aju pleaded. This was the first time in her life that she had ever begged anyone for help. Being a strong-headed and strong-willed person, Aju had never let herself be in a situation where she had to implore anyone to listen to her. Aju was shocked at her own stupidity and carelessness. "Just when I had to be utmost careful, I dropped my guard."

The only time she could remember when she had shed tears in her life was at Nani's funeral. Displaying emotions in public was not part of her personality. She had been a fighter, a go-getter who never relied on anyone for things she wanted the most. She had to get it herself or forget about it. But now, tears were flowing freely just like the Jhelum River she had followed to complete

her mission. Yes, her mission was to look for Pa and not cry and be weak. Pa was not weak. He was strong, he also ventured into enemy territory all alone, he had no back up; no one helped him for 28 years. And no one will but her. Yes, she had to be strong.

Wiping away tears, she folded her hands once again. "Please let me go! Allah will bless you. Someone is waiting for me. I am just lost. Salim is a good friend. He will be looking for me. When I saw you, I thought you were Salim."

"Salim is a good friend," roared the man sitting next to her chewing *paan* and spitting on the road as the jeep sliced through the dead of the night. "Salim is a good friend and she does not even recognize him."

Their laughter sounded eerie and dangerous. *"Bhaijaan, yeh to koi gori mem lagti hai. Khub mazaa aayega,"* the man chewing *paan* said, trying to rub his hands with her. She immediately pulled away. "Madam, wearing a man's clothes will not make you a man. How can you hide these pretty hands Allah gave you in *baksheesh*." Another round of loud sniggering pinched her heart, releasing a stream of tears.

They had now reached the police station. The jeep came to a halt and cops sitting next to her and opposite her jumped out first. She was now alone in the jeep but they were watching her. Maybe if she could jump to the driver's seat who had also stepped down, she could drive the jeep away and buy herself some time. But the driver already had taken the keys out of the jeep.

"Come down or you want me to carry you," the passenger cop bellowed. "You know I would love to." Aju quickly got up from her seat and started to get down as the *paan* chewing man moved forward making lusty gestures as if taking her in his arms. She walked inside the police station with the cops pointing guns at her. The dilapidated building was stinking of urine, faeces, *paan* and sweat. Before entering, she looked up at the board, finally something in English – Police Station, Muzaffarabad. She heaved a sigh of relief – at least these animals in the garb of two-legged

human beings did bring her to the right place. Salim should be here, maybe he just sent the wrong people and he will be waiting for her inside. She thought of her four-legged friend. The dog was more humane than these human beings.

She walked in with a little more confidence, like she always did, head held high, shoulders back, stride fearless despite being weary and tired of all the walking and hiding. Now all she had to do was to make another call to Sultana and let her know she was close and to come and get her. She quickly glanced around the space as the two cops walked in front of her and two behind her. There was a couple of old creaky benches on one side and a couple of small old desks and chairs for the police on the other. There were 3-4 tiny cells with iron bars and some men and boys in torn, dirty clothes cramped together. It appeared like some kind of a lockup where people were held in temporary custody before being produced in court.

She saw a phone in front of an officer looking like a senior policeman, who had a couple of registers or files in front of him but was lazing with a glass of tea in his hands. Is he Salim, then? This potbellied man in a police uniform appeared to be in his late forties or early fifties. But Salim should be younger, Aju thought. Sultana is just a year or two older to me. Surely, this person was not Salim. She approached the chair placed right opposite and was about to sit down when the policemen behind her commanded, "Madam, where do you think you are going? Get in." He pushed her to a dark cell segregated from the others.

"Where are you taking me?" Aju asked slowly as she stopped walking. "I need to call my friend. Can I make one phone call please?"

Other cops who had followed them sniggered. "Not so soon. You can make as many calls as you want later. Get in first."

Pointing to a small stinky room with iron bars and doors, the *paan*-eating policeman asked her to get in there.

"Why are you putting me in jail? I am not a criminal." Aju protested and stopped walking despite the policeman wielding his weapon at her. He just pushed her into the empty cell.

"Move in, madam! You have no choice," he scoffed as the others watched him.

"I go first since she is fresh," the senior potbellied policeman said, getting up from his chair. "You guys watch and then take your turns."

Aju was horrified at this conversation. "What do you mean? All I need to do is make a phone call and then you will know who I am."

"We know who you are. You are Salim *bhaijaan*'s *khala*. He will come and get you once we are done with you." The paunch moved up and down vigorously. Aju was frightened to the core. Every cell in her body was in a panic mode but she didn't know what to do. Wasn't there any rule of law in this country? They haven't even asked me my name or where I am from or what did I do.

"Please O please, let me make a phone call. Please just once," Aju begged but to no avail. The big man was strong and he pushed her in the cell so hard that she fell on her hands and knees but saved her head from hitting the wall. There was no way she could match his strength. Though fat and flabby, this man's grip was forceful and firm.

She quickly picked herself up and looked at him. The cell was really small and the stench was overbearing. There was a small toilet where one could merely squat to do one's business, a big earthen pitcher on the far right and a bunk next to it made of cement and mortar. The walls were stained with *paan* spit, urine and maybe faeces at some places.

"On the floor," the man bellowed. "Now."

"No! You can't do that to me. It is illegal," Aju managed to say knowing fully well what plans he had. And she was terrified.

"Illegal! My foot. Everything that happens here is illegal."

"You don't know my friend. She is a lawyer. She won't leave you," she tried, knowing fully well that her pleas were going to fall on deaf years. The *paan*-eating monster had locked the iron cage from outside and had moved away, thoroughly enjoying himself.

The big man was now undressing himself – his belt, shirt, his undershirt, his shoes, and his pants all came off in a jiffy, as if he was so experienced in undressing himself like a bat out of hell. He didn't have to see where his hands were going. His gaze was stuck at Aju. "Take off your clothes or I will rip them apart."

Terrified, she squeezed herself in the corner of the cell saying slowly, "No, this is not right. You can't do this to me. You don't even know who I am. Please let me go."

"All we need to know is that you are a woman and a good catch. It is not very often we get pretty women with as fair skin as you in this police station. I know you are not from here because I have seen all the women around here," he barked. "You can tell us who you are once we are done with you, my darling."

And with just his stripped underwear on, he jumped at her and pulled at her shirt. Forcefully holding both her hands with his one, he pulled her to the floor and lay on top of her trying to rip her shirt and then pulled at her salwar and underwear, pushing them around her ankles. Aju was screaming so hard that she herself could not recognize her own voice. After all, she had never screamed so hard before – ever. All her struggles and strength she had worked so hard to build had come to naught. The brute was able to hold her down with just his one hand and was now biting her all over before entering.

At that point, Aju realized that all her attempts were worthless but she kept struggling and screaming. "No, I am not giving up. Maybe someone will hear my screams and come to help or try to find out where the screams are coming from. My screams should go out of the police station." She had read somewhere that if you can't resist, just submit. Suddenly, she started having thoughts of her friend Rajni, who had told her about her own

experiences growing up; about the sexual assaults by her uncle. Since Rajni could not fight, she had resorted to submitting. But nothing could be compared to what she herself was going through. At least her uncle never penetrated her or hurt her.

Thinking about Rajni distracted her from the pathetic state she was in. She was still trying her best to fight but she needed her hands, which were tied on top of her head. She kept struggling, wiggling, screaming, and trying to free her hands and legs, which he had held close together with his own legs. The pain was excruciating, she could feel warm liquids flowing around her body – could be her own blood or this man's sweat or her own tears and sweat or semen. She had never smelt a man so closely before and now she felt like vomiting. The odour emanating from his body was worse than the cell she was in.

Finally he released her and stood up, looking down at her. "You are a beautiful tigress. But can't fight me," he said, panting. She lay there tired, bleeding, crying and exposed. The tattoo of her Pa, which she had got engraved on her thigh, lay bared for everyone to see. For the first time in her life, she regretted the decision of getting the tattoo on her thigh. She was breathing heavily, sobbing; tears, blood and her own hair covered her face – the only part of her body, which was covered. Aju finally got on her bruised elbows to collect her clothes when the driver of the jeep came into the cell smiling. "Ha! My turn," he chortled.

"No, please no," Aju managed to shriek. "Go away. Leave me alone, you morons."

Taking off his clothes he laughed. "Alone! That is not why you are here."

"You don't even know who I am," she managed again, this time trying to sound threatening.

"Yes, you are Salim's *saali*" (sister-in-law). "Don't worry, when he comes, he will treat you like one."

She was subjected to another round of torture and by the time the *paanwala* beast got his turn, she had passed out.

The monstrosity continued for the next 3 days. Shifts changed, policemen changed but none spared themselves the free opportunity to violate her. She had not only lost the strength to fight, but also the will. Her own body was not hers anymore. The badly beaten, bruised and bloody body was not hers. "This piece of meat does not belong to me anymore. It's not mine. It cannot be for this body is so dirty, defiled, disarrayed and destroyed. This cannot be Flight Lieutenant Ajita Singh, daughter of Flight Lieutenant Ajay Singh. No, never."

Neither was her soul, as even that was contaminated and soiled. Only her mind was hers. It was awake sometimes and dead sometimes. Actually, only her subconscious mind was hers, not the conscious mind, for the latter felt the excruciating pain her body was going through while the subconscious guided her to stay calm and that time will pass, that there is a light at the end of the tunnel, that every human being has a heart and that every man is not a beast. "Please let me make one call," she would mutter when she was awake and there was someone on top of her. "Please, my friend is waiting." And would lose consciousness again.

Whenever she awoke, she would cover herself up to the best of her beaten body's ability with a blanket, which someone had thrown at her. A few times, she had found some food in a dirty plate lying next to her. Sometimes it was *roti* with some onion, sometimes just a pack of biscuits and a glass of tea, which would be cold, but she would gobble it all. Not only because she was hungry but also because she wanted to keep her energy going. She needed the strength to fight, to heal. She did not want to die like an unknown and be called an anonymous body. She had to get home to her mother with her father. She needed the strength to look for her Pa – the reason she had submitted herself to this torture. Whenever she was awake, she would think hard, think of a way to get out of the situation she was in. Now that she was already violated, now that she was already desecrated, now that

her soul was already tarnished and tainted, she had nothing to lose anyway. Think Aju, think!

Her mind, which was the only functional organ in her body, was telling her to take advantage of her miserable situation and make friends with these monsters and try to get out. After all, she was not in their police record, they had not framed charges against her, and they had no plans of bringing her in front of a judge. They just wanted to abuse her till they could. She had read and heard about stories of women being raped and tortured in custody but that stuff happens to other people. It happens in other parts of the world. Those were just news items about people, which everyone read and forgot about. Newspapers made this kind of news sensational, made money and then no one would give those stories a second thought. Even the journalists who had first written about the incident would not do any follow-ups. No one cared.

Society had made women's lives so dispensable, she thought. "Why did my mother make me feel so special? Why did my mother always tell me that I was God's gift? No, I am not special. My mother is special. She made me feel special." Thinking about her mother made her cry more. "Oh Mummy! I miss you so much. I am sorry I never told you about my plans. I am sorry for hiding my heart from you. Why doesn't life give a rewind button so I could go back and tell Mummy everything?"

During her stay at this god-forsaken hellhole, she realized that this was a small police station where there would be no more than 3-4 policemen at a time. Her mind laughed at of the word "stay", as if she was staying in a five-star hotel. People use that word to describe a comfortable, cozy and happy environment and not a solitary dungeon. Whenever a beast was on top of her, she regretted her decision of crossing the border the way she did. Should she have listened to Rajni or Col. Mattu, who kept saying that they are trying to get Pa back? But his name was not even on the list of missing personnel. He had already been declared dead

or Missing in Action, which meant that no one was looking for him. "No time for regrets," she scolded herself. "I knew I could land myself in this kind of situation. I prepared for it physically though not mentally. That is why I had that IUD put in. But I never thought it would be so painful and strike at my soul." She cajoled herself that she did not have to give up. "This is no time to give up. Fight, Aju, fight. You have to live, if not for yourself but for your Pa. He is lost and I have to look for him."

It was maybe Day 4, or so she thought. Her day as usual started with a lot of "excitement" with another smelly creature on top of her. "People start their mornings with prayers and then eating breakfast of *aloo ka parathas* or eggs and toast. But these brutes start their mornings by violating a helpless woman. At least, let me eat my breakfast, you carnivorous heartless creatures before drowning me in a tsunami of semen," she tried to rationalize her obscene situation. "This body is not mine any more. Do whatever you want but my mission of seeing a smile on my mother's face will remain alive. This is just a small price to pay, Aju." She had never let her mind and heart talk to each other and that is where she drew her strength. Now she had to break the network between her body, mind, heart and even the soul. Each one of these items has their own identities. They are not connected to each other. The only item that belongs to me and is intact is my spirit. "You beasts. You can't break my spirit. Do what you have to with this piece of flesh. Don't worry, Pa, I will find you."

Just like her state of consciousness and unconsciousness, her thoughts too played hide and seek with her. She was alive one moment, lost to the world in another as the new shift policemen took their turns. She could gauge that these were not her "regular customers". "Oh boy! I have started thinking like a whore. No, I am not one," she assured herself. "I am a victim of rape and whatever is happening, is against my wishes. No, I am not

a prostitute. I am Flight Lieutenant Ajita Singh and will remain so forever." Will I?

No one at the station even asked her name or address. As of now they were presuming her to be a woman who had lost her way. She could not imagine what they would do to an Indian woman if they treat their own like this, she thought. And that too from the armed forces of India. Just the thought of the repercussions sent shivers down her spine.

Most of the time she would close her eyes if she was conscious when she was being raped. Then it occurred to her, "How would I ever recognize my rapists if I had not seen them? What if I could file a complaint and then not recognize my rapists?" When the next policeman was on top of her, she tried to look at his face as he came closer.

"What are you staring at? Close your eyes or I will shut the light out of you," he had roared. And when she did not, he hit her so hard on her face that she not only lost consciousness but also could feel the blood coming out of her lips, nose and ear. Whenever she was conscious, she would sneak a peek at them when they were about to leave or when they came in. "You bastards. Why would I even want to look at you?" And then she would be in cursing mode till she fainted.

Third down, fourth one to go before she would attempt to cover herself. She managed to pull the blanket closer to cover the top half of her naked body when she heard the door of her cage shut and another of those bastards come in. She could barely turn to her side or sit up. Her back was bruised and maybe the skin had peeled with all that friction the beasts put her through. She looked at this new policeman who was not taking off his shirt and his belt but looking down at her in pity. A new shift, Aju thought. She had never seen this person before.

He was staring not at her nakedness, but at the tattoo of her Pa on her thigh. Slowly, he bent down and tried to get a closer

look at it. Pointing at it without touching her with his fingers, he asked, "Who is this?"

Aju tried to get up, but her broken back wouldn't let her. And her hips hurt like a mound of rocks had fallen on them. She said hoarsely, "Why do you care? Do your business and get lost."

He looked at her strangely as if trying to recognize her. He shifted his gaze from her thigh to her face and helped in removing her hair from her blue and black face, with puffy eyelids, fresh and dried blood on her nose and upper lip which was protruding too far from the lower lip due to the swelling. The harsh gaze with which he had walked into her cell was now softening. For a few minutes, he just sat there looking at her and her Pa, then stood up, turned his back on her and walked to the far left corner of the cell, threw her own clothes at her and walked out.

Finally, someone had a change of heart, she thought. Maybe this is the person I should have asked to make a call, she thought. He did appear to be someone who was higher up in the ladder of hierarchy at this station. Or maybe he is Salim and this is my lucky day, she prayed. She had never prayed before and did not even know how. She had always seen her mother and Nani go to temples, pray at the little temple at home, sing hymns, but Aju was always too busy to really understand its importance. Another regret of her life – she should have at least learnt to pray the right way. But don't worry, God, I will get to you. One day!

Slowly she put on her clothes. The mundane activity had become a herculean task. It felt like hours as every part of her body was sore, scratched and lacerated. She could feel the clothes on her back touching the bone. Lifting her hips to put on her salwar was the most painful. She couldn't lift them anymore. She managed to drag herself closer to the wall panting. Her cries of pain seemed to have been heard by the officer who had not touched her. He came back with a glass of hot tea and a packet of biscuits and stood on top of her. She could not look up at him

as her neck would not move. It was too sore. She sat looking at his shoes instead, waiting for him to say something.

He bent down and looked at her. Putting the tea down and handing her the biscuits, he whispered, "I am sorry at what they did to you. I am so sorry."

She looked at him confused. Finally, she whispered, "Really, why? Aren't you one of those bastards?"

Not meeting her gaze, he said, "Don't worry. I will take you out of here. This is no place for you."

She merely looked at him with a confused gaze as this man tried to avoid it, looking down at the pack of biscuits he had in his hand. The look of embarrassment and shame was writ large on his face.

"You are Salim, right? You are Sultana's husband?" Aju was now sobbing like a baby. These were the kindest words she had heard in days. "Where have you been? You know I took the risk of coming here like this because I trusted Sultana and she trusted you. She told me you would help but…"

"Shhh…not so loud. No one here knows who you are because if they do, they will just kill you. Give me a few hours. I have called Sultana. We will get you out of here."

"Thank you, God, for hearing my prayers," she said slowly but couldn't bring her hands together as her elbows hurt. She felt as if her right elbow was broken.

"I know what they have done to you. This is nothing new here. Any woman who gets caught or files a complaint is meted out the same treatment. Even when no complaint is filed and there is just a grudge…" Salim trailed off. "Sultana did not know that I had gone to Islamabad for an urgent matter. When I got back today, she told me all about you and when I came to the police station, I heard these bastards talking about a woman they had in their custody. I didn't have to go too far to look for you. I am sorry, very very sorry."

Taking out a strip of painkillers from his pocket, he said, "Take these till we can arrange for some medical help. You will need a lot of fixing." Aju passed out again after taking two pills and a sip of tea. She realized later that those pills were not painkillers but were her escape route.

Chapter 26

Pursuit

Aju spent the next three weeks slipping in and out of consciousness. Every bone, every muscle, every organ and every cell in her body needed healing. She had a broken right arm, dislocated pelvis and innumerable bruises. She had to take at least 200 stitches and every visible part of her body needed healing. Salim was right, she needed a lot of fixing. The medicines kept her sleeping. They did not want her to move too much as her dislocated hip and shoulder needed to heal.

Salim had arranged for a stretcher to take her out. Two employees of the local mortuary had gone inside the cell, picked up her body as if dead and brought it out covered with a blanket. Salim had told the other policemen of the station that she was dead and he would arrange for her burial. No one had doubted his statement.

"In that condition, how long can a woman live anyway," Salim had sounded casual.

The others merely nodded in agreement. "She kept us all entertained for a week, though. But it is kind of strange that no one came looking for her all this time," one constable said.

"Yeah and she kept mentioning Salim every time she came to her senses," the other policeman said, looking at Salim. "Was it you she mentioned or someone else?"

"I am not the only Salim in this world. I have never seen her before," Salim sounded honest. The statement itself was true. It was the first time he had seen her.

The staff of the mortuary had left her "dead body" on the stretcher at the mortuary from where Sultana and Salim transported her in her unconscious state to a private hospital. Salim did wield a lot of influence in the area and was able to convince a doctor, who was also a friend from college, to silence. "This is my wife's cousin Razia. She was coming to meet her and just happened to ask some policemen about the next bus. Since she was alone, they tortured her. I don't want anyone to know what happened to her or her family will disown her. Please, can you just treat her and then I will take her home."

For the first three weeks, the doctor had put her on IV. A nurse would come once a week to give her a sponge bath and change her clothes and the rest was taken care of by Sultana and Salim in their house. Sultana was right all along, Salim was a good husband.

Sultana confirmed that Salim had to go to Islamabad on an urgent matter and she could not get in touch with him. "After you called from Madina Market, I called the police station and they told me he had gone there on an urgent matter. I did not tell anyone about you. So I went looking for you myself. But it was the next day because I know even I wasn't safe on the streets of Muzaffarabad at that hour. The police is the biggest violator of citizens' rights. A lone woman can easily fall prey to a man's beastly instincts in this part of Pakistan and no one will know about it. Women here have to be very careful. And when I couldn't find you, I knew you were in danger and something bad had happened."

"I understand why you couldn't go to the police station to lodge a complaint," Aju tried to assure her friend to free her from her guilt. "You knew very well what they did to me, would do the same to you too."

Sultana nodded. "Not only that. I could not have answered their questions about you. What could I have told them – that I am looking for an Indian Air Force woman pilot who had illegally crossed the border and is now lost in Pakistan? All hell would have been let loose and you can't imagine what they would have done to me and Salim too."

Aju smiled. "I know, my dear. And thank you a lot for helping me. Had it not been for you, I would not have been here."

"Of course. And then you wouldn't have had to go through the torture you did," Sultana hugged her friend as the dam of tears broke and flooded her face. This was their first hug since they had known each other since childhood. "You know I have been dying to meet you forever but not in this state. I am so sorry, my dear friend. I had warned you but you wouldn't listen. You are so stubborn, Aju."

The friends cried for a few minutes in each other's arms. Now that Aju's arms, back and pelvis were healing, she was able to lift herself up to hug her friend. "I should be the one to thank you for doing so much for me. I had always wondered how both of us could be friends when our countries are always fighting. But my mother had always told me that good people exist everywhere and Pa used to say that the enmity between our countries is due to politicians who try to keep the bickering alive to gain votes. They don't care about the common man."

Salim had walked into the room and unknown to the two friends, had stood there silently watching the two friends in each other's arms, crying like babies. "How is our patient healing," he finally broke the silence.

The two hugging buddies released their grips around each other and looked at Salim. "When did you come?" Sultana asked, wiping tears.

"Been here at least 5 minutes watching two friends in each other's arms. I never realized you were such good friends. I considered you were mere acquaintances and you wanted to help

someone look for their relatives as part of your job, Sultana," Salim said, pulling a chair close to the bed.

Sultana smiled, wiping away tears. "Part of my job, yes, but now more than my job. I have to help Aju find her father. I wanted to ask you, Salim, how did you recognize Aju?"

Without looking at Sultana, Salim said hurriedly, "I told you, those bastards were abusing her and I had to get her out. They were bragging about a precious bird in the cage. I just put two and two together since you also said Aju was missing."

"I understand, Salim, that you wanted to help a lone lady in distress. Like you always do. But how did you know that it was her?" Sultana pressed further.

"Sultana, I was telling every monster who came to 'visit' me at the station, to call Salim. When he came, one of them told him that I was asking for Salim. Anyway, what matters now is that I am here and safe," Aju said matter-of-factly.

Later, Aju asked, "Salim, when you first met me, you looked at the tattoo of my Pa painted on my thigh. How you looked at it, was a little weird. Like you have seen him or someone like him before?"

"Is that your Pa? Is he the one you are looking for?" Salim said quickly. Salim was a fair, handsome almost six feet tall man in his early thirties. Any girl would have fallen for this dude, Aju thought. Sultana is lucky.

"Yes, Salim. I could not have carried a picture of him with me for I was never sure it would ever reach its destination. So a few years ago, I got a tattoo of him on my body, which was not visible to the outside world. I could never have imagined anyone would see that in a way you did. I am sorry Salim, you had to see me like that." Now Aju was sincere. She would never have wanted anyone she knew to see her naked but she was hapless.

"Since I saw that tattoo, Aju, I have been thinking. I have seen this man somewhere. In fact, I met him once in my life," Salim said slowly.

Aju sat up. "What? When? Where," Aju almost screamed with pleasure. "Why haven't you told me before?"

"It has been so long that it was not clear in my head. I think he was the man who I thought fell from the sky."

"Fell from the sky? What do you mean?" Aju effused.

"During the 1971 war, when we lived near Abbaspur, I was playing near the woods when I heard a blast and saw a parachute come down. I was too young to understand what was going on but knew that we had to steer clear of the area as it was close to the border. Many in the village had left to escape the bombings but a few stayed back. My family owned a lot of cattle and hens and there was no way all that could be transported safely anywhere. My grandmother too was sick and not able to move. My father and few other elders in the village decided to stay back."

"But where did you meet Pa?" Aju was now excited.

"Yes, I am getting to that. I saw this man come down. He was dressed like an Air Force officer. But if I remember well, he said he was a Pakistani Air Force pilot. No one questioned him about that, neither did I, though I had doubts right then. But he seemed a nice man. I remember I asked him if he would teach me to fly planes and he said he would. But I thought he was really injured and bleeding and that was not the right time."

"Did he say his name was Ajay Singh? Did you ask him his name?" Aju was curious.

"Yes, the elders in the village did. If I remember correctly, he said his name was Maqbool or Maqsood or something like that."

Salim continued. "You know everyone that time was confused as to how could a Pakistani Air Force pilot fall to the Pakistani side of the border but thankfully no one pursued the matter as they believed him. Before he came out of the bushes, I saw him hiding something underneath covering whatever it was, with leaves and sand. So, when the elders had taken him to the *hakim* for treatment, I went back to the bushes where I thought he was hiding something. And he sure was."

"Wha...what did you find," Aju was now on the verge of tears.

"Wait. I will be back." Salim walked out of the room, leaving Aju in an anxious mood. Suddenly, her stomach had started rumbling and her heart was running full speed.

Salim came back in a few minutes and opened the button of his shirt's left pocket and pulled out an old newspaper folded with something inside. Carefully, he opened the brittle yellowing newspaper and took out two pieces of cloth with rugged edges. One had the Indian flag and the other read "Flight Lt Ajay Singh" written on it. Salim gave them to Aju.

For a long time Aju looked at those pieces of cloth and wept silently. She kissed and kissed them and cried. "Oh! Salim, thank you so much for keeping these and giving them to me. I can never thank you enough. I owe you a lot Salim. Thank you."

They told Sultana part of the story, avoiding mention of the tattoo. "Salim, you never told me about this. And why have you kept these for long? What did your family and others in the village do when they found out that Ajay was an Indian?" Correcting herself, she said, "I mean Aju's Pa".

Aju looked at Salim for an answer as he sat quietly looking at his hands. Then said calmly, "Aju, I never told anyone. Now, don't ask me why. Because I don't know. I was a child and my family always talked highly about India. Since childhood, I have been told that Pakistan would have been better off had it remained with India. I think at the time I was aware of the fact that had I told anyone that he was an Indian, they definitely would have killed him. But I did not want that because he had told me he would teach me how to fly. I kind of liked him and as a child wanted to be like him."

Aju was now sobbing silently, "Really?"

Salim nodded. "He was tall, handsome, fair and so smart. I never realized that at one point he was my role model and I too wanted to fly planes. But I got rejected when I tried for the Pakistan Air Force and therefore, compromised by joining

the police. Anyway, when I first looked at you, I was reminded of someone I had seen before. You resemble him a lot. I joined the dots together and here we are."

"Mummy always told me Pa was very handsome. But then what happened? Where did they take him?"

"Frankly, no one knows. When I went to meet him the next day, I was told he had left the night before and no one knew, where or how. But Aju, till that point in time, he was alive. And he was not arrested," Salim affirmed.

"How badly was he hurt? Was Pa bleeding a lot?"

"I do remember there was some blood. But when I think back, he was not injured badly. I mean, there were some bruises and blood coming from his temple and from a child's point of view, it was a lot but now I think, it wasn't too much for an adult. I always thought he feigned being injured badly. He sort of fainted when a lot of people gathered around him and were asking too many questions. I could gather he was not comfortable in answering them and so he just acted like he fainted. I was a child and was not supposed to speak in front of elders. But now, I am glad I did not say anything as I was the only one who had doubts about his story."

"What happened afterwards? Where did Pa go after?" persisted Aju.

"I wish I knew. I went to see him next day at the *hakim*'s house and I was told that he had left the night before. Some people in the village also said that clothes left hanging outside the house had gone missing. Things never got stolen even if you left them outside for days, back then. People did not even lock their houses. That is why, everyone presumed that the pilot had left at night and just picked one or two clothes for himself, as it was cold that night."

"Did anyone try to find out what really happened to him? Like where did he go? If he was injured, he couldn't have just walked away in the night," Sultana queried.

"That is why I always presumed that he was not injured that badly. He wanted to escape in the middle of the night so he did not have to answer any questions or face anyone -- for how long could he tell lies?" Salim clarified. "Under the situation, whatever he did was right. He was a very wise man and was trained well to handle difficult situations."

I am sure he was alive and well for a long time to come. Yes, that is why he kept writing letters that he was fine and that he was just lost. He was trying to find his way out," whispered Aju. "I always knew that Pa is alive. He has to be found. He needs help. That is why his name never appeared on any of the lists. Because he was never in jail."

"You know what, Aju," Sultana said, getting up as if she has just been aroused from a stupor. "Both you and your father are in the same situation. Right in front of our eyes, history is repeating itself."

Wiping away tears and trying to get up from her bed, where she had been lying for almost three weeks she whispered, "If he survived the fall from his plane, and the last letter he wrote was 20 years ago, he certainly is alive. He said he was trying to get home. Salim, he told Mummy to wait for him in all his letters."

"Salim, if he was able to send letters, does it mean that he is not in any jail here? Would a PoW be able to write letter from any jail?" asked Sultana.

"Sometimes convicts are able to sneak out letters with people who are being released or who are going to courts or have visitors. PoWs are not criminals and they are in jails because their governments have disowned them, because they were merely doing their duty and because they were patriots. While some prisoners would play the India-Pakistan card and can be violent, most hold these people in high esteem and if they can help, many do. So, to say that he could not have written letters from inside the jail, cannot be entirely right or wrong," Salim said.

"But aren't the PoWs segregated from the common convicts," asked Aju.

"Yes, they are that is why it is not easy for them to mix with the general population. But not impossible."

"Do you remember what the postage stamp said on the letters?" asked Sultana.

"Not really. But both the letters had different stamps," Aju said slowly, thinking hard.

"Yes, one said Sialkot. Where is Sialkot?"

"Not too far from here, actually," said Sultana. "Just shows at one point of time he did reach Sialkot and was safe enough to send another letter. When did you receive the second letter, Aju?"

"We received it 12 years after it was sent. I think it was stamped 1977 though we received it later," Aju remembered. "He had said the same thing that he will be back soon. My heart always said that Pa is alive. He needs to be found."

The three sat quietly for a few minutes. Salim broke the silence. "Aju, how are you feeling? I have asked Dr Usman to come and check you up tomorrow."

"I think it's time for me to get going. Now that I know Pa is alive, tell me Salim, how do I go around looking for him?" Aju asked, getting back to her former exuberant self.

Chapter 27

Clues

It took another three weeks before her medication was reduced to painkillers only. Which meant she was just not a vegetable any more. Sultana, Salim and Dr Usman had worked hard to "fix" her. They told her she was lucky to have escaped the tyranny alive but her nightmares continued. Most women never see the light of day once they enter a police station in this part of the world, she was told.

One day, Salim asked her to take a picture of her tattoo. He got prints made so it would be easy for him to look for Ajay. "After all, I can't keep asking you to lift up your pants when we need to show someone, or search a database or every time I make enquiries," Salim joked.

"I know. That would be so weird and embarrassing when women here wear veils and you are asking a woman to lift her pants up to her thigh," Aju laughed.

Aju was awake when Sultana and Salim walked into her room, Sultana carrying a hot cup of spicy tea and biscuits. Salim carried a few prints of her Pa to show to Aju. The prints were not very sharp but the studio had done a good job. Aju had told Sultana about her tattoo, who in turn told Salim. Salim pretended not to know about it but suggested Aju take a photograph that they would get developed and printed.

"Usman said though you can walk, you still will not be able to walk without a walker for another couple of weeks," said Salim. "I have made 50 copies of these pictures and have started circulating in as many jails/police stations as possible."

"Thank you, Salim," said Aju slowly, her excitement waning. They had decided a week earlier to make a list of possible jails her father could be in, though she did not believe at all that he might be rotting there. "We have to start somewhere."

"Salim, can we advertise in newspapers?" asked Sultana. "Maybe if he is not in jail, he is living somewhere or if someone has seen him on the road or maybe a doctor might remember treating someone that resembles him."

Aju looked at Salim hopefully. "Can we, please?"

Salim was quiet. He said slowly thinking hard, "I guess we could. But what are we going to say? We cannot say that an Indian pilot is missing and have you seen him."

"Yes, if we do that and people have seen him, then they will know he is an Indian. They will just get to him before we can reach him," Sultana sounded grim.

The three nodded and sat there quietly.

All of a sudden Aju jumped up with excitement. "Hey! I have an idea. We could say something like 'a mentally unstable man is missing for 25 years. If anyone has seen him, please stay away from him. Just call this number etc., etc'. Then we can give your number. This way, no one will suspect that he is an Indian and they will not harm him."

"We could do that but there is no guarantee that they will not harm him. You know how they treat people with mental illnesses," cautioned Salim.

"Maybe if we announce an award for reporting him alive, they won't harm him," suggested Sultana.

Agreed Salim. "Decided then, we will do that. How much reward should we come up with?"

Aju burst into tears. She hugged Sultana. "Oh! Thank you both of you. I don't know how I will ever repay you. I will definitely pay you the money when I get back but will never be able to repay your kindness. What both of you have done for me, I am sure even my best of friends back home would never have done. Thank you so much."

"Hey, warrior! Aren't you stronger than this? I am going out to buy you a walking stick or a walker and then let's take our fighter for a little sightseeing trip. I will take you to the best biryani place round here. This guy's food is amazing. You will never eat biryani anywhere again once you eat this," Salim declared. "Get dressed, both of you."

It had been a week since Salim had given the advertisement in the local newspapers but received no response. Aju's hopes were running low. The Kargil War had ended. India had recaptured most of the positions on its side of Line of Control which Pakistani troops or militants had infiltrated, resulting in the skirmish between the two countries. She was glad that the Indian Air Force had played a major part in India's win. News in the Pakistan media was censored. Therefore, she got only Pakistan's side of the story, which always held India in bad light. It was all India's fault that Pakistan lost anywhere between 450 to 4,000 soldiers. Every report had different figures. India had lied that Pakistan had sent soldiers across the Indian side of LoC. Pakistan had to withdraw troops due to international pressure. Other nations were worried that if the confrontation continued, it might result in a nuclear war.

The advertisements had not worked. There were no calls and no information from police stations. She had been sitting next to the phone for the past week with no result. She also was thinking about her mother. She would be worried about her. But hopefully Rajni had convinced her. How could she be sure that her mother was convinced about her plan? She could never have been able to persuade her mother that the legal process

was not the right way; that it would never lead anywhere; that the government of India had never given any answers; in fact it refused to accept that he was alive.

"Don't you think you should talk to your mother, Aju? It has been about two months. She must be thinking about you," Sultana suggested, walking into the living room where Aju sat watching TV, next to the phone and her walking stick. Walking was not an easy task any more for her. Dr Usman had suggested further rest to let the hip heal as it had gone through a lot of torture.

"I am sure Rajni would have explained my mission to her," Aju said matter-of-factly.

"Maybe, but don't you want to know how she is doing? At least let her know that Salim had met him once and that he did not die during the war. I think she has a right to know as much information as possible when our governments have failed here."

Aju just sat there listening to her friend. She was right. Mummy would be happy to know that Pa was alive when he landed. "I know she would be happy to learn that he was alive then. After all, even I had never accepted that Pa had died. Then those letters had always kept her hopes up," Aju said slowly. "I am not sure how I will face her, Sultana. I lied to her throughout. I told her I was joining the Indian Air Force as I wanted to serve our country and follow Pa instead of Pa's trail. I told her I am going to save lives, that our people needed my services. And what did I do? I abandoned the injured soldiers and gave my personal mission priority. I can't help but feel like a traitor."

Touching Aju's shoulders lovingly, Sultana tried to talk reason. "Don't harbour so much guilt, Aju. Your mother understands how you love your Pa and how you have always wanted to learn more about him. And that you have been planning your mission forever. I am pretty sure she will understand."

"I am not sure. I am scared that she will force me to give up my quest and come home. I just hope she is fine," said Aju, her voice hoarse from unshed tears.

"I will place the trunk call. You should talk to her. She deserves to know your whereabouts. She will be relieved to hear your voice."

Aju looked at Sultana and slowly took the receiver from Sultana's hand. Finally, it rang on the side of the border. But no one picked up. It rang and rang and no one picked up.

"I hope she is alright. She is not picking up," Aju stared at the receiver. "She is not home."

"Maybe she went out or she hasn't returned from school," suggested Sultana.

"It must be four in the afternoon there. She never goes out anywhere when she comes back from school," Aju was now tense but did not continue calling.

"Try again tomorrow," said Sultana.

At dinner that night, Aju talked to both Salim and Sultana. "Salim, I can't sit around doing nothing forever. I cannot live in your house like this. My presence here can put both of you in danger too. Either I should leave or do something to find Pa. How about if I retrace Pa's steps?"

"What do you mean?" asked Salim.

"I mean, I will go where you last saw him, Salim. Follow the trail he might have pursued. And from there, go to surrounding areas showing Pa's picture. Maybe someone will remember seeing him. He might have asked someone the way, or bought some food from a shop or got treated by a doctor. Someone might remember him and any little information might lead me somewhere."

"I don't think it will be helpful, Aju. It has been so long, things have changed. People in that area move a lot because of its proximity to the border. Old shopkeepers left the area or would be dead by now. Then you can't even walk straight. That is a rough terrain," said Sultana.

"She is right, Aju," said Salim. "And don't you worry about us. No one suspects anything. Everyone believes you are Sultana's cousin going through rough times. So we will not be in trouble."

"And why can't you live in our house, Aju?" asked Sultana. "Don't worry. We will stay in your house when we come to Delhi. Then we will be even."

"Thank you. I will never be able to return your hospitality. But I have to do something. Salim, can I at least visit some of the jails where Indian PoWs were kept or are kept. Maybe I can talk to some of them and they might remember Pa. Even the jailors might remember when they see Pa's picture."

"May be possible," said Sultana. "Salim, till now you have been asking with just a name. A picture speaks a thousand words. It might jolt someone's memory."

"I understand, Sullu. But it will be difficult to convince the higher officials about the reason of visiting these jails. What will we tell them?" asked Salim.

"Maybe I can use my contacts this time. I have been working for NGOs, trying to uphold the rights of women, children, the old and the weak, trying to fight their cases in court. I have also filed petitions in court on behalf of these people. Also some missing persons," said Sultana.

"The cells of PoWs are segregated from regular prisoners. We cannot enter those premises unless there is special permission from Islamabad. And that will raise a lot of eyebrows and could turn dangerous," said Salim. "Once Islamabad comes to know that someone is looking for an Indian PoW, and that too within Pakistan, all plans will fall through."

"I think you are right," said Aju slowly. "That will cause a lot of trouble for you. I can see how dangerous this could turn out."

"But there is something else we can do. Getting inside the jails will not be difficult. I can file a Missing Persons report at Salim's police station. Then convince the Yezdi Foundation or

any other NGO that we have to look for this person as the family is looking for him." Sultana worked for the Yezdi Foundation.

"But that will not get you access to the cells where he could be lodged," said Salim.

"Better still, I could say we are looking for a lost Indian fisherman," said Sultana excitedly. "Yes, that is better. Fishermen from both sides of the border easily get lost in the waters and have been captured by both countries and thrown behind bars for years. I got two of them freed last year with the help of Yezdi Foundation and sent back to India. Yes, that is a good idea."

That brought a smile to Aju's face. "Really, Sultana. Did you get the fishermen freed?"

"Yes, my dear. We made sure they were sent home across the border. Our volunteers had gone with them to the Wagah border and saw to it that they made it across safely. One of them called me after reaching home to thank me. The satisfaction and happiness I got after that call, I cannot compare with any other event in my life."

"Not even when you got married to me, my darling Sullu," Salim teased.

"Yes, my dear husband, not even that," winked Sultana. "Finally our warrior is smiling."

"You will have to be patient, Aju," said Salim. "This might take time."

"Not too long, though. I will start the process tomorrow morning. Hopefully by next week, we can visit some of the jails," said Sultana. "We have to shortlist only the jails where they keep fishermen, even if we don't suspect he might be in any of them, to appear genuine."

It took another week before they could visit their first jail. Sultana had used her contacts with the volunteer groups to gain admission. *We are looking for at least 10 missing Indian fishermen and at least 10 more people who might have crossed the border unintentionally and have been missing for more than 20 years.*

Their families have claimed that they were captured by Pakistani police and have been held in Pakistan. We have a photo of just one fisherman but it will not be difficult to find more once inside the jails. Please allow me and my colleague from the Foundation to visit these jails and try to talk to the prisoners there."

Deliberately, they did not give any dates or any other details about Ajay, giving the excuse that they have been missing for 20 years or more. It was not difficult for Sultana to get an ID as a volunteer human rights activist made for Aju. After all, she needed an ID to live in Pakistan, and getting a government-issued ID would be next to impossible.

They had to start local first to look authentic. Salim accompanied the two women not only for security purposes but also so he could strike up a friendship with the local policemen and jailors and try to get information off the record. "If you are looking for fishermen, this is not the right place," the jailor at Muzzaffarabad jail had opined. "Fishermen are not brought to the mountain jails."

"But you would be getting people who unintentionally cross the border," asked Aju. "Where are they kept?"

"It depends. Some are kept here with the local prisoners; others are locked up in isolated cells if they become too dangerous. After 20 years, most of them are just useless as they have lost their mental balance and are mostly just a burden on our system. I don't know why the government still wants us to keep them alive," the jailor said casually.

"What do you mean alive," Sultana asked a little curtly. "What do you do with them if they lose their mental balance?"

"*Mohturma*, no need to get angry. We don't kill them or anything. But you tell me, how long will a sane person survive solitary confinement? Living in dark, dingy airless confines – anyone can lose their mental balance. What I meant was, if they are incapable of giving us any information, that is, those who have been Indian

spies, why should we keep them and feed them? Why can't the government send them back to India? Get rid of them!"

"At least, their families will be happy to see them," said Aju slowly.

"Exactly! That is what I meant. For us their lives have no value. But their families will welcome them, take care of them as they mean the world to them," smiled the jailor. Phew! He thought, "This woman saved me or I would have been lynched right there. How can I tell them the inhumanity the poor Indians go through?"

"How many Indians do you have here? Do you keep any records? "Aju asked. Then, showing Ajay's picture, "Is this person here or was ever here or any other jail you might have been posted to?"

The jailor looked at the picture. "This is a very old picture and not clear. But I don't think I have seen this person around. No, never. And don't waste your time looking around here. I have been posted to a few jails in my 20 years of service around here and never seen him. I would suggest trying in Lahore, Karachi, Rawalpindi jails. Or even Multan. Salim *bhaijaan*, if you need any unofficial help, call me. I know people with some feelings for our neighbor, despite what they have done to our country."

Aju's jaws clenched in anger but before she could say anything, Salim took control of the situation. "Thank you, *bhaijaan*. I have been told there are quite a few such people in jails of Lahore, especially Kot Lakhpat and Gujranwala. There are reports of some of them still being held there."

"Yeah, reports," the jailor, Raza Hussain, sneered. "It is true. The bloody Indians are still there. We hear stories about them all the time. It is because of these people that some of our police constables don't last in their postings for too long. It's human nature, Salimji. The government does not understand that we are human beings too and don't like to torture another human being, especially when we know it is useless. They have no information

to give and even if they did, after living like dogs for so many years, they won't recognize their own mother, what to talk about any information for the benefit of our country. Let me know when you go there, Salim. I will call the jailor: he might be able to sneak you in the isolated cells too. Anyway, I don't even think it will be worth it. They don't remember anything, and look so different from when they went in. But I wish you best of luck."

The jailor's honest, helpful streak, cooled Aju's temper. She and the others got up, thanked the jailor and stepped out of the heavily gated area. Henceforth, every prison they went to and the conditions there, reminded Aju of her own confinement and the barbarism she had herself endured. The stink of dry fish, sweat, urine, feaces, onion, garlic and *garam masala* still lingered in her nostrils.

"Nani always said everything happens for a reason and that God has a plan. So that I could appreciate what Pa and others had to go through just to survive, God put me through the brutality that happens routinely behind these walls. Imagine, just a few days of such tyranny took a month for me to heal physically while mentally; I don't think I ever will. After spending twenty or thirty years here, one is just left a vegetable, they are comatose," she said, walking out of the Central Jail in Multan where they were told about at least five Indians who were rotting there for a couple of years. But none was her Pa. Sultana would be taking up their cases with her foundation soon.

Chapter 28

The reward

S alim would easily befriend jailors in about ten or twelve jails they visited. He would talk to them about his cases like they were old friends. Both Sultana and Aju would wear a light veil over their faces, more so Aju, to be as discreet as possible. The five Indians they met looked unkempt, like they had not showered for days, their clothes like their hands and feet were dirty and all of them were crammed in the smallest cell available. Their hair and beards were overgrown and matted.

The jailor had proudly walked them across the big open courtyard with cells all around, to the farthest part of the property where the five were kept. They were greeted with surprise but when the prisoners realized who they were, three of them got down on their knees and started pleading, "Please send us to India. It was a mistake. I crossed the border by mistake. I had no intentions to cross. Please don't punish us for just one little mistake. Our families are waiting for us. These people are barbarians. They beat us, torture us but don't kill us. They don't give us food or water but still keep us alive so we can suffer." The other two appeared too confused as to what was going on. The jailor informed the group that the two were now mentally challenged and no matter what was done to them, they remained unresponsive.

"But we are told to keep them alive so one day these people might come in handy when negotiating with India. Whenever that happens," the jailor informed them. "I should not have brought you here but Raza Hussain is a good friend. And sometimes, we do each other favours as everything cannot be done officially."

Sultana was taking notes about all the Indian prisoners they came across as she had plans to fight for their freedom in courts. She was interviewing them as well as the jailors specifically for that purpose. "Now that I know where these people are, I cannot sleep till they go back," Sultana vowed.

Finally, after a month of the visiting prisons where they got access, they found themselves outside Kot Lakhpat jail, the most controversial and the place from which the threesome had the most expectation. "Don't get your hopes too high, Aju," warned Salim. "These people are not only known for being very strict, they have a lot to hide too."

"I know. But these massive walls also shroud the worst secrets. The stories emerging out of the four walls of these structures too are ruthless and savage," said Aju, waiting outside the building to be escorted in.

"Be very careful here. Talk less, listen more," warned Sultana.

After all security formalities had been completed, Salim started chit-chatting with the jailor as if they were long lost friends. Parveen Ahmed, a big thickset man with a small goatee, was the very epitome of a god-fearing man who valued his service to his country – his only goal in life. They were served tea and biscuits, a rare occurrence. While Aju merely nodded as the conversation meandered around Salim's difficult cases, which included looking for missing persons, Sultana's humanitarian efforts, the weather and finally the political situation in Pakistan. "There is simmering tension between Nawaz Sharif and Pervez Musharraf after Kargil. Pakistan had to withdraw because of

the Prime Minister. Musharraf thinks if they had the political backing, things would have been different," Ahmed was saying.

"*Kya pata*, Mian," Salim said casually, sipping his tea. "One cannot clap with one hand. Prime Minister has to bow to international pressure. We know that Clinton was so mad at Nawaz that he refused to meet him at the White House. In fact, Washington did not invite Sharif Mian to visit. He went on his own, as he was scared that there might be another military coup. I read somewhere that Clinton was mad at Pakistan for having started the war, which could turn nuclear anytime."

"But Clinton could have asked India to withdraw too," continued Ahmed.

"Why would India have withdrawn," countered Sultana. "India was winning the war militarily. They were on safer ground. Had we not withdrawn, India would have killed so many of our soldiers or the *mujahideen*, whatever India calls them."

"India can say what it wants. But in the end, it was our soldiers' morale that went down," said Ahmed.

"Had Pakistan not bowed to Clinton pressure, the United States had threatened to shift its historic alliance with Pakistan publicly towards India, which would be a big blow on our economy and reputation," said Salim.

Aju had merely nodded at the conversation, doing her best to stay calm and not arouse suspicion at the portrayal of India as a villain. Finally, they were escorted inside the prison. Aju looked around the sprawling ground and high brick walls, with so many people crammed inside like stuffed dolls. It was very noisy, with guards patrolling the area. "We don't keep Indian prisoners with the locals," the jailor was saying. "Sometimes local convicts read the news and attack them. We have to be careful."

Aju knew the jailor was lying. It was not only the convicts who beat up Indian prisoners, but the staff themselves was known to treat Indians like animals. She had read and heard about the

treatment meted out to Indian prisoners in this and other jails of Pakistan. Political enmity prevailed inside the high walls big time.

"For how long are the Indian people kept here?" Aju asked.

"It depends. Till the time the court sentences them, depending on their crimes. The rule is, once they have served their sentence, they cannot be kept here. We have to send them back to India," the jailor informed.

"Is every person who is arrested produced before the courts?" Sultana asked.

"Of course," the jailor said proudly. "That is the law."

Both Aju and Sultana made eye contact through their veils. "How long have you been here?" Aju asked, trying to sound casual.

"Not too long. Just about two years now," said the jailor. "In this jail there are seven people on record who were arrested for smuggling through the border."

"What did they smuggle?" asked Salim.

"Anything. Could be drugs, guns, gold or even people. But since I came, my priority has been to produce these people in court first so they can start their sentence and go home as soon as they can. I have no intentions of keeping them here as they are a threat not only to themselves but can create riots."

To look genuine, the jailor went up to every cell and shouted, "Is there an Indian among you?"

"No, no. We would have killed him if there was," the crowd of people shouted back. The jailor looked at Salim who nodded, as if agreeing with the crowd. After moving along a couple of cells, Aju asked to be taken to the cells where they kept the Indians.

They walked along a few corridors, turning in and out, left or right, for what felt like an eternity to Aju. The jailor was right at least about the segregation part. There was no way a lone person could survive with the locals in this crowd and they had to be kept segregated. "Every time we let them out, we have to issue warnings and remain vigilant so these people are not harmed in any way," the jailor was boasting.

Once outside the small cell where the 7 Indians were kept, Sultana started interviewing them. Every time they answered a question, they looked at the jailor standing at a little distance, who was glaring at them threateningly. These people were anywhere between twenty and fifty years old. Sultana listened to their stories – three had drifted in their boats when they were fishing, two were caught crossing the border with drugs while two of them said their sheep had ventured across the border and they did not realize that they were in Pakistan. All of them denied seeing Ajay inside this jail or anywhere outside.

Though, these were not the people the group was looking for nor give any information, yet Sultana had to interview them, which would take her an hour or longer. Casually, Aju left the group and started walking towards the end of the corridor, lined with cells but quieter. The calm in this part of the dark corridor in comparison to the rest of the premises was eerie. The deadly silence was frighteningly creepy. Her heart went out to those who languished here and knew they would never see the light of day.

She thought about the good work Sultana was doing. That is what I will do too, she promised herself. "If I go back alive, I will go to law school and then help the Pakistanis in Indian jails. This is how I will repay Sultana and Salim."

As she reached the end of the corridor, she heard soft humming. As she came closer, she saw an old man with a blanket around his shoulders sitting with his eyes glued to the door of the cage, as if waiting for it to open any time. His salt and pepper hair was longer than Aju's and his beard touching his chest as if he had not seen a barber in decades. Aju stared at him for a long time. She bent down to his level and looked in his eyes straight. He diverted his gaze to her without moving or even flinching. He did not say anything, just stared back at her.

"What is your name," Aju asked softly. "Where are you from?"

No response. His face was expressionless but his eyes were trying to say something. She had seen these eyes before. "Please tell me. Where are you from?" Aju tried again.

Still nothing. "Are you from India?" she asked. A faint smile played on his lips but he did not say anything. Aju lifted her veil and put her face in between the iron bars, as far as the bars allowed. Aju saw a spark in his eyes when he looked at her face.

"Please tell me your name. I can help you, Uncle," Aju said softly again. She looked around the cell. The stink of sweat and urine was yet another reminder of her own ordeal. On the wall behind him, she could see some writing – like scribbling of a child. Looking closely in the faint light, she realized all the three walls had writing up to the highest point his hand could go. But the light was too dim for her to read.

"I don't know who you are, Uncle, but I will help you as you look familiar," Aju said. "I have seen you somewhere."

From the corner of her eye, she saw the jailor come to her. "Don't worry about this one, *mohturma*," he called out. "He has been here forever. We don't even know if he is a Pakistani or Indian or Libyan. Like they put him here first and then built the cell around him." The jailor and three other guards who were sitting nearby roared with laughter.

"How long, sir?" Aju asked as politely as she could while pulling down her veil. She did not want to disturb the informal friendship Salim had built as a result of which she was able to stand where she was at the moment.

They looked at each other, then one said, "I think even before I was born," one guard said and laughed hard. Others joined him.

"What did he do to stay here for so long?" Aju asked the jailor trying not to sound rude. "I thought you follow rules and you said you are not allowed to keep them here after they have served their sentences. So why is he still here?"

Everyone was quiet and the jailor now looked embarrassed; his gaze was becoming harsh. Aju had to be careful not to make

an enemy of him, for he had the authority to throw them out without batting an eyelid.

"Oh! I just wanted to know for my own knowledge what he had done to deserve this kind of punishment because he is alone in this cell while the seven of them are in one cell. I know you are a strict follower of rules and nothing wrong can happen with you at the helm of affairs. You know sir, during my research, this is the first jail I found where records were kept straight and people are treated well. I can see from their condition, don't get me wrong."

The jailor's face softened as he looked at Aju with pride. "Yes, of course. You won't believe what the condition of this place was when I had first came to this jail. It was a horrible mess – no records, no proper drinking water for the inmates, no proper meals and some had been here for 5 years without being taken to court. I got twenty of them released without charges, asking for the President's pardon." Aju's trick had worked.

"You would have his records in your office, right?" Aju asked. "What is his name?"

"I will have to go and check. I cannot remember every inmate's name, you see," the jailor said politely. "And he won't tell you anything. He hasn't spoken a single word since I came here."

"Not a problem. We can do that once we go back to your office. I was wondering if you have a torch with you. I can see some writing on the walls."

"Oh! That is gibberish. Even I tried to read but can't understand. But you can try yourself." He asked one of the guards to bring a torch and pointed at the writing. "See, it's neither Urdu nor English. Who knows what language that is."

But Aju guessed it was written in Hindi. She took the torch from the jailor and pointed at the writing on the wall closest to her. Sure it was Hindi written with pieces of red brick or just engraved with a sharp pebble inside the cemented wall. And it read *Ajay Amar bhai bhai, Ajay Amar bhai bhai, Ajay Amar*

bhai bhai. At some places was written *Meri Shikha* a few times. My Shikha.

Every inch of space on the three walls of the cell had the same scrawl. She knew at once who this man must be: Shikha Aunty's husband. Tears welled in her eyes. Pa had promised that he would bring Amar Chacha back, but he never got around to fulfilling his promise.

Aju just stook there – dazed, benumbed. She had never expected this outcome to her relentless pursuit of her missing father. Maybe God chose her to fulfill Pa's promise. "If not you, Pa, at least I will take your favorite brother home. Thank you, God."

As tears rolled down her cheeks, the jailor looked at her. "Do you know this man?"

Wiping away the waterfall under the veil, she nodded. "That is good news," the jailor said smiling. "Is he one of the guys you have been looking for?"

Not sure what to say, she nodded again. Then she mustered up the courage to say, "Can we take him with us, sir?"

"Not like that, *mohturma*. There is a process that needs to be followed. First, I have to look up his file and see on what charges he was convicted. And how long before his sentence is over."

"But I am sure his sentence would have been over by now. He has been missing for more than 25 years. He would have done even a life sentence…sir" Aju said, a little politely so as not to sound an alarm or show desperation, though her excitement knew no bounds and she was finding it difficult to control her emotions. She emphasized the word "sir", to keep him happy as giving more respect to people than they deserve, always turned a bad situation into a favorable one, at least in this part of the world. And she was not leaving any stone unturned to take Chacha home. She had to keep in mind that she was standing on soil that had been soaked with Indian war veterans' blood. Yet, revenge was not her mission and she had to control the seething fire inside.

Back in the office of the jailor, the threesome sat where they had before as the jailor and two other employees of the jail opened cupboards, dusting files, glancing at a few, putting them back, visibly frustrated at not finding the one they were looking for. The jailor gave up after an hour of searching.

"I cannot believe it, there is no file on this man. Finally, I had a chance to do a good deed, get this mentally deranged man out of here but no. I wonder why there are no records," the jailor said angrily, banging his fist on the desk. This man, whose moustache reminded Aju of the stern Pakistani dictator Zia-ul-Haq, whose jail was known to be the harshest and sternest, was proving to be otherwise. Or maybe, it is just this jailor who wanted to do some good deed before he retired after a long term of cruelty. Nani always believed that people do change, especially when they know they don't have too much time left. He wanted to do something good at the end of his career. Her heart couldn't stop thanking this man.

An office employee who was now covered in dust, was exasperated, "It is quite possible that he is a soldier from India. Maybe he was captured after the 1971 war and no one made a file on him. Before the last jailor retired, he had once mentioned that deliberately no files were created for these people so as not to leave any evidence."

"Quite possible," nodded Aju. "Absence of records leaves no trace of anyone's presence. Or absence"

"If this is true, how come he has been left alive?" asked Sultana. "Why didn't they kill him?"

"You don't need to kill a dead man. He is as good as dead anyway, so why would anyone take a murder on their conscience," countered the jailor.

There was pindrop silence in the office for a few minutes. Then the jailor said to Salim, "*Bhaijaan*, I have some work to do here. I will have to make a few calls and try to see how we can get him out of here. Sultana Begum, you are aware that there are

about 140 Indians soon to be sent home as a goodwill gesture by the government so India can release our people. You work with your Yezdi Foundation to get your seven people released. I will do my best to add their name to the list. And this Chacha of yours too," he smiled at Aju.

"But what will we say about him?" asked one of the guards. "We don't even know his name."

"If we say that he is an Indian soldier and has been rotting since the 1971 war, they will kill all of us," cautioned the other guard.

The jailor nodded. There was a pregnant silence. Then the jailor looked at the guards and said, "Is there a file on him? No. Do we know he is a PoW? No. Has anyone in the government ever inquired about him? No. He is just another fisherman who was caught long ago and no one bothered to look for him. Keep things simple so no eyebrows are raised".

"Since no one even knows he is here or not, he will definitely not be missed," Sultana assured. Everyone nodded.

"Now we will create a file for him," said the jailor happily. "What name do you want to give him? It should not be real for if he turns out to be an Indian who had fought a war against Pakistan, we are all doomed."

"Let's call him Maqsood," said Aju looking at Salim, who smiled back. This was the fictitious name Pa had used. "And he came to your jail sometime in 1975. Because he lost his mental balance, he was not able to give his real information, as a result of which he fell through the cracks."

As the threesome left the jail, Aju could not control the smile on her face. Her heart was smiling; she had never felt this happy before. "Sultana, I can't tell you how happy I am. Like for the first time I feel my life has meaning. I can't imagine how I will feel once I find Pa." And she hugged her friend tightly.

"Right, this was just so unexpected," chuckled Salim. "How could you recognize someone you have never met before, Aju?"

"It was not me who recognized him. It was him who seemed to recognize me," Aju said as they drove back to their hotel in Lahore. "You should have seen the spark in his eyes when I put my face through the bars and he saw me. Like something inside of him lit up. As if he was delighted to see me. But then, you too were able to relate me to Pa, Salim, because we are both so alike."

"True," agreed Salim. "Similarity between the two of you is so uncanny. No one can miss that."

"The writing on the wall which till now everyone thought was gibberish was actually Hindi," Sultana reminded them. "No one here can read Hindi so obviously, it never made sense to anyone."

"Amar Chacha! People at home have forgotten him. His parents are no more. They died waiting for him. Though I never got to meet them, I could feel their pain," said Aju sadly.

"But weren't they family? How come you never met them?" asked Sultana.

"Because after Pa disappeared, his family cut all ties with Mummy and Shikha Aunty. Their family believed that both of them were bad omens. We never got invited to any events or weddings. The only family I have known is my mother's, who supported us all along," Aju's short-term excitement had waned and she went back to her thoughts.

The plan was to visit Sialkot District Jail in, after which Salim had to rejoin duty. He disappeared to make a few calls to his station and some other government officials whom the jailor had mentioned as they reached the hotel. "I will meet you at the dhaba at the corner of Ghalib market. They have the best *dal chawal* in the world. Aju would be missing her favorite dish by now." They smiled at each other as he left.

When the two ladies got back to the hotel, Aju asked Sultana, "Should I call Shikha Aunty and let her know about him?"

"Not sure if it would be appropriate. You said she remarried and now has a family of her own."

"But not telling her would be hiding the fact. After all, Amar Chacha was her first love. She may have moved on because of societal pressure, but she always missed him," Aju was solemn. "Whenever Mummy and Shikha Aunty meet, they always talk about Chacha and Pa."

"Do they meet often?"

"At least once a year – in July for sure, was the initial plan. Along with another of their friends from school who died long ago. When the three got married, they had made a pact with each other to meet at least once a year in their home village. Two of them now continue the tradition but instead of meeting in the village, they meet at our house. Shikha Aunty's professor husband got a job in a college in Delhi a few years back, so meeting now is not restricted to once a year. But whenever they meet in July, they do pay homage to their lost friend."

Sultana nodded. Aju smiled, "Do you want to know how they pay homage to their friend?"

"How?" Sultana was now curious.

"By eating samosas," Aju chuckled.

"What?"

"Yeah! This friend of theirs apparently loved to eat samosas in school. Everyone in school would tease her that she had started looking like a samosa and no one talked to her. You know how girls that age can be mean. Despite living so far away, she would tag along Mummy and Shikha Aunty, as they were the only two in school who did not make fun of her. My mum has always been a very nice person, Sultana. But destiny has not been kind to her," said Aju glumly.

"Aju, I am not sure you should tell your aunt about Amar Chacha but I think you should leave that job to your mother. Let her know and leave it to her judgment," advised Sultana.

"I think you are right," Aju said, getting up and walking to the phone in the hotel room.

"No, no, Aju. Not from here," Sultana grabbed the receiver from Aju's hand. "It is not safe. You will have to ask the hotel reception to place a trunk call to India. It will raise red flags. People don't just pick up a phone and make a call to India here. The army here is very suspicious and everything connected to India attracts attention. Wait till we get home and then call."

Aju nodded.

By seven in the evening, the two went to the restaurant Salim had suggested and waited for him. They ordered lemonade to kill time, as it appeared that Salim had forgotten about them.

"Should we eat and go back to the hotel?" Sultana asked Aju, worried. "Maybe he forgot about us and went to the hotel."

"He could not have forgotten about us, Sultana," Aju rolled her eyes, teasing Sultana. "How can he forget his loving wife?"

"I am not joking. It is just not safe for women to be out alone here and soon it will be dark," Sultana cautioned. Both of them looked around the crowded restaurant. Every table was occupied by groups of men in traditional salwar kameez except for a table or two where families were just finishing dinner. Sultana was right. Their presence certainly was turning heads.

Aju agreed, "Let's order food, get some packed for Salim and go back to the hotel. You are right."

They saw Salim walk towards them as they reached the hotel. "So sorry to have kept you waiting. Hope you got some food for me."

Silence from the two women indicated their anger. "Okay okay, I get it. Just wait till I tell you why I got delayed," Salim gushed.

Once in the hotel room, Salim deliberately walked to the bathroom to freshen up as Aju and Sultana waited for him. They were hoping for some positive news.

After settling down with his plate of food, he started with a smile. "Aju, your patience and faith have paid off. I called my station just to let them know that I will be back in a couple

of days. The constable there told me that someone had called for me."

Sultana and Aju merely stared at him. "So," said Sultana gruffly. "People would always be calling for you."

"This call was different," Salim exulted. "The caller was a retired police officer who recognized your Pa, Aju. He said he had seen your Pa at Wagah police station."

"Really!" exclaimed Aju almost falling off the bed she was squatting on. "When? How? Where is he now?"

"Slow down," effused Salim. "It is true that he claimed to have met your Pa but don't forget, that was a long time ago."

"And," encouraged Sultana gesturing Salim to go on.

Putting another spoonful of *dal chawal* in his mouth and chewing slowly as if thinking hard, he said, "He told me, your Pa was caught close to the border, as if trying to sneak into India. He was brought to the police station, where he was beaten black and blue."

Aju's excitement immediately vanished. "Oh no! What did they do to him then? Was he hurt? Did they put him in jail?"

Getting up and putting his plate away, Salim exuded confidence. "This is just a start. Don't forget, Aju, this guy was talking about some time in the late seventies or early eighties. But no, they did not put him in jail, because someone had come and bailed him out."

"Bailed him out?" asked Sultana, confused.

"No, no, not that anyone gave bail in court or anything. What I mean is they did not lay charges against him. The police officer thinks someone had come to the police station and begged them to release him. He remembers that someone to be the father of the man they had arrested."

"Father? Grandfather wasn't in Pakistan, ever. That part I am sure about," said Aju slowly and thoughtfully. "He must be confusing Pa's picture with someone else."

"That is what came to my mind too. But he swore and confirmed that it was him. He said, this guy was a handsome dude who had no business being where he was. What he remembers most from the incident was that he did not want to beat him but had to. He also said that he was sort of glad that his father had come to take him. The father said that he was a wayward kid who had the habit of wandering away."

"Since he did not have a father here, who would claim Pa to be his son?" Aju was confused.

"You are not looking at the positive side of this information, Aju," gleamed Sultana. "That till then your Pa was alive and around. That he was really lost, as he wrote in those letters he sent to you. That he WAS trying to come home. That is why he tried to cross the border. That he KNEW he could not go back to India using the official channel and that is why he wanted to cross the border any which way."

"AND that you are truly your father's daughter, Aju," Salim continued as if trying to finish the trail Sultana had left off. "Just like him, you too did not believe in the official channel. Like him, you too crossed the border illegally."

"If we believe him, Pa is somewhere in Pakistan. Mummy was always right. She never believed that Pa was dead. His plane may have been shot down, but he was an excellent paratrooper. He may have been hurt a little, like you know, Salim. I have to find him," sobbed Aju as tears of joy flowed down her cheeks.

"Is it possible that he crossed the border and is somewhere in India," asked Sultana thoughtfully. "Maybe he lost his memory or something and not able to recollect, which is why he has not contacted you. Don't get me wrong, Aju. He would have aged too, while you are still looking for a youthful Pa, like the picture you have."

"Possible, Sultana, but 54-55 years is not so old that one loses memory," countered Salim. "Look at Amar Chacha. If you

give him decent clothes to wear and shave and give him a decent haircut, his appearance will change."

"Salim, you saw his condition. He does not remember anything. Not even his name," Aju demurred.

"Well, that could be because he has been in solitary confinement and we don't even know how long he has been there. We also don't know whether he was tortured, what conditions he had been kept in or under what circumstances he was kept. And doesn't look like we will ever know," said Salim.

"Yes and we shouldn't probe too much as it might cause suspicion," suggested Sultana. "Salim, what did the jailor say about getting Amar Chacha released?"

"It shouldn't take long, he said. He plans to make up a file about him and portray him as one of the fishermen the government is planning to release soon as a goodwill gesture between the two countries," effused Salim.

Sitting down with a sigh of relief, Aju opined, "There are good people everywhere. Right, Sultana? Indians badmouth Pakistanis and Pakistanis do the same. But it is all a farce; everyone just wants to be politically correct. But in their hearts, they know that we are all one."

Sultana and Salim agreed instantaneously.

Chapter 29

The hunt

They were not allowed to enter the high security prison of Mardan. That is where Aju suspected Pa could be, for it is only when people have something to hide that they shun transparency. Thanks to jailor Ahmed, who had kept in touch with Salim, they were able to get access to a couple of more high profile jails but all in vain. Not every jailor let them walk the grounds of their buildings, yet they had a good look at Ajay's picture and passed it around where they could.

Aju found another clue of Pa being in Pakistan in Quetta District Jail. The Assistant Inspector General of Prisons, Rizwan Qureshi, thought he had seen the man in the picture somewhere.

"In my career, I have met thousands of people and continue to meet them every month. Some are good, some are bad or very bad. This man appeared to be a good boy who was trying to be bad. And there was this sparkle, that flickering glow of something in his eyes, which I sort of remember," Qureshi said, holding Ajay's picture and sitting across the typical government desk under a picture of Jinnah staring down at the three.

"Where did you meet him?" Aju's curiosity was rising.

"If I remember correctly, I was posted at Sialkot police station. He was held in custody for a couple of days but did not stay long. He was let go as his relatives said something like he was retarded

or deaf and dumb and therefore was not in his senses when he was trying to cross the border."

"Hmm, you think he was caught crossing over to India or Bangladesh?" Salim asked.

"I have no clue about that. It was years ago and we did not make any file on him. There were no charges as he was let go really fast. I did try to ask him why he left his family who loved him so much but he couldn't speak," the AIG informed.

"Family?" asked Aju.

"Yes, I remember a group of people had come to save him. Some of them were really angry with him, as it appeared that he had the habit of running away. But his father had pleaded with us to let go of him as he was his only son."

Aju could not help but smile and cry at the same time. "Can you tell us when this was?" she prodded.

"I was posted there between 1979 to1984 or was it 1985, as I got an extension for a year because my wife was pregnant and too sick to travel. So, it has to be somewhere around that time. I'm sorry, I can't give you more information."

"What was so special in him that you remember him well enough to recognize him from this picture?" Aju was curious. Just the mention of her father invigorated her.

Qureshi looked at Aju dreamily. His forehead wrinkled and eyebrows coming closer, he asked to see the picture again. Rubbing his forehead, he said slowly, "I think there was something in his eyes that caught my attention. Those innocent childish eyes were conveying a message. And I tried to read the message but couldn't. Also, he did not seem to belong to that group. He looked different. Poor guy, he couldn't say anything."

Back at the hotel, the three of them sipped ginger tea. Sultana said, "Your belief now has been substantiated that your Pa is alive. Till the early eighties, he was in Pakistan."

"Another thing that is certain is that he was not in jail," asserted Salim. "Aju, we need to stop looking in jails now. There

is no point. I think we have enough evidence that he was never taken a PoW."

"Right," agreed Aju. "After all, there was no war after 1971. I think Pa was just drifting in Pakistan."

"Also that he seems to have been adopted by a family," queried Sultana.

"Adopted? Who would adopt a grown up man? He wasn't a child." Aju was confused.

"Yes, no one adopts a man! But every time he was caught, there was someone who rescued him. Just shows that he did have support from somewhere," Sultana's thoughts were floating in the same boat as Aju's.

"You cannot ignore the fact that his existence has come to light from different areas of the country. So, for sure, he was drifting," Salim finished his tea and put the cup down.

"He was right every time he sent those letters – he was lost and trying to find his way home. He was trying to cross the border so he could come home. But he got caught every time."

"Aju, you know. I need to congratulate you – you are the daughter of not only a fighter pilot but also an excellent actor. He deserves an Oscar for putting up such a façade for survival," laughed Sultana.

Three days later, they were back in Sultana's house after visiting another jail in Multan but all in vain. They were certain that Ajay had managed to stay away from authorities despite having a brush with them a couple of times. And he was right throughout – he was trying to find his way. He was lost. And wanted his family to wait for him.

Salim went back to his work the next day. The two women lounged on bamboo chairs in the balcony of Sultana's home, looking out at the hustle bustle of the morning rush in the busy Muzaffrabad Township. Children were walking to school, hawkers were selling their wares at the top of their voices, cycles,

tempos, rickshaws jostled with each other for a piece of that road as pedestrians struggled for survival.

Aju's hair was still wet from her shower and dripping water on the balcony as she bent towards the table to add sugar to her cup of tea. "I think it is time for me to go home."

"Already?"

"It has been more than 2 months since I left. Except for getting clues about his existence, there is nothing to look forward to," Aju lamented.

Sultana nodded. "The ad is still out there. Maybe someone somewhere will recognize him. Maybe we should advertise on TV this time."

Aju looked up smiling. "Why did we not think about that earlier? Everyone watches TV these days."

"Because we were being cautious. The media in Pakistan is not as free as in India. People are very scared of giving even a little information on TV as every little thing is scrutinized with a fine toothcomb."

"Hmm. I understand. Had this been in India, I would have advertised in at least a 100 different channels."

"I know. We don't even have that many anyway," laughed Sultana. "Shouldn't you call your mother to at least let her know that her belief had always been right? Her heart was always where your Pa was. The lines never got disconnected. Maybe that gave him strength and motivation to continue with his journey. I am sure, now, more than before, that he is alive and you will find him."

Aju merely nodded as she choked back tears.

"Don't, Aju. Cry your heart out. For those tears are for happiness. There is no sorrow in those tears," Sultana hugged her friend tightly.

A few hours later, they were heading to the Yezdi Foundation as Sultana had to report on the Indian fishermen she had found at the Kot Lakhpat jail in Multan. She urged Aju to make a call

from there, so that no eyebrows were raised. "The Foundation calls surrounding countries all the time and the authorities are aware that we are always looking for missing people, whether adults or children, be it in jails or outside. One of our missions is to unite families. Every day we get so many cases. It is easy to make a call to India from there."

It was just 11 in the morning. Her mother would still be in school. She had to wait till her mother got home. In all her excitement about getting some positive leads about Pa, she had forgotten what Ma would be going through. Undoubtedly, she would be missing her daughter. Undoubtedly, she would be angry with her. Undoubtedly, she did not expect her to disappear without a warning. As Aju sat in Sultana's office, dread was setting in. How will her mother react to the new information? Was she strong enough to accept the news? Time was supposed to heal wounds but it had not. Scars remained and with the news that Aju was about to give her, would she be just rubbing salt on them? After all, there was evidence that he was alive, yet Aju was no closer to finding out his whereabouts.

All of a sudden, she had butterflies in her stomach. She was jittery and her hands and legs were trembling. She was a bundle of nerves thinking about the right words to say to her mother. She made a couple of trips to the washroom. Aju could feel the flood of hormones in her body; her heart rate was increasing as her muscles tightened up. Her face turned red as she looked up and down the hall of the neat and well-kept hallway of the building. Through the glass door, Aju could see Sultana talking to a woman sitting in front of her and taking notes. Another woman who needed help finding her loved ones, Aju thought. Aju so wished she had a job like Sultana's, so she could help other people find their family and friends and bring smiles on their sad faces. She would feel so peaceful in her heart, realizing that she had helped someone find a parent or lost children. Why did I never think about a career like that? "How could I," she

cajoled herself, "because I wanted to find Pa and did not know any other way."

Sultana came out of her office.

"Are you ok?"

"Yeah, I am fine." Aju tried to turn her face so as not to meet Sultana's gaze.

"I can understand you are nervous, my dear. You are thinking about how to break the news to your mother. Right?"

Aju just nodded.

"Don't think too much. When you are talking to her, the words will just flow. She is your mother, she understands you. Till then, go with Maria who will show you around the building. We do a lot of work and there are children, women in the other wing of the building. If you want you can go help in the kitchen, read stories to children or even serve lunch in the kitchen. It is almost lunch time and they need all the help they can get."

Then turning to Maria, her assistant, Sultana requested, "Maria, can you please show my friend around a bit? She is new here and never been to this building. She will soon be joining our Lahore office if she likes it here." Sultana slyly smiled at Aju, who got the hint and smiled back.

Maria gestured Aju to follow her and started talking about the organization. "Did you know this place is run entirely by volunteers and donations by good people?"

"Really! I guess there are a lot of good people around here," Aju was impressed.

"Yes. I enjoy working here because there is a variety of work. They help people who are hungry, homeless, people who need medical help, help rehabilitate orphaned children, find homes for them and even help the dead. Some people donate just Rs 2 or 3 and some people can go up to Rs 5 lakh. That is how we are able to keep afloat. Why do you want to go to Lahore? We need good volunteers here. In Lahore, there are already so many people working for us. Do you belong to Lahore?"

"Yes."

"Yeah, I understand. You want to work where family is so you don't have to pay rent and still live with your family…"

Maria had gone on and on trying to impress Aju. For a few hours, Aju got so involved with the people of the Foundation that time just flew by. She helped in the kitchen serving food, then washed dishes, read English story books to little children and even played hide-and-seek with them before going out on the swings with them. Being with the children reminded her of her own childhood, where she missed out on so many pleasures as she was focused on her operation of finding Pa. On this day, with these innocent children, Aju thought of the mistake she had made. She regretted having sacrificed her childhood and even adulthood for just this one agenda of her life. Yet she wasn't sure that regret was the right word. "Wish I had a carefree childhood like these children," she was thinking as she was pushing a 6-year-old girl on the swings who was shrieking with delight as she went higher and higher. These few hours were the happiest moments of her life till now. She didn't remember the last time she had laughed and smiled so much.

About 5 pm, Sultana came looking for Aju. "You seem to have forgotten the reason for your visit here," Sultana laughed as she saw Aju having a good time. "My work is almost done here."

Aju said goodbye to the children and walked with Sultana to her office. The children requested her to come again. "Please, Aapa. Come again tomorrow." They pleaded. Aju nodded as she laughed heartily and waved at the children.

"Aren't you popular here, Aju," Sultana teased.

"Children are innocent. They make friends easily, unlike adults. For a few hours, I almost forgot why I came here," Aju chirped. "Sultana, can I come every day as long as I am here? I thoroughly enjoyed myself today."

"Of course."

The phone in Aju's home back in New Delhi rang and rang but no one picked up. "This is weird. Mummy is not picking up. It should be 4 in the afternoon there and she doesn't go anywhere after coming back from school."

"Maybe she went out to buy vegetables or groceries."

"Highly unlikely, Sultana. If she has to buy anything, she does so on her way back from school. She never goes out again."

"Maybe her routine changed since you left. She might be feeling lonely or just went out for a walk."

Maria walked in clanking a bunch of keys. "Just five minutes, Maria. Can you come back?"

Maria nodded, walking out of the office. "Try one last time, Aju. Maybe your mum was in the shower or just went up to the terrace."

Another couple of rings and yet no answer. Maria came back again as both Sultana and Aju got up to leave the office. Aju looked worried.

"Don't worry, Aju. We will try again tomorrow."

Chapter 30

Watershed

Sometimes in 1998

Many a time it had occurred to him that he too should marry a girl from the group and like Raju, settle down somewhere in the city and then find his way. Now that he was almost a Pakistani, almost, he reminded himself, he too should try to get married, look for a steady job and at least live like a normal human being. Just the thought of marriage brought about vivid memories of Anita and he kicked the thought out of his mind. "No, maybe she is still waiting for me."

He knew her well enough to perceive that it would not be easy for her too to accept someone else in her life. However short a time they had together, they had started loving each other and he could not imagine living with someone else.

But then, he had lived for so long without her and so would she have lived without him. Situations change, people change, life changes and people have no choice but to move on. And if the army had declared him dead or Missing in Action, her parents might not have let her live alone. Would she have moved on too? No one waits for anyone for 27 years. Yes, that is a long time.

Finally, he made a pledge to himself – "I will tell Chaudhury that I want to get married and settle in a village or city. Just like

Raju, I will tell him I am capable of doing general labor, which I have been doing for so long anyway. Maybe they will ask me to marry one of the girls in the tribe. Yes, I will. I think they will ask Mousmi to marry me." On second thoughts, why would she marry someone at least 25-30 years her senior? "She is not stupid. If I had a daughter, she would be her age or older." As sleep dawned on him, he pushed the thought of marriage out of his mind and vowed to continue to find his way home.

Ajay awoke to the sound of people screaming and threatening. As usual, they were in the woods, hiding after a big heist at the local moneylender's house, near Shakar Garh. They had just got lucky. Mousmi was the spy who had alerted the group that somebody had brought bags of money to the house. She was dancing outside the house with crowds cheering and jeering at her. She prodded the crowd with her sensual moves and watched a man entering the house, hiding something under his massive shawl. As this was not the weather to wear a shawl, that aroused her suspicion.

She danced away casually and within seconds bumped into him before he could enter the house. The sudden crash knocked the bag out of his hands and to the street. Mousmi immediately bend down to help him. She had barely touched it when the man pushed her away, snatching the bag back, and cursing. Mousmi apologized and went back to her dancing. She saw the door of the house open and shut fast, further confirming her notion that the bag could hold money. Minutes later, she saw another man entering the house carrying a big heavy sack, which could not be money, of course.

The Kanjars struck the same night and unlike most of their routine burglaries, they planned ahead. Six strong young men were chosen, led by Chaudhury himself and a thin, lean child, who would be pushed inside the house through the window to open the door for the others. In all his association with the group, Ajay had seen Chaudhury take part in burglaries only

a few times, mostly when a lot was at stake. It was a successful operation, as Mousmi had described the moneybag and sack in detail, making it easy for the professional bandits to find. However, a shock awaited them when the two bags were opened on their return in the middle of the night. While the blue one had money as expected, that too lots of it, the big sack had guns and pistols of different sizes.

The group was beyond shock. The older women became hysterical and started screaming. "Allah-o-Akbar! What did you steal this time? Why did you bring guns here?"

"We don't touch such weapons. We only steal money. We don't kill anyone," another said with concern.

"Shhh," the Chaudhury whispered to shut the women up. "It is night and people can hear us farther than you think. Let us all go to sleep now. We will leave in the morning."

His eyes widened as Ajay looked up and saw a man dressed in camouflage with a scarf on his face, pointing a gun at him.

"Move," he shouted. "Put your hands behind your head and make a line with the men." He pointed at the other male members of the group who were standing with their hands up on one side, women and little children on the other. Some women and children were crying while others just appeared confused. In so many years since he left India, Ajay had never felt so scared and threatened in all his life – not even when he jumped from his burning plane.

There were at 15-20 people dressed like army men, holding guns, which looked like higher-calibre Kalashnikov rifles, pistols AK-47s and others he did not recognize. One of them held the big sack of weapons the group had stolen the night before and was looking inside, as if trying to count.

"They are all in here," he said loudly. "You people had the nerve to steal our weapons. How did you even dare?"

"We didn't know this bag had weapons. We didn't touch them. Take them... just let us go," stammered Chaudhury, who was standing first in the men's line up.

"Let you go! So you can go out and tell everyone where you found these!" screamed the guy pushing Ajay. "Never."

A big, burly man with large shoulders emerged from the darkness. He was bearded and tall, maybe taller than Ajay, with close-set eyes and flat nose. His face reflected cruelty and terror. Like the others, he too had wrapped a scarf around his head but not on his face, as if he did not care even if he was recognized. "Who are you people?" he yelled rudely.

Everyone looked at Chaudhury, too scared to open their mouths. That Chaudhury was paralyzed with fear was evident on his face. Ajay felt pity for that ageing frail man who looked like he could collapse anytime. He himself was in no situation to help the man who treated him like a son all these years, and to whom he had always given fatherly respect. "We...we are Kanjars, *Bhaijaan,*" the Chaudhury shuddered in a voice Ajay could barely hear. "We only steal, we don't harm people. Please let us go."

"And you had the courage to steal our guns and money?" the big man moved forward, slapping the Chaudhury so hard that he fell to the ground. Everyone in the group was now howling and crying. "You certainly are bold, *eh*! You thought you could get away with this! We followed you, old man! My men are spread in this area like insects. You couldn't have gone too far anyway."

"Don't beat him, please," Chaudhury's wife pleaded. "He is old and weak. You can take all the weapons and money we stole. Please. It was a mistake. Please let us go."

The group of marauders laughed loudly, breaking the silence of night as if they were the kings of this place and not scared of being seen or heard. But who are these people? And what is their agenda? Should I ask? Ajay was confused. He didn't want to be the first one to be killed. This group did look threatening and

it was clear that killing was their business. None of them would think twice before wiping them out.

"Do you even know where you are standing?" roared the big man. "*Yeh Mirpur, hamara ilaka hai. Yahan hamari hakumat chalti hai.*" (This Mirpur is our area. We rule here.)

Confused, the group looked at each other. As usual, they never knew where they were headed. The only aim had been to stay in the jungles, away from the cities and the police. Trying to get up, Chaudhury barely whispered, "We will go away. We didn't know this was your area. We will go right now."

The strangers sniggered. "Where will you go? Azad Kashmir is all ours. Now you have to help us get the other side of Kashmir."

"Why? How?" Chaudhury stammered.

He pulled Ajay towards himself so close that Ajay could clearly see his tormentor's scars. "By happily supplying us strong men like this one, who can do our dirty job."

"The women will come in handy too," smirked another who was pointing his gun at the women of the group, pulling a teenage girl dressed in pink salwar kameez towards himself, "We will keep the pretty ones like queens with us and the older ones can cook and clean. We have no use for older men like you." And then he pointed his gun at Chaudhury as other men huddled together. The women and children started screaming.

"They will do what you want, *beta*. Please don't kill them," wife of one of the older men screamed. "Whatever you say."

"Are you sure?" the man pointing his gun at Chaudhury grimaced. "Don't tell me later that it would have been better if he had died," they guffawed.

Ajay was confused. Who were these people? Robbers or bandits like those in India who loot trains and people travelling through their areas. They were dressed like the military in camouflage and their demeanor reflected authority. There were a group of muscular well-built men, who could be anywhere from twenty-five to fifty-five years of age. The oldest one appeared to

be around his own age but fitter and stronger. Though he had tried to keep himself fit, he couldn't fight the vagaries of nature.

There were times when he had felt hopeless, dejected at the meaningless passage of time. Then there were times when his will to see his family became stronger and he vowed to do everything he could to see them and would get back to exercising as much as he could, in the garb of looking after the carts and tents. He would even move large rocks and tree branches to keep his strength intact. He would squat a few times a day, do push-ups, the burpees and if asked to do a chore, would jog or run to get some cardio working. He knew that was not enough and he should have done more, as he had to cross the mountains to get home. He had to be fitter than he was. The only exercise he was regular with was meditation and over the years, he was able to stop breathing for 3 minutes or more.

Chapter 31

Odyssey continues

A year later, sometime in the spring of 1999, somewhere in the Kupwara district of India's part of Kashmir and somewhere around 5 or 6 in the morning, Ajay found himself standing on top of a hill, watching the orange ball of the sun trying to slowly rise from its bed, stretching its beautiful red and yellow rays on the glistening dew-soaked leaves, glittering like stars, which were just trying to bid goodnight in his homeland. During years of living in the wilderness and amongst nature, Ajay had never stood and marveled at this magnificent magic, played every day by nature. Every leaf glowed in a color of its own, the soil looked wet and smelled his favorite familiar earthy flavor – like an essence he had forgotten all about. The view was breathtaking; he couldn't take his eyes off this grandeur of nature.

An onslaught of tears was welling in his eyes. His throat was choking, his face turning red and blotchy as he tried to control his emotions. He knew that if he allowed just one tear to fall, the rest would run amok. He hadn't cried for years and emotions had been building up in him, looking for a conduit.

"Not now", he controlled himself. "But soon I will let the tide take its course."

"Hey, keep moving, Iqbal. It's a long way to Srinagar," shouted Fawaz, who was leading this group of 5 would-be-killers. Fawaz

had boasted on the way that he had taken this journey 3 times previously and never got caught.

"I know this place like the back of my hand," Fawaz had bragged. "I was responsible for killing at least twenty – twenty-five people on my last visit here. I have done the entire recce and have friends here. Don't you boys worry," he had tried to reassure the group he had been assigned to lead on their last leg of training not too far from the border. The other four in the group had been brought to the camp from different states of Pakistan and even from Afghanistan. They were asked not to share information with each other, as the consequences would be deadly if anyone was found to be too curious.

"Doesn't matter where you come from. Keep in mind your mission. You are the chosen few by Allah and he will take care of you and your family. Just concentrate on your work," everyone was instructed. Thus even during the journey, nothing of value was exchanged between the five people. They just followed the leader blindly, made small talk about the weather, food, and health and faked loud laughter at Fawaz's lousy jokes.

For years, he had wished to touch this soil and rub it on his forehead, just like he had done on the morning of December 15, 1971, before his final flight. The soil of his homeland had been calling him, the soil he had yearned to return to. And now finally he was there. He couldn't believe that he had survived the torture he was subjected to in the last couple of months or a year. He wanted to laugh out loud, he wanted to cry out loud, and he felt like smiling for his achievement but couldn't do anything for fear of raising suspicion. He knew that this might be the last opportunity for him to accomplish his Mission Home.

And it wasn't a cakewalk. The ordeal had lasted too long, and he had to make friends with his enemies to survive. After the group of Kanjars were herded together the night of their last heist, they were made to walk, tied together with ropes for hours till they reached the interiors where there were more people like

them, who had been picked up from various places. Some were crying, others bleeding. Men with guns and weapons surrounded them all the time. There were men, women and children of all ages. Some were families, others on their own.

It didn't take long Ajay to realize that he had landed himself in a dangerous situation, much more dangerous than the war he had fought. At least his seniors planned his job profile during the war, he was armed and the target was the enemy. Now, his seniors were cruel brutes who had no qualms about killing their own people. And they were training him to kill Indians, his own people, and the people he had vowed to protect.

The trainers were a mix of Pakistanis and Afghans, yet they would kill a fellow man without a second thought. These people had no scruples and their aim of bringing innocent people to their hideouts was to make an army of irregulars who would go inside the Indian part of Kashmir to destabilize it. "Azad Kashmir" was their motto by hook or by crook. These people were terrorists who had the official backing of ISI of Pakistan, which supplied them with training and material. Now that the Soviets had left, arms, ammunition and trained guerillas from Afghanistan were abundant. Till then, Ajay did not know about the Soviet occupation in Afghanistan and the reason why the Soviet Union would invade a small harmless country like Afghanistan. To defend their own country, insurgents groups called *mujahideen* popped up in the country. America helped the guerillas with arms, ammunitions and training to fight the Soviets, to diminish Soviet Union's influence in the region.

Ajay was dumbfounded by his own ignorance. He had gotten the information in bits and pieces through the guerrillas but it made him realize how much he had missed. Though his struggle to reach home had kept him going and the group of Kanjars had helped him survive, yet this was not the life he had planned to live. He was never able to decipher who was who among the crowds as they all dressed similarly, carried similar weapons,

spoke in a similarly threatening tone. Some referred to each other as Captain Shah, Brig Javed, Major Qureshi, Subedar Ali, etc., but not everyone had a title attached to their names. So he guessed that those with titles belonged to the ISI.

Once Ajay realized the gravity of the situation, he was a nervous wreck. He could not think straight, walk straight from all the beatings he had been subjected to nor utter a single word for the fear that if they realized he was Indian, nothing would stop them from killing him right away. He had to be cautious and very discreet, not that there was too much of an Indian left in him. He had picked up some easy Urdu words which were similar to Hindi, like *Subha-ba-khair, ruhaniyat, raftar (speed), taabiir (drams), lehja (way of speaking), ba-dastoor (unaltered), inaayat (blessing), sukoon (peace), noor (radiance), waqt (time), khuda hafiz (goodbye) and some phrases like Allah ka fazal ho* (May God bless you). He had practiced the right pronunciation by mimicking others during his quiet time with the Kanjars.

He learnt to open his mouth only when spoken to or to defend himself. For days, he was an observer who kept a keen eye on the activities of the training camp he was in. He observed that people who were subservient were tortured the least. The outspoken ones or those who would have to be pushed around were tortured the most. Ajay soon realized that to keep him safe, all he had to do was say "*Ji huzoor,*" and do what they asked. That was the least difficult task, as he was trained to follow orders. "Trained," he thought. "That seems like a previous birth."

Many a time, it was not a simple chore or task. His captors wanted every member of their group to become as brutal as they were. Once he was asked to kill an old man who was not able to pick heavy loads and was almost useless to the guerillas.

Ajay was getting used to saying "*Ji huzoor*", now without thinking, and mostly to escape the heavy beating he had endured previously for not heeding to their commands. One of the captors handed him an AK-47, a gun he had never seen before. And

commanded, "Kill the old man. He is just a burden on us. We don't want to feed anyone who has no use for us." The old gentleman, who must have been about seventy years old with soft kind features and long flowing beard, had pleaded with him and the commander to let him live. "I will go away from here. You don't have to kill me if I am of no use to you. Please *huzoor. Muaafi de do.*" Please forgive me.

"So you can go and tell the world where we are hiding? There is no scope of *muaafi* in this camp," roared the man who had handed Ajay the gun.

"I promise I won't. Never utter a single word to anyone. I swear on the same Allah who has directed you to your doings. Please," he had pleaded with folded hands to the captor and Ajay, who was holding the gun pointing towards him. If eyes could speak, Ajay was apologizing to the man, praying for him, apologizing to God and was also mad at God for making him do this. "God, why did you choose me? Haven't you made me suffer already? Why this?' And then he pressed the trigger.

The old man's pleading eyes and his blood-soaked body would keep him awake for nights. For days, Anita had been replaced by this fatherly figure in his dreams. Lately, someone accompanied Anita whenever he saw her; someone standing in the shadows, maybe a child or an adult. Maybe, she had been remarried and had moved on. His thoughts were ambivalent on the issue – while he wanted Anita to find happiness, he also wanted her to wait for him. He was on his way and now his hope of finding his way back had been rekindled. He knew the route he was about to take was not righteous but he had no choice. It was now or never.

The more time Ajay spent on the mountains with the captors, the more he learnt about their motives and *modus operandi*. There were a few training camps operating in this part of the Muzaffarabad area. There were others not too far away. Some of the training camps were temporary, others permanent and yet others jointly run by the ISI. There were 4,000-5,000

trained terrorists who were on the mission of creating unrest in India. The modus operandi seemed to be to recruit or kidnap eligible people and brainwash young men into believing that their mission of "*jihad*" was a message from God. And that they were the chosen few whom Allah had directed to accomplish His task of neutralizing those who did not believe in Islam or those who did not respect Islam. "So Allah directed them to kill innocent people? Did Allah ask them to snatch Kashmir from India? When did Allah start messing up in the political affairs of countries, bequeathing spiritual goals on these barbarians?" Ajay mused but stayed quiet.

After the group got to the beginner's camp, the Kanjars were split up. While all the men and only two older women and a young one were stationed at this camp, the rest were sent to different camps and Ajay never saw them again. The younger girls, as expected, were used as sex slaves. The plight of these hapless young girls, Ajay thought, was worse than his. Their plight would not change whether they said "*Ji huzoor*," or not. Sexual violence or rape was used by the brutes to victimize not only the women, but also the men of the same family, who too were held there as a means of subjugation. It could be vice versa too — men of the families were tortured if the women did not comply with their demands. Ajay so wished he could help these ill-fated women but he was no match for the captors and their weaponry. And he did not even know where he was as they were blindfolded when they were brought to the camp.

Every morning, for a couple of hours, the leaders of the camp spoke about "jihad" — a struggle against the enemies of Islam. These people, to justify killing of innocent people in India, termed it as a "holy war". Indoctrination was important for these people, as they wanted everyone to believe in their ideology.

At the second camp, Ajay's batch was introduced to some weapons, mainly AK-47 rifles, Chinese pistols and other smaller weapons. For months, they were taught to hit the target in the

bull's eye along with giving them tough physical training and escape routes in case of being caught. Ajay was in a rush to move on to the next camp, where, as he was told, they had to prepare to cross over to India and create mayhem there. "Don't think about who is being killed or what their religion is. Stay focused on your goals. Just follow orders and you will come back alive and I promise rewards for you and your families. You will get so much money that you or your next generation will not have to lift a finger to work. We will take care of everything," General Shah of the second camp had said. "Our mission is to free the people of Kashmir from India's clutches. Kashmir is ours and we will fight till the end…"

He is right. I have to stay focused on my goal – to reach India. "If I have to become like them to meet my family, I will. For trying to find my own way has not worked. Maybe this is God's route to send me home. He is showing me the path and I will follow it," Ajay swore under his breath.

It didn't take too long for Ajay to reach the last camp. The first camp was the toughest for him and took longer for he had to mentally prepare himself to take human lives. Lives he could never give back. After killing the old man, Ajay was forced to use a running child as target. The child could not more than 12 years old and was being taught how to become a human bomb when needed. For days, this child had been pleading and crying to let him go to his *Ammi*. He was beaten black and blue, denied food and made to pick garbage and clean after people. Nothing seemed to work. The child was too stubborn and Ajay gauged he had no family at the camp. Looked like he had been randomly kidnapped to be used as a suicide bomber.

There was no escape. Options were limited – toe the mark or perish. The child tried to run away in the middle of the night and Ajay was made to shoot at the running figure. "Good opportunity to practice, Iqbal! Go, get him," General Shah commanded. "Follow him." As Ajay ran down the mountain with the gun

given to him by the General, two of the General's men followed him, forming a chain. It occurred to Ajay to let the child go, but then these men would get not only the child but him too. The child was his second victim.

Seeking forgiveness from God or the child would be futile, Ajay thought, wiping away tears and trudging back to the camp, and gesturing to his pursuers that he had done the job. As expected, they didn't trust him and one of them went down to check the little boy's body. "Somewhere a mother will be missing her son, hoping that he will come back to her, looking out the window waiting for his little footsteps to enter the house and call her *Ammi* once again. Who would have the courage to break this sad news to her?" Ajay had sobbed all night, cursing his fate for having to sacrifice a child to keep alive.

Chapter 32

Familiar turf

Now that these bastards had helped him enter his own country, Ajay had to devise a plan to escape. Of course, the escape would not be easy, he knew. If he deserted them, they would definitely track him down and kill him for sure. He had to come up with a plan that did not leave a trail for the terrorists to follow. Till now, he had not been told about their next step. But from their talk, he had gauged that they had a lot of support from within the Indian part Kashmir. And that there would be more trained intruders, including ISI, who would soon enter India through different routes, to create mayhem in his country. Fawaz had led them via the Jhelum River and they were now hiding somewhere in Sopore district.

Ajay had seen Indian Army patrols on the roads when the group was walking through the streets. There was heavy army presence and movement of Army trucks carrying armaments or armory, ammo carriers or supplies, Ajay guessed. "Is my army aware of the impending danger? Do they know that more people would be coming to India to cause terror? Quite possible," he thought. "Otherwise, why would Indian Army men be patrolling the streets? They are supposed to be at the borders or in cantonments. Certainly, a lot has happened since I was away. I have a lot to catch up." There were lots of CRPF and BSF jawans

patrolling the streets and strategic points too. He hoped Fawaz would tell him about the plan of action so he could alert the Indian authorities. How, he did not know.

After few days of hiding in Sopore, where the locals served them food, the group took the local bus to Baramulla. Fawaz seemed to carry a lot of money in his pocket, Ajay had noticed. He presumed Indian currency was given to him by his contacts within India, which he seemed to have in plenty. Just like him, the other three in the group followed Fawaz blindly, never asking any questions. When they stopped to eat at a local stall, they were asked to order different foods and sit at different tables so as not to attract attention. Once in Sopore, they were given clothes similar to the ones worn by the locals and a fake ID in their pockets so they did not stand out.

Ajay decided that he had to win the confidence of Fawaz. Just like his *"Ji huzoor"* tactic had brought him this far; he had to find another strategy to win Fawaz's confidence to get information out of him. "I will not let outsiders destroy my country," Ajay pledged to himself. Next month, the group was led to another hideout on the outskirts of Nowshera area. Still, they heard nothing from Fawaz about what they were supposed to do.

The group that had entered India would constantly change locations. Every day, Fawaz would leave the hideout for a couple of hours and come back with food, soap and other items of daily use. Ajay wished he would also bring some newspapers. He never asked so as not to raise suspicion but would read whatever he could from wrappings. He did get the hint terrorists coming from across the border were creating mayhem in his country. Thousands had been killed, including security personnel. No wonder the presence of army and other security personnel on the streets felt so threatening. They were never told what was the name of their group, who was the main leader or where the headquarters were located. All he knew was that he was in a camp run by a Gen Shah, whom he had seen just once before leaving.

The general had complimented Ajay alias Iqbal for being very patient and the best shooter in the camp. "You will be an asset to the group." Then turning to Fawaz, he had said, "Use him wisely. Don't waste him." Thanks to the compliments, Fawaz and the others had given him some respect.

Apart from talk about the daily routine, conversation was limited. One day, Fawaz returned late in the night and got some guns, which he called Kalashnikov.

"Wah! What a beauty this is," picking up the gun, excitedly Ajay started to aim at the door.

"Stop," yelled Fawaz. "You are not to do anything right now. No shooting or noise. I know you are dying for some action, but now is not the time."

"Don't worry, *huzoor*. But I can tell you; my fingers are waiting for some dancing action. How long do we have to wait"?

"Not sure," Fawaz took the gun from Ajay's hand and kept it back in the big sack he carried. "I too am waiting for orders. These beauties should be used soon."

"The general said that we are to teach India a lesson and free the people of Kashmir," Ajay dared.

The others in the group looked at him in awe for his courage and then at Fawaz as if expecting him to pounce on Ajay.

"I said I don't know," yelled Fawaz angrily.

"Shhh…be quiet or the villagers will hear us," Ajay warned. He had to prove his loyalty and this was an opportunity. "I am sorry if I hurt you, *huzoor*, but we are getting impatient. We just want some action. So much training and hard work should not be wasted."

The others nodded, though Ajay knew none of them were looking for any action. Like him, they too were looking for an opportunity to run away or hide and were in no way in line with the ideology of "*jihad*". Like him, they too wanted to go back to their families but were apprehensive about their future. Ajay had heard them weep silently a few times, missing their families and

asking forgiveness for not having done their duty as a father and a son. In this game of terror, emotions had no role.

"They said we have to wait for more people who will join us soon. We have to keep weapons and bombs ready when they come so simultaneous attacks can be carried out in different parts of India."

"But I thought our aim was to free Kashmir only. Why different parts of India?"

"Aim is to show to Indian authorities our power and the damage we can do if they do not let Kashmir go. Simultaneous attacks will cause a lot of confusion and death. It will also attract international attention and then maybe *hukumat* will do something."

"And you don't know what we have to do till then?"

Fawaz looked frustrated. "I wasn't expecting this. I was just told to hold on. For how long, I don't know. I think they are planning something really big. No one is talking right now."

"Did plans change recently?" Ajay prodded casually, going back to his corner of the shack.

Fawaz nodded. "Something big is being planned. AND I DON'T KNOW everything. Rasheed told me something like India has got wind of our plans and is planning action. He said we should stay put." Fawaz was grinding his teeth and his voice was loud and strident. Rasheed was like a secretary to the boss giving directions.

Next day, Fawaz had come back more angry than usual. "Doesn't look like we will be getting any more people from the camp soon. India is alert and has already started firing. Villagers living along the borders have been asked to go to safer places. They are using Bofors gun against us. Rasheed said we should be fighting in the mountains but now we have moved too far inside to go back."

"So, what should we do now? Sit here and twiddle our thumbs?" asked Ajay.

"I don't know," Fawaz almost yelled angrily.

Picking up the packet of food that Fawaz had got for them, Ajay said slowly and deliberately, "If they are not telling you what their next move is, are they stopping you from doing what you want?"

Fawaz was pacing up and down. He stopped and looked down threateningly at Ajay, who was chewing the chicken biryani Fawaz had brought for them. The best part of joining this gang of bandits or terrorists the world called them, was that they fed him real delicious food. After years of eating just rice, lentil and bread, anything was welcome. Food was always in plenty with the group and Fawaz always carried with him dry food ingredients like nuts wherever they went. For the believers of Islam, diet plays a major role in the physical and spiritual well being of the human body. It is believed that for this reason Islam prohibits the eating of certain foods due to their ill effects. Ajay wasn't sure how chicken and meat fit into this pure category, though he knew there had to be a valid reason if he asked. But that would reveal his lack of knowledge about Islam and maybe his identity. Not that he had any Hinduism left in him anymore, he reminded himself.

"Where did you get this biryani from?" Ajay was trying to change the subject. "Amazing! Never had it before." Which was also true. He hadn't lived with Anita long enough to know whether she liked biryani but had missed her every single day and night of the last 28 years. But at this stage in his life, he did not care. He was feeling rejuvenated and energized with the new diet he was being fed. Fawaz always brought extras and there never was a dearth of food – neither at the camp nor where he was somewhere near Srinagar.

The others had stopped eating and were looking up at Fawaz. He sat down with a thud, grabbing his share of the food.

"What do you mean?"

"Hmmmmmm…I don't know. I was just thinking…" Ajay continued to chomp away at his chicken leg, trying to weigh his words cautiously, as Fawaz looked at him impatiently. "I mean look at us…all five of us, all trained to fight, to use guns and weapons and even fight with our hands. All five big and healthy men whiling away our time eating chicken biryani and waiting for orders."

The others were looking angrily at him now as Fawaz's frown relaxed. "What do you propose?"

"Oh no, *huzoor*! I don't propose anything. You are our leader and we will follow your lead."

Fawaz's demeanor relaxed. "Oh no, Iqbal. We are all friends here now. I am not the leader. Anyone has better plans than I do, we will all follow each other. Right?" He looked at the others, who nodded.

"I was thinking if not major or big ones, we can at least plan some small attacks like on a bus or a market or school wherever there are people. Just to create panic and send a message that we are serious."

"I think we could do that," Fawaz seemed to be accepting his followers as his friends. That was a good beginning.

"Can we arrange for some small bombs?"

"What do you want to do with bombs?" asked Ali who had always been the quieter member of the group.

"Nothing much. Just plant them here and there in the city and create some commotion."

"No, we can't do that. That will raise suspicion and the police will come after us," said Fawaz. "They won't be happy if they come to know."

"None of us have to tell them. Maybe it is Lashkar-a-Toiba or the Hizbul Mujahideen who is responsible. Or the Taliban who are always crossing over from Afghanistan. Not that we are going to leave clues around or claim responsibility," argued Ajay wrapping up the bones and leftovers in the newspapers the food

had come from. But he wasn't ready to throw the garbage away yet. He asked the others to give him theirs too so he could throw out all in one bag. Of course, he wanted to read the newspapers before tossing them away. He had learnt names of terrorist organizations from the scraps of newspaper he had come across whenever Fawaz brought goods.

"Not a bad idea. But first I should get approval from General Shah. I am dying for some action too. I will call him tomorrow. He has to understand. I cannot take a decision on my own."

Fawaz went out every day to call his bosses but it appeared they were not picking up his calls or were ignoring him. He was now apparently angry at being ignored and treated so shabbily. "For years I have given my everything to the dream of Azad Kashmir, for years I have been bringing people safely across the border and I have left my family. And now they don't want to talk to me. Tomorrow will be my last call. If they don't tell me anything tomorrow, we will go ahead with our plan."

Next day, Fawaz had had come back with big bags containing nails, some acid, salt and some other chemicals. He said, he knew how to make small intensity bomb or firecrackers. "I can make bombs with different intensities. Some will be high impact and some low impact. Rasheed told me it was a good idea to create mayhem in the city that might distract India from the borders. They are fighting at the borders now and so no more people can come in from there. I told him my men were too motivated and did not have the patience to wait."

"Right. We are fully motivated to achieve our dream of Azad Kashmir," Ajay sounded excited. He had to escape but also ensure that they don't come after him or try to find him. For if they tried to find him, they surely would. These were not just any other group of bandits who ruled just one area of the jungle. These people had international connections, the resources, men and weapons to annihilate anyone anywhere. His plan had to be long-term and safe. "Make me the biggest impact one."

Three days later, five of them scattered in different directions. Deliberately, Ajay had chosen the farthest point – Srinagar. In the last couple of days, Fawaz had started trusting Ajay more than the others. Ajay was even allowed to go to the village alone to buy utilities and do some recce of the possible targets. Every time, he had come back to their hideout, when he had ample opportunity to get into a local bus or train and disappear. But if he did that, they would come after him and kill him. Just like this small group, there were other tiny groups hiding in close vicinity and one wrong move would bring them all out from hiding. If he escaped, it had to look genuine and convincing enough so there would be no point in hunting him.

He was asked to go to Badami Bagh near the army cantonment and plant some bombs so that when army trucks passed by, they would blow up. Fawaz had given him the most powerful of the bombs he had made, teaching him how to assemble it near the target. "If I mix everything together, you never know when it will blow up. When chemicals move, they react with each other to cause an explosion. So, just mix these in the can of nails and stones I am giving you and leave right away. The last bus leaving Badami Bagh is 9:30 pm. Make sure you take it."

"Of course I will," assured Ajay. "And thank you for trusting us."

"We have been together for 4-5 months now. I know I can trust all of you. You are like my brothers and as motivated as I am for jihad. *Inshaallah*, biryani will be waiting for all of you tonight. And something else too," he gestured as if drinking a glass of liqour. Everyone laughed and hugged each other, bidding *Khuda hafiz!* Goodbye,

His plan worked. He was out of the group and alone, walking towards the army cantonment, which was at least 7 km away. He had taken the bus but had gotten off in the market so he could buy a change of clothes and shoes and a pair of scissors. He went behind the market and cut off his long beard and hair as close

as he could. When he was doing that, a beggar with long beard and hair appeared from nowhere and watched him in action. His beard and hair too were a matted mess.

"Do you want to do this too? I can help."

The beggar looked at him and merely touched his ears and crossed his hands, gesturing a no and looking up at the sky as if asking for forgiveness.

"Are you hungry?" Ajay asked politely. All beggars are hungry all the time. A plate full of good food will eliminate his short-term memory of seeing a 'Muslim' cutting his beard.

It was almost 5 in the evening. He went to the local barbershop with the beggar following him. Once in, he asked the barber to clean shave his beard, and cut his hair as short as possible. When coming out of the roadside salon and putting back his *topi*, Ajay looked a totally different man. The beggar stood there looking at him with dancing smiling eyes and gestured making a circle with his thumb and forefingers. Ajay laughed and patted the beggar on the back. "I am going home. Don't want to shock the *biwi* (wife). Come let's eat."

After having a hearty meal of mutton kabab, roti and rice, the duo went to a clothes store to buy some clothes from the money Fawaz had given him for the trip. Ajay himself bought a beige salwar suit and gave his old black one to the beggar to wear. The beggar happily put it on as both of them matched in height and size – the beggar being a little skinnier and shorter. Ajay also gave him his shoes and bought new ones for himself from the nearest Bata store. How he had missed shopping for these items, he thought. This is how normal human beings should live. "Not like the life I have led with no family, friends and no one to care for. No one came searching for a missing soldier. But they will always remain precious for their families."

Now it was time to walk towards his destination. It was getting dark and the sun was ready to leave its golden brightness behind and make way for pale gray silver lining of the moon in

the sky. The stars were ready to twinkle and the array of colors dancing in the sky appeared as a harbinger of a calm night ahead. Tomorrow again, the sun will rise from its horizon and stretch its orange red crepuscular rays like blessings from the sky on the beings rising from a peaceful night of dreamy sleep. Will there be a tomorrow for me? Where will I be tomorrow? Anita, my beloved, are you still waiting for me? Even if not, I want to see you just once. God, whether you are Allah or Krishna, Ram or Rahim, this is my last wish.

A few meters before the gate of the cantonment, Ajay stopped and looked for the darkest spot. The sky was dark, but there was enough light coming from the buildings nearby and the street posts, that he had to look for a darker spot to mix the acid he was carrying in his bag. All this while he had been very careful with his bag and at times carried it in his arms like a valuable item.

Without too much noise, he moved behind the darkest corner of the boundary wall and sat down. He took the ingredients out of the bag and very slowly poured the different chemicals he was carrying in the can full of nails and pebbles. Though he was supposed to cause a high intensity explosion, Ajay deliberately did not use all the chemicals he was given. His plan was to cause a small explosion, enough to injure him and attract attention. Very slowly, he closed the can the way Fawaz had shown him. He was putting the can back in his bag when two hands pushed him back and dived at the bag. Ajay fell over.

Startled, Ajay sat there for a couple of seconds trying to understand what had just hit him. Not once did it occur to him that he could be followed and arrested before finishing his agenda. No, this was not the police as it was not him running away, but this person who had grabbed his bag.

Coming back to his senses, he got up and ran behind the black figure running with his bag. Maybe he was a thief who just wanted his bag, presuming it be containing valuables.

"Hey, come back. Give me the bag," yelled Ajay. "There is nothing of value in it."

The figure was now running towards the well-lit street. Oh my God! Thought Ajay. This can't be happening. I had not planned for this. The can might blow up in this man's hands, hurting him badly. That was not the plan.

Under the dim light, Ajay recognized the man to be the beggar he had met earlier in the day. And he had followed him throughout! Was he a spy or security personnel in the guise of a beggar? "Why did I not think about that? How can I be so naïve as to trust anyone like this? What should I do now?"

Whatever happens, he had to get this bag from him before it exploded. "No, I cannot have another murder on my conscience. I had planned to injure only myself so I can be close to people who can help me."

He soon caught up with the beggar and tried to snatch the bag, causing a lot of commotion on the streets. Soon, people will be coming out to investigate what was happening. Ajay and the beggar had now stopped running and both of them were pulling at the bag. He could have easily overpowered the bum by giving him one punch but he did not want to hurt him.

The beggar kept tugging at the bag and loudly asking him to let go. His eyes were wide and scary and in that second Ajay realized that the man may have seen him mixing the chemicals and was preventing him from harming people. But before Ajay could talk to the man, the beggar kicked him so hard in the groin that he fell back screaming with pain. The beggar too fell on the other side of the road, tightly holding the bag.

"BOOM"!

Chapter 33

Reunion

It was pitch dark, barren trees were letting the violet rays of the moon, or was it the sun, cast dark shadows on a group of people huddled together around a bonfire, trying to keep warm on the chilly night. Far away, a woman in a pretty pink saree and coal black flowing hair is walking with her arms stretched, calling him "Come to me. Come to me." The moon was now on top of her and as she emerged from the shadows, the white light of the moon shone her face brightly. A figure with sunken eyes, long hair and beard, huddled around the fire, looks up and stretches his arms too, ready to take the woman in his embrace. Suddenly he stops. Another shadow lurking behind the woman steps out of nowhere and looks questioningly at him with innocent eyes. He is trying to embrace the woman calling out in a quivering voice "Anita, Anita, Anita…."

Someone was shaking him, touching him on his cheeks. "What is your name? How are you feeling?"

"Anita Anita…"

"Who is Anita?" a voice asked.

"My Anita, come to me."

"Open your eyes, dear. How are you feeling? Does your leg hurt? What is your name?"

"Ajay." Or was I Maqbool or Iqbal today. He didn't remember where he was.

"Where am I?" He slowly opened his eyes and looked around to gauge his surroundings. This looked like a hospital. There were some tubes in his arm and he could see a bottle hanging near his bed. A doctor and a nurse with a tray in her hand were standing near him. A policeman was sitting in the corner of the small room looking at him. His mouth was dry and he felt like he had eaten plastic.

"Is he coming to?" he asked, still sitting on the bench where he was.

"Looks like," the doctor was checking his heartbeat. "What is your name?"

"My name! Where am I?"

"In the Army hospital."

"Where?"

"You mean which city? You are in Srinagar, if that is what you want to know."

Ajay relaxed. "Thank God!"

He tried to get back up but the pain in his back and legs was unbearable. He looked down at his legs, which were heavily bandaged. "What happened to my legs?"

"You were hurt in a blast. Don't you remember?"

Ajay lay back on the bed and closed his eyes, trying to remember the sequence of events that led him to the hospital.

"Okay, come out with it now. Who do you belong to? Where did you plan to plant that bomb that blew up on your face and killed your friend," the policeman asked rudely.

"Killed?" So, the poor beggar lost his life because of him. "Oh no," Ajay regretted. Another murder on my conscience.

"Are you saying you don't know your friend died?" the policeman bellowed.

"Be gentle. Don't push too hard," the nurse admonished the policeman. "He is coming around after a week. Don't expect him to remember everything right away. Go away. Come back tomorrow. With those legs, he can't run anywhere."

The kind nurse with eyes as big as her bosom and proportionate hips, glasses sitting on the edge of her nose, softly brushed his hair and pulled up his sheet up to his chest.

"What happened to my legs," Ajay wanted to know. He felt like his feet had blown up like balloons.

"Don't worry, dear. Your legs will be fine. You should consider yourself lucky that you still have legs and feet. They are severely burnt. You are lucky that you were just outside the Army hospital and the good doctors saved your life. You will need a couple of more surgeries and then you will walk again. Your friend died right away."

"Yes, walking straight into jail. Your friend Iqbal could give us no information. Good that you are alive," the policeman said walking out. "I will be back tomorrow with my seniors. Sister, make sure he can talk by tomorrow."

Ajay realized that the beggar had been given the name Iqbal. He was heavy-headed and groggy and it took him a while to clear his mind, which was running double speed to understand the reason. If the beggar died instantly, how come they are calling him Iqbal. He had not even introduced himself to the vagrant. As his mind raced, he remembered the fake ID Fawaz had given him when they had entered India, which he had forgotten in the pockets of the shirt he had given to the tramp. The beggar's death had freed Ajay of his jihadist connections. He felt a big burden lift off his shoulders, but not from his soul.

Time to go back to Anita. He had to talk to higher authorities and not to the local policeman, who will not be able comprehend the enormity of the situation. He wasn't sure if Amar had come back, so no point in looking for him. His Commander may have retired and forgotten about him. "I am not sure if Anita still lives in Rajpura." As Ajay's mind raced, he remembered Anita's brothers talking about following their dad into the army. "Yes," he thought. "Shyam or Sunny.

Even if they joined the Army or Air Force 5 years after he left, they might still be working. I have to look for Shyam Mathur or Sunny Mathur. But he couldn't remember Sunny's real name. Anita had just called him Sunny."

When the nurse came back to give him his next dose of medicine, he asked her if she would help him.

"Of course, my dear," the kind nurse pricked a needle in his arm. "That is why I am a nurse. To help people. What do you want?"

"No one will believe me if I tell them about myself. The only person who will understand my situation is Shyam Mathur or Sunny Mathur. Can you help me locate them?"

"Where do I look for them?"

"He might be posted anywhere in the Indian Army or Air Force. I don't know the details."

"And who do I say is looking for them?"

"Flight Lieutenant Ajay Singh".

The nurse gave him a shocked look. Ajay smiled and nodded. "Only between you and me, my dear. Not the policemen. They won't understand."

"And you are not running away from here?" the nurse made Ajay promise. "Because if you do, I will not only lose my job but they will kill me and my family. We live in very dangerous times."

"Sister, I have been running for twenty-eight years. I am too tired to run anymore. I am home."

After promising to look for Shyam and Sunny, the sister locked the door and for the next two days, kept the police away by telling them her patient was in no condition to talk.

On the third day, he had a visitor. It was Major General Shyam Mathur, dressed in his uniform and looking as professional as Ajay had once looked. Ajay sized him up and down as Shyam came closer to his bed.

"I am told you are looking for me. I am sorry, do I know you?"

Ajay could not control his tears as he tried to sit up with the nurse's help. "He has been waiting for you, sir. He had not talked to anyone since he came to his senses."

Ajay looked at Shyam, who was staring at him. Of course they both had changed. Ajay's coal black hair had been replaced with salt and pepper hair, his fair skin did not glow any more. Age had caught up with him. His eyes and cheeks were sunken, he had dark circles under his eyes, a broken tooth, a hundred wrinkles and so on. But Shyam too was not the chubby tall handsome 16-year old boy he remembered. His paunch had started making its presence felt and his gold-rimmed glasses could not hide the lack of spark in his eyes. Yet, he was Shyam all right.

Shyam came closer to Ajay. Yes, he was his sister's missing husband. "Is that you Jijaji? Ajay?"

Ajay simply nodded. The big lump in his throat was bursting at its seams and then the dam burst. Both of them hugged each other and stayed in that position for a long time. The nurse gave them privacy and walked out of the room with a big smile of achievement on her face.

"How is everyone at home?" Ajay managed. He could not bring himself to ask about Anita only.

"We all missed you, Ajay. Life has not been easy for Anita. She has missed you every single day. But like you asked, she waited for you." In the next couple of hours, Shyam filled Ajay on everything that had happened in their lives. While Ajay was excited to learn that he had a daughter, he was sad when told that his parents had disowned his family. But they were not alive any more.

"Finally, I know who that shadow was lurking behind Anita," Ajay heaved a sigh of relief.

"Shadow?"

"Never mind," Ajay wiped tears from his eyes. "I hurt Anita more than anyone else. If I had known it would take me this long to come home, I would never have asked Anita to wait for me."

"I just hope you are not too late."

"What do you mean," Ajay's anxiety was at its peak. "Shyam, please take me to Anita."

It was now Shyam's turn to cry. "Your daughter Aju has been missing. First you, now her child – how can Anu take two big shocks in her life. She is in the hospital, waiting for her daughter. I can't bear to see my sister like that. When you went missing, I somehow managed to support Anu. But not anymore." And Shyam sobbed like a baby as Ajay took him in his arms.

It took three days before Shyam could finish official formalities to take Ajay to Delhi, despite medical advice, to meet Anita, who was struggling for her life in the Army hospital. Shyam had called the hospital many times and was in touch with the doctors. Shikha and Pinky, Prema's daughter, were taking care of Anita. Tina too had come down to take care of Anita. There had been no improvement in Anita's condition. "Maybe if she sees Ajay, she might wake up and get better," Shikha was excited about Ajay's news. "Maybe Ajay knows about Amar too," Shikha wished.

Ajay was excited and apprehensive at the same time. Ajay's legs and feet were still bandaged and Shyam was pushing his wheelchair as they approached Anita's room in the hospital. Shikha and Tina sat on chairs, either side of the bed Anita lay on. Tina jumped up when she saw Ajay and ran to hug him.

"I can't believe, *Jijoo* (brother-in-law) you are back. Miracles happen. You are God's gift to us," Tina continued to hold Ajay tightly in her arms.

"And I can't believe that little girl with two piggy tails and favorite red skirt, can wear a saree and turn out to be a Mumtaz," Ajay joked. Tina took great care of herself and looked as gorgeous as any Bollywood actress.

"You are outdated, *Jijaji*. It's Madhuri Dixit now," Tina joked as everyone else merely smiled.

Shikha was now standing quietly on the further side of Anita's bed and sheepishly just smiled at Ajay, who smiled back. "I am

sorry, Shikha. I did not keep my promise. I could not bring Amar back with me."

"I know. It is not your fault, Ajay. It is my destiny. No one can change that."

"But I am glad, Shikha, you found happiness. Are you happy in your life my dear?"

Shikha nodded, almost ready to cry. "Not as happy as I would have been with Amar." She ran out of the room. Pinky followed her.

Anita was lying on the bed with an oxygen mask attached to a tank and IV fluids flowing through the veins of her hands. Lying there, she looked just like a child who forgot to grow. He did not remember his Anita so thin and lean. Not once did he have a vision of his Anita lying in a hospital bed with white walls and chords, in a hospital gown, waiting for him. What happened to the pink saree she always wore?

Ajay took her hand in his and kissed it, sobbing uncontrollably. "I asked you to wait, Anita, but not like this. I am sorry, Anita. I did my best. Please talk to me."

The doctor walked into the room and shook hands with Shyam. Shyam introduced Ajay. "This is Flight Lieutenant Ajay, Anita's husband. He has been missing for a long time."

"Welcome back, Lieutenant Ajay. Welcome back," the doctor smiled at Ajay. "Your arrival is timely and might help in Anita's recovery."

"What happened?" Ajay asked wiping away tears.

"She was brought here unconscious. It seemed like she had not eaten for days and had multi-organ failure. We have been able to restore normal functioning of her heart and brain but it is her kidneys and liver we are worried about. Most of all, she needs the will to get better. She suffered a trauma after her daughter went missing. Mr Ajay, you can understand the trauma she had to go through after you went missing and now your daughter."

Shikha and Pinky came back after the doctor left. "I had been calling Anita for three days as we had missed our July meeting. I kept calling and calling but she never picked up. I then called Shyam at Rajpura to find out if she had gone there. Shyam came running the next day and we found her sitting in Aju's room, holding the Court martial letter. How long she had been sitting there, we don't know."

"Court martial?"

Chapter 34

August 14, 1999

She always believed that it is better to light a candle than curse the darkness. Her mother had spent her entire life in darkness waiting for power to be restored.

The bus had just passed the Wagah transit post in Pakistan en route to Delhi from Lahore, from where she had boarded the bus to go home. Salim and Sultana had come to see her off. Under international pressure, both India and Pakistan were feigning to restart their friendship afresh after Kargil war ended. Pakistan promised to release every Indian who had mistakenly crossed the border and was in Pakistan jails, whether they had any documents or not. Salim, with the help of IG Rashid, pushed Aju's name along with Amar's, who was going by the name of Maqbool and was able to get them both on the bus to Delhi.

Aju looked at her watch. It was 9 in the morning. She should be in Delhi by 3-4 in the afternoon. Amar Chachu was sitting next to her. After days of calling her home in Delhi and getting no answer, she had called Shikha's house. Fortunately for her, Anita had always relied on her daughter to dial numbers for her so she did not have to keep checking her phone diary.

"Mom, you are so lazy. Why don't you check the diary I made for you?"

"Why should I? I have a walking talking diary," Anita had teased. "Next time I will check the diary. This last time, please. I have to speak to Shikha urgently."

That is how she memorized Shikha Aunty's number. The professor had picked up the phone and was astonished to hear her voice. They had never met each other, as it was Shikha who had come visiting with the kids. There never was any opportunity to go to their house. From Shikha's conversations with Anita, Aju had gauged that he wanted Shikha to stay away from Anita and her family. Maybe, so she doesn't fall prey to the evil eye.

"Are you Aju, Anita's daughter?"

'Yes."

"You are the one who flew over the border to Pakistan and now is missing?"

The professor did not wait for an answer but went on. "I am glad I kept my kids away from you. You brought shame to our country and our people. Armed forces is to protect people and not leave them injured on the mountains and fly over to enemy territory…"

"Please, sir," Aju tried to reason with the Professor. "My mother is not picking up her phone in so many days. Can I please talk to Shikha Aunty?" She wanted to give the news about Amar too.

"Shikha is not here. She is in the hospital."

"What happened to her?"

"Nothing happened to her, you dimwit! It's your mother who is sick because you left her. *Wah*! What a family! When the father comes back, the daughter decides to go missing!" The professor certainly was angry at her for abandoning her mother but more because Shikha was spending time with Anita.

"What do you mean father comes back? Sir, please tell me what is going on?"

"Well, your father or your Pa, who you went looking for, is back. He is in the hospital with your mother. Why don't you too go to her and be one happy family and live happily ever after. AND LEAVE SHIKHA ALONE." The professor had hung up.

298

She didn't know if she should cry or laugh. Should she be sad or happy? "Oh my god! Pa is back, Sultana. He is with Ma," she hugged Sultana tightly and kept saying "Thank God thank God".

"Sultana, I have to go home right now."

"We will do something. Relax."

If the professor said her mother was in hospital, then she must be at the Army hospital. After the bus crossed Panipat, Aju went up to the conductor to ask if the bus stopped near Delhi Cantt. He said it did. If Ma was in the hospital, there is no point going home. Plus Shikha Aunty was in the hospital too. She had to unite Amar with Shikha.

Aju was holding Amar Chacha's hands, which still were as strong as a soldier's. He held her very tightly, making her hand sweat but she did not let go of his hand. In fact, he was a source of support to her anxious moments. She had butterflies in her stomach. And she thought she must use the bathroom before meeting everyone. She was jittery and shaking. Amar felt her anxiety and held her tighter, looking down at her.

And he said his first words since they met. "*Ghabrao mat. Sab teekh ho jayga ab* (Don't panic. Everything will be fine now.)"

Amar wrapped Aju in the warm blanket of his arms and kissed her forehead again and again. "Thank you, *beta*. Thank you for saving my life."

Shikha and Shyam were sitting on each side of Anita's bed while Ajay was propped up on the next bed, which was placed in a way so he could see Anita's face. Every few minutes he would come down and stroke and kiss Anita's hands. They saw movements in Anita's eyelids and fingers when he did that, giving doctors hope that she would come around. Shikha almost screamed when she saw Aju walk in.

She ran to hug her. "Aju, you are back, oh my God! I am so glad." Then pointing at Ajay, "See who is back? Your Pa is here and you have been wandering the streets of Pakistan looking for him. Rajni told us everything"

Aju and Ajay stared at each other. "I should have showered before meeting my Pa. God! I look such a mess, not pretty at all." Aju was thinking and admonished herself at trivializing this once-in-a-lifetime moment. Ajay jumped up from his bed and was about to fall to the floor as his legs were still bandaged and weak, when Aju caught him tightly.

"I won't let you fall again, Pa. Never."

There was silence for a few minutes as the father daughter looked at each other for the first time and stayed in a tight embrace. Amar was smiling as he approached them. Touching Ajay on his shoulder, he said, "Remember me?"

Ajay let go of Aju. He looked at this frail man with long beard and hair, dressed in a blue pathani suit Salim had brought for him. "Amarua!!! Is that you?"

Amar nodded and another round of hugs and embraces continued as Aju looked at her mother lying there with the oxygen mask.

"Wake up, Ma. Look who is here. Our family is complete. Pa is back. You were always right that he would come back on his own. You were always right when you said that I need not go looking for him, Ma. You believed in your heart and your faith. Now wake up and see. I also got Amar Chachu back."

"Amar? What are you saying Aju?" Shikha was curious.

Without saying anything, Aju pointed towards Amar Chacha, who was still hugging her Pa. Amar helped Ajay get back to his bed and then looked at Shikha.

"Remember me?"

"Amar! My Amar," Shikha shrieked and ran to hug Amar, who was caught off guard. Both of them fell on the floor, with Shikha on top of this bearded aging man. Everyone laughed but Anita. Aju saw tears rolling down the corner of her Ma's eyes.

"Don't cry, Ma. These should be tears of joy. Everything will be fine. Pa will make everything fine. He is here now," Aju held Anita's left hand and Ajay her right.

The doctor had said, "Her tears are an indication that she is aware of her surroundings. That she is listening to you all. Keep talking to her. She might come around or she might not."

Anita beat all odds and regained consciousness, as Ajay took good care of her, while still healing from the blast. He talked to her every hour, every minute and every second he could. Just like in his younger days, it was his habit of sharing every little detail about his life, he told her everything.

She regained consciousness in the middle of the night, when Ajay was sitting on his wheelchair holding her hand and as his wont, talking to her. Now he was running out of topics to talk about so he had picked up an English newspaper and was reading.

"You know Anita, I not only missed you in the jungles, but also these newspapers. I feel like an alien now as I don't know anything about anything."

"I know." Ajay heard a frail voice.

He looked around the room. There was just a faint light at the bed stand near Anita which Ajay had requested to be set up so he could read to her whenever he wanted.

He felt Anita's fingers moving, or shivering beneath his hands. He looked at her. She was slowly trying to open her eyes, with tears still flowing.

Ajay was so excited that he wanted to run and call the doctors to come and examine Anita. Run he couldn't but scream he could. So he did but not loud enough for anyone outside the room to hear. He did not want to spoil the moment. This was his moment, a moment he had waited for his entire life. No, the doctors can deal with this later but just five minutes; I want my Anita to myself.

"O Anita! My dear! See it's me, your Ajay!"

"I know."

"I am sorry Anu. So sorry for making you wait for so long. I was selfish, my dear. I did not let you move on," sobbed Ajay holding Anita's hands tightly and kissing them all over. Then

he bent down and hugged her, lifting her from the bed and supporting her.

The nurse walked in to see what the commotion was all about and ran to call the doctor.

"Aju," said Anita in a shaky voice. "Your daughter."

"Shhh...don't talk too much. I know about her."

"She is lost. I lost her. I could not keep her safe," Anita was crying now.

"Don't worry. She is safe. She is back. And now all three of us can live happily together."

Epilogue

A year later

Amar and Ajay were awarded with Vir Chakra for their heroic tales of survival but both refused to take anything from the government which had abandoned them and declared them missing. "We will accept the Vir Chakra only when the Prime Minister or the President's child enters the armed forces and fights a war for our country. Sitting in cushy air-conditioned offices and commanding the soldiers to sacrifice their lives, is not bravery."

Shikha had left the Professor and started living with Amar. Her children, who were grown up now and were on their own, accepted Amar and Shikha's decision to leave the Professor. They knew she had never been happy and that the relationship was a mere compromise.

General Court Martial proceedings were initiated against Aju. She was charged with deserting her post, failure to report to duty, failure to follow orders and posing a threat to colleagues. Since Aju pleaded guilty, the trial did not last long but she was sentenced for a year of detention and dismissal from the Air Force. She was also forbidden to use her designation for any purpose for the rest of her life.

While still in detention, Pinki helped Aju register at Delhi University to pursue a career as a Human Rights lawyer like Sultana. Rajni apologized to Aju for not being able to convey her message on time.

"I am so sorry, Aju. If only I had been able to give your message to your mother before they decided to Court martial you, she would not be in this state today."

"It's not your fault, Rajni. I dragged you into this."

Unbeknownst to Aju, Salim was arrested in Pakistan for helping an Indian look for an Indian Prisoner of War and helping them leave Pakistan. And so was Praveen Ahmed, who had let Amar go. Sultana was fighting to get them out.

And as for Anita, finally, her nightmares ended.

Glossary

Aloo gobi	Potato cauliflower
Amma	Mother
Appa	Big Sister
Ayah	Nanny
Bauji	Father
Behenji	Sister
Beta	Dear child
Biradri	Community
Bitiya	Dear daughter
Bhiya	Brother
Chacha	Uncle
Chula	Oven
Chunni	Scarf
Dada	Grandfather
Dadi	Grandmother
Dakhhana	Post Office
Dal	Lentil
Golguppa	Indian snack
Inshaallah	If Allah wills it
Kirtan	Religious hymns
Madrasa	School
Masi	Mother's sister
Masterji	Teachers

Mohturma	Madam
Motabhai	Big Brother
Paan	Preparation of betal leaf and areca nut
Paanwallas	Seller of Paan
Sarbala	Best man
Sherwani	A knee-length coat buttoning to the neck
Tauji	Uncle

Research

Letters/interviews/information provided by Missing Defense personnel Relatives Association and families.

Wikepedia & published newspaper articles on the subject.

Dr Neelam Batra-Verma has been writing professionally for about 30 years and published thousands of articles in national and international mainstream newspapers and magazines. After earning a doctorate degree in Forensic Science, she decided to indulge her passion for writing and took up journalism as a career. She wrote on social and political issues till she moved to Vancouver with her family in 2002. While working for print and electronic media for decades in India and Canada, she successfully published and edited the first Hindi magazine in Canada. This is her first work of fiction based on true events.